rooster

rooster

an american tragedy

brian fielding

Bodhisattva Press
Providence, Rhode Island

Published by Bodhisattva Press
35 Oxford Street
Providence, Rhode Island 02905

PUBLISHER'S NOTE: This is a work of fiction. Names, characters, places, and incidents either are the product of the author's imagination or are used fictitiously, and any resemblace to actual persons, living or dead, events, or locales is entirely coincidental.

Publisher's Cataloging-in-Publication Data
Fielding, Brian.
    Rooster: an american tragedy / by Brian Fielding. Providence, Rhode Island: Bodhisattva Press, 2000.

        p. cm.

    ISBN 0-9676590-0-0
        1. Artists—Fiction. I. Title.
PS3556.I453 R66   2000
813'.54—dc21   99-66596

Printed in the United States of America

03 02 01 00 ▼   5 4 3 2 1

TO MY MENTOR

*"It taught us that, contrary to what we sometimes used to think,
the spirit is of no avail against the sword,
but the spirit together with the sword
will always win out over the sword alone."*

— CAMUS

Prologue

by MARCEL PHRENOL

IN THE DAYS BETWEEN Solzhenitsyn's death and *I Give You My Word,* Rooster, born Alexi Albert Rodriguez, completed a total of fifteen paintings. Of the period preceding Soli's death, he painted forty-two paintings considered mentionable. Twenty-one of these forty-two — exactly half — were painted prior to Soli's masterful tutelage, leaving twenty-one paintings considered directly influenced by Solzhenitsyn. *Songbird* was a transitional painting. Begun under Soli's tutelage, Rooster brought it to completion only several months after Soli's death; for this reason it is generally identified as being of the Post-Soli period, though many conservative art historians have eloquently argued that *Songbird* is a Soli period piece. Of the fifteen paintings completed between Soli's death and *I Give You My Word,* only three were finished after the completion of *Songbird.* These were *Af Taken, Sastruga,* and *Blue Hands,* and these represent the first of the paintings titled by Rooster. The order in which these three were painted has never been established. Between the completion of *I Give You My Word* (the only overtly religious portrait he ever painted) and his own untimely death, Rooster Rodriguez completed an astounding thirty-seven paintings, each of masterpiece quality, among them *Sublime Awe* and *Study of the Beautiful,* in just sixteen days. Thirty-six of these thirty-seven were completed in ten days' time. Number thirty-seven, Rooster's final masterpiece, entitled *Black Mask*, consumed days eleven through sixteen. In the time that followed, some claimed that the inconceivable exertion of these sixteen days killed Rooster; others said it was the sudden and accelerated spread of leprosy upon his body; a few honestly believe it was just an accident; still others, and I count myself among this lot, believe he died of a broken heart. This is his story.

1

ROOSTER STARED BLANKLY at the yawning blackness of stretched canvas. He waited for a voice to whisper direction. Staccato strokes. More blue. Sharper lines. Distinction. Cultural discernment. The lustrous colors stiffened on the palette. Exposure to air threatened to dull, dim the thing that would be. Inside himself, Rooster knew, the painting painted itself before the first brushstroke, before even the tubes of color were purchased. The brush, immobile, unruffled, remained vigilant, poised and ready. Only twitches of his hand, balanced on the hickory maulstick, revealed that the painter had not himself become a still life.

Soli, his mentor, like the echo of a ghost, spoke to him very softly from the corner. "You make a conscious decision to travel deeper, beyond the demons of desperation, through the gate of solitude and past depression's throne. A conscious pilgrimage is required to journey into the garden of inner being. There, Rooster, if you have the courage to make it, roses, innocent gardens of yellow roses, perpetually bloom. But be careful. The dreams within, they live their own lives. Sometimes seductive, sometimes selfish, always indifferent, they arrive only when convenience suits them most. Blame the inner dream for lingering too long and you blame yourself for faulty expectation. And promises? What promises have your dreams made you? That the dreamer knows the dream means only that the dream knows the world of the dreamer. In this, all innocence is forfeited. All innocence, Rooster, all . . ."

The voice fell silent and Rooster was again alone with the expansive void. It was a small canvas, appropriate for his skills, completely his to create, his to shape. Why did it feel so large, so inexplicable and large? Coarser canvas, rejected for this project, lay on the floor in unorganized piles. Such crumpled sights gave a man something to do on desperate days, futures unresolved. At any time the pile could be put aright. Such myths were necessary.

"These achievements deserve recognition," the voice began again, "bringing harmony from chaos. Never can we call such miracles minor, even when the chaotic simply contains itself within the circle of our own careful craft. Michaelangelo spent five years on the Cistene Chapel, on his back, looking upwards and upside down. Is there any wonder left why he was great? Still, you must never compare. You will never be Michaelangelo. Be thankful." The old master chuckled. "He probably slept standing."

Finer canvas, the kind that reveals true strength in the moment of being broken, leaned upon the easel. An aluminum necklet held strands of horsehair stiff about the wooden shaft. The blade of the brush addressing the canvas possessed a power so distinct, so poignant, that Rooster tremored with fear as his left hand balanced its weight. What if the canvas, expressive in its own right, yielded to the severity of color, unable to receive? Rooster wondered if thought itself might be sufficient to dapple canvas. His leprous hand could certainly accomplish nothing today.

"Besides," Solzhenitsyn added, "you would be dreadfully old."

Utilizing a scythe-shaped shard of glass clasped in the fingers of his right hand, Rooster blended small amounts of chromium red with magenta. An emboldened fuchsia that hinted of an impenetrable, metallic substratum emerged. Rooster envisioned the color as capable of sustaining an unerring resistance to violence. More subtle corrosives would also be well opposed. He had heard of such a color, not quite mauve, described in the sunsets of New Mexico and Tibet.

The brush tickled in his hand, itching to begin. With discipline he kept himself still, unmoving, patient as an absolute.

New Mexico and Tibet, polar global opposites. Why should such spiritual manifestations come to fruition at opposite ends of the earth, he reflected as the brush began slowly twirling before the canvas. Of what unique zeitgeist did it speak? If the pure and unbending axis of Earth were extended beyond the limits of Taos and Nepal, where would the endpoints be? What strange cultures would greet the human race? How enduring would their kindness be? Are there two cultures? Is Earth in the direct line of their communications? Do we distort their data? Kill their truth? Or do we serve a more benign purpose, acting as a medium, a mediator, an unknowing interpreter, a living cipher between alien forces stretched across the cosmos, mountaintop to mountaintop? Or is it all one culture, one galactic, universal ancestry dancing in the forgotten corners of the mind?

Rooster raised the transparent shard of glass to the brush, dabbed its horsehair tip, and snapped a watermark of the rich new color into the heart of the composition. It was the first mark of paint that Rooster had applied to the canvas in well over an hour. The deliberate effort pleased Rooster, drew a confidence to his spirit. He felt cool, forged, as one does in the aftermath of apologies and war.

"You have a unique style, Rooster. It may take years before they begin to understand it, appreciate it. This again is a good thing. Be thankful for it. Be thankful that you are anonymous. It allows you the privilege of being an observer. Once you are known, you will be the observed."

"If I live."

"You will live."

Solzhenitsyn, the master, quietly bowed his head, praying upon the varnished curve of his varnished cane. To what he prayed, he did not know. Snug in the corner, his hunched shoulders still convincing, he was a figure reminiscent of the first cave dweller of Southern France, that early dreamer, deep within the hallowed Earth, whose imagination, by drawing images of beasts and symbols of hope on cave walls and stone ceilings, midwived civilization. Early man had painted grazing herds and wild, dangerous animals felled by stick figures that had discovered the use of tools — even then, after God and the sun, these were the forms children first learned to paint.

Given free will, Solzhenitsyn would have lived forever. Sometimes, studying the morose work of a developing artist, Solzhenitsyn, absorbed, would forget the ridiculous prospect of mortality. He would envision within the canvas an opportunity for safe passage, hegira, escape from the inevitable. Such desires of old age echoed constantly of a Joycean pornographic where one wants what one sees. True art, he knew, makes one content with what is, exactly as it is. It does not leave the admirer yearning to possess the depiction in some other, somehow more tangible, more consumable, form.

Lifting his head, Solzhenitsyn shrugged the blades of his shoulders, cranky propellers forsaken to the age of the Mig fighter and the aplomb Stealth bomber. He experienced the depleted currency of his body, the body of an ever-reducing galaxy, aged and rigid — fluid only from a lost but monumental distance — mechanical, predictable, rhythmic, unschismatic, safe, academic, routine. *With all routine comes death*, he thought. He had no trouble meditating upon death in church or by candlelight, by sea or a simple meal, with a paint brush in his hand. But to accept it? To infinitely resign oneself to it? No, it was the same renegade spirit that inspired primitive man to draw upon the ceilings of the pitch black caves, to draw for no purpose but to defy the boredom, to protest the endless sleep, to document the struggles to survive, to remember the dead, and to make a statement for all those who could not find the way; we have not lived in vain!

"I think I should like to go for lobster thermidor this evening. Would you join me?"

Rooster remained unmoving, dwindled by staunch concentration.

"I'd hoped to wait for November, but my powers of reflection grow dimmer. I can barely taste the memory now. The thing seems less and less real. Is lobster a dream? A crustacean, imagine, what a silly manifestation of life." Solzhenitsyn paused. "Or is it the interior skeleton that is a silly manifestation? Ah, Rooster, there might not be a November for me. Each second delivers the sting of economy. As my own values diminish from the world, it grows increasingly clear that so must I. Has it always gone according to such a rule? No one speaks of these types of laws and rules. How blind we all are, in fierce denial of our own sub-cultures. I hope to make one more mark, Rooster. Perhaps in your heart, as you have made in mine. Do you suppose such a thing is possible? In ancient days I'd not dare to express such a sentiment. You'd have thought me queer. But malice spares old men. Our frailty strips our thoughts of their more fearsome applications. The public is full aware, turning us into statesmen, into puppets. We so affect the cultural consciousness that we eventually are called to serve it; drafted is more like it, for there is no choice, no choice when it comes to the endless consumption of the common good. Still, I would be pleased if I could touch your heart. . . . Lobster thermidor, wouldn't you join me tonight? Do you know, Alexi, I think you actually thought about painting today, real thought! Who would believe?"

"Soli, please, I must concentrate."

Solzhenitsyn arose before speaking again. "In youth we enter servitude to the most benign of delights."

"I need inspiration."

"But in middle age the true value of our efforts becomes clear."

"This canvas mocks me."

"Only at full bloom do we see with what persistence our youth persists. Listen to me, Alexi, listen to me," Solzhenitsyn commanded as he hobbled closer with the aid of his varnished cane. "All of our lives they teach that the workings of our minds matter most. Those who change the fundamental molecular structure of the world perform their minor feats of ecesis through the focusing power of the mind; no greater gift can woman or man combined conceive. What a brave farce we humans perpetuate, Rooster, what a brave farce. Without the body to enact the mind, all force remains captive. At life's end, truth comes free of her shell.

"'Hecatomb,' 'edentulous.' Do you know the meaning of these words? Of course you don't. I'd worry if you did. Ha! One discovers the meaning of such words only at my age. Certain words match with the number, the condition of our lives. Before their time they wander like ghosts, phone calls without voices, great empty messengers, sensitive time-released capsules, aimless hobgoblins snatching up unwary travelers. Booo, Boooo! They wait and wait and wait to leap upon us with their new fear, the terrifying image we so easily, so readily, translate into our own possessive reality. They barely need to do anything. They understand the hidden, the iniquities of our pride and vanity. They just put it out there, their one hidden word of inspiration, mental ICBMs for the pious and the literate. Benevolent? Malevolent? Their Psalm 118. Their minor, ha-ha, prophets. *Kindness endures forever.* Hecatomb: a sacrifice to the gods, a slaughter, a grand offering, a holocaust rendered unto heaven. Remember that. Remember 'hecatomb'! Ah well, Rooster, no one takes us seriously anymore. Dive into the material but beware the seduction of materialism. The modern malaise. Add terrorism and the news of the tragic and you have a voice, a voice of God."

The old man rambled; the young man did his best to listen.

"At my age you begin to believe in luck. Did you know that, Rooster? You become a paranoid looking for symbols and omens in the bellies of birds, in the torn web of the common house spider, in fortune cookies and tea bags, in the turning of the seasons. Everyone is a prophet in this world. That is what no one understands. We have created an entire culture of prophets all declaring their little truths, but no one is listening.

"Our prophets all can see, but none can hear. Only nature can hear." Solzhenitsyn thumped the cane, planting himself decisively to turn in a new direction. "Nature has groomed our species, you see. We are a species of prophets of putative virtue. We talk to flowers and feed the pigeons, the ducks and the fish. I watch the lean of the highest tree limb for a movement that strikes me as a bit too unnatural. Where would you sit if you could fly? If you had no natural predators? If all knew you as the preternatural predator? Luck outshines talent on the grayest day. German intelligence, Parisian wit, Nigerian strength, Sicilian romance, American ingenuity . . . no, no, no, no to all. Polish your rusty horseshoe. Ha-ha! Old men find moral rectitude in the alms cup of dumb blind luck!"

The old sage raised his head, cocking it left so as to more critically spy the canvas. Detached, he surveyed the ambitious lines, too raw for a master's refined taste. Still. Yet. Maybe. The surface foreshadowed something, something pressing from below. Solzhenitsyn murmured in awe, "You know of these things so young, Rooster, so young."

And even as his lower lip grinned at the glimmer of promise, his cracked upper lip, harsh and domineering, suppressed all display of appreciation. In the past, Solzhenitsyn would have been more generous with his smiles, looser, less demanding. Lobster thermidor. But death, or the looming prospect of his death, altered his style by slight degrees. Besides, the old master reasoned, if his student exhibited less impatience and greater personal application, the necessity to push would vanish. So what if the young man knew enough of life to record the hunter's approach? Could he plant the spear in the heart of the beast, just below the shoulder where the thin muscle, like warm butter, slices?

"Do you hear me? You must try harder, Rooster. You must relax yourself into the belly of this beast we call creation, originality. It has consumed and spit out souls of significant authority, authorities far greater than you. You can be a cretin, a bastard, an asshole as they speak it in the language of today, but your paintings . . . each stroke must be pure in its moral base. Each and every brushstroke must be the application of a salve. From your hands you must faithfully issue Gilead's anointed balm."

Leaning forward, Solzhenitsyn pointed with his cane to a stripe of green paint that had dipped from its intended border into the main birth of canvas. To the knowing master, it indicated a desire to defy convention without demanding attention. On a deeper level, Solzhenitsyn wondered, did it represent the intentional betrayal that coincides with deliberate acculturation into the average and the mean? Solzhenitsyn pointed. "Why? Why this offense? Are you trying to be mediocre? Or are you simply trying to make an argument for quantity over quality? Why, why did you do this?"

Rooster's center of attention shifted aggressively. He expected to be questioned for the magenta spot at the center. The color, the placement, the divisive essence of the line he had just placed: this was worthy of attention. To have the focus shifted to a meaningless point, an error that would be easily corrected as the painting unfolded, this cheapened their creation. Rooster respected Solzhenitsyn. He revered the man as the father he had never had. But recently? Recently his instructor had stuttered into the haphazard and the unprincipled, both in the directions he gave and the suggestions he voiced. It tested Rooster's patience.

Ah well, the powers of every master fade, fall, decline. For months now, Rooster increasingly sensed that perhaps that mystical juncture where student outpaces master had arrived. Would Solzhenitsyn recognize it? Would Solzenhitsyn let go? Could he? Rooster recalled his first meeting with the frail postmodernist. He remembered himself as a healthy boy then, barely aware of the august connection between the brush and the hand, scarcely cognizant that no separation will keep an authentic artist from authentic art. Where would he have landed had Soli not taught him of such things? Many things, many things indeed had become clearer since that impetuous moment when he shoved a pad of charcoal sketches beneath the master's runny nose.

Soli could still remember that day. Russet leaves had been flattened from a nighttime rain. Drizzle had continued through morning, trick-

ling upon dark moss. Small mounds of dirty snow melted into the gut-
ter. The dignified cohort of the school had acted quickly to contain
Rooster, the impertinent, colorful youth who had exploded from the
dull, gray background, but not before Rooster had succeeded in securing the small pad in the willful grip of the old man. Only then, when
the sketches were safe in Solzhenitsyn's hands, had Rooster allowed
himself to be dragged away.

That was two years ago, November. The setting was upstate Vermont
at the Danforth Institute of Fine Art, a place that owed its reputation to
longevity and breeding, time-honored euphemisms for old money.
Established in 1843 by George S. Danforth, an agrarian patrician of the
South Carolina tobacco Danforths, the Danforth Institute of Fine Art
maintained a perpetual atmosphere of rectal austerity. When discussing
art at the Danforth Institute of Fine Art, impeccable pronunciation
abounded. Students rolled their RRR's, trilled their J's, and refused to
display emotion before even the most visceral paroxysm.

Rooster had attended the school on a special scholarship for the
economically challenged. At that time, his disease was still a mystery.
His arrival coincided, nearly, with the growing awareness that after 150
years in operation, the Danforth Institute of Fine Art had failed to produce one single artist of historical weight, height or cleft, though in
1966 there had been a stump-footed black girl in the linen factory who
had won the Emile Percy Award for an incendiary collection of short
stories which she had conceived while reading the memoirs of the dis-
tinguished abolitionist Frederick Douglas. In one of the stories, the girl
wrote of a torrid, erotically charged love affair between Douglas and
Harriet Tubman. Mutually impassioned, Douglas' words gave Tubman
the courage to continue her furtive and dangerous battle, while the
bravery she demonstrated through this battle was the cause of Douglas'
inspired words. Though the irony was somewhat superficial, the depth
of heartfelt emotion and the sheer appeal of the historically plausible
fiction, won acclaim for the stump-footed black girl.

On the evening that Rooster accosted the aged master, Solzhenitsyn
was slated to preside as a judge at a competition for the graduating students of Danforth. It would be a multi-media competition. The students had gotten quite *creative*; Solzhenitsyn did not know what else to
call it. Some worked with wood, others with metal, some with twine;

only a few painted. The eclectic array of mediums would have been fine if only there had existed the slight hint of pure reason underlying the choices. Solzhenitsyn found it bizarre; viscerally, he felt disgust. He could instantly assess that not a single one of the lot understood art to be a passionate lifelong affair.

That the great master, whose presence greatly enhanced the event, had agreed to preside on the selection committee had been a coup for the school. The Dean took it as definitive proof that the program deserved international recognition and ordered ten cases of champagne. Solzhenitsyn, who abhorred the whole affair, had agreed to the torturous event for the sole purpose of repaying an old debt. Other than the fact that the exterior of the buildings were gray and horribly old, Solzhenitsyn knew practically nothing about Danforth's Institute of Fine Art. He held no opinion of the place, nor did he care to formulate one. Then there came Rooster, thrusting his sketches, unsettling the sanitized experience, bringing life, hope and humor.

"Who was that?" he heard the escort coordinator angrily demand of the entourage. The embarrassment of the cocoon pleased Solzhenitsyn. It reminded him that evergreens could not be crushed by winter.

"Who was that?"

"Rooster, Rooster." The name gained tight, contemptuous utterance from several mouths before a hand slipped beneath Solzhenitsyn's arm to guide him away.

"We're horribly sorry. Forgive us, Meister. A student, an ex-student I should say. Failed out. He doesn't belong here. Never should have been here in the first place. A cretin. This sort of thing doesn't happen at Danforth. Forgive us, Meister Solzhenitsyn. Let me take those for you."

Until then Solzhenitsyn had watched the scene with a delighted sense of detachment. Not wholly present in the activities, Danforth had seemed to him like a dream that one does not struggle to retain. But now, with the appearance of the flailing undesirable, Danforth became a mite credible and interesting. This had been Solzhenitsyn's most pleasurable moment since arriving on the sheer and classical campus where white facades and manicured lawns insinuated an eternity of pedigree and virtue of the worst sort — unchallenged. When the hand of the escort reached for the sketch pad, Solzhenitsyn reacted violently, though outwardly all he was heard to modestly say was, "No. No . . . No."

"Meister Solzhenitsyn has been upset by the attack." That they were calling it an attack struck the old master as comedy of a high rank. He laughed as they ambled forward, drawing him into the seclusion of a cold building with vaulted, cathedral ceilings. A secretary with an oval smile brought hot cider with a cinnamon twist stirrer. They did not attempt a second time to take the sketch pad from his powerful hands.

Solzhenitsyn learned that the name of the boy was Alexi Rodriguez. He called himself "Rooster," as did all those who knew him even remotely. He had been in the program for two years before being thrown out — or had he walked out? Solzhenitsyn could not conclusively determine — for refusing to adhere to the standards of artistic decency and integrity that Danforth held as untractable plowshares of principle intended for the cultivation of the developing imagination.

Asking several people for a more precise articulation of these "untractable plowshares of principle," Solzhenitsyn suggested that he wanted to be sure his own imagination had been adequately cultivated. He could not quite figure out what the young man's offense must have been. After all, he had just been asked in earnest to judge the value of several pieces of mounted twine made to resemble a multitude of phalluses passing simultaneously through a twine hoop dipped in red paint. His stark, ivory humor unsettled the instrument upon which he played.

Rooster had earned his name for the habit of rising early each morning, earlier than anyone, like clockwork at 3:30 a.m., to begin a day of creation. It seemed in and of itself a nice reason to call a person "Rooster," but Solzhenitsyn received from a rather unusual source — an appetizer waitress at a reception following the judging — a nourishing morsel of information. The actual name "Rooster" had been given to him by a professor of medieval impressionist modality, a German by the name of Heinrich Sachs, who was quite proud to announce one fine afternoon before the classroom of thirteen that young Alexi Rodriguez, for all his seeming attentiveness to time and for all the cackle about his substantial talent, had produced for his final project, nothing. To make his point, the professor held up Alexi's final project, a canvas white as white could be. So much better, Professor Sachs gloated (he had never been a proponent of the low brow scholarship), for the fact that young Alexi could likely sell the canvas back to the campus art supply store. Roosters, it was finally asserted, rise early, cackle at the sun, and peck seed off the ground, seed that is thrown from the hands of those who are more capable.

Some students nervously laughed; most did not. One student, from a unique angle in the room, noticed a nearly imperceptible, chalcedony glaze on the canvas — dustlike, patterned. Stunned into silence, that one student could do nothing but witness, impotent before his knowledge.

Collecting his belongings, Rooster walked calmly from the back to the front of the classroom. Politely removing the painting from the professor's hands, Rooster quoted the one line of German that deep meditation upon Ludwig Wittgenstein's *Remarks on Colour* had permanently stippled within his mind: "Was soll der Maler malen, der die Wirkung eines weiß-durchsichtigen Glases hervorrufen will?"

Professor Heinrich Sachs' jaw dropped wide.

Leaving the room, Rooster seemed content, some thought relieved of a burden, as though he had just passed a critical test of his own making. After Rooster had left, the stunned student found his voice. Staring in awe into the professor's eyes, the student repeated twice, as a ghost drawn through a veil, "You have no idea what you just did."

Contrary to the student's pronouncement, Professor Sachs, overwhelmed, did know what he had done, but a moment too late.

"Why, why?" Solzhenitsyn's question jerked Rooster back into the present. "Why did you do this?" Steady, vigilant as a soldier keeping a sworn enemy at bay, the old master continued pointing at the stripe of green paint.

Without pause or reflection or even a glance at the master, Rooster picked up the glass shard with which he had formulated the emboldened fuchsia and slashed at the canvas. He slashed casually, obscenely casually. With a single stroke of his hand, he scored a hole in the fine canvas, exposing the wall behind the easel. He expressed no concern, no anxiety or frustration as he stated blandly, "For the same reason that I did that."

Wincing with a sudden spasm of pain, gripping his lame hand, Rooster dropped the paint brush. Shimmering oils stained the ugly shag rug.

"Debasing your own canvas, that's not art," the old master sighed. "That's immaturity, just like the hacks you would claim to despise."

For all the bravado the young man exhibited in the tense moments that followed, Solzhenitsyn knew that the boy's energy was absorbed in an act of desperate aggression designed to hide a child's tears. Solzhenitsyn knew for he had been there also. Lowering the austere remonstration of the raised cane, Solzhenitsyn steadied himself before edifying his young student. The master trembled. They were close, so very close. If only the young man would take his lessons to heart. "Leave that to those who haven't been given your talent, who haven't been called. You're not in the business of performance."

Viewing regret in the face of his young artist, the master added, placing a paternal hand on the young man's shoulder, "It's all right, Alexi. Never be afraid. Never succumb to it. All artists go there. But remember, Alexi: the great ones do not stay."

Picking the brush from the carpet Solzhenitsyn inspected it closely, weighing it in his gentle hand. He took mental note of the striking color: a lustrous, somehow metallic mauve, shimmering and fiery. He did not tell Rooster that it seemed to him an original color, one that he himself, in all his years of painting, had never seen. Simply, he commented, "It's a good brush. I don't believe it caused the outburst."

In the early days of their training, such a comment would have made Rooster laugh with a lightened heart. Now such statements, sincere reproaches that honestly acknowledged how far behind schedule he had fallen, stung. With a trembling hand, his good hand, his leprous hand, he reached out and touched the wound he had inflicted on the canvas. Regret alone could not heal what he had done. The gaping chasm left Rooster feeling hollow, plain.

"It makes me tired, Soli."

"It should make you tired," the old master chastised. "Painting should exhaust you. It should leave you empty, used, *worthless* . . . with nothing left to give. That is what painting demands, every time, always. It puts you through horrible storms, storms of the heart within, storms that rage with a fury far greater than your body or mind can withstand alone. That's how painting, the act of painting, affects little souls like you and me. You know that. You know it's not the painting; it's the act of painting, the will to paint, the need to paint yourself through the storm, a storm that exists for no reason and with no intention other than your destruction.

"That's why you paint, Rooster. It's not some grand metaphor or an abstract exercise. It's the moment-by-moment truth of life. It's what you are doing every time you stare at that canvas, every time you prepare your paints, every time you clean your utensils, every time you bare your soul upon that canvas, every time you acknowledge the limits of your body and then ignore those limits. It should make you tired, Rooster. It should make you tired. *At first.* For that's what it takes to slip into the dream work. Only when you fall asleep to this world will you be allowed to awake in the other. It's not enough to rise early, Rooster. You must also work late!"

Rooster shook his head, scratched his scalp and watched the white flakes of dandruff drift from light into shadow, into a worldly chiaroscuro so complex that sight becomes ineffectual and frozen. The words of the old man were like they always were: different, always the same, never quite believable, too ethereal, spellbinding, utterly undeniable. He listened to each word. Closing his eyes, he tried with all his might to truly hear the meaning beyond the words, behind them. He didn't know how to listen. Sometimes he attempted to empty his mind of all effort. Inevitably he found himself floating away in his thoughts, lingering as a seraph above a warm field of brilliant colors, where red-billed ducks with orange paddles for feet have cerulean blue bodies. Floating above his canvas, the fiery sun radiated off his back. He was like a spectator who creates the game he watches, in perfect control of playful juxtaposition. Where all that should have been green was red, and all red became yellow, and black turned clear as crystal, and pink auburn and pale ivory turned to sand, and indigo to glowing, opulent pearl. Chocolate to mocha and vanilla to caramel, brittle gray to smooth azure, magenta to mustard, carmine to vermilion, sienna to ash, crimson to brick, tan to tawny, bronze to periwinkle, shimmer to shade. Granite to dust to dust. Pleading and lost, Rooster looked to Solzhenitsyn.

"I can see it, Soli. Sometimes right here in front of me. It's real, but I can't paint it. It's too big. It's too big for me."

"Then cut it down to size," the old man snapped, lunging forward, ripping the polycarbonate palette from the young boy's trembling hand in a manner that would have convinced anyone that the old master's age endured as a by-product not of reality but of bizarre illusion. "Look here, Alexi, look here." The master waved his arm.

"You take the time to manifest a wonderful background but you utterly lack the courage to fill it. You create a beautiful setting, but then you leave it blank. You try to dupe your audience into believing that the majesty of the thing should lie in the background. Or, perhaps worse," and here the master pointed at the seemingly haphazard dash of green, "you try to sneak in a foreground so inconspicuous, so circumspect, that it won't be noticed for anything but what it isn't. In a word, you ask the canvas to lie for you, and it does. It's a pure reflection of you. And what I see in this painting is a man who lacks the courage to step into the foreground. A man utterly, utterly afraid to grasp the mantle of his life and beat away all that would oppose the reality you extend."

Solzhenitsyn pointed with his cane to the rip. "I see a man desperate to escape, so desperate that he attempts to hide behind the background while parading such fraud as boldness, intrepidity, brazen moxie. That's what you did, isn't it? You hadn't the guts to put yourself on the canvas prominently for others to see, so you fabricated an escape hatch, a release valve, a gambit, a black hole back into yourself." The old master stared at Rooster with boring, meaningful eyes that shined brightly. "It's not great yet. It's extremely good, Alexi, but not great. And it won't be until you place yourself firmly at the center, in the foreground of a background that you intend to protect with your very life. No reversals, no projections into the future, no regressions into the past. No inversions or paradoxes or contradictions. Just the honest you, smack dab there." The master pointed with his cane to the center of the canvas. "There!"

An iron-willed hand extended, the old man offered to the young artist the brush he had picked from the floor. Rooster stopped asking questions. He stopped protesting. There were a thousand reasons and more why he could not do this thing which was asked of him. There was one old man, an old master perhaps in the grip of madness, telling him that he could.

"Come Rooster, try again, essai, this time with wisdom."

Rooster stared into Soli's eyes, neither searching nor hopeful. Something different, more noble within, caused him to look. In that instant Soli's eyes seemed to Rooster the most solid material the world would ever fashion. Rooster dipped his brush into whatever color struck his fancy. On the canvas he painted the number "37" in thick, linear blocks. For once, the colors seemed unimportant. The tear in the center of the canvas was a senseless act of destruction. Could it be made beautiful?

Again, Rooster stabilized his leprous arm upon a custom made, hickory maulstick. With his free hand, he squeezed a half tube of verdant green upon the palette and dipped the brush full.

"It seems to be going into remission again," Solzhenitsyn suggested.

Rooster glanced down, unconcerned by the chalky scales and the grayish puss that oozed from beneath. His hand was grotesque, but Soli did not think so. Soli could not think of anything that produced such beauty, as Rooster's hand did, as grotesque, unnatural and sick.

"It might be."

"It is." Solzhenitsyn attempted to sound positive, knowing that when it came to this topic, leprosy, he was no master.

For a moment, Rooster clenched the fist, remembering the pain. The brush now in hand wavered like a rapidly beating metronome before landing upon the canvas. He spoke softly to Soli, unconsciously raptured. "Green shall be my suture."

Solzhenitsyn sat back in a corner, breathed deeply, content that age had not yet seen fit to betray him.

♂

"I'm castrated. Castrated!" Marcel Phrenol was an evil man. "I cannot write another word. It is hopeless, hopeless."

The sumptuous woman lay in bed, tangled in percale sheets, stretching in the lazy sunshine that entered through cracked windows. The frustration of a writer she could not take too seriously. He had, after all, been a great lay, an athletic, giving lover who knew just what to take and where. The sudden transformation of the morning could do little to convince her that the curiously bold proclamation possessed true meaning. Closing her leonine eyes and settling deeply into the luxury of the bed, she tuned the man out and thought, "So this is what it's like to be rich."

The fifty-year-old novelist with confident hands that could be as soft as any woman, stripped the sheets away, exposing her naked body. Until now, she had not felt how cool the air truly was. He boxed her to the head. "Get out! Get up and get out of here!"

"Marcie! Marcie!" she called as she had the prior night. This time the cry did not cause him to melt in transcendent delight. "What is it? What's wrong?"

Gripping her arm, he ripped her from the bed and tossed her to the floor. "Are you deaf? Are you as cheap and stupid as you look? Get out! Get out with the trash!"

"Marcie." Confusion spread across her eyes as she looked past him to the bed, craving, despite his vengeance, to return to its comfort, the glorious sill of its cocoon.

"Don't call me that. You're a stupid skank. A cheap, stupid, miserable slut. How little you know. How little you understand." She saw the pen in his hand, the manuscript on the desk.

"Marcie please. I don't have to. . . ."

"Do you listen?" he shouted above her, snatching at her clothes, so recently enticing. "Out! Get yourself out with the trash. I am ruined, ruined!"

Naked and afraid, breasts bouncing, scampering for scattered articles of clothing, she scurried to the bathroom, running from the nightmare into which the day had dragged her.

Despite the fugue of warnings with regard to his reputation, she had found Marcel Phrenol charming, delicious, wonderful — like the salient perfume that covered her own stubborn carcass. Her cheek smarted. She studied the spot in the mirror quickly. It had only been meant to sting. And now she knew, for she had always wondered, what it was like to be with a great artist. If he had called her back to bed now, she would have gone, given herself completely, without restriction.

On the other side of the door, a fury raged. "Salamander. A rotten salamander. A rotten salamander!" She had no idea what had him. She would have gladly sat and listened, deemed herself blessed with the opportunity to bear witness.

Something cracked against the door as he hollered venomously, "Get out of here! Now! Get out of here now!"

It amazed her how comfortable she had become, how much, despite everything, she desired to stay. Quickening her pace, she pulled on her nylons and panties, her slip and her skirt. The bra she tossed aside, knowing fully why — to leave something behind. She gazed outside the bathroom window; a perfect bubble sky spun round. *Azure*. She smiled. It had been Marcel who taught her the meaning of the word. Before him, she had thought it just a word, different from blue only in its poetic cache. But azure is different than blue, and though it is found mostly in the sky, it is elsewhere also, in neon reflections and chilled, waxen lips and the gray hair of old women near death. She had fallen in love with Marcel for his mind — his sexy, glorious, insightful mind so that even now she could not bear to leave; and this, she already understood, was the very reason he drove her out so fatally.

He pounded upon the door with blind fists. "Do you hear me? Get out of here! Get out before I kill you! Before I destroy you! Get out! Do you hear me? Get out! Get out!"

She pressed the tears away from her cheekbones with the flat edge of her fist. She pulled the blouse over her head, the silver shimmering blouse that had caught his eye as she had known it would. She only had one heel; the other she could not find.

"Get out, you miserable little thing!"

Fearful now, genuinely, almost unsure, she opened the door. Marcel backed away, surprised by her pluck. For a brief moment, staring into the icy flame of his pale eyes, she wondered if he had intended to keep guard, to keep her with his threats from ever leaving again. The flashing thought faded in an instant. Marcel would never permit a thought of such mercy to exist undefiled.

"Don't think it. Don't think it," he shouted. "Don't think it. You're a whore!"

Racing across the room, she seized her bag. The other heel was nowhere to be found and she did not intend to search under the bed. Marcel, having temporarily escaped her view, returned, casting the silk, leopard-print bra in her face. "Trash for trash, salamander. Take your trash."

"Marcel," she began, but ceased upon sight of his passionate face, a contradiction to all his cruel assertions.

In the hall she almost broke down, holding the single pump by the heel. No, she thought, Marcel would hate that — or would he love it? She snapped the heel in strong, sudden violence, hurling the pieces at the door with both arms, shouting back, her own marvelous voice more powerful than ever. "It's your trash! Yours!"

⌒

By his own account, Rooster judged his tonal selections to be per-
fidious, deliberate breaches of faith. Horrible color, crooked lines, dis-
proportioned shapes, thematic distortions lost within the essential
dimension: distance. Madness, incompetent madness. A streak of zinc
yellow, suppressed imagination, broke down the middle of the canvas.
The mark was not sufficiently bold to declare itself a shaman's bolt of
lightning, so Rooster instead created a blunted dagger slashing the
intestines of space open wide. And just what did the universe consume? Nothing, nothing, nothing. Using a brittle, stained thumbnail,
Rooster dabbed at the glinting fringe of the line, pressing and dragging,
pressing and dragging, until contrast between light and dark softened,
flattened like a mist. And what had his mind been thinking to choose
a bold red to navigate the margins of the canvas? He cursed, submis-
sive to the profane, not too proud to pursue hell for an insight into
heaven. He had taken abstraction too far. It was rubbish and he knew
it. Abstraction had taken him. "What now?" he questioned. No density. No gravity. No weight. Sheer and superficial, ready to pop. With a
plastic scalpel he scraped away at clumpy red patches. It's like a spreading sickness, he thought. What he left behind resembled lava flows
stretched to an unnatural, deceptive end. At least this game brought
him peace; anything can be derealized. Lava flows, liquid bricks. It
shouldn't resemble anything, he scolded himself, tossing the scalpel
aside in defeat. It was supposed to be simple. Why did he have to make
it so, so much harder?

No, it wasn't supposed to be simple. It was supposed to be hard.
Only constant vigilance could protect the integrity of his work. It
should exhaust you; that's what Soli had said. How quickly the lessons
could be forgotten.

From a wider prospectus he searched deeper into the heart of the
painting. How many idols had his imagination tarnished, how many
defiled, how many razed? Between thick strokes of black and red black,
like the middle firmament of an Egyptian pyramid, a rectangle of lumi-
nescent green, like a radioactive toxin, spilled forth, threatening to consume the entire canvas. The color had Rooster thinking about alien
blood, of some thin, invertebrate worm from the pages of science fic-

tion. Goopy, gummy, viscous, gelatinous, genocidal plasma. The headache that itched in his arm was coming on. Artists were supposed to think about great things. They were supposed to be concerned with the bottomless suffering of humanity and the changing of the world, with utopias and government and oppression, with war and senseless violence, with existential dread, meaningful iconoclasm, homelessness, euthanasia, apocalypse . . . and what else? Rooster didn't know.

It was abysmal.

At the bottom of the painting, where a signature might go, Rooster pasted a horizontal collage, a sestina he had scribbled free hand in blue ink. Corrections scratched in red felt, only the center of the poem survived his own fiendish critic. The borders of the paper he'd torn away, creating a ragged fringe. Running a hand through his hair, he used a fan brush to dust over the poem, rendering a smoky illusion, a shroud. Spirits swept along the page in dim purple streaks.

Why couldn't he just paint like Renoir or Miró? Hell, to be that good would have been respectable. But those, those names of history, he could never join them. The religious magic that happened on their canvases resided more in their brushes than in their souls. They were more human, more real, more authentic than he. They had reason and purpose, something more than mere existence, more than the passing of one day into the next without going mad, without breaking down in recognition of the enigmatic, random and hopeless nature of all being. Sutured, just below the center of the canvas, there stretched the long slice he had inflicted upon the canvas when Soli had asked him "Why?"

Soli had warned Rooster that this hour would come, the hour when the art of painting stopped mattering, when form became a joke and all effort a tedious louse. Another thirteen hours had passed without a single eruption of genius — or even promise. It did not matter if he continued. It did not matter if he stopped. How terrible the world had made itself for him. He turned out the light, picked up his utensils for cleaning. Opening his mouth wide, he yawned in terror and exhaustion both.

Three months had passed since Solzhenitsyn's death, three empty months without the voice of the master in his ear. *Trust yourself,* Soli would have urged with full, heartbreaking earnest. Rooster missed the old man. Inspired by the memory of his mentor, rising against the exhaustion, feeling his way though the darkness, he approached the canvas once more. His hands reached for the palette and two tubes of paint. He moved precisely, like a calibrated machine, knowing exactly where everything was. Squeezing the paints upon the palette, he settled his leprous arm in the maulstick and raised a brush to the canvas. He knew what was there and the landscape he sought to create, knew it by heart. *Trust yourself.* Rooster dipped the brush and began painting. He needed no external light; the vision, the purpose existed within.

⌐

Inside Marcel Phrenol one goal existed. He desired to win the Nobel Prize in Literature. Three times he had been rumored to be on the short list, then passed over. His most recent novel, entitled *Another Day of Loving*, had been received to the most lavish and momentously positive critical acclaim of his career. A cumulative consensus seemed to be swelling that if Marcel were passed over a fourth time, politics alone could be to blame. Despite the stinging rejection of the prior years, confidence did have a grip on him. So good was *Another Day of Loving*, so named after a line from Kahlil Gibran's classic, *The Prophet* — "To know the pain of too much tenderness, To be wounded by your own understanding of love; And to bleed willingly and joyfully. To wake at dawn with a winged heart and give thanks for another day of loving" — that Marcel Phrenol believed himself used up.

Marcel shaved slowly in the mirror, content to let the steam fade the wrinkles of his stern cheeks into clean white clouds. The blade he used was dull. Of habit, he shaved without foam or gel. At most he would use a sparse soap lather. He found the idea of shaving cream to be a particularly feminine expense, reserved for the men he had been reading about lately who attempted to justify their manicures and facials as anything less than a slow swelling movement towards the fulfillment of a latent homosexuality. There were things, he reasoned, that in both life and in his writing could be too elegant. The skin of his neck and face served as rough contrast to the tenderness within his hands.

From the other room a crow cawed. "Quiet, Prophet," he scolded. Officially, the hotel did not allow pets of any kind. Marcel doubted that they would dare grieve him about the bird, so fierce was his reputation for getting what he wanted. The bird cawed again — a long, shrill trochee, one long note immediately followed by one short note. "I know," Marcel assented. "She is a special woman." Wiping away the few soapy bubbles that collected by his ears, Marcel slipped into a laundered, button down oxford. Entering the study, he raised his arm to the bird, pressing the shirtsleeve against the perched talons. Responding to the touch, the crow stepped upon Marcel's arm, sidling up the forearm, past the elbow and to the shoulder. Picking a few peanuts from his pants pocket Marcel fed them directly into the beak of the bird. "Passionate as hell, she is."

Marcel claimed the ability to speak the language of the bird, American crow. When lubricated with alcohol, he would sometimes demonstrate the talent with a proficiency that others found eerily convincing. Prophet often seemed inclined to agree with Marcel's claim, responding to Marcel's assortment of caws at thoughtful intervals that many accepted as sufficient proof that a single, continuous line of communication did in fact exist between the bird and the man. Sometimes, almost unconsciously, Marcel would slip from English to crow and back again. The bird doted through it all, as attentive to Marcel as a devoted wife.

What made the relationship more astounding was that Prophet was as blind as Milton. The poor bird had had both eyes shot out with a pistol — a snub pellet that struck askance, traveling in one eye and exiting through the other, leaving neither behind. From 60 yards in the wind and with an unsighted pistol, his friend, Everett Duman, the European marksman, had shot the bird on a drunken wager. Despite the fact that Marcel had not pulled the silver trigger, he may as well have; the idea for the contest had originated in his mind. Marcel loved tests of skill and talent. He loved being the best almost as much as he loved being with those who were the best. When the whistling bullet left the chamber, both men grew silent, watching the bird in the distance, perched upon the lonely dogwood bough, a single limb stretched into the wintry sky. Both expected the bird to fall, to drop like so much dead weight into the slushy snow. Instead, they witnessed only a disturbing shudder, defiant and horrid, dense and sobering as a psychic scream. For a fleeting moment the crow appeared destined to plunge downward into death, just as the two men expected. The legs buckled, its strength drained, but then all motion stopped and the bird grew steady, appallingly steady, a dark, stable, motionless omen against the steel-gray landscape.

Breathing heavily into the frosty winter air, both men stared, unsure. The great European marksman raised the pistol a second time, insulted. Marcel placed his hand before the muzzle.

"There's no need."

As in a trance, the author dragged himself through the slush. His vintage leather shoes were no defense against the cold ice melting against his foot. He felt numb, unaware of anything and everything except the crow, the only living thing in his dead world. The European marksman cursed the shot but did not follow. Marcel walked a step behind the heated breath smoking from his mouth, a breath rising into the air so crisply quiet that angel songs could be heard within the desolation.

Approaching, Marcel knew the crow would stay. It would not fly away. He understood that they were connected to each other as surely as a child is connected to its mother, each giving birth to the other, each dying in simultaneity. The black bird waited on the white limb against the gray horizon, waited for Marcel to cup it round the wings and place it beneath his arm. Marcel did not attempt to wipe away the tears that fell from his eyes and the bird's sockets, tears of saltwater and blood. The bullet had passed through clean and pure, precise and perfect, just as one would expect from the masterful aim of a European marksman of noble descent. It was then that Marcel saw his future. The docile crow never struggled. It neither cawed in pain nor fought as Marcel tucked it beneath his arm. Marcel often told people that he had wavered between two names for his familiar, Prophet and Tiresias. In the end he chose Prophet. The name, to him, seemed freer of symbolism.

"Passionate as hell," Marcel again repeated, returning from his fog of memory at the behest of the bird who was seeking more peanuts. "That's it, Prophet, they're all gone," the man stated lovingly to the bird as it nipped at his gentle fingertips. The bird released a single admonishing caw, and Marcel stroked the black feathers. "Yes, yes. I promise. We'll get more."

☞

Pressing a loose curl of blonde hair over an ear, Dorothia Rodriguez stood before the most recent work of her son, Alexi. With pious concentration, her watchful gaze scrutinized each brushstroke. This work he had not named. In fact, he never named anything; he found the concept of naming a painting to be an odious, needless repetition. "That's what frames are for," he would assert.

Since the death of her husband, Dorothia had raised her son alone. At the time of his father's death, Alexi was only four, barely of an age to retain coherent memories of the talented man who had hunted spectacular, exotic photos from around the globe for National Geographic magazine. Having sacrificed all of her own dreams to support her late husband's passions, passions that died when he died, she considered and accepted her own life to be a failure. Alexi's life she vowed to make a masterpiece. This vow, made as pall bearers lowered the casket of her husband into the hallowed ground, she revered with the zealous devotion of a martyr and the stoicism of a saint. It had been her relentless pestering that had brought the special scholarship for the economically disadvantaged to Rooster. It had been her insistence that drove Rooster to accost the master with his sketches. Now, with Soli dead, her son rejected from Danforth, disconnected and unknown, she needed to fight harder than ever before.

Alexi's talents had burgeoned under Soli's tutelage. He now painted with a virtue of patience sorely absent from his earlier efforts. Standing before the current painting, she could recognize the gift that Soli had planted in her son — wisdom. The wisdom of a lifetime of being an honored painter, the secret confidences that come with the ability to judge value truly. It was a quiet, self-assured energy that ached from the canvas. For the first time Dorothia suspected the depth of her son's being. She did not comprehend what was there, nor did she try. She understood only that a depth had been sown which the greatest artists and critics would be capable of perceiving. Yes, this alone mattered.

No longer, as in earlier years, did Dorothia have to worry or concern herself with her son's talent. As surely as roots exist for a tree that stands, it existed. But she did now have cause to concern herself with the critical issue of recognition for her son's considerable talent, and this proved the first and foremost reason for which she placed herself so conspicuously in the path of Marcel Phrenol.

"It's glorious, Alexi."

Rooster sat in the corner, defeated, exhausted. "It's trash, Mother. I can do nothing without Soli."

The abject description warmed Dorothia's heart. Her son no longer needed Soli and she knew it just as surely as Soli had. She could feel the swell of progress. "Why do you call it trash, Alexi? It's magnificent, better than anything you have done."

Rooster rubbed at his arm, feeling the shingles peel back, exposing raw flesh.

"You mustn't rub," his mother warned.

The boy exploded, choked with energy, pointing at the canvas, "Look at it! Look at the center, at the green in the center. It's useless, my own flaw. I can't correct it, can't go back. There, there forever, ruining everything I do and everything I touch. Look at it. That's why it's trash. That's why. There, the center, the core. Everything else is background to it."

Dorothia found herself both scared and thrilled by Alexi's outburst as she directed her attention to the canvas center. There she saw, for the first time, the sutured rip, painstakingly integrated into the landscape of original and unexpected color, a centerpoint completely missed. The cut had been synthesized into the artist's rendering, transformed into a natural expression.

"Soli tried. He tried to teach me."

Dorothia caught her breath. The seamless suture of green made the painting more, not less of a wonder.

"I wouldn't listen."

"Rooster, there is a man, a man you must meet for me." Rooster did not argue. He didn't care. He was too exhausted, and at least his mother had called him by the name he preferred. Again he returned to the corner, slumping into the chair from which Soli had so often chided.

"Alexi, do you listen? There is a man you must meet for me."

"Whatever you wish, Mother. Bring him to me. I'll meet him. Bring him to me." Rooster drifted off into sleep, muttering words the old man would have spoken.

Dorothia turned quickly to protest, but her son's gaping mouth stopped her. Yes, she thought, Marcel must be brought here. The reasons were beyond her now, but the mission was clear. "You'll call it *Songbird*."

"What?" Rooster summoned the voice to ask, his eyelids closed and his head tilted back.

"*Songbird*. This painting, you'll call it *Songbird*."

Rooster peered from his seat to the painting that mocked him, his vanity and all his desire. "Why?" He was not opposed. Anything would have been acceptable. The words ascribed to the painting were for those who could not read the painting in-itself, of-itself. He resented his own curiosity.

"Did you know," Dorothia began, "that the crow is a songbird? It's considered quite a beast by many. We shout 'Stupid bird' and all sorts of horrible things like that at crows. But, in fact, they're not stupid at all. They've been proven to be at least as smart as monkeys, maybe smarter. And loyal as dogs if you can believe that. They mate for life and they can recognize distinct humans. Interesting, isn't it? We all look the same to them, but they don't look the same to us. No, no, that's not it, it's the other way around. *They* look the same to us, but we don't look the same to them. They recognize individual humans, and they remember us too, even out of context. Imagine that. They're considered a songbird, but I already said that, didn't I? When they are alone, so the myth goes, they sing a beautiful song, but they won't do that, of course, unless you're very special . . . and they recognize you." Dorothia extended her hand and touched the canvas, the green suture, the anguished tear. "Even out of context."

Rooster stared from the chair at his mother. Soli would not have spoken so simply, but he would have said the same kind of things. He rose again and reached against the wall for a fresh canvas. *Songbird* he placed aside, complete. The weariness evaporated magically. His brushes were laid out, the pallet clean.

"Bring him to me," Rooster ordered, a request with authority. With a piece of charcoal in his hand, he settled his leprous arm upon the maulstick and addressed the easel. "Now leave me, Mother. I have work that must be done." The hand applied to the new canvas looked odd, deformed, warped and surreal. He sketched hastily. Already Rooster's face displayed signs of strain from the effort it required to hold the black chalk. Dorothia kissed her son on the temple. "My magnificent son," she said as she left the room that smelled of turpentine.

2

MARCEL ROSE FROM the grave. The clean, white Alabama marble slab was encircled by thirteen yellow roses, fanning out from the stone in a half-moon arch. The darkest months had passed. More would come. The grass was green, freshly cut. When do they cut the grass at a cemetery? The hole in Marcel's heart had not healed as all wounds are said to do. Time had only gouged him deeper.

A family passed him. Two children and a mother holding hands. "What pretty flowers," the little girl uttered. Marcel noticed only the innocent face and the woolen coat with torn pockets.

Every Sunday for five years Marcel had come to this spot. He searched for signs. In the first year they had been plentiful. Butterflies, birds, a wild growing columbine. All of life became a speaking symbol of minor miracles. Only later did the reality of dirt arrive; the reality that the roses rotted, were sometimes stolen; the reality that weather did soil the stone, that uncut grass grew thick with weeds; the reality that six feet below the ground nothing changed. This Sunday was special, though still not a sign. This Sunday marked the eighth anniversary of their wedding. Eight, such a number of completion, so steady, stable, sure and infinite.

Had he been unfaithful last night sleeping with that woman, that lovely, vivacious woman? He had made her believe — made himself believe — it was standard fare. In truth, he had not been with a woman since his wife's death.

He did not cry or apologize. He did not even pray. He simply stood dumbly, expecting nothing, unsure of why he still came and knowing that he would not stop. A plane passed overhead, a large one with the icon for Continental Airlines, a geometric globe, on its tail. He watched it pass across the wide sky, roaring dully. He found himself thinking about terrorists and death. He found himself imagining the plane exploding in a brilliant conflagration overhead, a display to fill the sky and create a new series of spinning, swirling clouds. That is all it would do, all that it would mean. He had no taste in his mouth for tragedy.

He would see the woman again, sleep with her, throw her out. It would be a good routine: simple, clean. He would not tell her that he cared for her, that she touched him somehow. He would not reveal to her in any way that she could not be replaced. It would be like business, like writing a book. Total attachment without attachment.

"Life does not have to go on," Marcel said aloud. Two chickadees darted by, but it was not affirmation. "Life can end for we, the living. In mid-stride we can lift a gun to our head and terminate this thing."

At a dank bar at the end of Beacon Street, Marcel drank gin and tonics. They were weak. He chewed on the limes, sucking for pulp until his face went pug with bitterness and the rind was stripped clean. Baseball games showed on the tubes, one at each end of the bar.

"Give me another." The bartender poured slowly. Sapphire gin. Another hit. Double off the Green Monster. Two runs score. Two RBIs. Pitching change. No. Hang in there. Get that last out. Yankees winning again. Fuck Ruth.

"Damn Red Sox," the bartender cursed. "It's like they don't want to win."

"They can't," Marcel responded, his mournful eyes glued to the hazy screen. The bartender tipped the bottle higher.

Dorothia knew she would find him here. He knew she would find him. Such predictions had become easy since Prophet had entered his life.

"Marcel." She placed her hand intimately on his arm. "Let's go. You don't have to. . . ." But she knew he did, and that it was all right.

"Drink?"

"A little early for me." She had a gin fizz.

"Angry?"

"I'm not angry," she stated calmly, compassionately. Another double, this one spinning down the line, careening in the corner, chalk flying.

They watched in silence as another Yankee rounded third, waved home, another nail in the coffin.

He touched her cheek, the slight bruise covered by a thick foundation. "I'm sorry."

She held his fingertips against her cheek, against the sorest spot, each sharing in the unspoken depth of the other's pain, mollifying both if only for the passing moment. The touch felt good, healing, a reminder that the one who delivers the wound can most profoundly heal the wounded.

They left the bar and returned by cab to the penthouse suite. After sex, they smoked cigarettes as Marcel read aloud from William Blake's mystic poem, "America: A Prophecy." The sun descended slowly over the city, consuming Cambridge, Kenmore Square, the Prudential, the Commons, the afternoon of Sunday.

> *Then had America been lost, o'erwhelm'd by the*
> *Atlantic,*
> *And Earth had lost another portion of the infinite,*

Dorothia read the newspapers. They were like an old couple of many years, comfortable and equal in their turns, individual texts that fuse into a common text more beautiful and somehow less fragile for the idiosyncratic. They ordered dinner and drinks, not in that order.

Tossing the news aside, Dorothia mused with a finger upon Marcel's body, lean and hairy with supple, sturdy thighs. He had a slight belly that she imagined indicative of wealth but not indulgence; the kind that comes from living the good life without ever wholly entering the good life, like a boy raised poor who never forgives the sting of economy, never forgetting the possibility of return. There were scars on his body. A long knife wound just below the abdomen. Salvador, he had told her without machismo. He continued reading Blake.

> *Albion's Guardian writhed in torment on the eastern*
> *Sky*
> *Pale, quiv'ring toward the brain his glimmering eyes,*
> *Teeth chattering,*
> *Howling & shuddering, his legs quivering, convuls'd*
> *Each muscle and sinew:*

She ran her fingers along the abdominal scar, down to his flaccid penis, where she studied the thick blue veins. Pressing aside the pubic hair, she explored the intense geography.

> *And, rough with black scales, all his Angels fright their*
> > *Ancient heavens.*
> *The doors of marriage are open, and the Priests in*
> > *Rustling scales*
> *Rush into reptile coverts, hiding from the fires of Orc,*
> *That play around the golden roofs in wreaths of fierce*
> > *Desire,*
> *Leaving the females naked and glowing with the lusts*
> > *Of youth.*

The penis glistened with her own dried juices, like a crackling sugar glaze. Bow-legged, she thought, brushing the backs of her painted fingernails along the thighs. She liked a bow-legged man. Moving upward, through the forest of hair upon his chest, Dorothia pressed her hand, tugging lightly at the flattened nipples. It was a masculine body, established with the signs of a rugged, natural youth lived with vigorous purpose. Still, she could not avoid the awareness that this body, not quite old, no longer was young.

Fanning curls of flaxen hair across his chest, she listened for his heartbeat.

> *The heavens melted from north to south; and Urizen,*
> > *Who sat*
> *Above all heavens, in thunders wrap'd, emerg'd his*
> > *Leprous head*
> *From out his holy shrine, his tears in deluge piteous*
> *Falling into the deep sublime; flag'd with grey-brow'd*
> > *Snows*

Finding rhythm in his beating heart and the strong, metered cadence of his voice, Dorothia, hungry eyes turned downward, stroked his member, watching it grow as his voice, secure and unchanged, completed the passage.

> *His stored snows he poured forth, and his icy magazines*
> *He open'd on the deep, and on the Atlantic sea white*
> > *Shiv'ring*

Leprous his limbs, all over white, and hoary was his
    Visage,
Weeping in dismal howlings before the stern Americans,

What does Orc represent to America, she would later ask. Her own
heart pounded with excitement as the pace quickened, a desperate,
feverish, demonstration of control. Who is Urizen? And why the leprous limbs?

Stiff shudderings shook the heav'nly thrones! France,
    Spain & Italy
In terror viewed the bands of Albion, and the ancient
    Guardians,
Fainting upon the elements, smitten with their own
    Plagues.
They slow advance to shut the five gates of their lawbuilt
    Heaven,
Filled with blasting fancies and with mildews of
    Despair,
With fierce disease and lust, unable to stem the fires of
    Orc.
But the five gates were consum'd, & their bolts and
    Hinges melted;
And the fierce flames burnt round the heavens & round
    The abodes of men.

Swallowing the last of Dorothia's drink, Marcel closed the book and
slipped it softly beneath his pillow. She didn't wipe or wash her hands.
A unique thing, Marcel thought, watching her on the phone ordering
more drinks. He adored her. When she returned he drew her into the
tangled sheets. Pressing her legs over his shoulders he buried his
tongue within her navel, playfully tickling his way downwards until his
tongue was dancing upon her clitoris. He held her firm, tight, as she
wriggled towards a mounting release. She bucked from the hips, pulling
his head, with force and vigor, into her wet, vaginal folds. Her sigh,
mingled with tears, filled the room with pleasure. The drinks arrived as
Marcel, with a hand on her womanly hips, softly suckled her breasts.

"I want you to meet my son," Dorothia proposed as Marcel rose from the bed to wrap himself in a hotel robe. Cracking the door he took the drinks. Two gins and tonic. Tall. Limes. Sapphire.

"Whatever the hell for?"

She deflected. "You know, I was reading in the papers about these genetic scientists who have discovered a way to override the cell's counting device, the mechanism of the cell that tells it when to stop replicating. Every cell has it, you know, except for the egg and sperm generating cells." Swirling the ice cubes, she licked her fingers thoughtfully. "And tumor cells."

Marcel quickly swallowed half his drink.

"They loosely call them 'immortality cells.' The ones with no replicative end life. The scientists. Where were they from? China? Or was it an American team led by a Chinese? Anyway, the scientists have learned to turn off the mechanism. It's called the telomere shortening system. They've actually taken cells that normally will divide only fifty times and divided them hundreds of times with the anti-cancer cells still working fine and dandy."

"The death of senescence," Marcel uttered ruefully.

"What's that?"

"Senescence. Aging. Growing old. The ultimate sickness. Why do you tell me this?"

"Why do you read Blake to me?"

"Yes," he acquiesced without offering an explanation. "Now drink your drink."

"I want you to meet my son." Plucking the lime from her glass, she fed it to Marcel.

"I hate children."

"He's not a little boy, Marcel."

Marcel rubbed his hands together for warmth. "Damn cold in here." Rising, he drew the shades without a glance at the scenery below. Withdrawing the hood that covered Prophet's cage, he whispered to the bird.

"Why do you keep it covered if it's blind?"

"Habit. Besides, Prophet can still hear. Did they send up the peanuts? Yes. Here we are."

Dorothia watched as Marcel fed the hungry bird by hand. There was something charming about the act, seeing the man dote upon the strange, blind bird, caressing the feathers with a thick thumb. She sensed that one had taken care of the other for a long time, that each had come to rely upon the other, growing, to the mutual comfort of each, dependent. A relationship of this nature would be simple to understand from the perspective of the blind bird. After all, Prophet would be unable to survive in freedom now. This was an assumption; she knew that nature likely had a multiplicity of secret codes at her disposal, codes even more arcane than a genetic sequence designed to ensure that a brilliant, if lonely, man would preserve a debilitated bird. Dorothia well understood how nature can be mysterious and cruel in similar, if not the very same, patterns of breath.

"So who is Urizen?" she asked. "And who is this Orc? Reminds me of Mork from Orc every time I hear the name. Do you remember that program? Robin Williams and who else? Who was that girl? Didn't she get killed? I remember a murder, something about her, or was it her sister? I can't remember her name."

Marcel went on to patiently explain that for William Blake, 1740-1828 (died the same year as Beethoven), the world was a solipsistic manifestation of mind-forged manacles. Everything, according to Blake, emerged from the imagination of men. Possessed by this belief, he refused to believe in any proclaimed state of separation between heaven and earth. He was the ultimate rebel, denying the validity of any institution that sought to *educate* the mind; religion, government and schooling were mere landscapes for training in a moral cosmology that had no reason for existence other than the control and subjugation of individual imagination and freedom.

All cultural morality was a prison. Even the stars, for Blake, were not necessary facts. They were only ideas generated by the mask of culture, illusions from which we should be able to escape, padlocks we will be sufficiently capable of picking when we reclaim the autonomous powers of an individuated imagination from the fetters of history and culture — both obvious and odious forms of institutional enslavement.

Blake himself, Marcel went on to explain, created his own mythic land where he was considered a prince of the mind; it was a landscape full of cosmic characters of his own creative process, a land where angels dropped by his doorstep to listen to his tales of the marriage of heaven and hell. In this mythic cosmology of Blake, Marcel declared, Albion represents the eternal man, the perpetual ideal to which we will return when the doors of our perception are cleansed. But in our imperfect land, the world we know, existence begins with Urizen.

Urizen is reason, the net of a powerful reason, a logic that fears all that is unknown, a logic so driven by fear of this unknown that it seeks to enforce "perfection" by controlling (or at least containing) the unknown. Urizen does not trust the emotions and feelings of the body; they don't make perfect sense. And because they don't make perfect sense, Urizen sees the emotions and feelings *and needs* of the body — and thus the body — as flawed and chaotic, in need of correction, discipline and infinite ordering. To perfect this imperfection, this inferiority that Urizen can interpret only as pain, Urizen casts reason's net over all feelings and emotions. All cravings and supposed needs are to be evaluated and censored. All feelings and emotions are to be scrutinized and judged. A strict disciplining of the body's irrational tendencies is Urizen's immediate prescription. Reason is efficient, stunningly so. Of course, Urizen sees only Urizen as capable of bringing order and thus an organized, reasonable shape to the cosmic body.

In the act of "ordering" Urizen binds Los. Los, Marcel clarified, represented imagination in Blake's world. By taming the wild flux of Los, of imagination, Urizen believes that the world will be unified once more, just as Plato once envisioned the perfect state as being achieved only through banishment of the poet. But in the process of subjugating or containing imagination, Urizen is also affected. The desired end is achieved for but a fleet moment before Los, in a final act of rebellion, energy and unfettered imagination, conceives — with the unwitting help of Urizen, whose fear of the body provides ephemeral Los with the very material needed for escape — and gives birth to Orc.

Marcel stared at Dorothia knowingly. Orc is pure libido, pure sexual drive. Pure, remember that. Libido, Orc, to Urizen, is an evil thing that, like the wild, chaotic, unpredictable imagination of Los, must be tamed, harnessed, controlled, brought under a single law and a single, supreme rule of reason. Urizen cannot appreciate these forces in their free state, for Urizen cannot understand that which is not Urizen.

Marcel finally began winding down to a conclusion.

"Orc, imagination as expressed in the libidinal, is the one force that Blake believes may be capable of overthrowing the dreadful, sterilized, totalitarian state of institutionalized, one-law-fits-all being that Urizen promotes. But Blake also is uttering a warning. Blake warns of the danger of an imagination that is reduced to mere libido. This too would be an imagination enslaved, a dangerous imagination that mindlessly serves another form of master, a dangerous imagination enslaved not by the logic of a reason that must know all but by the insatiable needs of a libidinal body — cosmic, instinctual, undiscriminating to the degree that Urizen is discriminating — that must consume all.

"In his visionary declaration, 'America: A Prophecy,' Blake proclaims that only Orc, pure libido, pure sexual energy that chooses not to express itself in expressly sexual ways, is capable of redeeming the America of the future. It is Orc that will save America in the moment of critical crisis when the overwrought law of reason threatens her very existence as a nation. Total collapse, implosion: this is Blake's oracular message; this is the warning, and this is how it comes. America's prudish psyche is nurturing social voyeurism, an economy of social voyeurism, social withdrawal, a fully fueled escape into ourselves from which there need be no return. Only Orc can safely lead us through the dreadful terrain of the most honest spiritual challenge of our day, diving into materiality without succumbing to its gravity, without becoming the total victims of what we think we see."

"And you get all that from this poem?"

The crow let out a shrill spondee and flapped its wings.

Marcel tapped the beak. "I do."

Walking away, Marcel left the cage open. He thought of his Ruth, five years dead. She was pregnant at the time, though they — he — had not known it until autopsy. What a shock it had been to learn of the deceased child. Double cruelty. Double tragedy. Was it a double funeral? Should it have been? What difference would it have made? A gray slab of marble with no moral significance, no symbolic power, no correlation to some imagined divine providence, not even a name.

"You'll have to go now. I must write."

"My son?" she pressed immediately.

"Yes, yes, fine. Just leave. Take your immortal cells and leave." Finishing the gin and tonic in full gulps, he did not look at Dorothia as she dressed. Their parting would be more dignified this time. As she left, he thought about calling her back, to throw her down on the ground and take her as an animal is taken, or perhaps to run about the room naked, screaming, "Nan-no, Nan-no," clowning as the best clown does, laughing through the unendurable, making sincere comedy of the purest sorrow pouring forth: unrestrained, unchecked, unevaluated, unburdened.

As she closed the door, he could remember that silly television show. He could remember Mork entering the dark egg in his red uniform, a silver triangle upon the chest. Mork, wearing white gloves, preparing to report to the great, all-powerful, omnipotent and omnipresent, the shazbat of the shazbat, the master of all that was, is, and will be, the zany zane, the triumphant, the glorious, the hippest of the hip, coolest of the cool, the one who listens and is heard. Most of all, Marcel could recall the silence of the egg in the moment before transmission, silence like a tomb buried beneath the earth, silence like a seed buried, fully alive, beneath a winter carpet, unsure of whether what it knows will ever come to light. Mork, for all of his humor, always entered the darkness with just a little bit of trembling fear and just a bit of courage, something learned from the most human lesson of the human race. *Orson, calling Orson. Mork calling Orson. Come in Orson. It's Mork from Ork; come in Orson.* It was Pam Dauber, and it was a young co-star of Pam Dauber, who had been murdered years later by a fan. Marcel sat at the desk. It was all material, all of it. The words flowed. Prophet, caught in the shazbat of the moment, flew into a wall.

ℐ

"Everyone gets depressed. It's the grand form of entertainment of our time. It's a sign that we are recognizing the world in a truthful manner, no longer deluding ourselves about what it is or what it may be. We are relinquishing our inveterate habits of half-truths and social narcotics. When our co-worker asks, 'How are you?' we don't say 'Fine.' We tell them 'Terrible.' The wife is having an affair and your teenage son never talks to you; your alimony rates have increased and your mother thinks you are a horrible hypocrite. To add to all of this your car needs a wash, the brakes are going and your underwear is ice cold.

It's not fine, it's terrible, and in the midst of this honesty, this refusal to partake of the social narcotic, you gain clarity, an insight into deeper reality. And for the very first time, you understand that you never learned what true love is. You suddenly take a very deep breath and look at your co-worker. They want to think you've gone crazy, but they know you haven't. And you suddenly understand why you are paying alimony and why your current wife is having an affair and why your teenage son doesn't talk to you. You still don't know why your mother thinks you're a hypocrite, but for the first time you suspect that you are and that she is too, and that maybe you can forgive her for this because maybe she never learned what true love is either. This realization is very freeing. It frees you, and it frees your co-worker, and sometimes, by the time you have finished with these wonderful revelations, you notice that your shorts have warmed up a bit."

Laughter.

"So you see, it is through this simple activity of embracing our own depression, of stepping into it, that we are able to step free of the over-whelming, oppressively vast world and comfortably set ourselves in the very center, as the core dramatic. Modern depression is a wonderful form of entertainment when you think about it; ultimately, it's the price and reward of complete social interconnectivity. The reward is that through the television and radio and newspapers we get to witness all of the things that we will never experience. We become culturally sophisticated, even the lowest among us. The price is that we are stripped of blissful ignorance. In becoming socially sophisticated we confront what buffoons we really are. It breaks our heart. We feel that again and again and again we must leave behind our childish ways. We are constantly letting go, constantly giving up. There is no end in sight. We look in the mirror and hate what we see. We have become so cul-turally sophisticated that we don't recognize ourselves. Maybe it is our cultural sophistication that has turned us into buffoons. We grow depressed. We lose our faith. We doubt, for we no longer know what is false and what is real, what is of value and what is worthless.

"But we should not tremble at this moment. In this moment of mindfulness, there is a vast and simple opportunity to choose. It is a valiant choice. We can choose to love ourselves as we are, with no hope that we will become better, with no hope that our condition is temporary or that it will ever become any clearer. We simply make the decision to love ourselves and love each other. There exists the wonderful possibility of awakening in this moment of confused recognition. Knowing that this is the condition of our time, we can enter it, embrace it, accept it. We will love our wife who is having the affair. We will love our son who hates us. We will pay the alimony without resentment. We will love our mother though she scorns us. We will wash our car, check the brakes, put fresh underwear on the radiator before going to bed. A tremendous mindfulness emerges from the awakening that comes intact with embracing our depression. We awaken to the reality that we do not need any God to depress us. This, we can do all by ourselves. My friends, thank you."

Guru Marubrishnubupu rose from his lotus of purple pillows to modestly accept the dignified ring of applause. Dark satchels hung beneath his lively eyes. He was a short, unshaven man with walnut skin that looked youthful and radiant beyond its years. The interlaced fingers propped upon the slight belly that swelled from beneath his robes helped to create a pleasant, non-threatening aura.

It had been a placid ninety minutes before the group of affluent Americans. Their desire to feel guilty was great. How could this group possibly represent the most powerful nation on the globe? In his native India the average person could think better, more independently, than they could here. For all the possessions of even the lowest caste, the Americans carried a sense of loss and desperation with them. How did one man so completely and darkly pierce their collective psyche, Marubrishnubupu wondered, thinking of Thoreau, the truest of the American seers. His single voice reflecting off of Walden had succeeded in crippling the American dream, revealing the shallow depth years before it *needed* to be acknowledged, exposing the nightmare just beneath the surface. But even in this there is a beauty, for it is through recognition of the wound's pain that the deeper dream, *now needed before its time*, is dreamed.

"Marubrishnubupu, please touch me."

He walked through the crowd smiling and lightly meeting the hands reaching into space. He never shook them in the American way. The Americans are like artists who feel shame that they are not bohemians. They seek to see a poverty that is not there, attempting to fight the real-

ity that certain ideas can only be discovered under a certain set of conditions, within certain cultures. Leaving the room, facing the congregation one last time, he bowed, his hands folded in supplication
beneath his chin. With sparkling eyes and a constant smile of humble
encouragement, he surveyed the room. Like a child, Marubrishnubupu
thought. His escorts guided him away by the arm, sliding silk screens
into place behind him, shunning the groping crowd that yearned for
one more word from the master.

In his private chamber, Marubrishnubupu lit incense sticks dipped
in oils of lavender, chamomile and marjoram. He watched the smoke,
the gentle, curling smoke that swirled with heavy mood. Legs crossed
in the center of a meditation circle, his eyes half-open as his free hand
pulled upon his long beard, he penned a few thoughts into a notebook,
thoughts that were seeds for future lectures, future questions and
future answers.

Marubrishnubupu liked America, and though they confused him,
he generally liked Americans — their dogmatic sense of liberty, their
fascination with the tragic hero, their strong desire for laughter, their
shrewd anti-intellectualism, their balanced approach to libertarianism,
their deeply concealed, self-deprecating spirit, their childlike love of
baseball. The game, the most endearing gift of the Americans, amazed
Marubrishnubupu. In many ways he found it more elegant than
Hinduism. It possessed a symmetry, unlike any other sport, that made
it most un-sport-like, something approaching the metaphysical. No
quarters, no halves, no periods. But nine segments, each of an indeter-
minable time. An eternity could exist within each inning. The only
other sports that Marubrishnubupu could think of that resembled it in
having no time limits, only a goal, were golf and tennis, track and field,
but these sports were individual; they were not collaborative, not team
sports. It was such a mystery to Marubrishnubupu. Nine innings, each
inning composed of three outs, nine defenders in the field against one
batter in the box. So indeed, it actually wavered, sometimes a team
sport, other times an individual sport.

Oddly, at the moments of being an individual sport, it was an individual against the team, but the individual represented the team.
Strange, deep paradox in baseball. A great deal of trinity and triads,
likely a Protestant influence on the game. Three strikes, three outs,

three sets of three innings. First third, second third, third third. Extra innings. Three bases, only one home plate. No time limit. No time in baseball. Marubrishnubupu thought it a wonderful game, although he'd only watched it on television and listened to it on the radio, furtively each time, almost embarrassed, unsure whether his embarrassment came from his fascination or his lack of understanding.

Twenty-seven outs for a perfect game. Three cubed. Profoundly mysterious.

Hailing from India, people often asked Master Marubrishnubupu if he were Hindu or Buddhist. Typically, he would answer by asking in turn something deflective, reflective and true: "But for what reason do you ask? What do you know of either? They are just words to you, near synonyms that indicate little beyond geography. Will naming the place of my home mean you know my home? Does listening to me make you a Mahayana Buddhist or a Hindu? Does addressing a group of Christians make me a Christian? No, we are simply discussing, learning more. It is not yet time for delineations."

The Bodhisattva's Gate Spiritual Life Center of Boulder, Colorado undoubtedly presented to the world a Buddhist frame; however, the beliefs and theories discussed within were something unique. Some claimed that the explosion of popular interest in Buddhism conjoined by a general naïveté about Buddhism had enabled Marubrishnubupu to exploit the market need by muddying the waters and selling what amounted to Hinduism with a frail, Buddhist façade. Some considered Marubrishnubupu to be nothing more than a shameless opportunist, a charlatan; others, more concerned with discovering something meaningful than defending dogma, openly and proudly called Marubrishnubupu their world spiritual guide.

In his private chamber the radio was on. He tuned the dial to reduce static. At high altitude Coors Stadium, the Rockies were taking on the Baltimore Orioles in inter-league play. The bottom half of the third inning was thirty-six pitches old.

3

"**N**O. I DON'T THINK SO."

"No. I'm not sufficiently enthusiastic about it."

"No. But you must understand this is a purely subjective decision."

"No. We are just too busy at this time."

"No. It's just not for me."

"No. Have you tried down the street?"

"No. It's unnecessarily pretentious."

"No. I don't have the wall space."

"No."

"Yes. I'll take those two."

"Excuse me?"

"I said, I'll take those two. *Songbird* and, what's the other one? That one there, with the dark cross above the silver triangle."

"*Urizen's Leprosy*," Dorothia answered helpfully.

"I'll give this Rooster a try. He's different. Shockingly intense in his own way." The art dealer picked up the two selections and placed them aside from the others. "It's all I'll take right now. We'll see what they fetch. I'll give them sixty days. That's reasonable. If they don't go, I send them back to you. No skin off either of our noses. Not too much anyway."

"The painter tutored under Solzhenitsyn."

From behind glasses, the dealer with penetrating eyes stared directly into Dorothia's face, searching the lines for validation of a doubted fact.

"That so?" There was more cynicism than appreciation in the woman's tone. Dorothia feared that she had blundered in the negotiation. She now regretted that Solzhenitsyn had succeeded in dissuading her from photographing his image.

"It's true."

The owner of the store on Canyon Road in Santa Fe, New Mexico studied the two paintings once more. She shrugged. "Either way. I'm not paying anything up front for them. You get thirty percent of gross."

"Thirty percent!" Dorothia protested. "That's hardly worth our effort."

The owner lifted the paintings by their frames, moved them aside. "Perhaps Solzhenitsyn can get you better?"

The owner stood in the light of her gallery. Reflecting off the pearl white walls and shine of lacquered wood floors, the sunlight, piercing through the window panes — an unexpected number of windows for a place where wall space is a prized commodity — warmed the small gallery. Attractive, meaningful paintings, thoughtful paintings, generous paintings spanned the walls. Dorothia enjoyed this place. It was not cluttered; it was selective.

"I'm expecting some space to clear. I'll place these on the east wall. It's a good space; it gives the viewer distance."

The shop owner, Irene Smythe, was like a small, smartly cut piece of polished jade. She seemed a remarkable reflection of the gallery or, the more Dorothia noticed Irene, the more it seemed that the gallery might be a remarkable reflection of her. From her cropped black hair to the exquisitely tasteful gold rings on her fingers, the woman projected serenity, purpose and class.

"Thirty percent is just fine."

"Excellent! Then we'll be in touch. Here is my card. If things go well, I'd eventually like to meet the artist."

"Meet the artist?"

"Yes, of course, that's the nature of representation."

"But you have the paintings? That's what . . ."

"Well, yes," the art seller chimed in with ease. "The paintings are what the buyers take home. But we sell the artist. It's not just about representing a painting. If I wanted to sell a product on a hook I could work for K-Mart. It's what the product represents, and the painting represents the artist."

"Yes, I see," Dorothia answered, though she did not.

Irene's penetrating eyes watched Dorothia, seeking to evaluate her curious body language. Why was this woman deflated after she had just gained the artist representation in a prominent gallery?

"But what about dead painters? That's just a painting, isn't it?" Dorothia proposed.

"No," Irene replied with expert certainty. "No, it is not."

A fog swept over Dorothia's mind. She felt outdone — or even worse — outclassed as she mumbled defensively, without thinking, "It doesn't matter. You can't meet him."

"Ms. Rodriguez, don't be unreasonable. I don't mean to be immodest, but . . ."

"He never leaves the house. My son is dying."

On that odd note, disrobed of pretension, Dorothia turned and sought the exit. Bells overhead tinkled as she closed the door to the gallery. Though she had accomplished at least part of her task in finally placing some of Rooster's work, all she felt was shame and inadequacy. Indelicately placing the remaining eight paintings into the trunk and back seat of her car, Dorothia conceded that her trip to Santa Fe had not been as successful as she had hoped. Rooster's paintings had not somehow stood above the crowd. Instead, they were swallowed like a name within the phone book, undifferentiated. Everyone agreed that the works evinced a genuine talent. No one denied this fact; what they denied was any claim that the paintings merited immediate approval, affirmative judgment, active advocacy. If the art sellers would not take a stand, who would?

Despite the glorious setting, she felt numb. A dull, aching depression throbbed throughout the entire world. All of her promises were slipping into the order of the unfulfilled. Her son was dying. In the rearview mirror she glanced into the listless eyes of her own face. Wrinkle lines, the kind that no skin cream could deny, were beginning to appear. She heard Marcel screaming, echoing about in the chambers of her head, "I'm castrated. I'm castrated!" In her car she stared at the dashboard, at the various meters that measured and regulated the vehicle, extensions of control, telomere shortening system. My son is dying, she thought. There is nothing to regulate death, no way to turn it off, to intervene. The dashboard was just a dumb thing. Two paintings at thirty percent. My son is dying. Why is Urizen's face leprous, ghastly? Urizen is reason; my son is dying. Immortal cells. Fuck Ruth.

There was a knock at the window. Dorothia pressed the button to no effect. She gazed through the glass. Looking past Irene she noticed the pantiled roof of the sand-colored, adobe gallery. Dorothia mused, almost with indifference, that Rooster would have painted a wonderful scene with such material, material the likes of which his eyes would never know and see. The woman knocked again. Mechanically, Dorothia inserted the key into the ignition. Electricity coursed and the window zoomed down. She said nothing. The window was down. That's what the woman wanted. Wasn't it? Who was this woman? Such impeccable taste. My son is dying. Two paintings at thirty percent. The window is down. What more could she want?

"You believe he's that good?" the woman asked.

Dorothia nodded.

"It's still the opinion of a mother."

Dorothia remained silent.

"I'll take the others. I'll take whatever he can produce."

Dorothia unloaded the car.

Irene Smythe had been an art seller for twenty-two years so she knew well what she sought. As soon as she had seen Rooster's paintings, she had known that she would represent him, at least enter a process to slowly engage the artist. What had her leery in the opening negotiations with Dorothia was that the art seemed a bit too well matched, too perfect. In essence, it was exactly what she wanted, and this, of course, made her suspicious.

"I love an artist who has no respect for death," Irene related to Dorothia, back inside the gallery. "But this is such a rare quality, seldom found even in Holocaust art. I wanted the art because of what I saw on the canvas, of course; but it's what you said as you were leaving that really captured my attention. Until then I would have been content to believe that the art was a mistake, like a monkey that types a line of Shakespeare. Personally, I never cared for Solzhenitsyn, so it wouldn't have mattered a great deal to me whether your son did or did not train under the Master, though in a way it certainly affirms something. I would suspect that Solzhenitsyn needed Rooster more than Rooster needed Solzhenitsyn. I find Solzhenitsyn's work marred by a bitter regret, don't you?"

Dorothia sipped her tea as Irene addressed a browsing customer.

Upon returning, she continued, "He really has no fear of death, you know."

"What?"

"Your son. He has no fear of death. He doesn't believe in it."

"He believes in it."

Over the course of the afternoon they discussed the paintings one by one, Dorothia explaining as best she could the conditions of their creation, Rooster's state of mind at the time, how long it took, the themes and ideas and questions that Rooster was considering over the course of each creation. Irene asked little about Solzhenitsyn, although she had already begun to categorize the various paintings into Rooster's Soli and post-Soli periods. "So *Songbird* began in the Soli period and was completed post-Soli? And *Urizen's Leprosy* is all post-Soli? All of the others are Soli period paintings? Perfect, that makes perfect sense." Irene nodded as she sipped her tea, as though now in possession of an elusive comprehension. "That's why those were the only two I originally selected. They're the only post-Soli works. That's when Rooster was finally completely free to paint in his own style. Though the Soli period pieces are inferior, for now they'll be more valuable."

"I don't even see the difference between them," Dorothia admitted.

"I'm not surprised. Your being so close to the production, you're not looking at or for the same things I am. You already have an understanding of the art and the artist. I don't, and right now, temporarily at least, that's my luxury."

Dorothia put down her tea. It was growing cool. "Why would the Soli period pieces be more valuable if they're of an inferior quality?"

"It's simple, Dorothia. Now that Rooster has been discovered — and I assure you he has been discovered; this is my life's work — the paintings that foretell of his emergence are of greater value because they are limited in number. There will never be another Soli period piece. He can't go back and paint like that." Tugging at a gold hoop earring, Irene reflected aloud, offering Dorothia a direct look into her conscious stream. "Eventually the post-Soli works will be of the upmost value, but not right now because he is still in the post-Soli period. As long as he is in the post-Soli period the market will fluctuate. Until he is past the post-Soli period the scope of the market is open and undefined.

Once he enters the next phase in his painting, the post-Soli phase will be closed, thus setting the market's limits. Don't worry about this though. There are always art investors who will speculate on an undefined market in which they personally find value. My job is to know these people, and I do. Rooster can stay in the post-Soli period for quite a long time if he likes." She glanced at the paintings, seemingly uninterested in their content now. "They'll be quite lucrative."

Dorothia gulped her tea in a futile attempt to conceal her delight. Eyes downward cast, she asked, "Will he be known?"

"Don't be afraid to ask that question. There's no shame in wanting fame. Don't confuse a desire for what is deserved with greed. Your son will be known. I won't say he'll be revered; that depends on him, but he'll be known. The name will be recognized." Irene looked at the work with a scandalous glint of delight in her eyes. "I'll make sure that he's known. Is he attractive? That matters to some prospective . . ."

"He's a leper."

"A leper?"

"Hansen's disease. Twelve million worldwide."

"Leprosy?"

"Yes."

"It still exists?"

"It still exists."

"It explains a lot."

"How?"

"About the paintings, I mean."

"Yes, I suppose." Both had their eyes upon *Songbird*.

"Divine energy."

"Please, don't say that."

⚘

The work was a realistic depiction, a personal piece that gave Rooster a sense of harmony and well-being. Leaning back against the metal of the stool, he released a tremendous sigh of relief. His body, those parts of himself that he still felt, ached with exhaustion. His wrists were swollen as were his eyes; blinking had become painful in the last hours of the afternoon. It was all worth it now, the painting

being complete. He thought, this is how art should make one feel —
content, regardless of one's condition.

He set aside the paints and the hickory maulstick that he used to
stabilize his painting hand. Each finger he unwrapped and rewrapped
individually, applying antibiotic and clean gauze. The carbuncular
wounds on the hand had transitioned from coal black to pale white.
The way the wounds transformed without feeling, as they changed
from hard, symmetrical scales to open sores, never ceased to amaze
him. The rawer the wounds became, the less he felt. How metaphorical could God be?

The painting — he considered it self-indulgent — depicted an
overtly religious scene, the first of the type that Rooster had ever completed, based on a short story within the Hasidic sect. According to legend, Rabbi Baal Shem Tov, founder of the Hasidic order, made a pilgrimage one dry summer with a student to the Holy City of Jerusalem.
Along the way, the Rabbi took a detour down a forsaken, unmarked
and overgrown road. The young student could get no answer from the
Rabbi when he asked where they were going and why they were traveling along an unmarked road that did not lead directly to the Holy
City. They arrived at the hut of an old leper, hideously scarred by the
disease.

Terrified, the young student refused to enter the impure hut, the
home of the unclean and forsaken. Ignoring his young student's
protests, the Rabbi Baal Shem Tov, welcomed by the cloaked and veiled
leper, entered the scant, thatched hut where, for many hours, the two
spoke privately. Returning to the road, the waiting student asked who
the poor leper was and why the rabbi had visited with him. As they
walked away, back towards the road to Jerusalem, the Rabbi explained
to the young student that in every generation there is a Messiah with
us, prepared to reveal himself if the generation proves worthy of the
teaching. The rabbi explained to the student that the leper with whom
he had met was that Messiah but sadly, once more, the generation was
not worthy. Thus, he would not be revealed.

The student found this, even from the mouth of his beloved Rabbi,
impossible to believe and argued that if the man were truly the Messiah
then he would not be a leper, and also that if this were the Messiah it
would be their religious responsibility to reveal his presence before the

world so that the Kingdom could be fulfilled. They walked for a long time in silence. The student felt quite proud, confident that his point had been made and that its wisdom was being reflected upon by the Rabbi. After many miles of silence were between where they had been and where they were going, Rabbi Baal Shem Tov, emerging from a deep contemplation and smiling at the way nature hides her tracks, answered the student, "And that is why we are not worthy."

As Rooster envisioned the scene, imposing his own fertile imagination upon the rich story to recreate a single moment, the Rabbi Baal Shem Tov sat in the thatch hut by a small fire with the old leper who sat on the ground in a russet tunic. Like a Muslim woman who exposes only the eyes, the tunic was wrapped about the face and head. Drawn back from the fire light, the old hermit remains in the shadow, intentionally positioned so as to hide even the accidental glimpse or a direct gaze upon the flesh about the eyes. The rabbi, for his part, bends close, eager to capture a slight glimpse of the divine face. Emergent from the shadow, the sole extremity revealed is a single peering eye temporarily illuminated by a flicker of firelight. Oversized, sharp and discerning, the opaque orb, unexpected as a thief, breaks through the shades of darkness. The Rabbi, for all his vigilance, pulls back in surprise, unprepared for what he has sought, afraid and astonished by the truthful glimpse which has come, always as the absolute does, a moment too soon. In the background, peering through a tiny window from the outside, curious and frightened, attracted and repulsed, is the Rabbi's student: long, curling black sideburns, a handsome face anxious with fear, comely eyes enthralled and wide, transfixed, seeing also what the teacher sees, incapable of comprehending.

The hands and feet of the leper are swaddled to conceal the oddly shaped disfigurements. Charred, a single wooden cup and bowl are by the fire. It was a wonderful trinity dynamic that Rooster succeeded in conveying through delicate, finespun gestures and expressions. The Rabbi is a student to the leper as the Rabbi's student watches the leper with curiosity and disgust, unsure of what his eyes are seeing, indignant. Two are in and one is out; yet the deeper Rooster reflected on the painting the less clear it became as to who the two were who were in and who the one was who was out. The dynamic reminded Rooster of Soli, and he imagined that the spirit of the old man was with him as he admired the completed work. How often had he felt that Soli and the painting were in a conspiracy, clearly understanding what he did not? How often did he think that he and painting were engaged in a profound communion no observer could comprehend? And finally, how often did he believe that he and Soli were co-creators and that the painting was nothing more than a disconnected manifestation of what they already were? Regardless, the utter interdependency remained clear; all three were bound, each by their own unique form of concealment. Rooster hoped that even if others did not know the names, they would see these things.

The disease had begun to manifest itself during his last months at Danforth, though a full year passed before diagnosis. It is more than curiously strange what we are willing to pass off as a rash; besides, Rooster immersed himself in painting, willfully omitting the physicality of being. The painting, the channeled creation on a canvas, was the only true world, the only world worthy of sincere attention. Rather than see a doctor, he raised a brush. Rather than identify a problem, he depicted a condition. Others have done this, he was sure, have used the arts to transcend — or hide — their maladies from the world. Art is a solitary act; it reduces the risks that others will have to witness the embarrassing fits of epilepsy, the manic bipolar depression, the schizophrenia, the alcoholism. The arts provide sanctuary for the damned, a plausible explanation for the abnormal who wants only to be normal. An artist can live on the fringe, and yet be culturally accepted, even socially respected. Artists can place themselves in exile, for the greater good, and still contribute. Properly channeled, given time, the damned can be transformed, the accursed, blessed.

There were other reasons too, of course, but these encapsulated the thoughts that Rooster had been thinking upon as he brightened the fire of the painting with orange scythes and blue-white scimitars reaching above the flame. Art allowed him to live in isolation, yet it gave him the opportunity to live in a socially meaningful way. He wondered about others who may have enfolded themselves in their art in this way. Thinking about the modern dancer, Martha Graham, who lived a horrible alcoholic life full of violence and shattered relationships and substance abuse, Rooster marveled. As terrible as her life seemed to have been, what would it have been without dancing, without those few precious minutes of "interpretive dance" when her true being, a being scorned and rejected in daily life, received not only unconditional acceptance but momentary tribute? What would life be without those sparkling moments of recognition, moments which acknowledge, moments which confirm that God creates each of us for a specific reason? Rooster could only sense the answer with a shudder of dread. What would his own life be like — a modern leper — without his paintings, meaningful communications to the world?

"I live not for the totality of life but for moments like this, moments of clarity. In a way I suppose that this affirms the totality of life. That is a romantic thought, but all that I am really trying to do in getting to this moment is to believe in a life without pain, without suffering. It is in the moments when I believe in this life that my purpose is clear, that I willingly carry the burdens of my disease."

"Why can't you stay there?"

"I don't know, Soli. It is so hard to say, 'It is finished,' to acknowledge that it must begin all over again, to confront the possibility that another moment of clarity may never arise, to convince oneself to forget what was."

"The memory causes the pain. It's not what is or what will be. It is what was that is killing you."

"I know you are right. You're just a ghost in my mind."

"Transitions are all important. Transitions. Put all of your attention on the transition. On the transition from 'It is finished,' to 'It now begins.' This will help you, Rooster. I give you my word."

Rooster chuckled. These imaginary communions with his deceased mentor, Soli, acted as a salve to his troubled soul. This time he would name the painting. It would surprise his mother, he was sure, for him to take an interest in such a thing, for him to give meaning to that which always had been meaningless.

"Wake up, Rooster, wake up!" The ghost of Soli chided him from the corner, rapping the heel of the cane upon the floor. "It's time to open your door to the world. . . . Wake up!"

Rooster had been stretched upon the floor when a knock came at the door. Twisting languidly, he began to arise from a deep, refreshing sleep. Still disoriented, he opened his eyes and searched for the source of the disturbance. The knock came a second time, soft and unsure.

Rooster looked to the empty chair in the corner of the room. Soli's cane leaned upon it. "Just a dream," Rooster told himself and not without dismay. "Just a dream." Gazing at the corner he shook his head for the foolishness of believing. The knock at the door came a third time.

Glancing at the time, he knew it was the delivery of supplies he had ordered: tubes of verdant, indigo and white paint, new brushes, thinner, charcoal, flaxseed oil, also lunch, pepperoni pizza. He paid so well that the store would run small errands with the deliveries.

"Just leave everything by the door," he called lazily from the floor, waking, reentering the painful reality that only painting and sleep helped him to escape.

"You have to sign." Not the words but the voice impelled Rooster to push himself off the floor. It was a female's voice, gentle and strong, carrying through the door.

"I have an account."

Rooster waited silently for a reply. Nothing. He strained to listen for the sweet voice again, the beautiful sound of the feminine. Had she left? Why hadn't he opened the door? He knew why.

"You still have to sign."

"I've never had to sign before." He could hear but could not control the anxiety in his voice.

"They didn't tell me that. Far as I'm concerned everyone signs."

Rooster stood nervously, staring at the door, pressing his wrapped hands upon his pants as though to dry the palms of sweat. The patterned response was unconsciously performed. "Come on in." It amazed Rooster that he said it, that he did not deliberate, hem and haw, contemplate his skin or the possibility of an odor. He was thankful for the pungency of turpentine.

The door opened with a slow creak and Rooster wondered if this person knew, if she had heard rumors about the leprous recluse of 113 Progress Street. The usual delivery person, a young man who never asked questions, who simply knocked and yelled that the supplies would be billed to his account, now seemed, already, a phantom to Rooster, a messenger never seen and now replaced, like a spirit sent to the answering of prayers. The cleanliness, the barren nature of the transaction was like the feeding of a zoo animal — banging on iron bars to make the contained species aware of its meal but not lingering for the exhibition, possessed of no desire to be close, to understand the quality of the consumption, the nature of the destination, the determination of the unseen creature within. With the usual delivery person, with the delivery person of the past, it was the relationship of an animal, as it should be, an animal being kept alive for the sport and benefit of others. Only the paintings emerged from the room.

His heart pounded as the door swung in. Like a creature in the zoo, he watched with heightened senses as the outer world, the promise of freedom and all the dangers to which freedom was obliged, entered. Carefully, never releasing the knob of the door, she maintained a functional safety line that would help her, if it became necessary, to escape. The way she protected her avenue of retreat, this was the first thing Rooster noticed. It answered his question. She knew of him, what he did and what he had. No gift of prophecy is required for the purpose of extrapolating the obvious. Solitude attunes one to the subtle simply by removing the common stimuli that function to excite a conditioned sensitivity to the gross. She moved slowly, understanding that every movement she made would be interpreted at a hundred fold its meaning.

He fell in love with her hands.

They were small and wonderful hands.

They did not clutch the knob of the door for safety but only touched it lightly, as though a reminder of a her daring.

Rooster stood dumbly, dumb as a goat. Unmoving, hesitant, like a creature redefining instinct, he gave pause, trapped in her spell. The room belonged to her, the paintings to her, his life to her.

"Where do you want this?" she asked, dipping her head to force eye contact and raise his sight.

The question pulled him out of his meditation on her hands. "Oh, yes, anywhere, anywhere at all."

She stepped wholly into the room, letting go of the gold, gleaming doorknob. Carefully pushing aside a pile of rough coal sketches, she placed the pizza and the bag of supplies on a table. She lingered over the sketches, allowing her fingers to touch the paper, to be marked by smudges of coal.

"I've heard of you."

Rooster watched the way she turned her hand to note the charcoal that lingered on her fingertips. With her thumb, she spread the dusty chalk along the sensuous length of her fingers. She stretched the black color, extending the shade with circular movements designed to last. The black chalk filled the crevices within her skin, lifting the swirling lines, the unique pattern that belonged to her alone. The black chalk created contrast, a wonderful contrast that helped her to see, and thus remember, the depth of her own being, the purposive miracle of her own inimitable genetic construction. Rooster honed in on the fingernails, white at the tips, hard and long, unpainted, simple, unadorned and natural. Much time had passed since he had seen clean, strong nails. To Rooster, they spoke of health. His own mother left hers in a perpetually painted state, covered by an outer shell. The condition of his own nails varied, possessing a world of seasons unto themselves: sometimes soft and pulpy, other times cracked and brittle, sometimes tawny as pollen, other times blackened with dried blood beneath, but rarely, very rarely, healthy. Her palms were small but deep, like an earthen well with moist, pink fissures, a vessel willing to be filled, to carry a precious load within the cherishing, womblike cup that can only be formed by human hands.

From the bag she emptied the contents of supplies.

"I can do that."

But she didn't listen. With the bag in hand she bent down to where the soiled gauze lay strewn on the floor before the empty easel. With both hands she collected the garbage into clumps and quickly pushed it into the bag. Avoiding the blood-congealed ointments and the tawny brown stains, her intense, somehow angry movements, exhibited no fear of contact. To Rooster it seemed that she was a rebellion against the very existence of the sullied gauze. He felt that he should have stopped her, but he didn't. He watched. On the floor she was face-to-face with his recently finished painting. Seeing the painting at eye level, she paused.

"It's beautiful."

Only then did Rooster advance with the step he had almost taken to restrain her from picking up his soiled bandages.

"It's just been finished," he told her, able to smile comfortably as she was not watching him. "The paint is still wet."

"You didn't sign it," she noted as she picked up the last bandage from the floor and discarded it in the bag. "You should sign your paintings."

"I never sign them."

"Do you have a bathroom?" She stared at him now, directly into his eyes. She had a thin, curveless body with small breasts that were probably peach-colored and freckled like her cheeks. Thick, caramel hair, tied in a pony tail, dropped in a straight line below the center of her back. Everything about her was small except the fearless force of her being.

He stood dumbly, fantasizing that her tiny ears made her lips appear inexperienced and full.

"I should wash my hands."

It was a grim reminder of reality. He gazed away again, feeling a backlash of shame. What had he been thinking? How had he allowed this? "Down the hall. Use hot water."

When she was gone Rooster pulled on a dark turtle neck that concealed his neck and lower chin where earlier outbreaks had left portions of his body with permanent scars. He found relief in the fact that with the exception of his arms and a slim peninsula of raw, scaly tissue extending from the left side of his stomach to the armpit, the disease was currently in check.

"Is there anything else I can do for you?" she asked upon returning.

"No, no nothing." With his bulky white fingers, Rooster scratched his head. "Where is the other delivery person? You're new, aren't you?"

She nodded. "I asked to deliver here."

"Why?"

"You don't remember me."

He stared at her unabashed, exploring for some clue. "No. Should I?"

"No. I didn't suspect you would. I'm Tamara. Tamara Browne."

She did not extend her hand which relieved Rooster from the awkwardness such a display would have necessitated. Without any proof, he believed that she understood this.

"I'm . . ."

"You're Alexi Rodriguez."

Rooster, growing defensive, glanced at the supplies. "Do I have to sign anything?"

"You're also known as Rooster."

She had his attention. "How do you know?"

"That doesn't matter, does it?" She walked over to the painting on the floor and lifted it to the easel so that she could study it better. "Do you mind?"

"No," he admitted.

"Does it have a name?"

Rooster had always hated the question in the past. He battled his initial instinct, to scoff in arrogance at the notion, and overcame it. He was no longer the same person he had been at Danforth, finding ways to challenge professors and peers alike, selecting minutia from which to launch his claim of superiority. Soli had taught him what a waste of time such posturing proved in the end to be; though perhaps necessary in its own way as a single lesson of the artist's journey, such forms of personal arrogance grounded in intolerant, broad-based, categorical judgments, ultimately required a soulful transcendence. Does it have a name? Rooster smiled self-consciously, unsure, yet confident that it would be liked and appreciated, confident not in his own powers but in the source of those powers that told him even now not to worry.

"I Give You My Word."

She bowed her head, acknowledging that to her the painting's title, with its multiple inflections of meaning, functioned as a well-intended invitation. Rooster could see her now, whole and unabashed, as she admired the painting. Standing at the edge of the canvas, he believed she truly saw him: not the tainted creature in a zoo, not a bacterial, leprous time bomb, not even a man talented with paint — but him.

Moving from the beauty of her hands, her arms appeared as fragile sheaves of wheat. Her neck was creamy white with the large and common hollow below the windpipe where the inner edges of the collarbone come to meet. Peering about her, Rooster watched so as not to disturb her. Having drawn back the long flowing line of her gorgeous, Godiva hair, her tiny ears, filled with space, were revealed. Her nose was so shaped as to suggest that it would end in a sharp point, but it did not. Instead, it resembled a Greek sculpture worked in marble, deliberately chipped, making the viewer feel not a sense of loss or absence but a yearning for antiquity. He noticed, through the contrast of her presence, the quality of the light.

"Let me." Rooster opened a shade, snapping it up so that it spun with dissipating momentum on the silver rod. With the shade furled, the illumination of a glorious day spilled through the window, washing the room with a stronger light. She thanked him, and as the words lifted from her beautiful lips, he tingled, knowing that he had opened the shade not for her but for himself.

She reached out to the painting, her fingertips so close to the surface that no touch was demanded for contact. In the improved light, she found a new layer of detail that served to enhance the old layers of what she mistakenly surmised she had seen and understood. To think that he had painted this today, that the colors were still wet, amazed her. That something so young should be so old could be only one of two things: an illusion of seeming or an expression of a completely progressive concept of time.

"I adored your work even before I saw it."

"Who are you?" he asked in marvel, stunned into an exploration of her deepening mystery.

"Yes, who the hell are you?" demanded a hoarse voice. In the doorway Dorothia stood with her hands firmly planted akimbo on swaggering hips. Rooster and the young woman both turned from the light, towards the source of the sudden intrusion. Silence of the ages penetrated as all three stood in revelation, their true selves in the center of the floor between them. Raw hearts make for raw meat in a lion's den, where no one holds the advantage of surprise. Dorothia, a bit sharper in her wit, spoke first.

"What are they delivering today?" Walking over to the supplies, she shoved them across the table. "Concupiscent whores?" The woman who could appear stunning with desire, sent a ferocious glare in the direction of the girl. "Is there a reason that you're in this room?"

Tamara said nothing. She simply stared back, fearless and knowing, as though she comprehended the implications and difference between two and three, between the direct and the indirect, between resolution and mediation, between love and control. It was a moment's passage between the two that communicated all to Dorothia that she would ever care to know. In tersely deliberate, controlled sentences, Dorothia made her intentions clear. "You go back to your store and tell Sal Gentiles that the Rodriguez family is done doing business with The Amber Artist. Done! Have Sal make up a bill to close out the account and tell him that I will be there within the hour. Do you understand what I expect of you?"

Tamara stepped forward and faced Dorothia with strong, square shoulders. Dorothia was much larger. Yet, as Rooster watched he could not help but feel that in a contest between the two, his mother would lose.

"I understand," was Tamara's answer. Kneeling, she picked up the bag of bandages. Dorothia stood aside, strongly promoting her exit.

"I was showing her my painting, *I Give You My Word*."

"What?" Dorothia asked, displeased that her son had broken his numb silence.

"*I Give You My Word*, I was showing it to her."

"It's beautiful," Tamara attempted. "Your son has a great gift."

Responding to the girl, Dorothia turned from frigid to ice cold. "You can shut up and leave. I know my son's talent." She added spitefully, as though Rooster were not there, "Who do you think made him what he is?"

Tamara stepped toward the door. Her eyes locking, her tiny, fearless frame quivering with anger, she replied, "He did!"

"No!" a zealous Rooster blared. "You can't talk to her like that!"

Dorothia beamed. "Do you hear that? You're upsetting my son."

He stepped forward emphatically, gut churning with fear as he spit the words forward from his constricting throat. "No, Mother, you. You can't talk to Tamara like that. She's my guest."

"The delivery girl is your guest!" Dorothia mocked. "I go out to sell your paintings and you want to take up with the delivery girl? Are you trying to ruin everything we've done? Is that what you're seeking to do? Destroy everything?"

"Don't worry, Rooster. This doesn't change anything. I'll see you around."

Her long mane of hair sensuously whipping as she turned, Tamara walked from the room with Dorothia charging at her heels.

"To hell you will!" she shouted. "You won't see him around. Do you understand that? You won't see him around!"

The front door closed, leaving Dorothia to leer across the empty antechamber. Re-entering Rooster's room she shut the door, immediately launching a fierce counter-offensive. "My Lord, Alexi, what has gotten into you?" Racing across the room, she yanked the shade shut. "You know how sensitive you are to the strong light."

"You had no right to do that." Her son spoke with an edge Dorothia found difficult to appreciate.

"No right?" Clutching her heart, she repeated his opprobrious phrase with an affected exaggeration. "Since when does a mother have 'No right' to protect her son? Since when? Since a pretty little whore comes in and turns your head? A . . . A . . . A concupiscent salamander!"

Reflectively, his mind incapable of even hearing such ludicrous terms, Rooster approached the easeled painting. "She liked my paintings. We were talking about them; that's all."

"Rooster, don't be naïve. She sees money in you. That grubby Jew down the street knows you're a goldmine waiting to happen. Maybe they even know about Soli's inheritance. That little girl finds out and she makes a play for it. She gets close to you. You're susceptible to a pretty face. That Jew probably paid her to do it. We're not getting our supplies from them anymore; it's that simple. Not after today."

"Stop it." Rooster dropped into his chair, numb and quiet. His whole body felt weary, drained. He stared at the painting. Without the light, it now disgusted him. "There's no need to talk about people like that."

Dropping slices of pepperoni into the oily cardboard, Dorothia chewed on a slice of pizza. "Now what's this? Is this what you've been working on while I was away?" She scanned it. "Oh God, Rooster, you're not doing religious again, are you? You know that's not where you shine. You're an abstract painter, an abstract painter." She pointed, dismissive. "They don't want that. Keep it surreal: defiant insincerity, calculated fancy, intellectual disorder. That's what people are looking for, paintings they don't understand. Emotional paintings without people. It's good, but anyone could do this. Think about it, Rooster. Think how hard this makes life for me."

"I think it's one of the best things I've done."

"Maybe it is," she scoffed, tossing the crust aside. "But I just met a woman who thinks your two last works are the best you've ever done, and she wants to see more just like it. She wants to represent you. She can do things for us, Rooster. I can tell. She's good! She can get your name out there. Make you known. But she likes what you were doing before I left. She wants more of that. Not this. The last thing she needs is more realism. People don't want it. It's too . . . prescriptive."

Rooster sat silently before *I Give You My Word*, giving no indication of whether her dwindling harangue was having an effect.

"My God, Rooster, we finally begin to make some progress and you want to change your style completely. How can I represent you if I don't even know what your painting means from day to day? You'll have me looking like a fool is what you'll have me looking like."

Rooster scratched at the irritation at his side. "It's only one painting." Raising an arm, he sought relief from the searing pain of the shingled infection. "I'm not changing my style completely. It's hardly even a painting. It's . . . it's an exercise in composition."

She watched him wince with pain. The depression of seeing her son struggle in this way pierced her soul. Refusing to submit to even a moment's despair, fighting to protect her son's very sense of hope, she chirped cheerily, working hard to distract him from over-reflection. "Thank goodness, reason! Now have some pizza. Let me tell you all about the dealer I met. Irene, she took all ten and she'll take more. She's glorious. A Godsend. An absolute Godsend. She raved about your paintings."

For the next twenty minutes Dorothia spoke in a single, unbroken, long-winded, brainwashing monologue. "She wants to meet you, of course. She's very impressed by your discipline, by the way you completely immerse yourself. Your whole life is painting. No distractions. It shows, you know? People out there, people who know exactly what they're looking for, can see it: no distractions." Rooster could scarcely tell whether the words were observation, command or deep suggestion.

Saying nothing, he began to plan his next work, a smaller project, in his mind. His hands were wrapped with fresh gauze. Second skin was learning how to feel.

⌘

That afternoon Dorothia Rodriguez spoke with the owner of The Amber Artist. On the condition that the new delivery girl's employment come to a swift end, she did not close her account as threatened. Sal Gentiles, the pallid owner, liked the young, dependable woman who had worked for him for two weeks; however, the Rodriguez account drew a respectable share of annual revenue which, understandably, Sal liked more. As Miss Rodriguez and Sal spoke in the back, Tamara locked the register and walked out, bells jingling on the front door. As has always been the case for the egoless, finding other work presented no challenge. For instance, Tamara had been the appetizer waitress at Danforth's judges' party on the evening that Rooster had pressed the charcoal sketches into Solzhenitsyn's grip. She was the one who had given Solzhenitsyn the intriguing information that had persuaded the old master to actively seek out the young exile.

Jobless, returning to her second floor apartment that evening, Tamara sat quietly before the muted television, working on a puzzle of a Bavarian landscape in the winter time. Off center a large stone castle arose from the verdant fjords that peeked from the snow. Snow was beginning to melt, or had it just fallen? Were the fjords re-emerging at the tail end of a long winter's spell or were they just being covered? Was it a time for blooming or hibernation? It bothered her that she could not tell when looking at the picture cover whether the scene was spring or autumn. Were they entering the hard season or being finally relieved of it? Constructing the puzzle piece by piece gave her ample opportunity to reflect upon these questions and formulate her answers.

At the zoo a week earlier, she had read a sign by the zebra pen stating that in Africa the natives believe that the stripes are white. She was surprised by the profound simplicity of the idea and the cultural commentary it contained. It took her a moment of conscious, thinking effort to affirm that, yes, she had always thought of the stripes as being black. Only after much more reflection did it occur to her that perhaps, in reality, there was no base color. It was not a matter of black stripes on a white beast, or white stripes on a black beast; instead, it was something far more simple and far more complex, two sets of wholly independent stripes interlocked, two bases compromised into a balanced pattern, each picking their natural points of advance, of give and take, each with an equal claim, each with a valid perspective, each so intertwined that they could never be divided, if, in fact, they ever had been. The snow-covered fjords were similar. Without the context of time — of something like history — the season's tone is lost: the tone being something different from the mood which is distinct and pure, appreciated singly, not for what it promises or for what it has been through, but solely for what it is. Somewhere, she reflected, searching for the puzzle's tone, there must be a clue.

Tamara recalled her days at Danforth after Rooster had left at the behest of the school. Rumors abounded, rumors that grew. He became the campus legend after his expulsion; that legend swelled pursuant to his "attack" on Solzhenitsyn. The first wave of campus opinion took the event as a clear sign that Rooster had always been wrong and the establishment always right. Rooster's "attack" affirmed the social code and galvanized the entrenched community in its assessment of what was and was not art. But it did not take long for opinion to shift. A second wave of rumors spread, informed rumors that Solzhenitsyn had actually sought out Rooster and taken him on as a personal student, an unprecedented move from a cantankerous master with a reputation for defending his own quietude with the fervid care of a recluse. The legend grew as legends do, through wild elaboration. Of the many fabrications, one of the most popular related that Rooster was amassing all his works for a grand, posthumous release. He needed only to prevent their release until after he died of a mysterious disease that had been slowly killing him for years. Even Professor Sachs, who had first used the name "Rooster" publicly, gained a strange, underground cache in the evolving mythology. Amidst this mad swirl, the perception of Danforth as a legitimate institute of fine art spread.

Tamara worked methodically from the bottom left hand corner towards the upper right hand corner of the puzzle. Not one of those to do the outside frame first, she could perceive no point in such a shackling approach. Once a frame is done, she reasoned, it's a closed system, self-limited and complete. And even if it had to end that way, she did not have to succumb from the very beginning. She could fight. How often does at least one piece of a puzzle get lost? Statistically, what were the odds? She yearned for the lost piece; she wanted to complete the puzzle and discover the fatefully fitted right hand corner piece splendidly missing. To her mind, losing a piece from the middle meant little; that was an accepted part of the human condition. But to lose a flat edge, a border, a limit that must serve some grand cosmology of the hyperbolic function, to lose an edge — or even a corner — now that would be wonderful! She wanted to lose a piece of the frame. That would make the puzzle interesting again, would make it more than a mood. With a piece from the middle the shape remains fully defined. A complete outline exists. We can see into the nothingness of the void exactly what we have lost, and in this at least there is a full satisfaction, a wholeness with which we can sleep. But a piece from the edge strips away that tranquillity; definition in absentia sends us spilling directly into the abyss, into the mystery of the unwavering, perfect contrast between the known and the unknown. Occasionally glancing at the television set, she watched current fashion, picking her cues. At the very least, she relieved her sense of lonesomeness by acknowledging the lonesome, voiceless prophecy of the hazy screen. She snapped a shingle of white snow snugly into place, interlocking the pieces, coming closer to a unity of vision.

That night, leaving her second floor flat, she prowled the streets for hours in search of something new, something truly original. Snow was falling laterally. Tamara found this sensual, the odd idea that it would never fall, but rather blow round and round the surface of the earth, never touching ground, perhaps spinning back into the atmosphere, returning to the place from which it came, a virgin snow that never fell.

Before her life came together, Tamara had been a math major at Stanford and a graduate student in physics. She had been working on her thesis, a relatively minor study applying the Lorentz contraction through vector analysis within distortions of conic shapes. It was to be a fairly unoriginal work, designed to meet requirements while raising a few non-prescriptive yet slightly provocative points for speculation. It was unambitious and uninspired graduate work. She had been writing her conclusion, experimenting with the pithy, quirky, ironic close when someone mentioned Heisenberg's uncertainty principle. She knew of the concept, standard book definition stuff that she had never thought about too deeply. The uncertainty principle states that it is impossible to measure two properties of a quantum object simultaneously with infinite precision. Maybe it had been two sleepless nights; she could remember a thunderstorm with lightning, a warm, hard rain rattling in the street. She had listened in utter darkness, sheets pulled down, her body beaded with sweat. The statement of uncertainty had disturbed Tamara.

Her entire project was junk. If she could not define a single relationship with infinite precision, then she had no meaningful contrast upon which to base a single speculation. Proofs be damned! There were no relationships, just individual, unique entities that must be considered in the totality of their unique being. She saw herself in the roiling thunder as nothing more than one who very carefully catalogues the items of a room, giving names and descriptions to items with which one has no personal attachment or knowledge, no relationship whatsoever. It appeared to her a veiled form of psychological materialism, and she knew that she could not live this way any longer. She could not be a collector, living to plant a flag on every street corner in space. What value is there in that with no beginning? She abandoned her thesis. It concluded mid-sentence of what could liberally be read as a final paragraph. She turned it in with a single sentence letter that announced her withdrawal from the university. The incomplete thesis was never graded.

After that choice she followed art, though she refused to allow herself the illusion of practicing art herself. No, she preferred to watch others, to study them, to discover what they were after. What she respected was that there were no grand and universal claims to truth and that there never had been. A work of art was by its very nature ambiguous and incomplete, a paradox, faultless and breached all at once: uncertain.

At 8:37 p.m. she stood pressed against the gate of Rooster's brownstone home. A dusting of snow, cottonseed wraiths, tumbled along the gray sidewalk. Some landed after all. Light radiated from the curtained cracks of the street level window where Rooster painted. She could have jumped the gate and knocked at the window. Iron palisades, aesthetic and capable of impaling, stood guard. She could have even leaned over and unlatched the lock. Not tonight, she thought quietly. Soon, but not tonight. Let him rest. Paint. He knows that I am; it's enough for now. I won't pin him down, won't even try. I'll learn her schedule, her way, memorize it. Her routine, perfect it. I'll replace her, day by day. I know she doesn't want to, but she'll have to face it.

Picking up a pebble, Tamara threw it at the window before dashing away, lateral to the street called Progress.

4

MARUBRISHNUBUPU WOKE FROM a distressing dream of import. Upshot, prone in the darkness, sweating pearly rivulets of salt, he slipped from his bed and hurried to the temple shrine. Illuminated by red votive candles, shadows undulating within the dome, the shining Bodhisattva danced, chaffs of wheat swaying from his hands, one leg raised, a tightrope walker circumnavigating the shores of life and death, pleasure and pain. To the sides, attending to the statue of the Bodhisattva, an entourage of golden Buddhas were reposed in grave meditation. A curious shrine, sacrosanct in its own way, the arrangement selected to honor the Bodhisattva, the earthly prince of compassion, of the awakened heart, over the transcendent Buddha.

Marubrishnubupu bowed to both sides and then to center. He lit incense before laying himself upon the terrazzo alter before the feet of the dancing Bodhisattva. Mumbling nervous chant, he remained motionless, in humble, desperate meditation. "What have I seen? What have I seen?" The fearful question broke through the chants, directly imploring the dancing god to answer. Marubrishnubupu was like a novice to his own mind. The shrine maintained its vigil — noble, knowing, hushed.

Pressed flat upon his belly on the cold stone floor for hours, arms raised above his head in a gesture of supplication, Marubrishnubupu prayed for the return of a state of peace to his mind. Willfully releasing all that he knew to be a source of agitation, he did not pray so much as empty himself of the nightmarish dream that had come to him. In the

dream, he had been seated cross-legged upon a purple lotus of a thousand and one blooming petals, serenely floating above a sparkling,
crystal city. Twinkling light radiated from the planet. The azure sky was
vivid and spotless, free of all pollution. Marubrishnubupu could probe
the world with his feelings from the purple lotus; wherever he sensed
a seed of discord, he would channel the discord through his mind,
purifying it of the pain and sorrow that comes with confusion. He
would bring clarity to the confusion before sending the seed back to its
source, corrected through all the love of his swelling heart. In the
dream he spent an eternity in this blissful state, probing the crystal
planet and purifying confusions.

It was a happy state, meaningful and peaceful. The discords he
resolved were ever minor, never challenging. A simple impulse of his
intellect restored perfection to the universe of the purple lotus of which
Marubrishnubupu was but a single, harmonized petal. It was as the
dream of the dreamer, probing always the perfection of the perfect, perpetually in a state of maintenance rather than correction, as a window
cleaner making love to clarity, that Marubrishnubupu came across a
seed of true discord. As he had done a thousand and one times before,
the perched sage brought the seed within his mind so as to make the
necessary correction, to wipe away the speck of sorrow or confusion.
With the seed in his mind, Marubrishnubupu did as he always did; he
lived the life of the seed forwards and then backwards. He grew the
seed in his mind as it would grow to the end of its life — for all discord
was originated in the idea of death — and then, where the seed thought
life ended, Marubrishnubupu would plant another seed, one based in
love and life, that would, like a great mystery of promise, short-circuit
any lack of faith, any doubt, any confusion with regards to the right-
ness of things. Marubrishnubupu opened the seed of this dream and
began to live the life forward. This was a life filled with simple plea-
sures: a bright red cardinal, a field of virgin snow, a sparkling lake in
moonlight, a campfire, the burnt scent of roasted pine nuts, the mouth
of a dark cave.

At the mouth of the dark cave, Marubrishnubupu shuddered. Never
before had he shuddered in this dream. Looking about him in this
sweet world he saw the pleasing scenes of the past still lingering, but
he sensed something else with him; everything he had passed (the red

cardinal, the virgin snow, the sparkling lake) seemed to be nervously watching to see what he would do, to see what would come next. That such an ominous feeling of anxiety should abound in the midst of such an idyllic setting was unsettling and, Marubrishnubupu knew, not to be taken lightly. Adjacent to the cave's opening, a massive triangle of stone stood balanced upon one of its pointed angles. With a heave he might have been able to tip it, thus covering the dark, forbidding mouth of the hungry cave. Marubrishnubupu attempted to peer inside. He used the light of his mind to illuminate the entrance. But where his light entered, it did not illuminate; it disappeared, swallowed completely within the dark void. Never before, in all of Marubrishnubupu's dreams, had such a thing happened. At this point Marubrishnubupu knew that he was dreaming, lucid dreaming, aware that he was asleep, but cognizant that the world of the dream meant something to the world of his waking.

To illuminate such points of darkness was Marubrishnubupu's role. He called into the cave, listening for an echo, but his voice only died, murdered it seemed, before the full word had been uttered from his lips. He attempted to remain calm. He glanced at the stone triangle that would so perfectly fit across the dark mouth of the cave.

Temptation.

Stepping forward, actually stepping away from the purple lotus, Marubrishnubupu tested the balanced triangle with his hands. He sensed enough to believe that if he pushed, it would topple without resistance. The darkness would be covered, concealed . . . but not resolved. Such a path he had never walked before. With a hand on the massive stone triangle he contemplated the implications of his act; he felt the fear in his own belly.

"I wouldn't do that if I were you."

It was strange to hear the gruff-sounding voice of another. After all, never before had another voice been present in his dreams. Always it was just Marubrishnubupu and nature, and that absence of humans, he thought for the first time, was what made it so perfect. Turning in the direction of the voice, Marubrishnubupu saw a man approaching him, a man colored completely gray and white. The figure had a large pot belly and a pudgy, squinted face. Black swirls of short, oily hair poked out from beneath a tightly fitted ball cap. Slung upon the man's right shoulder, a thick, wooden bat rested. He was dressed in a pinstripe baseball jersey, tight about the hips, with knickers drawn high over the calves. Only as Marubrishnubupu realized that the figure was wearing a baseball uniform did he see the beaming red socks, the only patch of color attributed by the dream to the gray man. Following that first impression other details fell into place. Marubrishnubupu saw the "B" on the ball cap and the word "BOSTON" stitched across the pinstriped chest.

"I mean, I really wouldn't do that if I were you." The man had a slow drawl to his speech that possessed a charming, confident quality. He stepped forward. No, Marubrishnubupu thought, the man had swaggered.

Marubrishnubupu studied the man carefully. He sensed that he knew the man, though he could not recall from where. The powerful arms, the barrel chest, the confidence, the swagger, that baby face. The man, apparently bored for the moment, swatted at the empty air with the thick bat.

"You're Babe Ruth," Marubrishnubupu whispered in amazement, quite pleased that he had been able to pull the connection from the annals of myth and lore.

"Yours truly. But . . ." he looked around, admiring the scenery outside the cave. "They call me the Bambino here."

"And where exactly are we?"

The Babe leaned his thick bat against the stone triangle and walked to the mouth of the cave. He stared into it wordlessly, his back turned to Marubrishnubupu.

He spoke quietly, with a melancholy in his voice, the gruffness gone. "Did you ever want something more than everything else in your life? I mean want it so badly that it consumes you, eats you up. It's all that you can think about, even if it keeps you from seeing everything else around you?"

Marubrishnubupu watched the legendary figure in silence. Every so often, in spite of himself, his eyes returned to the red socks in the sleek black cleats upon the Babe's feet.

"I am a Hindu," Marubrishnubupu answered after a pause. "We believe in letting go, that life is found in not wanting. We hold that in relinquishing our need to possess objects of desire we find true bliss."

The Babe laughed. "And I'm the greatest ballplayer that ever lived. I'm the very heart of the game. I'm not supposed to strike out, or have a bad day, or lose the big one."

"I don't understand," Marubrishnubupu stated flatly.

"What I mean, Kid, is that sometimes, even when you're the best, you're going to strike out. You're going to make some mistakes."

"I'm sorry, Mr. Ruth, but I don't . . ."

"You don't know much about baseball do you?" Ruth picked up his bat. "I mean, you like the game, but you don't have a clue as to what it's really all about. You don't know what it is to step into the batter's box, what it is to dig in to face a pitch with the bases loaded and the home team down by a bucket of runs. You don't know what it is to face a 90-mile-an-hour fastball or a nasty curve. You don't understand what it is to *want* to knock the snot out of a ball, to hit it into the bleachers for some little boy who believes you're a really swell hero. You don't know what it is to step out on a baseball diamond, to feel the freshly cut grass, to smell the chalk and the hotdogs, to chase down a fly ball or hit the cutoff man for a close play at the plate. That's the kind of thing, Kid, that you just don't understand. Isn't it, Kid? You ever held a baseball bat, Kid?"

Ruth extended the thick piece of Louisville pine to Marubrishnubupu. Marubrishnubupu balked, raising his hands in protest. "No, I couldn't. I mean, I don't need to."

"You mean you don't know how to."

"Well . . ."

Running a hand across his soft chin, the Babe shook his head. "Listen, Kid, I know you don't *need* to. But do you *want* to? That's the point of baseball. I know you don't need to. None of us need to. Take the bat, Kid. Feel it in your hands. This is the finest wood in the whole wide world, a genuine Louisville Slugger."

Tentatively, Marubrishnubupu reached out his hand. He felt the sticky pine tar as he wrapped his palm about the neck of the extended bat.

"That's right, Kid, don't be shy. Your baseball bat is your best friend."

Forgetting his protests, Marubrishnubupu grinned like a little boy as he hefted the club awkwardly in front of himself. With both hands about the neck, he tightened his grip, wringing his wrists together as he had watched ballplayers do on the television screen.

"That's right, get a good grip. Choke up on the bat a little bit if it's too heavy. You want to be able to snap the wrists. You're looking for head speed. Now let's see your swing."

The guru held the bat before him; he noted the worn marks on the thickest part of the round wood where contact had been made with hundreds of balls. Each mark was a scar that memorialized a battle at the plate, a struggle against the will of a pitcher and all nine men in the field. Each mark was an assertion of victory, an assertion stating, "Home plate belongs to me." Marubrishnubupu swung the bat uncomfortably before him.

"Bend your elbows. You get no power if you don't bend your elbows. And you have to bend your knees a little too."

Marubrishnubupu brought the bat over his shoulder with his back elbow bent. He turned his head to face an imaginary pitcher. Bending his knees, he dug into an imaginary plate.

"That's it. That's a good strong stance!"

He waited, staring straight and sure into the eyes of his opponent. He heard the crowd's roar and he saw the fences far away. The windup. The pitch. His heart raced. His palms sweated. He saw the white ball released from the tight clutch of the pitcher's hand. He saw the slow rotation of the red stitches. He raised his lead leg and stepped into the ball, swinging with all his might. He heard the crack of wood upon the leather canvas. He heard the zip of physics and felt the sharp jolt of contact in his wrists, a jolt that only made him stronger, more sure of himself. The bat followed through, driving the ball as far as it would go. He twisted, pivoting off of his back foot, spinning himself into a corkscrew as he watched the ball sail into the distance, higher and higher, getting lost in the lights.

"That's pretty good, Kid," the voice interrupted. "That's a solid swing." Marubrishnubupu held the stance for just a second of indulgence. Then he grew embarrassed, self-conscious. Handing the bat back to the Babe, he mumbled an apology.

"What are you apologizing for? That felt good, didn't it?"

"Yes," Marubrishnubupu smiled, blushing. "Yes, it did."

"That's a good thing, see."

"I . . . I . . ."

"You hit the snot out of it. Say it. That's what you wanted to do, isn't it?"

Marubrishnubupu didn't answer. He simply looked at his hands, rubbing his fingers, pleasantly lingering over the pine tar that had helped him to keep his grip firm.

Ruth patted his belly. "I ate too many of the hotdogs, Kid. You ever have a hotdog at a ballpark?"

"What?"

"I said, you ever have a ballpark hotdog?"

"No. No, I never have."

"I eat too many of them, Kid. It was fun to watch you swing that bat. You got a good natural stance."

"I do?"

"Sure, sure you do, Kid. You could be a heck of a hitter. You just have to be willing to dig in and protect home plate. Remember, you own it. Home plate belongs to you."

Marubrishnubupu was about to reply when Ruth interrupted. "And don't tell me you're a Hindu and you don't believe in owning anything. You own home plate. Get it?"

Marubrishnubupu bowed his head. "All right."

"That a way, Kid. Now you're talking. You don't know what it means to the kids to watch their heroes fight for home plate. That's what you always have to remember. What you do up there, you do for the kids. You're fighting for the kids."

Marubrishnubupu watched as a tear dripped down the cheek of the big man.

"Aw shucks . . ." the Babe added.

"Is that what this is about?" Marubrishnubupu asked. "The kids? What is it, Mr. Ruth? What's wrong?"

The Babe bravely brushed the tear away from his pudgy cheek as he stared Master Marubrishnubupu in the eyes, slinging the thick piece of wood over his shoulder. "You just remember it's for the kids. You got that?"

"I'll remember, Mr. Ruth."

Suddenly the Bambino looked off into the mouth of the cave as though he had heard a call. "It's gametime, Kid."

Staring into the distance as he adjusted his cap, the old sultan smiled as he again rubbed his cheek dry; it was a brave smile that Marubrishnubupu felt overwhelm him at the bottom of his heart. He understood why this lovable man was a hero to millions. Stepping towards the mouth of the dark cave, the Babe paused. Marubrishnubupu saw the number on the back of the jersey. The number he saw caused his heart to leap into his throat: 3. Leaning with a hand upon the cold triangle stone, Ruth turned back before entering. He spoke softly, honestly, gazing down at his own feet.

"When I was a kid at St. Mary's I dreamt of playing baseball, of playing in the bigs. That's all I ever wanted. That first day I walked into Fenway, my first day as a big-leaguer, stepping onto the fresh cut grass of that field, let me tell you, it was heaven. After being an orphan for all those years, I knew I was finally home. I didn't ever want to leave. I don't think anyone really understood that."

He paused, shyly kicking at the dirt before continuing. "My last Fenway game. I can remember it like yesterday. It was 1934, the year they redid the park and put up the Green Monster, a hitter's dream. We were playing a double header. Sunny day, light breeze to center. In the sixth inning of the second game, my team had to come off the field. I trotted from the outfield straight into the Red Sox dugout. I was halfway there before I remembered that I was a Yankee. The fans, they kept cheering me so I didn't stop. It's where I wanted to be, Kid. It's where I always wanted to be. That's the year I retired, kind of. 1935 is a different story altogether. . . . Anyway, it was a mistake heading into the Red Sox dugout, but you know, it wasn't, Kid. That was the dugout through which I first entered the bigs twenty years earlier. I guess on that last day, I just wanted to exit the game the way I entered it, on the home team. I was always a Red Sox at heart. I never meant the curse, but it stuck. . . . Gotta go, Kid. You remember to protect that plate. It belongs to you." With a wink the Babe turned towards the cave. His jersey, Marubrishnubupu suddenly noticed as he caught a last glimpse of the noble sultan, now displayed the word "YANKEES" across the barreled, pinstripe chest. An "NY" was on his lid. Entering the darkness, the mystical number across his back, the Bambino's red socks were last to disappear.

Marubrishnubupu stood at the threshold of the dark void, calling in, "Ruth. Mr. Ruth. Babe." With a bold heart, taking a deep breath, Marubrishnubupu stepped forward. From within he peered back. He could see the crystal city in the distance. The bright cardinal perched on a branch appeared to be singing a song, though Marubrishnubupu could hear nothing. The field of snow appeared to be melting.

Marubrishnubupu saw short cut grass, patches of smoothed out dirt, and a rounded tumuli in the center of the flat field. Instantly he understood. It was the pitcher's mound that rose from the ground and beneath the snow was a baseball diamond.

"Mr. Ruth. Mr. Ruth?" he called out as the darkness within rumbled. Marubrishnubupu watched as the cardinal flapped away in fear, as the crystal city quaked and collapsed, as the purple lotus died, as the triangle of stone tipped, extinguishing the light and locking the sage within.

"*Ruth! Ruth!*" Turning to face the darkness, Marubrishnubupu saw the first vague patterns of unfamiliar forms. He saw a man weeping by a gravestone bellowing the name, "*Ruth, Ruth!*"

Marubrishnubupu realized that it was not he who was calling for Ruth but the frightened man clinging to the gravestone. In a nearby sphere, Marubrishnubupu saw a woman with horns removing her clothes, wrapping her legs about the man's head and pulling him forward. The salacious nature of the image caused Marubrishnubupu to look away in fear of his own attraction to the image. Turning once more, the images collapsing one atop the other, collage-like, Marubrishnubupu witnessed a young boy shivering in the nude with a paintbrush in his hand before an empty canvas. Transfixed, Marubrishnubupu stepped closer, attempting to peer at the canvas. On it, in dynamic colors, was the ideal depiction of the man to whom he had just spoken, Babe Ruth, corked in the classic pose, immediately after a swing, watching the ball sail into the distance for a home run. The shivering boy had scarified, wounded flesh. His skin was pale and blue, ice cold. His eyes were listless and lost. Gazing into the eyes drained of spirit, Marubrishnubupu felt a deeper sadness than he had ever known. He was paralyzed, unable to respond to the shivering child. In the eyes he saw an all-consuming grief that could only come from an all forgiving love — the love of a dying Messiah. Stunned by the sense of revelation, Marubrishnubupu felt a pair of hands clasp him by the shoulders. He jumped with fright, surprised to see a young, plain girl with a freckled face and caramel hair desperately imploring him, her terror real, "Stop it! Stop it! Please, break it! Break this curse!"

Overwhelmed, Marubrishnubupu felt himself suffocating, drowning, sucked downward. As he pushed the girl aside in horror, he realized that he was drowning. Flailing madly, losing control, he fought the bone cold water, fought to a surface covered by thick, black ice. Spinning in the icy water, unable to breathe, losing consciousness, he saw in the distance a painted canvas. It displayed the image of Babe Ruth hanging from a pitching mound gallows in his gray pinstripe Yankees uniform, his limp feet dangling, his red socks exposed to a crowd of angry faces that were about him jeering epithets of invective hatred. "Go home, Yankee! Yankee, go home!" Snow fell softly. The crowd faded. Hushed.

Still much disturbed the next morning, Marubrishnubupu, scheduled to host a weekend spiritual retreat seminar, boarded a single engine charter plane for Taos, New Mexico. The dream, like an unfinished palinode of import, lingered with the master. Gripped in inner turmoil, his own emotions were garbled and confused, his mind unfocused. Still, he would lead. Those who traveled from miles away expected him to do so. He would address the seminar participants. They sought him for his wisdom, and he would serve in this capacity to the utmost of his ability. He accepted these recent dreams and the ambiguity they brought to his waking hours as a spiritual fire, a test of integrity and commitment to the difficult path of inner peace. Oddly to him, it was the most fleeting of the images that pierced his mind: the young, plain girl who had grabbed him by the shoulders, shaking him, as though to wake him from ignorant slumber.

"Break the Curse! Break it! Break this Curse!"

℘

The audience gathered. Marubrishnubupu began his address; he opened a seed, allowed it to live its natural life, drew it back within and closed it, sealing it for a future birth. In between he watched the contents flow, following a path all their own. Where that life seemed to end he spoke of promise and hope, uttering simple reminders that all which dies must live again. Drawing the contents of the seed once more inward to their shell, Marubrishnubupu brought his spellbinding address to a close. "And so, my friends, we can say with confidence that a soul and spirit does reside in each of us, a soul and spirit that wishes to serve a greater, universal good. All that we need do is place aside our ego, our sense of hurt, our sense that this world has treated us unfairly. Think of these words, my friends. For so it is with each of us in our great and little lives. We begin when despair has stripped us of all hope. We are still aware of the hopelessness, feel its force, but we are not overwhelmed by it; we are not defeated by the suffering of this life."

He wanted to speak of baseball but he did not. What could he possibly say about the game he did not understand to a group of Americans who had grown up with the game? How silly would it have sounded if he told them that Ruth had begun with a curse because he understood blessings? Gulping down an uncharacteristic nervousness, Marubrishnubupu concluded, "Put up your white picket fences. Take care of your home. My friends, thank you."

Remaining seated on the stage, Marubrishnubupu adjusted his maroon robe, pulling it higher upon his shoulders. The audience clapped energetically. The sound of aching sea waves resounded in the applause; he understood that this was nature's way of speaking through the human throng — like the Fenway faithful that had applauded Ruth in 1934 as he trotted to the dugout where he had always belonged, even after the ill-fated trade. The host of the Taos seminar, a thin, wispy vegetarian who at the age of thirty-five had changed his own name from Todd Mark Anderson to Gregory Life, stood up from the front row. Quelling the applause, he announced that Master Marubrishnubupu would answer a few brief questions. Hands shot up, excited hands full of desire and need. The master surveyed the sea of faces and shrugged. Everyone laughed, so proud to be undifferentiated; the moderator selected someone as nondescript as possible to ask the first question.

"Master Marubrishnubupu, you said that all we need to do is put aside our ego, our sense of self-righteous hurt, and our will will guide us. I think I understand, but this seems to me like saying that all we need to do is move a mountain out of our way. It seems like such a large task. How can we simplify it?"

The master bowed. He himself felt happier than he had in a long time addressing the group and could sense the infectious nature of the spirit moving him. This resembled life on the purple lotus. He spoke slowly, taking full advantage of the fact that English was not his native tongue. Broken English done well is far more eloquent than average use of the language, the struggle of the speaker somehow imbuing the words with a greater depth, a freshness lost to the native speaker.

"That is a very good question. You see, the questioner understands that number does not matter. The number of tasks we accomplish in a given day or life is insignificant to the quality of the tasks. And when we realize that the number of tasks is not significant, then we are prepared to accept that even one task may be too many. Receptive to such reality, we can sit and let the great mountain of ego wear away with the erosion of the tides that eventually come. This is what our will is, a patient tide that sets itself to a single task of quality with unrelenting vigor and defiant joy. I do not wish to be esoteric, but it may help some to realize that all you need is to focus on the quality of your wave, and you will soon recognize that it was never a mountain after all but only a very manageable mound magnified by a very clever ego. Focus on the quality of the wave, not the quantity of the mountain."

The questioner nodded happily, apparently finally maneuvering past a troublesome obstacle that had long plagued his mind.

"Next question for Master Marubrishnubupu."

A raven-haired woman in an ivory dress and black pearls stood. She did not flatteringly smile or placate; she gazed hard at the master as though cognizant of standing not before a man but before a large book of answers that required no personal attention. Marubrishnubupu, for his part, had the curious thought that he was looking at a polished piece of jade.

"Master Marubrishnubupu," she began. "I know that we have talked much about dismantling ego. Still, to me, there are beings deserving of special consideration, recognition. I find this can be a difficult task. We don't want to be wrong in such things. How does one identify greatness? A gift from God?"

Weighing the woman's sincerity, Marubrishnubupu examined her as she examined him: for truth and answers. Within his breast he held a portentous boding that connected this woman to his recent dream. The audience grew uneasy with the deafening gulf of silence between the master and the sharply dressed woman. Many quickly began casting disapproving glances at the questioner, subtle accusations that held her responsible for the sudden, unexplainable declension of their high spirits.

The moderator, who had worn an apple pie smile all day, attempted to steer the question clear of the master. "Obviously, Master

Marubrishnubupu, the questioner fails to comprehend the whole spirit of the day. The whole point is that we are all great, all equal when we
listen to our spirits." The host spoke with a confident veneer that
crackled from the strain of nervous cheer. Others in the audience
bobbed their heads, pleased to swiftly depart from such a misguided
intrusion. Still as alabaster, Irene Smythe remained standing, staring,
bold, unabashed, fully present, into the master's eyes.

"Let's take another question," Gregory Life gaily intervened.

"No," Marubrishnubupu finally asserted, relieving the tension in
the room and in himself with a light tug at his beard. "This woman asks
a deeply significant question." He did not remove his eyes from hers.
"And I am tempted to believe she knows how significant a question this
is."

Slowly as an alligator, the master slipped into his standard voice, the
voice that everyone appreciated for its ability to make entry into the
complex appear as simple. "The questioner asks about the nature of
greatness, about whether, all ego removed, there are differences between
us. She is right. This is a dangerous question, but a very important one
that we should not seek to ignore, to sweep under the rug."

"First of all, it is important to affirm that from a Buddhist perspective, we do not believe in God. Thus, the idea of a being as a gift from
God is extremely difficult to rationalize. We simply are what we are,
more as a matter of personal merit than bestowed gift." The master was
choosing his words carefully, more carefully than usual, though his
occasional lapses with English made the distinctions difficult to detect.
"We are all equal in being what we are; however, in essence you ask the
question, 'Are we all equal in what we are to one another?' I would
answer this by saying that as long as we are different in what we are to
ourselves, we cannot be wholly equal to what we are to one another."

Marubrishnubupu sought for a definite sign of comprehension in the
focused eyes of the inquisitioner. "If, for instance, I have a dream of a
man drowning in the middle of a frozen lake, that man will have a
meaning for me that he does not have for a person who has not had that
dream. What others mean comes down to who we are. Theoretically, of
course, it is possible that a single being has more meaning to more of us
than any other single being, though this does not necessarily make this
being innately more meaningful than the rest of us. Do you see?

Regardless of the numbers, greatness must still be a matter of quality. At heart, our own relationship to our self is the determinant factor. If you desire to identify greatness, there is only one way to do it; you must accurately surmise the relationship of the appraised unto itself."

Irene inclined her head in acknowledgment. White knuckles alone betrayed the true extent of the tension in her mind. Though not yet stripped of all doubt, she was a bit closer to what she needed to unravel. The master watched as Irene took her seat; he found her compact, efficient, elegant and daring. Good control, he noted as she ascended in presence above the crowd, tremendous self-discipline. As the next questioner dutifully probed the issue of joyous, unconscious service, Marubrishnubupu sat unblinking, unsure himself of what had been revealed and what discovered.

In the cloistered vestibule following the afternoon lecture, a disciple of Marubrishnubupu approached Irene. He was a young man with narrow, mischievous eyes that she found unusually petulant and resentful for one who claimed deep affiliation with a Spiritual Life Center. The cheeks of his rootbeer skin were round and soft. Irene wondered about the boy's birthplace. She believed spirituality a difficult concept for a child, and where it was easy, she feared indoctrination. In this boy, she sensed the arrogance that resulted from the memorization of lengthy text from aged scrolls, an arrogance that often comes when one is fortunate enough to be born directly into a rich culture for which outsiders yearn. The spirituality of his position filled him with a repulsive self-respect that accompanies the righteous who have never fallen from grace, and thus, sadly, have never known redemption. She admired the course tan robes wrapped at the waist with a thick cord. The young man went barefoot, of course, life being viewed as more spiritual without shoes.

"The master requests your presence as his personal guest."

Curiously, Irene experienced no surprise as she twisted her heel free of a crack in the stone; she had not expected to leave the place without a clearer revelation of whatever mystery had brought her here.

But already she knew. It was the paintings of that boy, the dying leper boy. She thought of him as a boy now. How else could she hold him in her mind, a specimen so clearly under the domineer of that woman? Without having yet met him, she felt she knew his life: controlled, oppressed, subjugated, shame ridden — and through it all — unhindered, unhampered, free. How could such contradiction be possible? Those paintings from a boy, she mused, amazed. But maybe he's not a boy. This facet of leprosy confounds me, transforms this production into something more than I am ready to take on. Yet here it is, these paintings, the paintings of which I always dreamed, and by a mere boy of twenty-two calling upon me to be his herald, his tightrope-walking impresario. Is he dying or isn't he? Dorothia could lay it on thick or take it off, leaving Irene with the impression that the disease was more a tool of mawkish convenience than a source of misery. The messages from the mother were conflicted, but those damn paintings were real.

Now here she was, on a spiritual retreat — of all the places possible! — seeking to disengage a paradox, to reason it out. How could a boy paint those? I don't care if the great Solzhenitsyn did serve as his mentor, she brooded. They're not imitations; they're complete, authentic originals. They're not concepts; they're fully bloomed ideas. They're not attempts; they're achievements. How was it feasible? Was it her one need? Had she lost her perspective, her solid artistic judgment? She couldn't take the chance of being wrong. For the first time she sought affirmation that her own mind remained clear. Who better, she decided, than a Buddhist master. They like to slice through delusions with quick cuts of subtle truth. She'd gladly take that now, if it would prevent an embarrassing fall, a misjudgment. Talk of spirit was fine, but a Buddhist never forgets reason. That's what she told herself in order to bring herself to Taos.

Irene noticed the novice before her, still waiting for her answer. "I'd be delighted to be the Master's guest."

"Follow me." The boy turned, indifferent to the woman, dragging the long, maundering cord on the ground beside him.

After descending a flight of stairs that led to a cool basement, she followed the young acolyte through a long, tired hall with several turns. Irene thought it a converted bomb shelter, though its sheer size and maze-like, catacomb structure caused her to doubt the theory. It seemed more likely to her, as imagination fed her delighted curiosity and the walk became a minor adventure, that these were covert pathways that led to the inner sanctum of a secret sect. After only a few turns through the moist walled chambers, they came to a solid, iron door. The boy knocked gently, exhibiting a sudden humility that he had not thought necessary to waste in his dealings with Irene. "Master, the American woman."

Inside, Marubrishnubupu reposed cross-legged on a vast purple pillow.

"Please, come in. Do not be shy." The boy bowed to the master and removed himself. Closing the door, a thunderous echo refracted through the underground channels.

"Please sit. You are my guest. Would you like tea?" Marubrishnubupu rose from the floor to pour tea from a steaming pot of fine china. A hand painted pattern of tiny warbling birds, flitting amongst winding blue ivy, decorated the china. Irene glanced about the room. It was simple, sparse, acetic; by no means luxurious living. An iron framed cot, with a pillow atop a folded blanket, had been constructed in the corner of the room.

"I have stayed here before. They are kind enough to give me my own room so that I am able to continue my work while visiting. Do you like sugar or cream?"

"A little cream."

"I quite enjoy my visits here. They refresh my soul. I have never witnessed sunsets quite so spectacular. The sun glows as though struggling to communicate the fragility of existence, mauve and pink and lavender. These colors come from elsewhere." He delivered her tea. "Please sit. Be comfortable. This room is sparse, I know; it enables us to think more clearly, with less distraction. Complexity distracts us, but it does not help us to become better human beings." A single chair had been placed before his pillow. It offered no comfort; she smiled, balancing the tea in both hands.

"Why did you request to see me, Master Marubrishnubupu?" To her own surprise the name rolled off her tongue with the ease of rainwater flowing down a wide sluice.

"I drink my tea plain, though I prefer it with a touch of sugar. People don't think a spiritual leader should wish for anything in his tea." For an unknown reason the words, in the simplicity of what they confessed, touched Irene. She understood in some small way that the constant requirement of humility was just that — constant, and capable of an infinitude of demanding manifestations that an outsider to the life could likely never conceive. Every idiosyncrasy of the multitude magnified, multiplied, absorbed and assimilated into an active modeling to others of the viability of perfection, simplicity, total acceptance, tolerance and pacifism, an emotional straight jacket fit to the purgation of all desire. This was spiritual leadership through self-denial, public and personal tests a thousand times harder than anything the social world could construct. These were tests of eternity, tests with no beginning and with no end.

She did not know why, not fully, but she experienced a thoroughly unanticipated surge of respect that bristled within the very marrow of her bones. Spontaneously she rose, placing her own tea on the table. From the cart she took up the sugar bowl and carefully poured a heaping spoonful of the white crystal into the Master's cup. She dipped the spoon and stirred as the Master remained motionless with the cup extended upward to her, a child's pleasure gleaming in his eyes.

She found Marubrishnubupu to be an attractive man, likely over fifty, though he appeared not a day older than thirty-nine. She knew of the propensity of these monks to defy traditional laws of aging, an effect of meditation and living in accordance with the fundamental doctrine of ahimsa. Groomed with a haircut and a shave it would have been relatively simple to imagine Marubrishnubupu as quite dashing. He sipped the tea in merriment, smiling in serene appreciation for the melliferous flavor that for him was decadence.

"You have done my soul a generous service." With eyes closed he held his lips to the lip of the cup, allowing the tranquilizing elixir to enter his mouth in small, lingering increments.

"You're welcome."

They sat silently for several moments, and Irene knew that the invitation extended to her had not been common. A gravity attached itself to the invitation as surely as the compelling impulse that had put her behind the wheel and on the rising road to the tiny mountain hamlet of Taos. It was late September; in an hour the sun would be setting and her heart suddenly ached to see one of the glorious, elliptical sunsets of which Marubrishnubupu had spoken. She had been here before. But she had never truly thought of the sunsets as more blessed than those of Santa Fe, or all of New Mexico for that matter. Until now she'd not given any sincere consideration to the idea that Taos was somehow special. The aura that surrounded the place was for tourists, a carefully constructed social agenda, a native conspiracy based in enlightened self-interest. As though enlightenment would ever modify or be modified.

Her own eyes gazed past the cot, directly into the cement wall. She imagined clouds rolling past in the brilliant sky and a blood-red, mandarin sun, the colors one would see on a Japanese flag. Did Buddhist masters take vows of celibacy? She could make his tea and be very pleased in a place like this, fortified and protected from the daily cares of the world. In time she could easily forget about the activities of her life, about selecting artists and keeping food on their tables, about hosting showings and organizing wall space, about maintaining an impeccable image. Sipping at her own tea, she felt warm inside, sparse and vast as the room, atop the spinning globe. She sighed.

"You wish to know why I have called you here." The calm statement exuded profundity — as though he had already said something meaningful.

To linger a bit longer without purpose, to absorb the warmth, would have been Irene's sole wish. Marubrishnubupu was simply responding to her earlier question, a question she would gladly retract for the opportunity to simply sit and enjoy this steaming tea, all secular matters left behind, trivial and far away; they could live on tea and sleep in this cot with a single blanket and pillow, dreaming of sunsets and moonlight, making sensuous love instructed by the Kama Sutra for hours upon end. It was an absurd, trivial little romance, and she knew it. But, she reflected to herself, isn't this what love sought, a happy state of simplicity that puts an end to all of time?

"I don't have to know right now."

"I have had a dream," Master Marubrishnubupu began. "In the audience today, when you asked your question, I understood that you are connected to that dream." He placed the tea aside. The rising vapors grew dimmer, tamer. "At first, I am shamed to say," and she could see that he was, "in my cynicism, I doubted my cosmic intuition. But you have, through your question from the audience today, confirmed the deeper truth. You and the dream are connected."

Irene studied the Guru with foxlike eyes, the eyes of a discerning art critic, deciphering the code not for content but legibility.

"How am I part of your dream? What was this dream?"

"It may seem odd to you," he warned her.

"No more odd than me being here."

"You are honest. I respect that." After a brief pause, he met her eyes and spoke intently, "I have dreamed that Atman has incarnated. That the true Brahmin is here. The Great One. The Great Oneness."

Irene glanced to her tea, suppressing a patronizing smile behind her teacup. "I've heard the terms, but I'm not thoroughly familiar with your religious icons."

Marubrishnubupu nodded, speaking slower so as to give her time to absorb the impact of the meanings. "In the West you are mainly a culture of Christians and Jews. You believe in your Yahweh and your Jesus, primarily your Christ. And even those who don't believe in anything are saturated by these forces: your Old and New Testaments, your Torah, your Koran. They are all evolutions of the same consciousness, of the same basic understanding. Is this correct?"

As an agnostic and a meliorist, Irene chose not to cavil over minor points of contention. "Basically, yes, I suppose it is one tradition."

"Good, very good. Hinduism and Buddhism are similar. We are different, but we emerge of the same source. In your Western world you wait for your Messiah to come, either for the first or second time. It is really the same. You are waiting for an arrival that will save you, fulfill your prophecy, that sort of thing. In our beliefs there is no such physical manifestation that we seek or expect. Souls are recycled through reincarnation. We seek perpetual improvement, but we are not waiting for the One true being to come to us. We have our venerable teachers, this is true, our incarnations; however, these are not the same thing as your Messiah. They are teachers, symbolic representatives, not corner-stones of salvation, not Messianic in function. Do you understand the distinction I am making?"

"I think so. You're saying that we in the West harbor a hope to touch God and you do not."

"Yes, this is a respectable manner of saying it."

"That your gods on earth are not really gods on earth, but ours are, or at least we genuinely expect them to be." The comment conveyed a satirical edge that Irene did not wholly intend. She suspected that it stemmed from a subtle resentment at being lumped together in some simplistic mishmash of Western religion that did not exist. An agnostic is not a Christian or a Jew or a Moslem in disguise. An agnostic is not an atheist. An agnostic is an agnostic is an agnostic. It's as true a faith as any. The only difference is that it has no Sunday church and it does not take collection.

Marubrishnubupu reflected on her assessment, unaffected by the tone. "Yes, that's accurate."

Irene was feeling an increased skepticism fermenting within. For all of his esoteric comprehension, this was just another man who could not face his own brand of particular, amusing and patronizing arrogance. Only art could be trusted, a religion safely burrowed within capitalism, and never the other way around.

"So tell me more about this dream," she prompted.

"Atman is here!" Marubrishnubupu announced in a passionate voice, far more forceful than anything she had anticipated from this man of peace, this man of indifference to the samsaric wheel, this man who freely blended Hinduism with Buddhism — perhaps even other traditions — without shame or apology.

"Atman is the uncreated created, the formless form. The one that need not be one. You have your Father, Son and Holy Spirit." Irene bit down on her tongue. "Father sends the Son. Now imagine that the Father has come. Not the Son, but the Father. This is what it means to say that Atman has come. I have dreamed that Atman has taken form. The ultimate Brahmin. Siddhartha's father was a Brahmin, did you know that?"

"I don't even know who Siddhartha is," Irene replied, growing more disinterested by the moment by this man who knew how to bullshit in religious garb. She suspected him, for the first time, as a cult leader.

"Siddhartha Guatama is the boy who grew to be Buddha. And this is why the religions are connected, just as Islam is connected to Christianity. The same angel who echoed words of revelation to the Virgin Mary dictated the sacred text of the Koran to Mohammed."

"Gabriel."

"Yes, Gabriel," Marubrishnubupu bowed. His face glazed over with strength. "Irene, the angel Gabriel has now visited me."

"I didn't think you believed in angels."

"He has come from the void to reveal a mysterious message. The religions are converging into one, returning to their source. Atman has incarnated! Atman has come to destroy the wheel of samsara, to free us."

It was difficult, if not impossible, for Irene to understand what the man sought to communicate. For several moments her mind played ping-pong. Was he a crackpot? A religious zealot driven over the edge by psychological narcissism? Or was he just another man clinging too tightly to hope?

"And just what is samsara?" Irene leaned forward not to listen but to ease the discomfort that the aluminum folding chair caused her lower back.

"Yes, I am sorry. I sometimes forget that our specific languages are separated by centuries of tradition. Samsara is what the Buddhists know as the wheel of confusion, the vicious circle of life and death, the never-ending cycle of desire and fulfillment and desire again, the seasons of pleasure and pain, birth and re-birth. The notion is communicated in the image of the snake that perpetually feeds upon its own tail; it is existence as we know it. The Buddhists seek Nirvana which is a state that transcends the samsaric wheel and frees the soul from eternal rebirth."

"That sounds like death to me."

"It is very complex," the sage replied. He had confused himself.

"I'm sure it is." She paused, unsure of whether to continue in patronizing the fantasy. "But we were really talking about your visitation. You said the angel Gabriel came to you. I'm wondering, what does Gabriel have to do with Atman?"

"Before now, nothing." Marubrishnubupu spoke with such enthusiasm, such certainty regarding the obvious nature of that which he expressed, that Irene felt pity for him. How could a person be so lucid before the crowds and so lost within the golden canvas of his own solitude? She decided in that moment to listen, to be open-minded and to learn, to at least offer her compassion as solace to his insentience.

"So you've had a divinely inspired vision?" she asked.

"I believe the answer is yes."

"And Gabriel came to you?"

"No, Atman came to me as Gabriel."

"So Atman is Gabriel?"

"There has never been a Gabriel; there has only been Atman."

"So Atman revealed the Koran."

"It would seem so."

"And Atman announced the conception of John the Baptist to Mary."

"Again, it would seem to be the logical conclusion."

"So you had a dream. What do you do with it? It doesn't mean much to me."

Marubrishnubupu pressed forward on his purple pillow. The narrow bridge of his nose functioned to exaggerate the lively eyes. His gaze was so strong, so meaningful, that Irene wavered and questioned for a flint flash who had sense and who was senseless.

"But you see that is but a small part of the dream, almost insignificant. I have often thought the world religions are one, like a family that gets fragmented by time and dust, unable to recognize the return of their own sisters and brothers and children. Deceived by clothing, fooled by dialect. Damned to the angry perversions of unwitting incest. But never have I had such vivid confirmation until now. In the dream, Atman was guised as Gabriel."

"So you did see Gabriel?"

"No," he answered hurriedly. "I saw Babe Ruth."

To this new twist, Irene dropped her mouth in open disbelief. "Babe Ruth?"

He stumbled impatiently in his speech, trying to bring her back to the point and realizing that it would probably be impossible now. "Well, it wasn't Babe Ruth, of course. It was only Atman coming forward as Babe Ruth to communicate a deep truth symbolically."

Irene shook her head in near disgust, dismissing the latest lunacy as too inane to validate through a response. "O.K., whatever, let's say for the sake of argument that it was Atman disguised as Gabriel, disguised as Babe Ruth." Her eyes rolled to the ceiling. "Is that right?"

"Yes, yes," Marubrishnubupu coaxed, thrilled that he had not lost her.

"Well, how do you know it wasn't God the Father disguised at Atman?" Irene was prepared for a game of quibble now; a game often played by all-too-slick ironists in the world of art.

"They are just words. False, invented boundaries designed to create imaginary distinction."

"If they're just words then why don't you just say that God the Father visited you disguised as Atman or even that Babe Ruth is God the Father!"

"That would defeat the whole intent of what I am required to communicate."

"Which is that Atman rules over God the Father and Babe Ruth?"

"Forget Babe Ruth!" he blurted out.

"You brought him into this," she retorted sharply.

"No, no. You misunderstand. I need to show that these religions are linked for the modern mind, that God the Father leads to Atman and that Atman leads to God the Father."

"So they can be used interchangeably?"

"Eventually."

"When?"

"When people understand that they are the same."

"You understand that they're the same. Why don't you begin for us? Begin to just use God the Father. If God the Father and Atman are the same and you know this, then this should be easy."

"Yes, yes, it would be easy." He was growing frustrated. "But then what kind of connection would I have shown? Speaking to an American audience you already understand God the Father. It is the correlation to Atman that is new and must be stressed."

Irene took a deep breath, deciding to cease the escalation towards mutual destruction. "Master Marubrishnubupu, I need to interpose. Honestly, I don't care what you want to call your Godhead. When it comes right down to it, I'm an agnostic. I believe that when all is said and done, I'm agnostic because it frees me from having to defend God I over God II. Whatever you want to call *It* is fine with me. I've never experienced God directly and I don't expect to. The only reason I'm here is that you asked me to be your guest. I've enjoyed the repartee; it's been witty, but I really don't care all that much about the answers. So you probably shouldn't invest too much in trying to convince me."

"I see," the master replied pensively. "So the very idea that Atman . . . God the Father . . . could manifest here on earth is unbelievable to you?"

"Yes."

"I have made a grave error, Irene, and I am sorry for this. It leaves me quite embarrassed. I have assumed your interest in these theological matters. Atman continues to astound me in Its workings. I have spoken too much when I should have been listening. May I ask you a question?"

Irene felt her whole body relax. Marubrishnubupu had been right; the sparseness of the square room did help her to think more clearly; she could exist on an equal plain now; this was all that she ever wanted in her relationships with any person. "Of course."

"At the seminar today, why did you ask me that question about identifying 'the great'?"

Now they were arriving at the willowy heart of the matter. Softening, Irene gazed into Marubrishnubupu's eyes. Her own turn to be embarrassed had come. "It seems silly now."

"Please, tell me."

She sipped at her tea to cause delay. "I'm an art dealer. A woman came to me early this week seeking representation for her son. He's a painter."

Marubrishnubupu, listening with extreme interest, kept his face under taut control.

"Truly glorious works, wondrous for the age. Twenty-two years old and they demonstrate a maturity, a mastery over the canvas that rarely comes from a lifetime of painful experience."

Irene was gazing into her tea cup at the beige liquid that flowed from edge to edge, a competing, flowing wave in a three-inch world, a dynamic similar to the oceans extending from shore to shore. Waves, repetitions, bouncing upon one boundary and reflecting back, arriving to the other shore yet barely recognizable, changed not by the motion of the ever-consistent sea but by the shore, its own unique geography. And this is how things change, she thought, things that are the same, eternal and invariant. What they are never changes, only what receives them.

"I don't know why I came here per se. I haven't met the boy yet. I'm not sure that I want to."

The master leaned forward. "Why?"

"It's difficult to explain. It's like there are two types of artist. There are those artists who are improved and perfected through their work. Their work I always see as a promise of what they wish to become and what they might be. Their paintings are an indication of the path they

have chosen to walk and the destination to which they may with diligence and courage one day arrive. Their paintings are where they wish
to go, more than where they are."

"I think I understand."

"And that's the way I see most artists. Their art is the best of what
they are; the person, though not a letdown, is still, well, *a letdown*."

"Like a guru off the stage."

Irene smiled. It was an extremely kind thing for Marubrishnubupu
to say.

"There is another kind of artist though, the rarest type of artist, who
transcends his or her own art. This kind of artist, though I hedge away
from the use of such terms, is superior to their own artwork. The medium, noble as it is, fails to wholly and truly represent the individual
artist. I've only met a few whom I have ventured to put into this category. These are artists of such a brilliant sensitivity that the medium
channels their energy and in the process of channeling, diminishes
rather than clarifies the light of their vision. It's as though they know
and can recall a far better place than this world but the materials of this
world are too crude to enable them to communicate its beauty. They are
heightened. They possess a sensitivity scant and beautiful. They're the
ones who can make you believe not that a better place could exist but
that it does exist, and they've come here to let us know about it. Like I
said, I've only met a few artists who fall into this category. And of those
few, I've turned out to be wrong as often as I was right. I've almost
stopped believing that this second category really exists."

"It gets harder to believe, does it not?" Marubrishnubupu asked, a
remarkable empathy in his voice that helped Irene to understand that
his experiences with debilitating disappointment were similar — and
likely, his experiences with doubt.

"One starts thinking that there is no better place, that we can dream
of it, but we can never be there. And after being let down so much, it
becomes easier just to stop believing in the living, just to place all our
faith in the dead; they can't let us down any more. If we desire, after
their death, we can even make them into more than they were. That's
why we love the dead artists, the dead prophets, the dead leaders. It's
because they can't hurt us anymore. We always reserve our greatest love
for the dead because they can't touch us, can't let us down."

"And we can't touch them."

"Yes," Irene responded, sadly torn.

"So what is it about this young painter that so affects you?"

Irene pressed her eyes against tears. "I want him to die, Marubrishnubupu. I don't want him to let me down. I want him to be what he is in my mind right now. I want him to die before I discover that I am wrong."

"And what is he in your mind right now?"

Her body was shaking. Tears welled up that she could not fight. She could not hold her voice steady; still she spoke. If he could do such paintings, she could at least speak. And yet, what was he in her mind right now? She didn't know. It was a threat beyond her comprehension.

The master passed her a Kleenex. She blew her nose and padded her eyes. "I'm sorry. This is foolish."

"To cry is not foolish. It is foolish not to cry, to repress our sorrow."

He was saying less now and she liked him more. *"Lachrymae Rerum,"* she said softly.

"Excuse me?"

"It's a Latin phrase."

"I'm afraid that I do not know Latin."

She laughed. "Something you don't know."

"Everything is known, but I am not the one to know it. What does this phrase mean? Teach me."

"It means 'the sorrow of things.' There's no reason for me to cry, and yet . . ." Lifting her head from the Kleenex, her eyes brightened with the illumination of insight. "I suppose you could say that *lachrymae rerum* comes when one gets re-acquainted with samsara. Oh, Master Marubrishnubupu, it's just that I feel I've been wrong about the whole world."

"Wrong about *everything*?"

The question was as simple and as clean as the room where, though below ground, one could not hide or pretend. In a different life, she could have loved a man like this. She looked to his face. His warm smile convinced her to believe. "No, probably not *everything*."

Outside the sky was filled with distinct bars of mandarin red and pale gold. The indigo sun wrapped its childhood rays about the childish world.

"Do you believe in heaven?" she asked.

"I don't know," he replied. The very indication that he might seemed to rub against his Eastern doctrines.

For the first time, Irene knew that she did.

Extending his hand to her, they rose together. Marubrishnubupu invited her. "Come, it is a good time. Let us go watch a sunset."

They walked the cool maze together. At their feet, a draft traveled like a holy ghost through the underground channels. Marubrishnubupu guided her left and right as her hand traced their path through the caverns, collecting upon her fingers drips of sweet moisture that seeped through the concrete walls. Emerging from a different door than that by which Irene had entered, they stepped into the mountain desert, beyond the ashram. The sky, transmitter to another species altogether, was as radiant as she had imagined. Having issued forth from the hallowed earth, Irene felt the friendship of life, his hand in hers, spring again. Purple, pink, azure, gold: such a tincture of colors filtered through a whisper of cloud as the blood-red mandarin sun slipped beneath the horizon. They walked past parched arroyos to a place where they sat in the warm sand, silently gazing at the bars of colored light that filled the sky. Yes, she thought, there is a heaven. There must be. A green lizard with a flickering tail scampered beneath a rock.

"You must see this young painter," the sage declared. "There is no choice in the matter."

"I know."

♒

Marcel sat in the hotel bar. Prophet strode the edges of the black lacquer table, sidling upon repousse designs like Braille, stretching wings but never flying, occasionally maundering to the bowl of salted peanuts, beak pecking upwards, taking no more than half a nut at any given time.

"Eat slowly, Prophet."

"Caw-caw!"

Marcel was waiting for his publisher who had given him a hurried call an hour ago, expressing an absolute need to speak with him immediately. *We're speaking now,* Marcel had said. *Meet with you, meet with you,* his publisher and longtime friend had shot back. Yawning into the phone, Marcel had agreed. *Fine, fine, meet me at the hotel bar, then. Are you writing?* Jack had asked. *Drinks first, writing later. Christ Marcel. Shut-up, Jack.*

"Another martini, Rose," he called from his corner table. 11:00 a.m. in the morning, he waited in the dimly lit bar, repairing lines in a journal — resuscitating lines was more like it. With his jaunty nose buried on the page he held a pimento olive in his free hand. Prophet arched forward, sensing something in the stillness before striding over with quick steps. The bird licked at the salty fingers before discovering the alcohol saturated olive. Gobbling the pimento from the center, Prophet sampled from the olive before walking away, uninterested in the bitter feast. Marcel dropped the remains in an empty martini glass with two other olives in a similar state.

The line with which he wrestled concluded the second chapter of his current work-in-progress. *"Eli ignored the fever and dipped an entire toe into the blood-lime juice of parricide." "Ignoring the fever, Eli draped an entire toe in the bloody lime juice of parricide."* He crossed the whole thing out with anger, began fresh, admonishing himself to keep it simpler. *"Eli had killed his mother. Fever subsiding, lime juice poured from the open bottle, translucent drape to the wound."*

It was more than just the last line that was crap. It was the whole thing. The bird sounded out and Marcel echoed in agreement. The bartender sauntered over, smiled, amused.

"I can hardly tell which is which."

"What's that?"

"You and the bird. You sound alike. I swear I can't tell the difference." She was tall for a woman, frumpy and in her forties. The oxford, black tie and vest could not conceal the buried dreams. She had a southern accent. Georgian, Marcel surmised, maybe Tennessee. "Sapphire martini, extra dry."

Marcel pushed the empty glass forward and slid the full one toward his mouth. "Thanks, Rose."

Marcel noticed her ass, sagging, a centerpoint of gravity after which all else would follow: hips, breasts, chin, cheeks. But this was only the small, rounded half of growing old. It was the dreams unfulfilled that caused the greatest sag, the heaviness of sluggard pupils, like a woman hypnotized once too often. He stared unabashedly at her. She had a thing for him which made it all right to look at her unabashed. Besides, this was the job. Men watch women and women watch the men watching them. Marcel had read this somewhere and found, to his amusement, that it held true and made sense. There were yellow stains beneath her arms. A woman, no woman, no matter how destitute, should not have to wear a shirt with pee-colored sweat stains beneath the arms, he thought. She noticed his stare and took it as a compliment.

"That bird is gonna get high blood pressure," she stated, stroking Prophet with a cautious finger. The bird bristled away, side stepping along the raised edge of the table, never crossing crow's feet.

Marcel gazed up from the woman's paunch.

"Everyone's different with salt. Some people need it."

"Yeah, I guess you're right. It's just when I was a kid they said too much salt was bad for anyone. Now they say it's all individual, everyone responds to it different. Pretty weird, huh?"

"Yeah, pretty weird," Marcel replied.

"You need anything else?"

"Nothing else. Wait. Where are you from?"

"Kentucky. Why?"

"No reason." Prophet cawed loudly through the dim, empty bar. *The Price is Right* was on TV. Bob Barker liked to keep himself surrounded with pretty blondes in their thirties, facial features all the same, Scandanavian descent, even the black one. A college girl from A&M agonized, watching the yodeling man on a stick in the mountain climber game. The crowd cheered as the placard covering the price dropped. She had $1.47 cents of slack and a box of Rice-a-Roni as the last item whose price she needed to absorb. The yodeler began climbing again, up and up. Only a dollar left, he approached the peak. The frenzied crowd was going gaga, screaming in fear and excitement. Fifty cents, would the yodeler stop, or would he plummet to his death? Prophet crowed. The yodeler never changed his pitch or tenor. He proceeded forward, singing his happy song, unaffected by the impending doom, twenty cents away. How much more could a damn box of Rice-a-Roni cost anyway? Where did they buy it, Marcel wondered, his own pulse racing, at some upscale yuppie store? Ten cents. Five. Marcel could not watch. He looked away, peered from between his fingers.

Three cents. My God, someone stop him! The yodeler plummeted to certain death as the steady song spiraled into sad oblivion. The college girl dropped her arms from supplication and prayer. The San Francisco disaster. Parting gifts.

"Life's a bitch." Rose retreated with the empty glass. Lingering unnecessarily at his table, she had wanted to tell him that she was reading his book, *Another Day of Loving*, but she'd gotten afraid that he would have asked a question about what she thought, her opinion, and she really didn't have one, though she liked it, even if it did get a bit heady sometimes. She followed what she could, even kept a dictionary with her to look up the words she didn't understand, words she'd heard before but never really used. It turned out, to her maudlin surprise, that her English wasn't all that good. She liked the characters though. They were like people she could have known. She thought it would have been stupid to tell him that his book was better than her favorite soap opera, even though the title sounded a lot like the title of a soap opera, something that Marcel had never noticed. Anyway, she would have felt stupid if he had asked for her opinion, so she said nothing. He would not have asked for her opinion.

"Eli plummeted into the heart of his fever. Lime juice, the old remedies and wive's tales of the Kentucky South evaporated into drowsy, midday matricide." Prophet nipped at the pen, playfully yanking the tip from the page.

"Marcel!"

"Jack, you old dog."

"Still keeping that filthy bird."

"Still not washing your ears with soap."

The publisher sat; he was an exuberant man with a well groomed taste for fine clothes and other things.

"Walker Blue, rocks," he called over to the bartender. He looked at the bird pecking at the peanuts. "Fresh bowl of snacks, too."

Marcel closed the journal and pushed it aside. Prophet, seemingly attuned to the very vibrations of the table, hopped forward in two bounces and landed on the book.

"Please, Marcel, you don't have to hide your writing from me. I'm your publisher. I love it when you write. There's nothing in the world I love more. For every word you write, the closer we both come to retirement."

"And death."

"Don't be so morbid."

"What is there to retire from?"

"How I do envy you, Marcie. No comprehension of the hell. Shit, that's not quite true. I'm sure you conjure your own. You've never liked me, have you? We've made each other rich men but you've never actually liked me, have you?"

"No."

"I wouldn't try to say that doesn't hurt. It does. I wish you would. I mean, I wish you did. But then, it's sort of academic as long as we're useful to each other, isn't it?" But the question was not so sure of itself, though it smiled grand and benevolently.

"Why were you in such a grievously dire need to see me?"

Her eyes on Marcel, Rose delivered the drink.

"More snacks, too, honey." Dropping his head to the drink, Jack tossed it back. It seemed to Marcel a hedonistic display, betraying a too severe excitement. "God, what a life. You drink all day and write. What I wouldn't give. Screw a little on the side, I'd wager. Perfection. Absolute perfection."

"Why were you in such dire need?"

"Look, Marcel. I'm still your publisher. Our lives are intertwined, like it or not." On the television, the time had come for the fabulous showcase showdown spin-off. It gave everyone a second chance to make something good happen, the winners and the losers alike. The girl from A&M whipped the wheel through a powerful spin that sent it round and round and round in a frenetic blur. Marcel liked that; nothing irritated him more than a contestant who spun the big wheel limply. Spinning, only the constant appearance of the red and green portion of the wheel enabled the viewer to identify completed rotations, revolutions, cycles. Gradually the wheel slowed, ticking past the numbers, single and double digits, the dollar symbol far away.

The first spin yielded fifteen cents.

"It's happening, Marcel."

"What's happening, Jack?" Marcel lifted his drink and sipped.

"The Nobel committee. Rumor has it that you're on a very short list. It's between you and two others. *Another Day of Loving* is having significant impact."

Marcel lifted the plastic spear and took one of the olives into his mouth with a greedy bite. Prophet pealed. "Who are the others?" he fired.

"Juliet Busche and Emil Freidberg."

"Busche? Good God! Freidberg makes sense, but Busche is a hack. Her book learning makes French look like a dead language, like the fucking Nazis won."

"Well, my sources tell me she has some strong proponents on the committee. In fact, it's being argued that her vernacular speaks to the average reader."

"The average reader! The average reader doesn't exist. I'm so sick of proselytizing myself for some imagined average reader. It's a damn straw man argument is what it is. God is dead, the author is dead, now the reader is dead. I wonder who they'll kill off next?" Prophet nipped for the second olive on the miniature dagger, missing badly.

"What are you talking about, Marcel?"

"Christ, Jack, I wish you knew, I really do. First the philosopher kills God, then the academic literary critics kill the author, now the publisher kills the reader. Only problem is, we miss the point that the philosopher only killed God to roil the people. They didn't expect to be met by apathy. Now it's a virtual killing spree, a subtle cultural conspiracy gone postal against the creative imagination, terrified to concede that any one individual has the right to conjure and retain their own idea. God is just a manifestation of the collective conscious. The author is nothing but a scribe of the collective will. The reader is nothing but a faceless, mindless placard without self-discriminating taste, there for no other reason but to consume the same formulaic stories again and again that have been mandated and canonized by *the average reader*. The average reader exists no place but in the wallet of the average publisher."

Jack sat back comfortably. Here was a role he knew, a role he could play. The patronizing, somewhat truculent publisher needling the out-of-touch, self-absorbed, too-good-for-his-own-good writer. Another full drink sat before him. This one he sipped. "Still on a crusade, after all these years. We've made each other rich. Let it go."

Prophet crowed. Marcel laughed good-naturedly, holding the olive between his thumb and forefinger as the bird nibbled away.

Jack shook his head. "Filthy thing."

Marcel glared at Jack with cold, appraising eyes. Jack could not help but feel his own words reflected.

"Hey, bartender, why do let him keep this filthy thing here?"

Rose lifted her head from the novel she hid behind the bar, Marcel's novel. It gave her a quiet sense of relief, of hope to read the words with him around, as though his presence, a simple glance in his direction, helped her better understand. She finished the sentence she was reading before looking up to Jack to answer. *Dipping at her feet, Vaja touched the sand between the toes as though to demonstrate that a woman or a man is very much defined by the audience.* Her eyes were stuck on Marcel, the quiet, eccentric man who so adored his bird.

Jack was pointing, a slight belligerence in the frenetic motion of the hand. "Why do you let him keep this filthy thing here?"

Rose did not like Jack and as Marcel was not paying him attention, she found just cause to like him even less. He was attempting to be charming, playful with the paid help. Rose slid the open book back into its concealed nook. The entire nature of his mannerisms communicated to Rose a desperate neediness, a yearning for love and appreciation. She stifled her own first impulse to wry sarcasm and thought to herself, *Another Day of Loving.*

She answered lightly, "A blind bird soars from heights we can't see." It was not the response Jack expected. He stiffened like a scolded child. Marcel's eyes were on the bartender who stood in a suspension, unsure of what to make of her own reply. Stroking the bird's feathers, he nodded in his own imperceptible fashion, deeply affirmed. Ashamed, not quite ashamed but unsure, the bartender lowered her eyes to the task of wiping down the bar for a third time that morning, wishing to cling in her own heart to the words that came from nowhere but her own mouth.

Jack kicked back the scotch. Flustered, aggravated, he rose to leave. "I don't get any of you."

"What don't you get?"

"Christ, you're on the short list. This was supposed to be a funny scene."

"Actually, it's been very amusing."

Jack threw his arms in the air after tossing a fifty on the table. "You're too subtle for your own damn good. You know that, don't you?"

Marcel shrugged indifferently. Truth was, Jack was about as close to a good friend as Marcel had and they both knew it. Talons gripping the notebook binding, Prophet let out a lengthy, shrill pitch, something they could all laugh at.

5

As a boy, Soli grew up in potato country in the southwestern corner of the Russian Federation. Born in 1925, he was raised in the midst of a world languishing in depression. Already filthy poor, far removed from the heart of economy and the treacherous politics of Moscow, daily life remained relatively unaffected by the state. Marx and Lenin were not required reading in the small hamlet of Krylov, west of Moscow and in a direct line between St. Petersburg and Kiev. Social consciousness, even economic determinism, will not accelerate the growth of an analphabetic potato.

Those who lived in the small hamlet attempted to live simple lives. They worked the flat plains together, sharing equally the results of their labor. A single leader from the community, selected by consensus, presided over the hamlet. This leader, a miller by trade, listened to the voices of Krylov before making decisions concluded to be in the best interests of the hamlet as a whole.

When, in 1927, the soldiers began arriving annually to collect tribute for the regime, the people decided to comply rather than fight. The vast majority of their yield they hid well to ensure that their own people never wanted. The soldiers thought the inhabitants of Krylov bad farmers, and the chief of the hamlet strongly reinforced this opinion with his shimmering act of stupidity and fear that more than fed the ego of the army officer before his troops each season. The people of the hamlet adored their leader. He cared for their needs, while caring little for his own. He traded with discreet hunters who also served as scouts. He devised and executed a brilliant method for crop planting and rotation and storage to assure that no matter when the soldiers came, their tax collection could never demoralize the well-being of the clan. But most of all, their leader swallowed his pride, choked on it to protect the hamlet and its people. This man, Michayl Maschovich, was Soli's father.

Michayl and the cruel army leader shared a heinous agreement, the type that is forged through a tacit, burning lock of the eyes. Other hamlets would make up for Krylov's poor farming year after year, but in exchange, the army leader demanded and received from Michayl a loathsome servility. For two days and one night of every year, Michayl exchanged his leadership for an unconditional yoke. He turned perfect fool without a brain, without an opinion, without a single notion of self. He would be beaten, laughed at, spit upon. Worst of all, he would be made to bathe the general upon his knees in conspicuous places both before and after *the night*. For on one night of each year when the army came, the general took — claimed — Michayl's wife. And it was Michayl who prepared the general to enter the bedroom upon twilight and Michayl who, upon his knees, washed the general the following morning. The stakes were high, a single slip in his performance and the whole village would be slaughtered. Such was the perilous, terrible nature of their locked gaze.

Those nights were the hardest, the cruelest. As Michayl cared in solitude for their son, his heart burned with rage. And the boy, too young to comprehend, could only feel the extreme passions of love and hate convoluting the fearless man. Had it not been for Soli on those nights, Michayl would have killed the despicable general, fighting to his own certain death and the death of every man, woman and child in Krylov. He hugged Soli on those nights, so tightly that Soli thought he would break. No boy ever knew such love. He hugged back, hard as he could, with all his might, pressing his lips against the rough skin of his father's cheek. The boy did not then understand what he saw in the village during those two grievous days of the year; however, he could understand his father's love, and perhaps even his father's pain, a pain he willfully shared, best as a wounded father would allow.

The army men were silent on those nights, their mettle quenched, their bellicose rage quelled. They did not celebrate or revel in wine. And though through the afternoons they participated in their mockery of the hamlet, represented by Michayl, at night they relented, slipping into a shameful self-reflection, aware that the man shouldered a burden for the sake of responsibility and love that they themselves as men could never dream to bear. The general believed these displays caused his troops to be inspired by him. In fact, the troops were inspired by Michayl's unconditional love for his people. When the general entered the sleeping chamber with Michayl's wife, the tone outside changed; many could see that the soldiers in their own subtle language were treating Michayl with genuine respect, their own humanity deepened by the sacrifice.

Following the annual performance, the people of his own village were not so kind. Some men always doubted his manhood, spoke of this in subversive whispers, though only once was it challenged, exceedingly unsuccessfully. Michayl was strong as the land, as was his beautiful wife, Naistika, born with the scent of henna in her skin, who lay for the general, dry and unmoved as a brittle salt lick. The general strutted in the morning, but not convincingly. Devilish, cruel words he whispered to the man on his knees who wrung the wet bathing towel. Then, by late morning, harsher with his men than with the village, the general and the soldiers departed, gone for another year.

Michayl never spoke of these days. As soon as the army left, he took Naistika to his chest, consoling her in the wake of the terrible ordeal, understanding the depth of her own steadfast sacrifice. Soli, young, closest to truth, internalized the passions of the father, the invective rage, the humility of willfully bending to an inferior opponent, a bending that required incomprehensible courage. It was the power of Michayl's mind that Soli learned to imitate, the ability to protect and shield the heavy terrorist heart. How could any man carry such depth of conflict so well? For the man who clutched Soli in the night, the barbarian who wanted vengeance, remained hidden from the world, exposing through neither a flicker nor a twitch the raw pride beneath. The true strength of Michayl's mind, his father's mind — from the sunset of all that makes life rich to the rooster's sacred vow at dawn — this is what Soli learned.

6

WATCHING THE ASCENT of a DC-10 lifting from the tarmac, Irene experienced a sharp stab of anxiety bleeding through her chest. As pain throbbed through her shoulder and into the bicep, she wondered if she might be having a heart attack. The line for boarding the flight from Albuquerque to Providence began surging forward. Did she truly want to board this plane?

It seemed that only a moment ago she had been imbibing a mauve sunset in Taos: mountainous peaks swathed in dull haze, the giant ember of the sun dying gently, Endymion's young, masculine beauty in slow dissolution, misty plains embalmed, low frequency ions charged, an inky electricity shimmering, heavenly peace intact. Leaving the ashram, she and Marubrishnubupu had walked a half mile, crossing an empty, stygian arroyo, to a place where no divisions of civilization muddled tolerance of thought. They had held hands; at first Irene thought this odd, but the farther they progressed away from the identities to which others held them, the more nature succeeded in arresting her cynicism. Resting on a boulder by a blooming cactus and a stiff, barbed fern, they had continued their discussion with less formality and a heightened equality. They had agreed that she needed to meet this new young painter.

Irene worked her arm, contracting it at the elbow, facilitating the flow of blood.

"Ticket please."

She boarded mechanically, without having answered the first of her questions. Did she truly want to board this plane?

She listened to crash instructions in English and then in Spanish. When being told to shove one's head between the knees, language, she decided, became irrelevant. Dangling from the manicured hand of the stewardess, the oxygen bag that would appear from the ceiling in the case of an emergency resembled a curious satchel of some synthetic beast's forsaken stomach. She flexed her hand, breathing deeply. Clasping her eyes against the throb, Irene found herself thinking about UFOs and aliens. Would their internal organ system be like ours? Would they bleed? Would they love? Could they suffer a broken heart? Would they be our gods and our heroes, our avatars and redeemers? Or would they be punishers, anti-Christs sent from the sky? How quickly could humankind be shifted from the top to the bottom of an expanding, cosmic food chain?

In the aisle diagonally across from Irene, a young student slowly turned the pages of a thin book. The jacket cover read *Someone Is Watching: A Case for Extraterrestrials*. The cover illustration demonstrated covariance. Calculus waves of varying intensity criss-crossed. Bright differentials of dancing color merged and radiated against a backdrop of empty space. The intense image of deeply patterned waves of color and light emerging from darkness in a swirling helix impacted Irene. At first glance, the optical curls of color seemed at odds. A moment's reflection revealed harmonization, fusion, the perceptual suggestion of at least a third, unifying wave.

A nomadic smile crossed her face. At least she could acknowledge that all of her thoughts were not thoroughly her own. The notion comforted her as she again closed her eyes, turning away from the stewardess and the young reader. There are effects, she mused, for which we never know the cause despite the absolute transparency of reality. What she found comforting in this notion was the correlative insight that insanity carries within it a socially directed mandate of the collective will. She rubbed her arm. The pain had begun to dissipate. As the steward droned on and on, she removed the red vomit bag from the rear pouch of the seat before her. On a whim she brought it close to her nose — cinnamon scented. The steward's vomit bag was ice blue. Peppermint perhaps? She laughed aloud. Designer vomit bags, another subtle mandate of the collective will. In a more civilized world, vomit should smell nice.

Less than twenty-four hours ago she had been watching the sub-limity of a sunset in Taos. Now, following a direct flight, her body would soon be touching down on the far side of two time zones. As an art dealer on a mission to meet her new artist, she appreciated the trip east. She had heard much talk that in the previous decade the northeast trinity (New York, Boston, Providence) had rediscovered itself. The region was experiencing a renaissance, unearthing — perhaps remem-bering — a cultural lodestone of artistic riches. Less steeped in the western mythos of frontier glamour, the northeast trinity honored the best of American heritage, the stalwart pilgrim's progress. A progress inspired not of adventure but of belief.

Irene recognized the art of the region as being less whimsical, more stable. Sometimes the region was stilted by the Puritanical, the Calvinist in particular, a bit too European at times and not as cultural-ly diverse as it would purport to be — weak in Native, Sino and Latino American culture. Still, she could not deny that the region evinced an art that functioned as a wonderful, weighted rudder, a plodding rudder that sought not to control the ship but only to moderate the velocity of grander turns.

Irene found her time in the northeast to be a grounding experience. Entering its world was like stepping upon a Shakespearean stage where all the characters take themselves seriously, even in the most meaning-less of their details. It was a noticeable, often laughable, wholly palpa-ble feature to an outsider, one that supported Irene's conviction that the western community, despite its love of freedom and often through its art, experienced and evinced vacuousness, a lack of dandelion-like, tenacious roots, a staggering sense of native loss that no flight of fancy, no imaginative impulse, however lofty, could fulfill.

In fact, Irene frequently found the opposite, that the will to fly with-out the burdens of what is left behind leads to self-annihilation, a genius so profound that it more than risks entry into an orbit deemed useless by the current age. It was as if, she often used the metaphor, her artists discovered new elements on Saturn that would make teleporta-tion possible here on Earth. The discovery, though amazing, even impressive, means nothing to the spirit of the time if we cannot get to Saturn to mine the minerals. It may be years before a visionary com-prehends that it is not the minerals that are the aim; it is the preparation for the expedition to Saturn, the redefinition of space, the estab-lishment of a new density to the solar system that provides the neces-sary teleportation system breakthrough. As a pure lover of the imagi-nation, Irene valued this type of artistic daring of oneself into the future.

Simultaneously, tempered in the spirit of a more common sense, she acknowledged the law of austerity: time will recognize in time that which must be acknowledged. All else, despite powerful merits, must wait in a state of suspension. Not always easy for an artist, and this is why, she conjectured, there was such a high rate of suicide amongst the artists in her salon. She could hawk the seeds of their greatness and acknowledge that greatness even as she recognized that critical accep-tance would not arrive for years. She sought to patronize these select few, their frangible, anachronistic, misfit souls. To protect them, cat-alyze them — best she could.

She had an address, a phone number and an overnight bag. After settling into a hotel downtown and refreshed by a nap and shower, she took a bite to eat and set out to find the home of Alexi Rodriguez. She spent an hour walking the downtown area, meandering along Waterplace Park, a river rerouted, literally sliced through the heart of the city. She sat on a bench gazing at the Rhode Island state house set in the capital city of Providence. A massive, glorious, monumental structure, it was said to have the second largest unsupported dome in the world, behind only the Vatican in Rome. She wondered if this were true. Atop the unsupported dome there stood a golden sentinel in loin-cloth; the figure reminded Irene of Michelangelo's *David*: calm, sub-dued, visionary. But instead of a sling, this confident young figure held a long spear in one arm and an anchor balanced on the ground in the other. Locals knew this statue as *The Independence Man*. So this is a mariner, she thought, in a place dubbed The Ocean State. A spear for defense and killing. An anchor for stability, roots and balance over the second largest unsupported dome in the world.

Irene was stalling. She had no particularly great interest in the city. This leprosy, she did not understand it. Hadn't doctors eradicated such an antiquated disease? Shouldn't they have?

This was the disease of the times of Christ and the middle ages, a disease that belonged to darkened histories, to chapters relaying notorious, scarcely believable tales of a long, long time ago. Leprosy seemed more like a disease conveniently made for Christ to heal than a living reality to be confronted.

In her own mind she attempted to compare leprosy with modern day AIDS, but it did not quite work. She knew many people from the AIDS community, worked with them on a fairly regular basis. They were unique but seldom terrifying. One of her artists, a close friend, Mary, had died from the disease two years prior. A bisexual artist, Mary had fought the disease for eight years before succumbing. Irene remembered her as a spirited fighter with an unparalleled zest, an eagerness for life. She never complained or moaned her fate, never once asked, "Why me?" The tension inside, the anger, if that was what it was, manifested itself only on the canvas. And even there, the paintings communicated a will to redemption, a will to hope, a deep understanding of love, forgiveness and compassion.

Mary had transcended her own work.

Irene was by Mary's side in her last hours. A routine cold degraded into a deep bronchitis that multiplied into minor ailments throughout the body. For two weeks, the body's defenses collapsed, losing each day the little battles that meant the war. The minor ailments led to the failure of major organs, the inability to take solid food, the loss of bowel control. Over a period of two weeks, Irene witnessed Mary's vibrant spirit fade away, unable to combat the invisible, microbiotic forces. She wanted to die with a brush in her hand. Lacking even the strength to hold it, Irene taped it within her friend's palm so that the horsehairs extended an inch beyond the bony index finger, perpetually straightened.

Mary needed only to move her finger to create a line of color in her mind. It kept her happy unto death; Irene believed this. Smiling in spite of weakness, Mary joyfully admired what Irene had done, turning her hand into a paintbrush, uniting flesh and wood, bringing artist and tool together, binding them so as to be one and inseparable. It was the way Mary wished to die, to enter the next world.

People try to turn it into something mysterious, Irene thought to herself, watching the steady flow of the canal. She let a tear roll down her cheek. Wilted yellow petals and dead brown leaves drifted past.

But there is nothing mysterious about it.

It's a human being facing the inevitability of death much sooner than expected.

It's a human being experiencing the twilight of their life at a time when they should be enjoying the full stride of the noontide sun.

It's a human being losing who they are just as they have learned to celebrate the person they have been.

It's a human being alone when they most need companionship.

It's a need for friendship, a need for love.

It's a disease that should not be.

Yet it is.

There is nothing mysterious about confronting death.

Nothing vague.

Irene hailed a cab and handed the driver the address. She was ready to meet this artist, this human being. Ready to love him for who he was, what he lived, what he did with the time he had. Ready to support him and promote him and sell him and be a friend as best she could. Ready for everything but to watch him die; though she was willing, if needed, to do this also. A spasm of stabbing pain again shot through her chest.

The cab rolled down the cobblestone street slowly, the shocks ill prepared to absorb the rough, uneven road. They came to stop before a three-story Victorian in a quaint, tightly packed residential community, the kind of place where students and professors and blue collar working folk co-exist in a fully integrated spectrum, representative of all that we are, magnified by who we could together be. Irene proceeded up the walkway, swinging open the rusty gate and entering the tiny courtyard where heavy wooden chairs were set in groomed alcoves amidst barren rose bushes, blooms dispensed for the impending season. Shades were drawn, but a light was on in one of the rooms, overlooking the rose garden, to the right of the porch. She took a breath and rang the buzzer.

After a patient wait, she pressed the button again. Listening more intently, she heard an interior chiming, a melodic pattern of tinny notes announcing a visitor's arrival. No answer. Dorothia said Rooster never left their home. Either he was not answering or Dorothia had not told the truth. First and foremost, Irene needed to know the answer to this question, and she had to find out now, today. This was her primary motive, the reason why she had not called in advance to communicate the plans for her visit. Irene sought to evaluate two things. One, she needed to verify the accuracy of Dorothia's perspective by bringing the second hand account into the first person. Second, and highly relevant to her first objective, she needed to meet the artist in a true, unaffected setting. The last thing Irene desired was a pre-arranged meeting with all sorts of unnatural preparation, preparations so often designed to create an illusion of the way it would be imagined that Irene would want it to be.

She rang the bell a third time before strolling along the deck and through the chilly air. As she stood upon the unvarnished planks of splintering pine, a movement behind the shade caught her attention. Peering from behind a peeled back crack, she saw the sterling eye of a man studying her, collecting features like a scientific probe that lives to consume and assimilate information. The face was young and harsh, concealed by the cowl of a gray hooded sweatshirt, pulled deliberately tight. The boring, cyclops-eye startled her. Catching her breath, she leapt backwards. The eye, steady and bold, kept her off balance, surveying her intrepidly, collecting information, gathering material.

"Rooster! Are you Rooster?" But she knew the answer as she jumped forward, pressing against the railing, all her trepidation gone as adrenaline took over. Already from that single eye she understood; this was not a boy freakish prodigy. Thank God! This was a fully trained, self-disciplined and stylized artist. The paintings were not drawn of the hand of slumbering innocence but of aware cognizance. Thank God! Stripped of the worst anxiety, her heart pounded freely. She forgot herself as she stretched out and rapped on the window with her fist, calling repetitively, desperately, "Rooster. Rooster. I need to talk with you! I'm Irene Smythe. I spoke with your mother. Rooster?"

Scuttling, she returned to the door and rung the buzzer — the chimes — in rapid succession. Already she had discovered an exciting possibility. So he never does leave the house. Confirmation of the artist's seclusion excited her. She needed to get closer to discern with reason that which her penetrating eyes had innately intimated. Was he the boy puppet of Dorothia, or was she his? Irene had not expected to see what she had seen in the eye, a density of form and matter, unafraid and consuming. She felt violated, sensuously pick-pocketed of a portion of her soul, as though it now belonged to him to do with as he desired. It stimulated her, thrilled her in an undeniably sexual way. This was her role in art, what she found so esoteric and erotic, to be the objectified subject. How wonderful, she thought with elation, that she had sought to sneak up on him and he had snuck up on her, contained her so completely, so gracefully, so fearlessly.

Enraptured, her optimism soared. This was the artist for whom she had been searching. She felt sure of it. She released her inhibition at the prospect that the art would be but a shadow of the larger artist. Like a chicken with its head lopped off, Irene scuttered back and forth attempting to spy through the window, ringing the bell, struggling with the locked knob, rapping at whatever would project her presence.

"Rooster," she cried. "Rooster, I need to talk to you."

The light went out in the room. Silence. Silence. Silence as Irene receded from her frenzy. A couple stopped on the sidewalk and watched her. Becoming aware of her own hysterics, she composed herself. The couple passed. She ran her hands over her face, felt the ridiculous pounding of the aortic muscles, the tight, wrenching pain in her right shoulder returning. She had been ambushed. Now he would know her. She would never again get a look so true.

One last time she rung the doorbell, listened to the chimes. Rooster, she muttered to herself in expiation, defeated.

In a state of shock she walked past the gate, leaving it unlatched, swinging. She drifted away from the home, striding down the center of the cobblestone street, lost in déjà vu. From the dark and lonely house an eye watched her. The eye studied the curved line of her back and the cracked phantom of heat she left trailing behind, a phantom that only an artist would see and only a visionary would understand.

cf

Marcel took a break from his reading of William Blake. He sought not for clues as much as he did for intimations of the immortal voice that guided the modern prophet, which Marcel thoroughly believed Blake to be. Blake's *Proverbs of Hell* disturbed Marcel, causing him significant melancholy. The particular line of distress: *"The eagle never lost so much time as when he submitted to learn from the crow."* Blake did not intend the proverbs ironically, nor were the proverbs designed to be strictly taken as the voice of a negative brimstone. The *Proverbs of Hell* functioned as one additional manifestation in a long series of works by Blake that expressed the belief that the false dualism of heaven and hell is the cause of sadness in the world and that true peace will and can only be attained when an individual accepts that the lessons taught by hell and heaven are component and complementary portions of a full body of wisdom, one reflecting off the surface of the other like a rippled moon upon a placid lake.

Clamping the cover shut, Marcel shoved the book aside in disgust. For all Blake's talk of heaven and hell, the meaning should have been clearer.

☞

The lights of Fenway warmed the night sky. Wisps of low white clouds stretched across the scarlet horizon in slight, insubstantial strips. Marcel checked the paper, a 7:35 start. If he left now he could make it for the opening pitch. He called the bar directly and ordered two Sapphire martinis. The drinks were waiting when he arrived.

Marcel pulled an empty flask and asked the bartender to fill it. Knowing who he was, the bartender protested without resolve. "We're not supposed to do this, you know."

On Yawkey Way Marcel haggled with scalpers. He wanted the third base side so he could heckle the Yankees. He found a pair of seats in the third row, right behind the dugout.

"Closer the better, Buddy."

"You'll be able to spit on those bastards, right on their heads."

Marcel liked that.

Taking both of the tickets, Marcel thought about giving the extra to one of the boys who always hang out by the gate, hustling their way into a game. He decided not to. He didn't need the hassle of feeling like a molester for making some kid's day. That's the society we live in. Can't be too nice, better to be a bastard; that, people understand. At a vendor he bought a hot salted pretzel and an Evian to push back the flask of gin.

He found his row just as a couple of underhanded Yankees were tossing warm-up balls into the crowd. Smart move, he thought, but it won't work.

Having two seats he got to choose whom he sat by. There was a man in his fifties with his family or a woman, early thirties, cute as hell, out to the game with her boyfriend. Marcel preferred to sit next to the family guy, maybe be able to comment on the game here and there. Then again, he was drinking and didn't much think the father would appreciate his kind of influence.

Marcel slid past the young couple as the players were being introduced. It was the none-too-subtle perfume that got him, diving into the hypothalamus or the cerebral cortex-something-or-other in the front lobe of the brain. He couldn't remember; all he knew was that deep emotional memories were activated most forcefully by the sense of smell. Settling in next to the woman, she smiled and said hello. Marcel could feel himself staring. The boyfriend was the jockish sort who could never apprehend the threat of a charming, aged intellect to the potent sexual vigor of youth. More and more, Marcel was beginning to feel why he had come, to get near the game, to close in.

The home team drew big applause, even if it was tentative and nervous, full of *here we go again* memories. This was the final night in a four-game homestand versus the Yankees. With just three games remaining in the regular season, the Sox were clinging to a half-game lead in the A.L. East. The Orioles were just off pace and the Yanks were two back. Just three days earlier and the Sox were holding all the cards. A three-game lead with six to play. The Yanks were five back. Three straight home beatings and it was a new season. Ruth loved the Yankees. They used to go to the ballgames together. It was their favorite pastime, one of the few places where he wasn't a writer and she wasn't a writer's wife. He smiled at the young woman to his right; he felt reconciled. Suddenly it seemed right to him that he had two seats and that he was sitting next to a woman. That damn scent.

He leaned over, his cheek touching strands of her long, curly hair, stiff with spray. "You a Yankees or a Red Sox fan?" Marcel inhaled, settled back.

"Red Sox," the girl replied.

"Oh," he sounded disappointed.

"I guess you're a Yankees fan, booo," she mocked playfully.

"No, Red Sox through and through. Diehard."

The boyfriend glanced over, square chin, solid, seemed like a nice enough guy. "These damn Yankees win tonight, and it's bye-bye Red Sox." Marcel nodded, though statistically he knew it wasn't true.

Marcel took it all in. The fresh cut Kentucky Blue grass, the raked dirt of the infield, the uniformed players limbering their arms on the sidelines and in the shallow outfield, the parabola of a simulated fly ball, the speckled sea of fans, faces left and right focused in the same direction, a dusty quarter moon, Venus, the North star, twilight, pink-gray clouds, the city skyline, the red Citgo triangle, the American flag, the bleachers, the hand-changed Fenway scoreboard, the warning track, white chalked lines from the foul poles to home plate, the netting to catch foul balls, the posted signs of "NO PEPPER."

They rose for the National Anthem.

"What so proudly we hailed . . . And the rockets red glare, the bombs bursting in air, gave proof through the night that our flag was still there. O say does that star spangled banner . . . Marcel was thinking of Blake; couldn't get him out of his head . . . *Sullen fires across the Atlantic glow America's shore, Piercing the souls of warlike men who rise in silent night. Washington, Franklin, Paine & Warren, Gates, Hancock & Green. Meet on the coast glowing with blood from Albion's fiery Prince. For the laaaaaaaa nnnnddd of the frrrreeeeee . . . Descend to generations that in future times forget. And the hooooommmmeeee ooofffff the bbbbraaaaavvveeeee!"*

-"Play Ball!"

The pretzel went down easy with the gin. The father with the family cast Marcel a dirty look. By the third inning the jock and the girl were getting loud, swigging from the flask with Marcel. Laughing at his jokes, the girl repeatedly tossed her hair over her shoulder, moving the air and the sweet scent of her perfume in Marcel's direction. Marcel had to shift his weight and rub his burning eyes.

Scoreless through four innings, in the fifth, Johnnie Jons, the Yankee starter, was showing signs of slipping, his pinpoint control faltering. The Sox were threatening, first and third with no outs and the top of the order coming to the plate. Ned Stimpel, the speedy center-fielder, rapped the first pitch down the third base line past the out-stretched glove of the Yankees' third baseman. The umpire waved wildly with his arms, shooing the ball out, bellowing, 'FOUL! FOUL!" The crowd jumped on him as Johnnie Jons said a silent prayer of thanks for a call that could have gone either way.

"You suck, ump," the boyfriend cried.

"Yeah, ya' stink," the girlfriend added.

Marcel was in the spirit. "Get some glasses, will ya!"

Even the father with the family was protesting, though less bluntly. Marcel swigged away and passed the flask down the line. They all drank and laughed and were in general agreement without ever having to make eye contact.

Ned Stimpel popped it up behind home, relinquishing the easy out. He bashed his bat in anger, sending it bouncing toward the leaping bat-boy.

Freddie Lanscaster dug into the plate next. He was the third base-man, a burly Polack with a .318 batting average and forearms that belonged to a construction worker. "Come on, Freddie," the crowd yelled. "Bring him in, Fred."

Johnnie Jons blew him off the plate with a rising slider to the chin. The Fenway faithful booed in disgust as the ump checked the ball, rub-bing it between his palms. "Don't take that crap, Freddie!" "Hit it right back at his face!" They were hungry for blood now, or runs. It was all pretty much the same to this crowd, ravingly hungry after six years without so much as a divisional pennant.

On the second pitch, the Red Sox called for the hit and run. Freddie swung hard and missed as Mike Bardick, the veteran catcher, the last person you'd expect to steal, got a great lead and a good jump at first. With a man on third, the Yanks didn't even challenge the advancing baserunner. Second and third. One out. "Come on, Fred." "Come on, Freddie!" "Show 'em how it's done." "Bring 'em home!"

Freddie ripped the third pitch up the middle, a blazing line drive on its way to center field. The crowd, in one fluid motion jumped to its feet, just in time to watch the Yanks' golden glover, Manny Herman, slide into the grass on one knee, snatching the sinking ball out of the air. The runners were fooled by the velocity of the ball off the bat, espe-cially the runner from third who was halfway down the baseline as the Yanks' gold glover lifted the snowcone and whipped the ball to third for a force-out to end the inning.

The Fenway faithful lavished the shabby baserunning with a chorus of angry boos.

"After four, and still no score." These were the words of the announcer that Marubrishnubupu heard as he switched on ESPN to watch the game of the week. The Colorado Rockies, his favorite team amidst this fascinating American game, were not playing tonight.

He had had an extremely busy day, his activities ranging from teaching and writing and inspiring to fundraising. Lately the expenses of his group were increasing at a rate far greater than collected contributions. As spiritual leader, it remained his responsibility to ensure that sufficient "food" filled the cupboards to allow the continuance of all the good works his organization had begun. He felt extremely proud of their mission and the manner in which he saw it enriching people and communities. Still, how had their growth outpaced contributions? As the numbers of followers grew, he reflected that at times he resembled a banker more than a guru, a setter of budgets and rates of interest rather than a supportive guide on the road to enlightenment. He wondered if something had been lost. Does an increase in quantity necessarily lead to a diminishment in quality of instruction? He wanted nothing more than to work directly with all of his people, his entire flock; but despite his best efforts, such a reality no longer remained a viable possibility. Not having enjoyed an escape for quite some time, tonight he decided to sneak off and enjoy a game for an hour or two, just enough to be reinvigorated. Patriotic Americans were very fortunate to have such an extraordinary game as a cornerstone of their nation.

By traditional standards, he should have been reading and writing, developing the philosophical body of his thought and teachings, and yet something inside persuaded him that watching the game possessed a relevancy to his teachings that no book would bring. If he could not understand the game of baseball, he would never reach the American audience. Perhaps he was fooling himself. He convinced himself not to concern himself with such thoughts; the Red Sox were again taking the field.

There were nine men to defend against one man armed with a stick of wood. The one man with the stick of wood must defend home plate against a single man attempting to hurl a ball past that home plate. All of the action takes place around home plate. Marubrishnubupu thought, these Americans make a religion of protecting this home plate. The greatest hit in the game is a *home* run when all of the defenders, nine of them, are transcended, incapable of doing anything as the one man leaves home plate and returns to it victorious and unmolested. A home run. A run home without intrusion — a moment of pure celebration. The run is not yet earned, but no one is capable of stopping it. The hitter of the home run controls time. No other sport has such a thing! They make a religion of the home, these Americans, they protect it and revere it in a way that those of us in other countries do not quite comprehend. He mused on these things, unsure if they were wholly true. He sought a breakthrough in awareness. As greatly as he desired to share the Buddhist and Hindu soul with Americans, in the secret depths of his heart, he desired that an American would share the wonders of this game with him.

In most sports there are two goals, one for each team. Both teams have their own goal and defend it accordingly. Both teams attempt, once their defense is strong, to attack the goal of the other and take it as their own. Not so in baseball. Both teams are protecting and striving to claim the same home plate. There are not two goals, both equal. There is only one goal, home plate, and each team aims to prove, one to the other, that they best deserve to own it, that their claim to it is stronger, more noble, more righteous. And yet both are defending the same home, protecting the same home, caring for the same home, loving the same home. Home plate. Marubrishnubupu drew its shape on a piece of paper. Didn't it resemble a simple house that a child would draw? Marubrishnubupu drew a door and two windows. He drew a line to complete the triangle and the square. He drew a chimney with smoke swirling from the roof. He drew a stick mother and a stick father holding hands. He drew two stick children and a stick dog. He drew a circle with short lines around it for the sun. Beneath home plate he drew a line for land. Below the sun he drew a tree that resembled a large piece of broccoli. In the tree he drew small circles, apples. Gazing at the simple, pleasant picture he had drawn, he outlined home plate once again with his pen.

The Yankees went down in order in the top of the fifth. Johnnie Jons reclaimed the pitcher's mound. Marubrishnubupu thought about that. What does this pitcher's mound represent? All sensible manifestations are manifestations of a truth. The pitcher's mound. A rising, rounded hill of dirt, perfectly centered in a diamond of tufted green grass. Marubrishnubupu watched closely. The pitcher always had to touch the white slab at the center of the mound as he released the ball. It served as a marker of some sort, an invisible lifeline. To what? I am thinking too much, Marubrishnubupu chided himself. It was only a game.

There was one out in the fifth when Boston's clean-up hitter, Max Slaine, drove a fast ball high and away into the center field bleachers, breaking the 0-0 tie. Marcel and Company jumped to their feet and literally danced in the aisles. *Ruth.* It marked Max's 59th home run of the season as he trotted about the bases triumphantly. High fives flew as the crowd cheered in delight. "Max, Max, Max, Max."

Right now Marcel would have been rubbing salt into his wife's wound, needling her about the obvious inferiority of the Yankees. She would have taken it in good humored fun, shaking her finger as though to say *Just wait* or, quoting Yogi, *It ain't over 'til it's over.*

God, he loved her. He would trade in all his books and the impending Nobel to have her back. There was little doubt that her death had made him a better writer. In words he relentlessly pursued her, traveling into hell to find her for just one more day — hell, one more moment — of loving. He would give it all up, the writing and what it brought, to have her back in his life. He knew it was inhuman to live for the dead; still, it was all that he could do, all that he knew how to do, to stand on a white page and hurl his best words, one after the other, in vain, desperate pursuit of what has been lost.

Grinning teammates greeted Max, slapping his rear end and his helmeted head as he planted himself upon home plate with two feet.

Johnnie Jons survived the inning and the sixth and seventh too. Marubrishnubupu loved the classic pitcher's duel, a low scoring affair where every ball, every strike, every swing had the potential to change the game's outcome. Every single was the tying run, leaving the man at the plate as the go ahead, and that's exactly what the Yankees had with one out in the eight: a man on first and their number five batter, Jared Small, stepping to the plate. A perfect misnomer, Jared Small was three for three on the day, one of the few Yankee hitters with any success off the lefty, Mike Killigraw. Checking the batter's box, Jared positioned himself by leveling his compact, powerful swats over the plate.

"They gotta get Killigraw out of there. His pitch count is way the hell up there. He's not a long distance starter." This assessment came from the girl to Marcel's left. He loved her more and more.

"Your girlfriend keeps talkin' so sexy and I'm gonna steal her away from you," Marcel warned, half-serious, the liquor having a sweetly intoxicating effect.

"Better watch it, Jennie, I think pops has got it in for you." They laughed. The girl, Jennie, sighed a longing. Marcel sipped from his beer. They had shifted to Budweiser when the flask went dry. Now they had to settle for what remained in their cups, as the sale of alcohol ceased following the seventh inning stretch.

Jared Small sent the first pitch bouncing between short and third for his fourth hit of the evening.

"How many outs?" Marcel asked.

"Two."

"No, one," she corrected her boyfriend.

"Two."

"Look at the board, dipshit," Jennie retorted. Marcel chuckled.

The pitching coach marched to the mound, a rotund beer-drinking guy, gray and old. Marcel wondered if this were how he looked to these two kids. In their thirties, hell, they were still kids, with no idea of how lucky they were to have each other.

Marubrishnubupu watched in suspense as the manager chatted on the mound with Killigraw. The announcers flapped away, informing the viewing audience of the bullpen's activity. Bardick got his two cents in and the thing was settled. The manager took the ball from Killigraw, and the weary warrior trudged off the mound. The manager signaled for the bullpen. The crowd rose to applaud the gutsy performance of their pitcher. Seven hits, one walk, no runs surrendered over 7-1/3 innings. It was a great performance in the midst of a tight pennant race, but it might not be enough.

The ESPN camera canvassed the crowd, from one side of the ballpark to the other, 46,468 people pounded their feet, a swelling mass of appreciation. It was an awe inspiring sight. Marubrishnubupu doubted that most understood what an extraordinary display of fellowship it was, and how rare. 46,468 people applauding a man who might not even win, a man who had simply done his job.

The Sox brought in their best closer, "Sparky" Martins, a wily eight-year veteran. The announcers filled the void with shards of information. "This has been a sensational season for Sparky. A 6-1 record, 34 saves in 36 opportunities. His second trip to the All-Star Team and his wife, Joyce, is home tonight expecting their second child any time. If he can close out this one for the Sox, it could be his most important outing of the season."

"That's right," the color man added. "If he can find a way to squeak this one through, it'll keep the Red Sox a game ahead of the Orioles, who won today at Texas. With just two to go that will keep the Sox in the driver's seat."

"And it'll push the Bronx Bombers three back, out of contention for anything but a long shot wild card."

"That's right, for the Yankees, they pretty much need to come up with at least one run if they want to keep their playoff hopes alive. So once again, it's first and second with one out in a nailbiter at Fenway. Red Sox lead 1-0. We'll be back right after this station break."

Captivated by the screen, Marubrishnubupu's hazy eyes religiously followed the unfolding of the game. He truly did not care who won in this particular contest. What fascinated him was the nature of the drama, how every pitch made a difference, how the actors were always different.

Sparky Martins zipped his first pitch down the center of the plate, bullishly challenging the hitter, Julio Gomez, who whiffed, swinging late on the blazing heater. The Bosox were past the meat of the Yankees order, but that meant little to Sparky. One hit and the game was tied.

For the second pitch he gave Julio some off-speed stuff. The lefty hitter got ahead of himself thinking long ball and pulled the change-up hard, foul of the first base line. This was the Sparky Martins who had carried the Red Sox all season with clutch pitching. Ahead on the count 0-2, he could work the plate, baiting Julio, holding back his best stuff, testing his self-discipline against Julio's.

The next pitch flirted with the outside corner and Julio swung, lurched, protecting the plate. He just nipped the ball, fouling it off. "That'a way, Sparky. Strike the bum out!"

The next two pitches were balls, the second a nasty, looping curve that nearly broke over the corner at the last second from a foot and a half out. The crowd broke into delirium as Bardick shot a glance to the third base umpire working to coax an overrule. The umpire waved it off. Two balls, two strikes.

Twisting his ankles aggressively, Julio dug into the packed trenches with his cleats. He came from the farm leagues of Havana where he had learned how to fight back into a count. The third pitch replicated the first, a testing heater down the middle. This time Julio jumped on it, timing it perfectly, snapping his wrists into the red stitches. The crack off the bat drove the hearts of Red Sox fans into their throats. Marubrishnubupu jumped to his toes. He watched the ball rise as Ned Stimpel dashed back, back, back. With a stab Stimpel took the ball over his shoulder for the out, but the runners were tagging, pressing for position. Stimpel's zippy throw into the cut-off man could not prevent the advancement of the runners. Sparky Martins tossed the resin bag to the back of the mound in disgust and relief. Marubrishnubupu, nervous with excitement, wiped his palms with a towel. "What a catch," he said under his breath. The announcer echoed the same words a moment later, and Marubrishnubupu felt a surge of pride in his growing ability to rightly appreciate the right things.

"Two outs. Men on second and third," Marubrishnubupu thought.

"Two outs, with men on second and third," the announcer sputtered as the Yankees' number seven hitter dug in. Calling time, the umpire stepped forward with a brush to dust the dirt off home plate.

Sparky opened the sequence with a slow breaking curve that missed the inside corner. Philip Rand, the switch hitting right fielder, watched the pitch into the mitt. These damn Yanks were being patient at the plate. For the second pitch, Sparky delivered a fork-fingered fastball. The pitch came in with dancing laces. Sparky worked the inside of the plate. Scouting reports on Rand said he couldn't protect the inside with any consistency. The split finger held the inner third. Rising into Bardick's mitt, Rand's healthy cut whiffed beneath the ball. Bardick grinned knowingly. The scouting reports were right on. Triple tapping his right inner thigh, Bardick called for Sparky to open up the plate. He wanted to bait Rand with a ball, maybe get him to chase a breaking curve. Keep him guessing, then they'd come back inside, exploiting the weakness after they'd opened up the whole plate. Bardick didn't want to make Rand's job any easier by sending the message that he only had half a plate to protect. Sparky nodded, reading Bardick's mind. They were going for the slow K, working to soften him up, grind him down. They had balls to give. Sparky delivered the curve well outside. Rand checked it but refrained. He definitely preferred the outside action, yearned for it. That's the last of the outside junk he'll see, Bardick thought, double tapping the left thigh and signaling for the change-up.

Jared Small took a small lead off second base. His eyes scrutinized the catcher in search of a clue to what Rand should be looking for.

Marubrishnubupu thought it through. *Two balls, one strike, two outs. They could give up the base on balls and gain a strategic advantage, having a force-out at any base with the number eight hitter. They don't lose much by giving up a walk.*

The pinpoint control on the change-up demonstrated why Sparky had earned a trip to the All-Stars. It was high and on the inner corner. Rand swung hard but found himself jammed tight. Even if he could have made contact, he would have had no power to squeeze through the bat.

"SSStttttttrrrrrriitwo!" the umpire hollered in the strange, constricted language of the sport.

The crowd bristled with delight.

Bardick called for the fastball.

Sparky shook him off.

Bardick threw for the curve.

Sparky shook him off again.

Bardick signaled for the change-up.

Sparky nodded. He wanted to strike him out with the same pitch. Small rubbed his thigh and the first base coach ran two fingers along his belly. Philip Rand stepped off the plate on delivery. Opening his stance, he pounded the ball with a massive, decisive cut. The echo of solid contact filled the stadium. Before the crowd could comprehend what had happened, the ball was soaring towards and then over the 37-foot-tall, green monster.

"*Yankees take the lead!*" the announcer screamed, as 46,467 moaning Red Sox fans slumped into their seats. "*Yankees take the lead!*"

"Home run!" Marubrishnubupu cheered before the ten-inch screen, waving the small drawing of a happy family in his hand. "Home run!"

"Damn Bambino!" Marcel shouted, alone, turning away from the empty seat, shaking a defiant fist into the sky. As the Yankee runners crossed home plate, Bardick, who had wanted to go with the fast ball, stared at Sparky Martins in disbelief, so much to say, *Wrong pitch.*

7

FRAME IS CONTENT. Tamara completed the puzzle of the Bavarian landscape. Not a single piece lacked from the final product. She found this fact not only uninspiring but wholly disappointing. The scene itself, a photographic imprint of yellow daffodils, white snow, green grass and cuts of gray stone, failed to captivate her imagination.

What she sought from life was not a pleasant landscape. She desired the personal poet who could soothe her mind with floating dreams, who could feed the imagination through more subtle means. People, Tamara believed, were the critical factors in the shaping of the universe. Individual people, these are the units that make the difference to the planet. Ideas do not emerge from nature, from genetics. They come from people who dare to see their world and the world of others in a different way. It seemed such a simple concept, just a farthing of common sense for a coffer. People were the currency, not a place or a thing, but a person with the congenital ability to alter the world through the sacred dance of imagination and will.

Plucking the upper right hand corner piece from the puzzle, she pulled on her coat and headed into the street. She knew her destination. Probability had it that Dorothia would be out, wherever she went to, for the night and into the morning. Tamara had nailed down Dorothia's schedule fairly well. Most nights, after preparing dinner for her son, Dorothia entered her Cabriolet with a travel bag and disappeared for the night. On those few nights when she did not follow this routine she tended to stay at home, doing very little as far as Tamara could tell besides watching television and occasionally checking on her son.

During the daytime, Tamara found Dorothia's schedule unpredictable and had decided to avoid 11:00 a.m. to 6:00 p.m. completely. Sometimes Dorothia would stay at home, though rarely. Other times she would amble about town, spending hours at the malls, purchasing pieces of clothing with selective aim, as though on a hunt for something specific, for which no substitution would be allowed.

Tamara had decided to see Rooster again. If the car were gone, then Dorothia would be absent until at least eight in the morning and tonight would be the night. If the car were there, then Tamara would be delayed another night. Two nights, three nights, whatever it would take. Patience alone was required; gravity's demands, density being true, the absolute determination of a course of action could not, over time, be denied. All factors entered into the equation, Tamara did not excessively worry about Dorothia. The mother was substantial but not insurmountable. Her influence, like the tension that builds torque, would be reduced or broken. As long as Dorothia desired to exhibit the obstinacy of their first meeting, it would remain a mathematical ultimatum — redefine your role or be factored out.

The gibbous moon walked easily through the sky. Leafless sycamores stood guard above the sidewalk, silent sentries with rhythmic swaying boughs. Tamara wore a heavy wool coat purchased from the Salvation Army store for five dollars. She wrapped the tan collar snugly about her neck. October had arrived, bringing temperatures only slightly unseasonable. Cloudy mushrooms of steam spun forward from her mouth even as she pressed her lips into the warm wool. There were holes in her mittens; still, they were better than nothing. By the time she arrived at the home of Alexi Rodriguez, she was praying that Dorothia would be gone. Her toes were numb. The prospect of having to turn around, retraveling the path she had just come, would have been disheartening.

At the address she scaled the palisades without thought or effort. Ignoring the door, pushing past the rose bushes, she went directly for the window. The space between the rose bushes and the house was slim. Thorns snagged the bulky fabric of her coat, hindering her progress. Pressing on her tiptoes to reach the glass, she pounded on the screen window harder than necessary, rattling the frame. The shade shot upward as though he knew who it would be, as though he expected her at such a time and in such a fashion. The illumination that glowed from the window poured soft and warm upon Tamara's uplifted face. Rooster stood at the glass with both hands raised to the panes. For just a moment they stared, one into the other's eyes. It was Tamara who broke the peaceful gaze, flapping her frozen arms, signaling him to raise the window. Grand smiles covered both their faces.

Rooster leaned out. "I didn't know if you'd . . ."

"Yes, you did," she rejoined before he could complete the sentiment.

Bending now, relaxed, Rooster stared into the night. "It's beautiful."

"It's freezing," she shivered.

Rooster breathed in the air and pressed it out from his lungs, admiring the long white mist that danced like chaos before him. "I suppose it is," he teased with indifference.

"You're insufferable," she protested.

"Wait." Shutting the window he dashed about within the room. Tamara jumped upon her toes, trying to spy the action inside. The light went off. She pressed against the rose bushes for leverage, attempting to improve her sight line. Nothing.

The front door opened and Rooster emerged, spinning in a joyous circle.

"What are you doing?" Tamara asked.

"Going for a walk."

Her mouth dropped. "But I'm freezing."

"Don't worry."

And she didn't. After all, wasn't this what she had wanted: an imagination that could alter the landscape? Still, she felt the need to communicate a few basic facts. "It's fifteen degrees. Do you know that?"

"No."

"Where are we going?"

"Anywhere but here."

"I'm going to transform into an icicle if I stay out any longer. You know that, don't you?"

"You'll be fine."

What more could she truly say? Did she have a right to complain about being cold? Though his condition was not hers, one did reflect

upon the other, revealing it in a truer light, pressing her to acknowledge an order of magnitude deserving regard. It takes a big noise or a
powerful jolt to wake a giant. Yes, she admitted, everything that happens takes place according to an order of magnitude.

Was it so cold, or was the extremity of cold an apparition, a physical force that entered the domain of being to promote the issue of her
need for entry into the home? But now he had exited the home, sharing the chilling night with her, a turn she had not expected. It communicated that the need which called him outward was greater than
the need which called her inward. In this fact she did, without doubt,
feel a warming effect throbbing throughout her body, as though her
cold had been dispersed by the intimate knowledge of a deeper, incomprehensible cold. It was the force of friction, esoteric at its core, at play,
creating heat.

In truth, perhaps Rooster had his own plan. Out of doors on a cold
night, he could keep his skin well covered without drawing attraction
to the need for coverage. He could wear thick mittens over his shingled
fingers, wear a hunter's cap with plaid earflaps to conceal the thick
scars on and about the left ear; he could release from his mind even the
slightest fear that an open wound, though treated and wrapped, might
still emit a stagnant odor, medicinal or other. His face remained
unmarred by the disease, though his eyes over the past weeks had been
experiencing a strain that caused concern. Any moist part of the body
necessitated extra care and attention. So far there were no signs of
mucus or soreness in the eye or eyelids, only the constant strain. The
battery of medicines were helping to stave off and contain the disease;
however, no treatment had succeeded in controlling it, rendering it
dormant. Instead, Rooster had spent the last two years of his life like
the tightrope walker in Nietzsche's *Thus Spake Zarathustra*, Death constantly at his shoulder, threatening to leapfrog over him, to overtake, to
surpass, never at too far a distance, never affording an opportunity to
let up, to rest, to relax from the work that has been done. Ever, ever he
remained in a state of double tension, fully aware that he was a deviation away from an unchecked leprosy that would do more than cause
pain, burning itches, numbness, scarring. Always on a trembling wire,
high above the ground without a net, the audience below waiting for
him to fall, to die, to satiate their need for the great drama; for as engag-

ing a spectacle as the dance with death may be, if it does not end with death victorious, the audience feels cheated, as though the spectacle is somehow inauthentic. Death, motley fool he is, loveless, must consummate.

For two years he had walked the wire with the urging and aid of his mother, of Soli, of a splendid team of doctors, but not once had he succeeded in coming off the wire, of finding a respite from an emergent "problem area to watch closely." A moment's inattention and all could be lost. The enemy was a silent killer, microbiotic and untiring, waiting, waiting for the vigil's end, when the giant would sleep and the meager feast, unimpeded, could begin.

Rooster clad himself in denim jeans and a navy style winter coat with large black buttons that had belonged to his father. Tamara watched him walk two steps before her, leading the way. To see him on this night, he could have been any self-assured young man, so thoroughly and convincingly did he convey his regularity. She sighed in delightful appreciation, for this made him all the more than she already believed him to be.

He whistled a slow fugue from Bach. The notes lifted the night. She suspected that he did not know that this itself, the whistling of Bach, could be construed as an oddity. So removed from the everyday had he become that he held no sense of the mainstream. Had he the desire to fit in, he would not have known the direction to take. She would not tell him. She wanted him just as he was, for the simple brilliance of the shorn seams. Could he believe this? This was what she wondered.

"Where are we going?" She found him handsome for his confidence, for the portrayal of confidence.

He grinned, though as he gazed at her, hands deep within his pockets, the fear of what they were doing trickled from him to her. Stepping into the street, he entered more fully the wan moonlight. Staring upwards, searching into the countless stars for reprieve, he confessed, "I don't know. I've never been out of that house."

The incredulous brow of thinking that shaped Tamara's features made her skepticism obvious.

Rooster paused. "I've been out. It's not quite that. It's just that I haven't been out like this, at night, for enjoyment, *for no reason.* Since the diagnosis I don't do more than paint. We go to the doctors some-

times, but that's about it. I prefer not to leave. It makes it easier."
Dropping his shoulders, fully feeling the heaviness of the cold night for
the first time, the heaviness that first follows every act of lightness, he
added, "Maybe this wasn't such a good idea."

Tamara stepped from the sidewalk into the street. Progress was a
road of little traffic, so they were safe. She wondered why he had
stepped upon the road. What do the small, unconscious incidents
reveal? Gently reassuring, she encouraged him, "It's a very good idea."

"I wouldn't even know where to go from here. Where to start."

"We've already started."

And he noticed that they had. Tamara had taken him by the arm;
they were moving forward in a direction with no sense of what lay
ahead, confident only that together, it was not what lay behind.

"But where are we going?" Rooster asked.

She tightened her grasp round his arm. "That's my question," she
chided. "Now stop being silly."

Down the center of the street, in perfect silence they walked past the
cars parked for the night on both sides of the cobblestone aisle. Cool air
entered them and came out warm. They were safe from all discomfort
and all disease. To Rooster, the bulky coats between them felt like a form
of impervious armor. The spacious sky, full and open, promised him
that no danger could linger upon his lips; on this night all threats were
dilute. He again whistled the fugue, this time releasing symphonic ener-
gies not of fear but of joy. The rich night pulsated with fulgurous messages designed for the discerning eye: satellites, radio transmission tow-
ers, distant jets. In the night there exists a calming stillness, defenseless
and open, more gracious than the enfeebled judgments of the burning
day where nothing is allowed to hide and thus, precious little to heal.
Under the circumspection of the charitable, wan moonlight, Rooster
experienced an emotion he had never known in all his life, even before
the dread disease came forth. He felt in tune, harmonized. The emotion
was peace. As they walked arm in arm, he felt enveloped in a purse of
well-being. He felt protected, safe, a profound safety that even his art
provided for only brief and transient moments. He turned slightly to
Tamara to watch her pouty lips and the slender line of her slicing nose.

The universal, so inscrutable from the beginning, tonight suggested
a reason for all the hardship and pain, for all the trials that purge the

soul. A reason, a purpose, a goal behind it all. Rooster finally understood what Soli had meant when he had told his sole pupil that Aristotle had been incorrect in *Metaphysics*. In that work by the ancient Greek, four candidates are proposed for the title of primary being, unmoved mover, progenitor of the universe, *essence*.

The four candidates Aristotle thoughtfully proposed were form, matter, agent and substratum. As simply as Soli had instructed Rooster — as well as he could recall — *form* was the shape that defined matter and non-matter, the setter of established limits. *Matter* was the content of a thing, that which filled the form. *Agent* served as a type of catalyst and enzyme all in one, acting to enable the transformation of non-being to being and back again when the twin forces of creation and destruction deemed fit. And *substratum*, well, for Aristotle, *substratum* was an underlying matter or form that could not be known through any means. It was something theoretical, below the surface, active but wholly unknowable. In the end, the old Greek championed for form as the truest expression of the essence of being and non-being.

But Soli disagreed. Soli believed that the true essence of a thing came forth from the unknowable substratum, an essence beneath the defined surface, perpetually concealed from the empiricist's probe, inexpressible, indemonstrable and undefined. Substratum was the ummoved mover, primary being, the first principle, essence (at least in Soli's mind, a mind less motivated by the principle drive of the Greeks: define the world). Soli believed, and it was a belief he shared with Rooster, that though making definitions may have been the central challenge of the ancient world, making definitions was not the primary challenge of the contemporary world, the modern mind. The primary challenge was not even to attempt a reflection of the substratum; rather, it was to honor the unseen without striving to make it seen.

Tonight Rooster felt that the unseen saw fit to honor him for the work he had performed, to grant a respite from the torturous journey, to provide a more lasting impression of the realm he served, the realm for which he existed. Rooster still did not understand substratum, but he believed in it, just as he believed in a God that loves us from an intimate distance too close to see.

"Where are you?" Tamara asked, noting the acute disfocus of his eyes.

He smiled, conscious that he had drifted away and unsure of how long he had been gone. "I was thinking of my teacher, Solzhenitsyn, something he taught me. Something I think I am only now beginning to understand."

"And what is that?" This is what she had sought to share, the inspiration of the far away gaze, the event of being overpowered by an imagination that one intuitively knows to be good.

They turned a corner and continued walking in the center of a new street. "It's difficult to explain, though I think Soli did much to help me understand. What he did was so hard, attempting to teach a boy the lessons he had accumulated over a lifetime. I don't think I ever fully appreciated what he sought to do. My gratitude was incomplete."

"You loved him."

"Yes. I think he knew. . . . I hope he did."

"He did." The words were exactly the ones Rooster needed to hear. She responded to his deepest longing as though the very cosmos had taken shape, guiding him by the arm to the place where pain would end. To where?

After several turns round corners and streets, they came to an unmarked dead end. Rooster smiled, accepting that here at least, the sublime intuition of freedom could not forever last. They stood at the edge of a darkened forest of trees and brush; patches of silvery snow radiated from within.

"I guess we should turn back," he stated, twisting upon his heel. But Tamara, holding him by the arm, tugging lightly, whispered one word only. Here, the gravity that pulled her inward was stronger than the gravity that pulled him outward.

"Why?"

The hush came from the forest itself, and Rooster knew that this was no narrow dream, that the substratum was with him — present, magical and real. It was not an imaginative event, not wishful thinking. Each time he stifled his desire with the snuff of reason, she coaxed him to trust, to take one more step in the direction of the unsubstantiated.

"We're lost now."

"No, we're not," she reproached.

"Why?" He surrendered.

"Because we're together." Grabbing his hand, she pulled him into the dense wooded patch of red maple and pine.

"Don't worry," she whispered, and he didn't.

They walked, mitten-covered hand in mitten-covered hand, over the frozen ground and through the scrunching pockets of snow. There was little light, but enough shimmered through the skeletal boughs to transform the pods of snow into soft glowing beacons. In the absence of a full line of light, Rooster and Tamara at least had summoning points of reference. They needed only to connect these points to form their own hallways. Leaping from patch to patch of glowing snow, they pretended that only the crunchy white knolls provided safe footing. They danced their way through the forest playing a child's game, foolishly laughing as they progressed, advancing deeper and deeper.

"Watch Out! Oh, you stepped on dirt. You're dead!" Tamara screamed as Rooster bound away, landing on a safe patch of snow.

"No, I stepped on a magic flake. It melts as soon as you step on it."

"No fair! How can I follow if you use up the magic flakes?"

"There's one; there's one. Jump now!" Without hesitating she jumped upon the magic flake and leapt to the safe pod where he waited. They laughed and continued forward, in the throes of mathematical imagination.

As the pace of their game quickened into a frenzied, frenetic samba of whirling delight, the thought occurred to Rooster that he felt wondrously clean and healthy. Looking up he spied a star twinkling through the windblown boughs and made a wish. Let this night never end. Panting heavily, he did not have time to linger on the thought, so far behind in the game had he fallen. Three pods ahead, Tamara was disappearing behind a thick grove of spotted dogwoods. He would have to use all of the magic flakes to catch her. He scattered them ahead, chasing her forward, slipping, never falling, her girlish giggle the most beautiful music he had ever heard.

When he reached the spot where she had been, he settled upon the snowy island, beaming with a grin, searching for Tamara's presence, a presence to define his next destination. Leaning against the bark of the sickly tree, he caught his breath, waiting for her to reappear from hiding, a new twist on their clever game of cat and mouse.

♔

During the bitter winter of 1934, sweeping famine ravaged Russia and Eastern Europe. The summer and autumn harvests of the prior seasons, stricken by drought and locust, produced pitiful yields of sickly crops. As the tributaries of the plains grew staid, the watermarks of the mighty Volga River descended. Darkened with feces and the locust decay, pestilence spread. The highland country, with its sprawling forests, howled like a dead reed. Bubonic plague (officially denied by the Ministry of Health) devastated western Russia killing cattle, pig, bear, deer, dogs and humans.

During these times, one small hamlet of Russia's western plains, led by a quiet miller, suffered less than the general population. Guided by Michayl's eerily prescient foresight, the hamlet of Krylov experienced discomfort but not destitution, sickness but not affliction. The practice of rationing food had begun months earlier in the village, well before individual incidents of calamity multiplied into national famine. There was much complaint when Michayl ordered the commencement of rationing and the salting of extra meat for the winter even if it meant no meat for the summer. Many protested openly, calling the measures extreme. Michayl implemented his plans, undeterred by the grumbling.

When first news of traveling hoards, scavenging for food, began to arrive from scouts, Michayl ordered all of the food transported from the hidden outposts to the center of the village. They could not take the chance of losing supplies to bandits. The few mules of the village, hitched to primitive sledges, "travoises" Michayl called them, were worked in shifts until all supplies were consolidated. In the center of Krylov, the villagers could protect their food from violent hoards that would think twice before attacking a village well organized if meagerly armed. The general's army was not expected again for seven months. Bringing the stores of food to the village represented a risk; Michayl thought it a good risk. Despite vocal dissenters, with the blessing of the majority his proposition won.

As the challenges of 1934 grew in scope and complexity, it became harder to shepherd the community. Many, less astute at reading the subtle signs of the time as Michayl, failed to appreciate the relative fortunes of their own village in comparison to the whole of Russia; thus, when they should have been praising their leader, they were criticizing. Unfortunately, some viewed times of strain as a perfect opportunity to launch their ego's drive for power. This above all was the principal reason that as the crisis intensified, Michayl continued to draw the village into a single, tight sphere about their food stores. In his own mind, he feared the dangers posed by marauding bandits less than he feared the treachery of an inside usurper. Through his strategy, the protection of the stability of the village, of the heart of Krylov, became everyone's equal and mutual responsibility.

As the winter crisis of 1934 deepened, Michayl took, in retrospect, a terrible gamble, calling the frontier scouts in from the plains. The chances, he thought, that the general would trudge forth from the capital in the midst of what had become an increasingly harsh winter were infinitesimal. In addition, the presence and utilization of the stalwart scouts within the village would be a great advantage to those who did not know the intimacy of true hardship as these wilderness men did. He assigned them to trapping locally for small game, anything, no matter how modest, that could bolster the village food stores. It appeared a solid plan with minimal risk, and as reports began to trickle in of the actual status of the region, even those envious of Michayl's position as leader found it difficult to criticize the effectiveness of his plans. For, as the region and seemingly all of Mother Russia struggled against the pervasive face of grim-spirited death, Krylov contested only with a mild hunger at night that would be satiated in the morning by a ration commensurate and reasonable to need.

It was in many ways a solid plan, as solid as any statistically valid plan can be. The general had never visited more than once in a year; this was true. Also, the general did not desire to trudge off into the raging winter on a campaign for food. As any native would know, winters in Mother Russia's womb were for hibernation. But despite the accuracy of these facts, in early January of 1935, just as it appeared that the worst could be coming to an end, the general, ice frozen in his beard, cruelty chiseled into his desperate features, arrived.

♔

His eyes accustomed to the wooded setting and pale strands of light that filtered independently from above, Rooster scanned the young grove of maples before him, searching for signs of Tamara. Pacing his breath, he strained his ears, listening for an indication of where she might be. Was she hiding? He waited.

After several moments he stepped from the pod. If she were hiding, the game had changed. If she were not hiding, this was not a game.

"Tamara," he called out, not shielding the concern of his heart. "Tamara?"

Nothing.

He moved forward now, taking concentrated steps in the general direction she had gone, trying to predict where she would have moved, what pods she would have pursued. Pressing on, he no longer grew anxious about stepping on dirt without a magic flake. "Tamara?" The name came from his lips like a whispered plea, unsure of the validity of its own request.

He discovered half a footprint in an edge of snow. The other half did not exist. Was she already disappearing? This glimpse, he'd found it too hard to believe. How could it be true? Had she fallen into the other world? Had their game become real? What existed beneath the form? Had she come from there? Like a will-o-wisp, had she returned?

"Tamara!" His voice grew in pitch and apprehension. The tempo of his steps doubled. "Tamara, where are you?"

He was lost. Not just lost, not just lost in a forest, but lost from the feeling of peace so recently felt, so precious and new. Rooster ran now, calling out her name as he rushed blindly into the forest, in a straight line with no sense of direction, passionate and uncaring but for the one goal. "Tamara!"

Flailing past brush and low hanging branches, he sprinted, unsure of whether he was approaching or departing. "Tamara!" Tripped by cragged roots, he fell flat on his face into snow and frozen mud. He did not rise. He felt his body like a sick sore as he mouthed her name without sound. "Tamara."

Rolling onto his back, he pressed the throbbing orbs of his eyes in a scouring act of castigation. The heavens gazed, opened; dumbed into awe, he experienced his first vision.

"Rooster!" He heard the cry and pushed upwards. "Rooster, where are you?"

Turning to the voice he saw her, scarcely thirty yards away, in a lustrous bath of light.

"Tamara?" He rose.

She saw him through the pattern of trees and smiled, calling to him with a gentle waving hand. "Come here," her summons came. "It's beautiful."

He walked in a daze, trodding on numb, clumsy feet, keeping his burning eyes steadfastly locked upon her figure, a radiant angel suspended in a misty aura of unearthly light.

"Come here, come here," she urged. "It's beautiful." Gazing upon her presence, her being, entering the opening where she stood alone, pure and untouched, Rooster could only agree.

Space, quiet as a tomb, unfurled as Rooster received Tamara's extended hand. Below them a placid lake, surrounded by a bowl of pines, appeared. The light of the moon glistened upon the rippled surface. Deflected upwards, the light danced towards the exact spot where they romantically stood hand in hand. Wafting upon water, the silver rays of moonlight stretched like a child yearning from the cradle.

"I thought I'd lost you."

She smiled, touching his cheek, "Did you truly?"

Together they drifted down the slope. Coming to the edge of the lake, the clean water lapped in slow luxury at the stony edge. The roots of a bowed birch were exposed to the winter, dipping into the lake through the subtle powers of erosion. The trunk of the tree was posed at a lean, like a tutored bonsai, horizontally cascading over the lake at a sensual angle. A humble bridge, still growing, beginning with no end. Tamara stepped upon the bowing trunk, inviting Rooster to follow with her.

Taking small steps they balanced their way to a thick, heavy branch where they were able to sit comfortably. The lake roiled softly beneath them, striding against the limbs that dipped so low as to meet the water.

"What is this place?" he asked her.

"Spirit Lake."

"Is that true?"

"I don't know," she answered.

Moonlight danced upon the pure liquid. The reflection caused a flicker of white flame to traipse unevenly upon their cheeks.

"I'm not cold anymore," Tamara told him as she watched the gentle water beneath her dangling feet.

"Soli used to say that the clouds in the sky are like the mind of man. The sky is the eternal truth, unchanged and unchanging, but the ideas of a man are like the clouds, whimsical and changing, impermanent. The mind is nothing more than a device of imagination. Our one task is to make it steady and even, to hold a shape, a pattern for as long as we can. He used to challenge me to keep my mind as steady as the sky. He told me that a cloud that disappears becomes one with the sky."

Tamara listened to the rhythms about. "I like that."

"You would have liked Soli."

She smiled, recollecting her memory. "Yes, I'm sure I would have," she concurred wistfully. Quietly, she asked, "What else did he teach you?"

She watched the pacific features of Rooster's face as he gazed to the center of the lake where the moon appeared positioned at a precise perpendicular. She noted how calm and pleased he looked as the loving memory of his master entered his thoughts.

"He was a father to me. He taught me about so much more than painting, though that's what we talked about most. He taught me how to use my mind to guide my work." Rooster laughed at the irony. "The next day he taught me how to use my work to guide my mind. I think that more than anything else, he wanted me to see nature in a different way."

"And how is that?"

Rooster dipped his toe, padding the water, sending ripples forth in continuous circles, one after the other, each following the next, each in order, each incapable of altering the order, each event in time an undeniable subset of the all that comes before, the last being closest to the source though the first may understand it best.

"I'm not quite sure. That's why I still paint. I think he wanted me to understand that nature challenges us to change her. Nature wants us to learn through her first and foremost. She wants to be our teacher. But to do that we need to engage her. Admiring her is not enough to know her."

"Her?" she joked, feigning jealousy.

Rooster grinned as he looked Tamara in the eye without concern for affect. "It's more intimate for me. See, I'll never know a woman in that way . . . so I have to create those intimacies elsewhere."

Tamara thought to challenge his assumptions, but she stopped herself. As close as she was willing to get to him, she knew that unless there existed a complete cure, intimacy of the type they were implying would never be possible.

She stared at his hands as they clung to the wood. "I know something about channeling energy." Removing a mitten, she drew closer. He stopped her as she raised an exposed hand to his cheek.

"Tamara?"

"It's all right."

"No skin to skin."

Her countenance was serious as she pressed his hand away and brought her palm to the skin of his cheek. "It's all right."

His eyes were closed. His body trembled. She moved her fingers lightly across his cheeks and to his lips. She traced their outline with a single finger, her own eyes now closed, memorizing their feel to her touch. Returning the other way, the back of her hand brushed his cleft chin, where the history of scarring caused rough ripples. She felt the pain deeply held within his shivers. This was as far as they could ever go; they both knew it. By far it was enough for each.

cℐ

The general arrived in a nasty mood. He and his men, armed with machine guns and spiteful resolve, appeared different this time. Though the majority of the men still traveled on horseback, three armored trucks, with wheels made for snow, accompanied the force. In the recent past most of the men had carried swords and pistols, but now a different time had come, when all men wielded the explosive capacity of the machine gun. The world had dramatically changed.

In the small, rural hamlet they'd heard of incredible devices that belied the imagination, but, holding faith against hope, they had not quite believed. Yet here were the machines, weapons of insanity, weapons of modernity that enabled one man to destroy an entire village. The general himself, like a dogmatic bulwark or a throwback, armed himself only with a cavalier's sword and a long, luger pistol. Through famine, his power and the hatred he nurtured in his lifeless eyes had grown.

Michayl, more unsure of himself than he had ever been but for the knowledge that he needed to find a way to protect the food, marched from the warm hearth of his home to greet the general. Before he could speak, the general, like a man who has predetermined all that is to be, launched his opprobrious slander.

"You grow fat, Cur. Your people must be eating well." Michayl bowed his head humbly; he knew that he had lost much weight since his previous encounter with the general and would not be goaded into public disagreement with him. Such stubbornness would make conditions worse for the village as the general would thrill in squashing even the slightest trace of rebelliousness that manifested itself before his troops.

Michayl waited for directions without a word. Villagers watched from their homes, hiding any scraps of bread and meat they still possessed, swallowing down what little they'd managed to preserve of individual rations.

"Mother Russia is bound by famine. All townships are to tithe to the great needs of the Motherland. Each takes according to need; each gives according to ability." With these words the general ordered his men to check the storehouses for food. Michayl's heart dropped. If their food stores were claimed the entire village would starve. All of their planning, all of their years — his own years — of sacrifice would come to this, to nothing.

"General, General." He threw himself down. "We have so little. Barely enough for the winter. Just enough to get by. General, please. We have worked so hard. Our children!" It was not an act. Not an act as all the other performances had been. The general reared back on his neighing horse, distancing himself from the shameless beggar supplicating himself in the powdery white snow.

Had anyone seen the general's eyes they would have seen something they had never before seen from the cold, vicious man — genuine surprise. Dismounting from his horse, he unsheathed his blade. "Get up. Get up, Cur!" the general shouted, kicking Michayl squarely in the mouth with his polished, black boot. Hot, crimson blood splattered upon the snow.

Pacing about Michayl, he studied the figure, attempting to discern what action to take, attempting to ascertain whether he was being fooled. Finally, the general decided that it simply did not matter. What mattered is what he did next, how he utilized this opportunity with the village, with the soldiers, with Naistika.

"You have worked so hard, this Cur claims," the general pronounced in a loud voice. "Is your work so much greater than the work of Mother Russia? Of the work of her great army that travels through the winter to feed her people, to meet the needs of the nation? Is your work, the work of a miserable Cur," and with this he spit on Michayl, "so much the greater? Do you think so much of yourself and so little of Mother Russia? Miserable, ungrateful Curs, all of you!"

Michayl began to rise. The general backhanded him to the ground with the stiff, brass hilt of his sword. The village was still, quiet as the thick crimson trickling from Michayl's gaping mouth.

"Is that the sentiment of this selfish township? Are you all of such a selfish, miserable stock? Do you all believe as this Cur? That your personal needs are so much greater than the needs of the greatest nation in the world? Is this your sentiment? And you wonder, and you wonder why this poor, little, nothing man suffers!"

The general paced more. Clearing his throat he recommenced his guttural tirade. "Should I kill this man? Should I kill this despicable creature that mocks our dear Mother? I wouldn't sully my blade! No . . . Mother Russia is merciful to her weak, her wretched, men . . . no, her CURS! Ignoble Curs . . . like this. My men have traveled long and hard for the cause of Mother Russia. Prepare us a meal and a bed. We leave in the morn to do the work of a great nation. Think on this."

With these words the general unclasped his belt. Dropping his pants, the cruel general relieved himself on Michayl's back. Urine mixed with blood. Soli watched from the stoop of their home, fighting Naistika's attempts to drag him within the house. She hid herself, so she thought, so as not to make it worse on her husband. In the silence of the village, above the wind, only the single, piercing scream of a child's trauma existed.

That night, beneath brave stars, Michayl slept in the snow, burrowing deep to stay barely alive, unwilling to enter the home of another as the general, intoxicated on henna, lay in Michayl's bed with Michayl's own warm wife.

In the morning, chipper and buoyant, the general ordered the villagers assembled for an address. One last time he admonished their choice of leaders. Then, in a public declaration of Mother Russia's grace and goodness, he announced that all of the village's food stores would be left behind, untouched and unmolested but for the meals necessary to keep his men strong. Great Mother Russia cared not for the scraps of a selfish village that could think of nothing but itself. The general stated that he intended this as a punishment and a lesson, so that with each morsel of food that fattened their own greedy stomachs — through guilt and the knowledge of their own pettiness — they would feel the pangs of starvation that plagued their loving mother, Russia.

The general's army left in a better mood than they had come. Despite their mission, the trucks were still empty of the food they were to bring back to the capital. Somewhere down the road there would be a next town.

As villagers rushed to gather Michayl's frozen body, scarcely alive, from the snow, the quartermaster set about to daily tasks, preparing healthy rations for the village that owed one man so much. Business as usual, he cleaved his knife.

♍

"It's beginning to freeze over."

"What's that?" Rooster asked her.

"The lake, it's freezing over from this cold spell. You can see it happening around the edges."

He had not noticed before, but her observation was correct. Solid patches were forming upon the lake, places where a dull sheen seemed to trap the light of the moon rather than reflect it. The placid lake had begun to grow hard and definitive. The color of palladium. Rooster contemplated the scene. Tamara wondered upon his attractive and knowing smile.

"What are you thinking?"

"That the substratum is hiding itself."

She laughed. "Even now, you're thinking about philosophy. Aristotle's *Metaphysics*. Does a girl have a chance?"

"Come here."

Directing her to turn, he ushered her closer, into the eaves of his arms. "You don't need a chance. It's a guarantee. . . . Besides, it's not really philosophy. It's nature that I'm thinking about. Soli wanted me to re-see nature. That's what I'm working towards. Philosophy is just language."

Tamara squeezed his hand. The pain of wrapped sores on the fingers beneath the mittens caused him to wince. It was barely perceptible, but she felt it. She had been on the verge of asking him how he could comprehend or "re-see" nature while never leaving his room, but she stopped. She had begun to understand that nature through the disease had done much to come to him.

"Can you help me to re-see nature?" she asked. High overhead a plane crossed in front of the gibbous moon, interrupting the splendor of their enchanted oasis. With a finger flipping at her lower lip in thought she mused, "To you, that's nature too, isn't it."

"Yes."

Leaving a silver trail of icy vapor to mark its path, the airplane split the sky. Tamara imagined the vapor line as a mark of chalk drawn in the sky, connecting two unrelated stars, creating a defined relationship where previously there had been none.

"This is our place," she stated eagerly. "This lake and all of the sky above."

"Yes, always," he assented. At the lake's center, the moonlight twinkled. In reflection, the silver stripe in the sky vanished completely, its oracular dividing mark meaningless before heavenly stars thus wed.

Tamara and Rooster departed speechlessly, in awe-breaking, sage serenity. They lingered slowly, less playful and more intense than their arrival. The innocence remained, now sealed in trust. Together they had created a labyrinth to get to this place. The path there, which seemed so random, unfolded on return as a straight laid piece of track. As they proceeded forward, each reasoned on their own that it could have been no other way; no other destination would have been possible. No combination of turns could have led them to any other place. The mystery of the thing faded, succumbing to prudence. Tamara in her mind redefined the Heisenberg Uncertainty Principle. It was the force of fate, the fate that moves all things, she thought. Fate is the essence, the *sine qua non*. No complex mathematics or physics can reason fate, though fate can be expressed in mathematics — just as it can be expressed in gravity or electricity or magnetism or engineering or chemistry or philosophy, poetry, music and painting. These are just modes through which we seek to prepare ourselves to meet our fate, the uncertainty that is certain. She smiled. For the moment, she didn't care if it would make sense to anyone else. It made sense to her, just as the substratum made sense to Rooster.

As they walked she stated, "I want to hold your hand, your real hand."

Rooster did not answer.

"All right then," she pursued, "I have something for you, but I have to put it in your hand. That's the only way I'll give it to you."

He paused and looked at her doubtfully. They had arrived at the edge of the forest; the street with its paved yellow lines lay just ahead.

She prodded him by parroting his own lesson. "It's a part of nature."

Tentatively he removed the mitten from his left hand. The tightly wrapped gauze beneath smelled of sebum and the ointments he applied to the scaly wounds in varying stages of denigration and healing. Wrapped from the wrist, the gauze covered the entire hand. Revealing even this, Rooster felt embarrassed.

"Please though," he pleaded, "it's for your protection."

Tamara thought of fate and limits and mysteries and puzzles, of certainty and certainty and certainty. Removing her own red mitten, she drew from her pocket the upper right hand corner piece of the puzzle she had completed, the Bavarian landscape on the cusp of a new season. Even complete, she could not discern from the picture whether winter was coming or going. The answer no longer caused her concern or consternation. The winter was not a season to resist or fear. It could be warm and loving, the most preferable place to be. She placed the corner frame in Rooster's hand. He looked at it, felt it. She did not need to explain. All creativity ends in common sense.

8

TWO DAYS PASSED before Irene succeeded in getting Dorothia on the phone. The imperative messages she had left on the machine, Rooster had erased. Irene protracted her stay in Rhode Island by visiting some of the local art enclaves and prowling RISD, the local arts school with an international reputation. The city possessed an undeniable charm, an enchanting allure that she could not recall from previous visits. She networked a bit, dead-end prospecting, all excuses to justify her time. The possibility of a wasted business trip disgusted her. In her business, the successful were defined for their ability to make the hard contacts, to effectively manage the eccentric and creative.

But this was different somehow, and in her heart she knew it.

Her own capacity for judgment in this matter she did not quite wholly trust. Having constructed a stalwart reputation for herself through her years as an independent art distributor, her opinion counted. What had made her judgments so substantial was the reality that, despite her love for art, she had never in all her years encountered a work of art that she loved. She sheltered in her consciousness a lofty ideal of such a height and crisp magnitude and meaning that none had ever attained it. Thus, experiencing art always from the perspective of her visionary ideal, her judgments never seemed to err or falter. She had a reputation for picking winners from the bowels of the rejected. Some viewed her magic touch as a run of uncommon luck bound to end. If they possessed any sense of the contrast that her personal ideal produced, they also could have pulled genius from the masses, so apparent would it become.

The ideal she held was her grail quest, and it empowered her frail physical figure with a nearly vatic sight when it came to the discernment of fine art. Her taste was known to be impeccable. That is why when her gallery on Canyon Road began displaying the works of a cubist impressionist from Nicaragua, works of the same style began to appear in patches all along Canyon Road. Like anything else, the profession of art dealers possessed its share of imitators and hacks incapable of critical thinking.

She valued no one style over any other. It could not be said, for instance, that she preferred naturalism to the impressionistic, or realism to post-realism. She did not search out period pieces or even art that exhibited a specific temperament or philosophical disposition. She sought that alone which approached her visionary ideal with the greatest zeal and promise. But the works of Rooster, and Rooster himself, were an anomaly. Always in the past the works of art, good as they were in comparison to the population of artists, left her fundamental vision, and her position as guardian of that vision, unchallenged. This fact left her free to nurture an artist's promise, to guide and mentor. Now, for the first time since her induction into art, since the coming of her vision, she felt that she was the one who needed to learn. And it was not simply that Rooster offered to her the possibility of an art that matched her ideal, no; this is what she had initially believed. It was more than this. Rooster's art exceeded her ideal, transcended it. It was as though from the sublime mountaintop of his art, he had shone an alchemical spotlight upon her mountaintop, revealing the reality that while her conception represented the embryo, his representations were fully developed actualizations. His art humbled her in the dignified manner she had always wished but never suspected possible. Excitement and terror abounded within her breast simultaneously. And her visit, anarchic as it had been, worked to convince her that this time, the artist at least equaled the art.

These thoughts caused her to stay in the city when the city bored her; these thoughts caused her to find reasons for beauty and goodness in all that surrounded her.

Sitting on the hotel room bed, she picked up the phone and dialed the number. She had already left two messages today.

As she dialed her mind wandered to Marubrishnubupu. If this were truly so important to him, if he believed his touted dreams, then why wasn't he here in Providence chasing down this leprous phantom with her? Where was his conviction? As much as she respected the proper values his asceticism exhibited, she quietly loathed the passivity that characterized his particularly popular brand of spiritualism. Stand at the center. Wait and see. If it is to be, it will come to me.

The attenuated, clicking dial tone ended abruptly. "Hello?"

"Hello, Dorothia?" Irene could hear the thrill her own voice emitted. She had not expected an answer to what had become grim routine. Calming herself, reclaiming composure, she added, "Dorothia, hello. This is Irene."

"Irene, oh yes, hello. What can I do for you? Are his works selling?"

"Yes, yes, that's all fine. I'm calling for another reason though."

"How much are they going for? Who are the buyers? Important buyers?"

"I'm in Rhode Island."

There was a long pause on the other end, then the words, slowly, "That's nice. What are you doing here?"

"I've been trying to see your son, Rooster. I've been calling and leaving messages. I stopped by the house."

"You came here?" The terse question retained no assuaging pall of social gallantry.

"Yes, a few days ago. I wanted to . . ."

"A few days ago!"

Irene did not reply. Her natural instincts were coming back. She did not intend to be bullied, dissuaded from her necessary course of action. "Yes. Two days ago. I wanted to meet the artist on his own terms."

"That was very stupid, Irene. Very stupid."

Resisting the urge to pursue this weak line of argument, Irene maintained her course. "Yes, well, he didn't seem to appreciate the visit. He wouldn't open the door." Dorothia began speaking again, but Irene talked over her. "Still. With the time I still have left I'd like to meet Rooster. We have some important matters to discuss if I am to represent him well and do for him the things I believe he deserves done."

"Anything you need to know you can learn from me." Dorothia threw herself forward as a gloomy rampart.

Scribbling on a pad, Irene wrote the word, "CONTROLLER!!!" She pressed down hard with the pen to amplify the exclamation points already screaming. "I don't think that's accurate, Ms. Rodriguez. You don't paint the paintings; Rooster does. He's the artist, not you. He's the one I need to be speaking to."

"He doesn't want to speak to you," she snapped.

"In New Mexico you told me that you wanted me to meet him."

"And I do, but you don't just show up out of the blue and disturb him. He has a schedule just like any of us. We don't try to surprise people."

At least on this score Dorothia was right. Irene had sought to ambush Rooster, for reasons she continued to believe were valid, such as avoiding this exact conversation she now found herself being sucked within.

Irene returned to the beginning, her simplest point. "I need to see your son."

"Well, you can't see him, not today."

"Tomorrow then."

"I'm not sure. I'll have to see."

"Ms. Rodriguez, I cannot stay here forever. Either today or tomorrow."

"It's not up to me," Dorothia protested, shifting to higher authority.

"Who is it up to?"

"Why Rooster, of course. Didn't you just say he's the one you want to see?"

"Yes. But didn't you tell me he can't see me today?"

"He can't."

"Did you ask him?"

"I don't appreciate your trying to get clever with me."

Irene sighed, "You know what, Ms. Rodriguez? I'm going back to New Mexico tonight. Tomorrow I'll wrap up the paintings and have them all shipped back to you. That should make this all much easier."

"You wouldn't do that?!" Dorothia blurted out in shock.

"Yes, I would."

Another long pause ensued. When Dorothia spoke again, she sounded downright chipper, "Tomorrow then, come at noon. He eats lunch then. We can talk then."

Irene spoke with a laser precision meant to cut. "We?"

"You and Rooster, I mean. Yes, you and Rooster."

"Thank you, Ms. Rodriguez. I'll be there at noon." Click!

Irene collapsed upon the bed, exhausted from the contentious conversation. She had won, accomplished what she had sought to accomplish, at least in theory.

Calling the airlines to cancel her ticket home, she wondered what would occur in that house between now and her visit, what illusions Dorothia would attempt to cast. Chimeras were exactly what Irene so desperately hungered to avoid. Tomorrow she would enter a home where all signs of the real Rooster were concealed and hidden behind the mask his controlling mother deemed would garner greatest approval. This would make ascertaining the truth more difficult, but like all paintings, there would be, for one who looked closely and knew exactly what to seek, discernible signs.

cP

Another Day of Loving spent 64 weeks atop the *New York Times Bestseller's Fiction List*. What pleased Marcel most was that on all post-first edition prints the publishing house had agreed not to place his photo on the jacket cover, finally conceding that the stripped down cover — nothing but the title and the author's name in red block letters upon a pearl mat, like blood in snow — best mirrored the soulful content. Marcel had argued for a simple cover from the start and lost. Jack only yielded the point after the novel had achieved international acclaim of such magnitude that wrapping the pages in a stinking, rotted cabbage leaf could not have negatively impacted sales.

On page 53 of the story, when Marta, a young Palestinian girl, the daughter of a diplomat, returns home to find her father assassinated by a bullet through the center of his head, she does a peculiar thing. Her father, Abdul ben-Shahid, had been signing official papers ordering the release of 150 prisoners of the Palestinian state. These prisoners, mostly Israeli dissidents who would not honor the terms of resettlement agreed upon by the two nations, had been a minor source of irritation to the peace process. To the dismay of the Palestinians, the Israeli state had done little to discourage the squatters. Israeli silence, a tacit complicity, fueled the political hot button. The squatters were being called "non-violent conscientious objectors" by sympathetic compatriots. Most of the squatters simply had no place to go.

With Mont Blanc pen in hand, the Palestinian diplomat was signing the release orders, effective immediately. No plan for redress, the Israeli dissidents would quite simply be freed. What would happen to the dissidents and the disputed lands following the release was a mystery to everyone, including Abdul ben-Shahid. In the complex world of international politics, the pundits struggled to interpret the maneuver. Was this a calculated form of antagonization or the genuine demonstration of a sincere commitment to use peaceful methods of resolution in the midst of destructive conflict?

Publicly and privately, the Palestinian diplomat sought to send the message that in progressing towards peace, prisoners of war could not be accepted as a necessary means to achieving regional stability. It was a bold move, some said, anticipating the release, motivated more by naiveté than a sophisticated comprehension of geopolitical ramifications.

Palestinian extremists deplored the move as weak pandering to the Zionists. In fact and truth, the diplomat was guilty of pandering not to the Zionists but to his eight-year-old daughter, Marta, whose classmate's father was one of the imprisoned. She had done nothing more than question why her friend's father was in prison. The man had refused to move his family from the home that had belonged to his father and his father's father. By virtue of the resettlement, that home now belonged to the Palestinian state. Marta ben-Shahid did not quite understand, could not. She only saw that her friend, half Palestinian by virtue of the mother, now living with Palestinian relatives, had been displaced from her home and ripped from her father's arms. "What if that were us, Papa?"

> The heads of state are our children, and our children's children. It is they, ignorant of power and prejudice, who best understand the process of peace, who are best informed to guide our nations and our peoples to the promise of a better land, the better land for which all our diverse religions so assiduously search. We must create for our children histories not of war but of peace. Histories of peace, that we have dared to dream and live, must become the lessons of our schools, our communities, our dinner tables, our proud nations and our international family.

These were the words that the diplomat had written in an official press release announcing his intentions to pardon the prisoners. Two days later he was dead. When the girl in *Another Day of Loving* finds her father dead, she does a peculiar thing. Marta hugs her father, removes the pen with which he has been signing the papers from his hand, and begins to meticulously imitate his signature. For hours, over and over again, until she can perfectly replicate his signature, she practices. Then, one by one, she signs the 132 release orders still awaiting his official approval in the center of his desk. Once completed, she places them in an envelope and walks to the embassy where she is known, asking to see her father. They inform her that he is not there. She informs the guards that she has some papers that he has forgotten. She is delivering them at his request. They let her in the office where she places the documents in the official "out" box as she has seen her father do many times before.

Or, in Gibran's words:

> *When love beckons you, follow him,*
> *Though his ways are hard and steep . . .*
> *And when he speaks to you believe in him,*
> *Though his voice may shatter your dreams . . .*

Marcel knew as surely as the sun does rise that *Another Day of Loving* was a special book. It possessed in its slim pages a capacity for selfless overcoming that is of the rarest quality. Seldom did a book appear with such a forceful moral imperative so subtly articulated, like the steady progression of nature, patient and undeniable, generous yet sublime in its economy.

Through his earlier works, Marcel had earned the rap of being a half turn too clever, a twist too ironic. The critical sentiment that plagued his work in the early years was that while technically masterful, the writing lacked something of the human dimension. It was too thorough in the head, while being deficient of the heart.

The first sign of a breakthrough came with the critical reception of his fifth book as his wife of two years, Ruth, battled breast cancer. They had scarcely been married a full year when the diagnosis shattered the dream of their world. In the beginning, Marcel had been more devastated than Ruth. Only later, as his wife vomited following the first treatment of chemotherapy, did the deeper reality begin to sink in: this was not about him. It affected him, but it was she who suffered most, she whose life was jeopardized. And he could do nothing, could write nothing to slow the spread of cancerous cells through the fatty tissue of the breast.

"We've been unable to control the spread. It is now inoperable. We're sorry, Mrs. Phrenol."

Marcel had stared at the doctor with cold, black eyes as Ruth sobbed softly, "I don't want to die. . . ."

"If we'd known earlier . . ." The doctor stopped himself short of completion. No "ifs" could change the reality of what was; Marcel's glare communicated this much, his stillborn rage directed at all the world. He had never wished to fall in love, had fought it savagely, had refused to open his heart and trust in another, had feared the betrayal, the abandonment all over again. He knew this would happen — *knew it*; that as soon as he loved, this vicious world would inflict its blow — a blow not meant solely to defeat or hurt but to demoralize through senseless annihilation of the best that is. What hurt now was not so much the blow but the fact that he had known it would come, that he had expected it, that he had opened a door in trust to be betrayed once again by nature's indifference.

"What are you trying to say, doctor?" Marcel growled fiercely. It had never occurred to him that it was not feelings he did not trust; hate he trusted well enough. "Are you saying that my wife is going to die?"

"Mr. Phrenol!" the doctor implored for discretion.

"Is that what you're saying, doctor?" The choleric sarcasm spewed, as though the medical certificates on the wall were as useless, meaningless and trite as the title page of a book.

The doctor placed his hand upon Ruth's as she wept in isolation. He stared boldly at Marcel. "You have some time left. Use it wisely."

Marcel disputed without perspective. "It's voodoo, doctor, mumbo-jumbo, voodoo!"

After the doctor left the room, Marcel turned his attention to his wife. "We'll get another doctor, someone better. We'll beat this. We can beat this. We can." On his knees, he clutched her hands in his and begged as a child. He talked, pressing on with words of inspiration to stop her from speaking the words he feared. "There are ways, there are ways and we'll find them. Alternative medicines. Rainforest cures. Chinese."

Ruth smiled, though Marcel could not know why. He was for the first time bringing to her the same vivid energy he brought to his craft, to his secret universe of fiction. She smiled for the doctor who thought her husband unfeeling and for the little boy before her who still believed in voodoo. She smiled for her husband and the child she saw born in his face. She smiled as she stroked Marcel's brow, the brow of this curious, fragile genius who could write of the most complex hearts with delicate ease and inspiring sensitivity, yet know not his own. She smiled for the life she had lived and the days she had left.

Marcel collapsed in her lap, tears streaming from his youthful, innocent face. "I don't want you to die, Ruth! I don't. Don't!"

She smiled for she was not alone. As he sobbed in her lap, the child born of the man, she felt at peace with life and death, fully consumed by a love more perfect than she had ever dared to dream to know.

cℐ

Irene awoke thankful that this would be her last day in Providence. The trip had already taken far more time than anticipated, and it was surely costing her money at home. In the streets of the city she met the wintry wind of the morning with a fresh sense of promise. She had an hour and a half before her meeting with Rooster. Deciding that this would not be a meeting where she would be well served by showing up early, she solicited directions to the Providence Library from the hotel doorman.

"Have you enjoyed your visit to the city, Ma'am?"

"Not particularly," she answered.

"I'm sorry to hear that, Ma'am. I guess you can't please everyone."

Arriving at the austere Providence Library, she conducted some quick and intensive research on the topic of leprosy. Seated in an oversized, Edwardian, cedar chair at an oversized, Edwardian, cedar table she plopped down a stack of books with a booming reverberation. Old libraries always leave room for ghosts. She had minimal time for this project; she suspected that she had purposefully imposed the time constraints upon herself. Ever since she had discovered this painter to be the victim of such an antiquated disease of deformity and malignant sores, she found herself on edge, off-balance and tense, unsure of what to expect. She wasn't sure how much she truly wanted to know, truly wanted to see. The reputation leprosy carried from the early Christian ages left her feeling heavy with despair and dread. She pushed the thought from her mind.

In the brief time available she learned enough of this wretched disease of the damned to prepare her for the idea, if not the reality. She learned that twelve million human beings live with the disease today, modern times. A quarter of the victims are younger than fifteen years old. In the thirteenth century the Catholic Church sanctioned a ritual for all lepers called the Mass of Separation. Sensory nerve loss tends to begin at the extremities. Toes. Fingertips. Nose. Armadillos often contract the disease in the wild. In medieval Europe lepers were made to carry a leper's rattle called a clapper. Rifampin can tint the patient's urine, causing a reddish shade sometimes confused for blood. From the moment of infection, it can take four to eight years for the disease to manifest. Leprosy causes severe nerve damage. There are eleven references to lepers and leprosy in the Old Testament, eight references in the New Testament. The prophet Elisha cured Naaman of leprosy by commanding the man to bathe in the river Jordan seven times.

Sulfa drugs were once used to treat the disease. Bathing in the smoke of burning, severed adders was a popular cure at one time. God turned Moses' hand white with leprosy as a demonstration of power. Secretions from the nose, mouth or respiratory systems of lepers should be carefully disposed of. Hand washing does help. Doctors are unsure of exactly how the disease is spread. Tuberculoid leprosy is less serious than the cutaneous or lepromatous forms which are also more easily spread. One half million cases are diagnosed every year. When the face is marred by leprosy, there can be a loss of eyebrows and eyelashes creating an odd, leonine appearance. God cured Moses' hand of leprosy in a display of power. Lagophthalmos is a condition that prevents the victim from being able to close his eyes. The skin ulcers of lepers can heal, though slowly, often leaving deep, deforming scars. Bacteria can invade the organs, causing a multiplicity of effects including atrophy, loss of sensation, paralysis and secretion of milk from the breasts of females and males alike. The body is able to mount a localizing defense against tuberculoid leprosy. Another drug used in the treatment of leprosy, Clofazimine, can cause a blackening discoloration of the skin. Autonomic nerve damage causes the skin to dehydrate, leaving it extremely dry and cracked, increasing the risk that an infected individual will develop open sores. In Europe, leprosy first occurred amongst the rich and upper classes and was viewed as a health issue. Later, leprosy became a disease of the lower classes, at which point leprosy was interpreted as proof of a corrupted morality. Hard, leathery nodules often proceed the appearance of ulcerated, suppurating, odorous wounds. Leprosy is commonly known as Hanson's disease. Native Americans have proven immune to the disease. Naaman is written of in Kings II, Chapter 5. A victim of the disease can die of suffocation, unable to breath due to bronchial swelling. Blindness, or an unblinking state called lagophthalmos, can result from leprosy. The first alms to be offered by a healed leper include two living birds (preferably doves), cedar wood, scarlet and blooming hyssop. Over seven billion bacteria can accumulate on one gram of skin tissue. In cases of significant nerve damage, patients are taught to care for themselves by performing frequent visual checks of their bodies. The difficulty of incubating the disease in animals has been a substantial roadblock in attempts to more closely study and monitor the disease. Twelfth century rhetoric claimed that leprosy was spread through sexual penetration. There are at least three different types of leprosy, each varying in severity. The disease is caused by Mycobacterium leprae and there is no known natural immunity. The World Health Organization recommends multi-drug therapy in combating the disease. Rifampin, Clofazimine and Dapsone are the predominant drugs used in treatments. Dapsone causes itchy skin, but is otherwise very safe. The clapper warned others of a leper's approach. In the past, lepers that touched others were severely beaten with wood. Armadillos are good hosts for the bacteria due to their ideal body temperature. Household members of a leper should be examined by a doctor every five years. Leper colonies and sanitariums were plentiful from the 13th to the 16th century; lepers went there to die in the company of others. The disease is identified through a simple biopsy. In the past it was nearly impossible to discern the difference between certain skin maladies and leprosy. Hansen's disease is rare in the United States; it is most prevalent in

India. In 12th century Western Christendom, the leper was regarded as a sinner, a tainted soul. At the same time, in Jerusalem and regions east, no such association between leprosy and sin existed. Following at the heels of nerve damage, gangrene can set in resulting in localized "necrosis." The Mass of Separation ceremoniously proclaimed the leper as dead to the world; lepers were often made to stand in graves as dirt was heaped upon them and sanctioned words were read by a priest. Translated from the Latin:

RITES OF THE MASS OF SEPARATION

I forbid you to ever enter a church, a monastery, a fair, a mill, a market or an assembly of people. I forbid you to leave your house unless dressed in your recognizable garb and also shod. I forbid you to wash your hands or to launder anything or to drink in any stream or fountain, unless using your own barrel or dipper. I forbid you to touch anything you buy or barter for, until it becomes your own. I forbid you to share a house with any woman but your wife. I command you, if accosted by anyone while traveling on a road, to set yourself downwind of them before you answer. I forbid you to enter any narrow passageway, lest a passerby bump into you. I forbid you, wherever you go, to touch the rim or the rope of a well without donning your glove. I forbid you to touch any child or to give them anything. I forbid you to eat and drink from any vessel but your own.

The church considered this sacrament a rite of honor for the leper who was deemed to represent, in metaphorical terms, the rejected Nazarene. It is not clear that the leper saw this ceremony as an honor.

"Necrosis," in laymen's terms, means that parts of the body die.

Hope for a leprosy vaccine, though unrealized, remains high.

Irene closed her books. Where would a modern leper find compassion, she wondered, drained by the list of facts. Glancing at her watch, she knew it was time to go.

The question stormed through Irene's head as she walked the angled streets towards the district where Rooster lived with his mother. Her nervousness about meeting this young man had faded, consumed into a miasmatic pool of sympathy. It was a horrible thing this boy was living through. How could selling art make sense in the face of a world where leprosy — *God dammit leprosy!* — still existed, hidden at the fringe?

She remembered her own grandmother in a nursing home, secluded from the world. As a girl, Irene used to go visiting with her own mother, always reluctantly. To see the shriveled creature struck fear in her heart — and disgust. She felt no desire to kiss the old creature or touch the dry, scaly skin, stricken with psoriasis. A tense, palpable energy ached as she would sit herself in a corner of the room, unmoving, willing herself into the invisible, praying for the end. Such feelings of horror and deep resentment before the inevitability of human decay could not have been uncommon for a child, and yet so many years later, Irene still carried the shame of her inability to respond with compassion.

She remembered wanting her grandmother to die, to stop persisting, to let the able move forward with their happy lives, untouched by the unclean. Even in the wild, a lame animal has sense enough to crawl away and quietly die.

I'm some sort of terrible person, Irene Smythe thought to herself. I'm a monster in a pretty shell. Inside ugly shells, the truest beauty resides. Irene thought of the images that this artist, Rooster, created; whatever resided on the inside, hidden beneath the dreary smear of enforced isolation, it was beautiful, and it revealed itself, with or without his consent, on canvas.

She arrived at five to noon with her travel bag slung over her shoulder. As soon as this visit concluded she was planning on heading to the airport to get the earliest flight possible back to Santa Fe. Passing through the gate, the memory of her recent, failed attempt returned to her mind full with the question that had brought her here in the first place: Is the art subordinate to the master or is the master subordinate to the art? To represent the magnificent art properly, she needed to know the answer.

She rung the doorbell. Familiar chimes filled her ears. Inside, she heard the rustle of hustling footsteps. A deep breath of the brisk autumn air relieved her persistent anxiety. The door opened and Dorothia, pale as a ghost, stood before Irene.

Surprised by the frightening specter who gaped at Irene without words, Irene sputtered, "What is it? What's happened?"

"Nothing. Nothing," Dorothia unsuccessfully assured her. "Please, please come in."

The amalgam of data of which she had just read spit through Irene's mind as she watched the sad creature who was telling unnatural lies.

"I hope I haven't come at a bad time. I know I'm a few minutes early."

Dorothia nodded without listening, her attention elsewhere, distracted. "Yes, a few minutes early. That's it. That's it," she declared.

Irene did not have the slightest conception of the 'it' to which Dorothia might be referring.

"A few minutes early," Dorothia repeated again, softly under her breath, attempting to convince herself that an obtuse problem had been satisfactorily solved.

"Please, please sit down. Can I get you some tea?" Dorothia stole a nervous glance at the closed door of the room that Irene assumed belonged to Rooster. Scurrying away before Irene could answer, Dorothia, shrouded in her mystery, disappeared down the hallway.

Disconcerted but patient, Irene seated herself on a divan in the entryway. The furniture piece seemed a throwback to an earlier period of history, when homes were designed to accentuate a prominent greeting room. She checked her make-up in the mirror, thinking the habit narcissistic, especially under these circumstances. Seated, she relaxed, dismissing the understandable and lingering tension. Wouldn't I be the same, Irene mused. My son, the leper. I'd be fearful of anyone coming too close to my home. I'd become overprotective too, wanting to protect others from the disease while protecting my son from the rejection of others. Quite understandable; she wondered why she had not reasoned to the cause of the odd behaviors earlier. In such a cruel world, paranoia could go easily unchecked. Visitors, she felt sure of her insights, were not common for a young man so uncommon. Listening to the apprehensive scurry in the kitchen, china clinking on silverware, Irene experienced empathy for the quiet desperation of another and their world. Her first instincts had not glowed beneficently upon Dorothia. She had concluded this mother to be controlling to an obsessive degree. Would I be different if I had a child in such a state, she sincerely asked herself, as her goodwill for the modern matriarch swelled.

"Can I give you a hand in there?" Irene called out.

"No, no. I'm fine," the voice chirped back with forced merriment.

Irene regretted that she had been so niggardly in her assessment of the mother and decided to repay her initial skepticism with the interest of a more personal kindness. With a finger wetted with saliva, she pressed down her eyebrows as her eyes wandered askance, glancing at the closed doorway in anticipation. There are many reasons, if I were the mother, that I would keep this boy locked in a room. The thought had crept upon Irene with the stealth of a butterfly; at its core a latent cruelty that caused her to shudder remained. She made up her mind, and it allowed the whole of her body to relax, free of the ungodly, unsustainable burden. The art is better than the artist. Dorothia emerged from the kitchen, smiling falsely, walking with an exaggerated slowness. Take a look around, Irene concluded — this is just a boy in the shadow of his mother.

℘

"Sugar?" Dorothia asked, placing a sterling tray of wine biscuits and tea between them. "Oh, I forgot the lemon," she cooed in a calming contralto.

"I don't use it," Irene assured her kindly, wishing to assuage Dorothia and display in clear terms that all was now well and easily understood between them. How could she possibly have opined this tender thing to be selfishly motivated by some despicable need to dominate?

Irene smiled kindly at Dorothia and, not seeking to impose a demand or press her own agenda unduly, only cast the subtlest glance in the direction of the closed doorway. This minor gesture seemed to cause Dorothia considerable unease as she wrung a napkin in a coquettish manner ill-matched to her age.

"I don't think it's quite possible for you to see Alexi today, Irene," she blurted out finally.

Irene nodded gracefully, almost as though she had expected it would come to this and happy that it had for the fact that it gave her a consummate opportunity to express and demonstrate the magnificence of her new insight and the generosity of her heart. She felt as though a cosmic simulacrum had conceded to grant mercy, all these years removed, allowing her a second opportunity to learn the lesson she could not accept as a child so frightfully fastened against the suffering of another: her long-deceased Grandmother Smythe.

"I understand completely, Dorothia," Irene responded, leaning closely to her companion on the couch, leaving her hand to linger on the supple arm of the soft-skinned woman.

"You do?"

"Of course, I do, Dorothia. I can understand how nervous you must be opening the doors of your home to a visitor. You work very hard to protect your son from what others might do or say. You want to protect him from being hurt. I respect that tremendously, tremendously." Irene felt a warm surge within, enough to convince her to continue with her courtly display of munificence. She looked deep into Dorothia's eyes in a manner that Dorothia found disturbingly intimate. "You don't have to worry though, Dorothia. You can trust me. I have the interests of you and your son at the front of my mind, and my heart. To me he's a talented artist whom I want to know better, nothing more. His disease, well, I'll treat him no differently than anyone else."

Irene sipped her tea, joyously relieved, convinced that words as these would open any doors that were shut, regardless of the padlock on the inside or out.

Had not Dorothia had her own pressing problems, she might have laughed — not with little contempt — at the ridiculous monologue.

"I have no doubt," Dorothia declared slowly, carefully measuring her words, while blurring the mockery of their meaning in melancholic sweetness, "that you would treat him *no differently* than anyone else." Dorothia acceded to a general condescension with a bow of her head as she moved her arm loose of Irene's touch.

"But you see," she continued more confidently, "it's not that I don't trust your every intention. There is not a thing in the world that I wish for more than for my son to meet you so that he can thoroughly convince you in every respect of his immeasurable talent. He has been nothing less than thrilled since I told him of your interest in his work. He's terribly excited to make your acquaintance."

The contrast of this statement to the phone conversation of the prior evening, Irene did not challenge, so swimmingly were they engaged.

"It's just that, well Irene, my son's health is poor as you know. Some

days he is very strong and other days he can scarcely rise from the bed."
As crocodile tears began to flow on cue, Dorothia pressed forward to her
full advantage. "We never know from one day to the next. Today is not
a good day. He painted through the night to surprise you, to honor you
with a special work for your visit. The effort exhausted him. He's such a
good boy, always pleasing others, no matter what the personal cost. He's
weakened his defenses. The doctors rushed over just this morning."

"How horrible! Is he all right? Is there anything I can do?" Irene
again placed her hand on Dorothia's arm. Dorothia controlled her urge
to cringe.

"He needs his rest, Irene. That's all any of us can do. I can't allow
anything to disturb him. Help me to accomplish that; that's what you
can do for him. What a charitable gesture it would be."

"What a toll it must take on you."

"It's a terrible toll, for any mother," Dorothia agreed, suppressing the
knowledge that currently had her seething.

Irene placed her tea on the table before them with a resoluteness far
too enthusiastic for the occasion. "If it means I have to return another
time for my visit, then that is just what I will do."

"Oh, thank you, thank you, you are a grand and understanding
woman."

Irene did not understand it, but she felt as though she had been
transported back in time to a far more civil and graceful age. And
though her own mission would not be accomplished today, she possessed a quiet conviction that by releasing her own needs she had won
something wonderful for herself and, perhaps, the whole of the human
race.

After some additional small talk and continued assurances that
Rooster's deteriorated health represented but a temporary setback and
nothing to be alarmed of in the grand scheme, Irene took her leave.
Only on the way out, as the door closed firmly, did she realize that she
had not even removed her coat. And what of that "special painting"
Rooster had worked through the night to finish in her honor? Standing
on the porch, Irene gravitated to the window that opened into Rooster's
room. Leaning over the railing she peered inside, conscientious of the
fact that she was spying, perhaps even breaching the amicable agreement between Dorothia and herself. Peering past the thick, hibernating

branches, it surprised Irene to see Dorothia, her pearly back to the window, stripping the bed pushed into the corner of the room.

Fearful of being caught, she pushed away and hustled down the walkway into the street.

The idea that she did not know where she would catch a cab did not phase her. What did bother her as she gazed back at the house, the curtains now drawn, was a sudden and gnawing feeling, a suspicion really, that she had just been swindled, masterfully.

⌒

It was early evening when Rooster returned home. A saturnine ambiance pervaded the entryway; the antiquated chandelier that hung from the cathedral ceiling, unlit, deftly demonstrated the capacity to cast gloom as well as merriment. The heartbeat of the hollow house drummed in an eerie, unwholesome silence. Rooster closed the door behind him and listened to the full echo of the hall, of the varnished floors well versed in the language of projecting solitude. He had hoped that she would be gone by the time he arrived home, pulled away by her mystery gentlemen, another pauper she wished for him to meet, to entertain, to impress with his motley, pathetic condition. He hated it, the very thought of what she asked him without words to do. Soli would have even dared to venture a slight profanity — *screw them, screw that servile ingratiation.* So why had Soli bound him to her? Why had Soli declared her executor of the trust?

Rooster sighed. To harbor ungrateful particles within his mind was not his intention. But moments as these, they were a hell, plain and simple. He waited in the darkness, like a bird in an egg, aware that already, somehow, even enclosed in a dark shell, he was not alone; the battle begins in the instant of mutual recognition. First stage probing tests commitment, resolve, conviction, preparation.

A single low-wattage light, pale amber in color, shone from his room. The door was wide open. She would be sitting in his chair, Soli's rocking chair, disdainfully, as though it belonged to her, as though it channeled oricular powers to her, insights into the realm of the dead which empowered her judgments with the supernatural, as though she were heir to a throne of wisdom and knowledge deemed hers even if she could comprehend neither the throne nor its teachings.

Rooster had been preparing himself for just such a dismal scene the whole way home from the lake, where he and Tamara had again walked, spending the warm, sunny afternoon in conversation, casually and easily laughing at the trivial and the complex. She could talk to him, understand him in ways that he failed to understand himself. In the darkness, standing at the front door, his hand still upon the cold, bronze knob, he smiled. Whatever his mother said, it would not matter; it could not defile the memory of the afternoon he now possessed. They had met at the lake, at the exact spot where she had glowed in the delicate moonlight two nights prior. Tamara was waiting when he arrived. On the trunk of a collapsed tree she sat, her slim back to his approach. She watched the sparkling light trip upon the serene water. All his worries, when he saw her waiting — for him — disappeared.

Tamara had packed a lunch of cheese and tomato sandwiches, Oreos, cola and mixed fruit. They had spread a red blanket by the lake's edge and eaten lunch slowly, talking seldom, watching each other, each wondering without asking what the other might be thinking. *She's beautiful,* Rooster had thought as she removed her twill jacket. The brilliant sun, the stillness of the air, caused an unseasonable warmth. He had noticed her hands, again, when she removed her mittens. She had worn little make-up, a light pink lipstick and a gentle layer of sparkling blush. A mandarin turtleneck with tears at the wrists and elbows had hugged her tightly round the neck as her caramel tresses fell round her shoulders. She had smallish eyes tightly set atop her filed nose, creating a stolid concentration that taken properly could put a person at ill ease. Her lips, as she sat facing the sun with her eyes closed, had curled upwards in the corners without quite smiling. Having caught him spying on her, she had tossed a grape at his face that landed in his shirt. The grape's cool peel rolled against his skin.

When she had rummaged in the basket for dessert, the sweater pulled away from her hips, uncovering her behind, which Rooster had studied in a most content manner. This last act of noticing had given Rooster the great pleasure of feeling normal.

They had talked loosely and freely through the afternoon. The red blanket, he had told her, reminded him of the story of how he was born.

"And how was that?" she had asked, coughing, as she swallowed a sip of cola down the wrong tube.

"My father," Rooster had begun, "was a photographer for National

Geographic. He took pictures of insects mostly, though he told everyone he was an ornithologist. My mom was a lot younger than him,
almost twenty years. She was in the Peace Corps in Ghana when they
met. They fell in love, I guess, and she traveled all over the world with
him. They were in South America when I was born. He used to go out
into the jungles of the rain forest."

"The Brazilian."

"Yeah, that's the one. He used to go out to search for new species of
bugs and worms and spiders, things like that. They lived in a village
with the Brazilians. They couldn't understand my parents, and my parents couldn't understand them. I guess my dad knew a few words, not
much really. When my mom was pregnant, just before I was born, they
decided on a signal so that if my mother went into labor, she could get
the news to my father, wherever he was in the rainforest."

"What did they do?" Tamara had asked, leaning forward with
interest.

"Every two hours my dad would send one of the hired natives
climbing up a tall tree from the floor of the forest. From there, just
above the canopy of trees, they could see for miles. They made a flagpole thirty feet tall in the village and flew a white sheet from it. The signal was that when my mother was about to have me, she would have a
villager replace the white sheet on the flagpole with her red blanket.
And it worked perfectly. They say my father was four miles into the
jungle when they spotted the red blanket on their makeshift flagpole.
He made it back to be at her side for my birth. He even discovered a
new species of wasp the same day, too."

"Is that all true?" she'd asked, not quite knowing whether to believe
the extraordinary tale.

"Every word of it," he'd answered, staring off into the shimmering
lake, "even the wasp." How easily they got along, how well they comprehended and accepted the essence of the other.

"What happened to your dad?" she'd asked finally, when a prolonged gap in the conversation merited a question of its type. "Is it all
right for me to ask?"

Rooster had nodded. "My dad got killed by a lioness in North
Africa. He chanced on some cubs and tried to sneak some photos. Baby
lions are rarely photographed in the wild. They say that the mother was

probably there all along, waiting to see how close he would come. Mom says that nothing made sense about it."

"What do you mean?"

"Well, a lioness doesn't usually let any threat get close to its cubs, but this one, at least this is what they say, lured him in with the cubs, actually drew him in using the cubs as bait."

"Which meant the lioness intentionally put the cubs in danger?"

"Yeah."

"It set a trap?" she'd asked in surprise.

Rooster had looked her in the eyes; it was a puzzled look that told her it still bothered him, not just the death, but the manner of the death that went against the grain. "That's right, she set a trap."

They had been silent, both embroiled in reflection, attempting to solve the riddle of the lioness. Tamara had wanted to ask if the lioness had eaten his father, but couldn't find it in herself to ask. Finally, as though to acknowledge that she couldn't figure a reason, she'd stated with linear simplicity, "I'm sorry."

"It's all right. It was a long time ago. I barely remember him."

"You were four," Tamara had stated, wrapping her hands about her arms, rubbing to ward off the chill inside.

Rooster had stared at her as he calculated the math inside his head, re-equating an answer he already knew by heart. "How did you know?"

He'd wondered whether she was a psychic. Tamara wondered whether she had dug too deeply into his life. "I'm sorry," she had repeated, adding, "I shouldn't have."

"But how did you know I was four?"

"It was a guess. I guessed," she'd lied.

He settled back upon his elastic arms, only slightly satisfied. "Oh, a guess." Rooster had grown quiet, self-quelled in provoked circumspection. His thoughts had been divided. "Anyway, my mom and I went back there when I turned fifteen. She told me she wanted me to know him now that I could appreciate him. She told me the same stories over and over and over; every place we went was another story about my father. She really loved him; she did. I remember she used to tell me that what made him so great was that every part of him was good. I'd almost forgotten about that; she hasn't said it in a long time."

With the sun settled high within the sky, water fowl and ducks drifted in squads over the center of the lake. The few patches of ice that had formed in prior days had melted away. Billowy, altocumulus puffs with steep stacks filled the heavens.

"It's peaceful out here."

"The doctors think that's when I was infected."

Tamara and Rooster had stared one to the other in a state of petrification, the source of which they could not conclusively determine. Their individual thoughts, so distinct and different, both offered without precognition, collided, stunning each.

"Why do I feel," she had dared to ask though it made little logical sense, "that we're both saying the same thing?"

Tamara and Rooster had eased into the second half of the afternoon, delighting in a more simple, less taxing conversation. Listening pleased Tamara; for the time being anyhow, he needed to be heard more than she needed to speak. Later, with his head upon her lap, she had read aloud to him from Marcel Phrenol's new book.

"Have you read it?" she'd asked.

"No," he'd answered.

She'd stroked his hair with her open fingers, and he had allowed her. Tamara's voice sung warm and true. Ducks and geese quacked in the background, overcoming all remnants of external intrusion.

"I haven't either."

Turning to a random page near the center of the book, she had broken a crease into the bind and begun in resolution.

"You're not going to start on the first page?"

"Of course not," she had laughed. "I never do."

"Ligaments of Orpheus emerged from the lyre open to the sky, grand as an ancient Greek temple, hyperfine in architecture, abnormal in sensitivity to the divine. Department store mannequins leapt at me. In their plastic I saw the swirl of hypodermic syringes, alkaloids and analgesics, white crystalline aiming for the bulging capillaries of my Christmas swollen tongue. I was choking on the tinsel birth of Christ.

"There were faint, fleeting indications, traced spheres to my love, a traveler's guidebook, an itinerary scorched by crooked flame. This absolute construction of neutrality failed to suit me. No alkaline. No acidity. Neither positive nor negative. And still, still my love wept for me. I waged as a warring nation upon myself, distilled and subatomic. Perfect hydrogen. Castrated of emotions, this is hell.

"Carnage accompanies me, a stench of blood and urine buried in my nocturnal breath. My sanguinary self discovers itself; you are there in promiscuous lines of Latin, Hindu, Sanskrit. The carpers holler, 'You are not sane.'

"'No, I am in love, consumed by love, a gem inlaid, bezel, gypsy style in love.' Say nothing. I drop beneath the seventh strata and see her image for the first time liberated of innuendo. Magnificat anima mea Dominum. Say nothing, but touch the lyre; bend thy tensile microwaves. Be mindful of thy Buddhist friend. This princess ranks above the rani and the rain. There is a Sanskrit word for 'power.'

"A single cut along the axial nerve and all phobia will be gone. All abnormal behavior and all anxiety, all emotions of the mind will be relieved. No disorder will remain. The department store clerks now indulge in neuropathology. My tendons strain from playing, but I am sure that she can hear, the passionate shepherd in Musac to his love. A kleptomaniac in Hades should not come as a great surprise nor should the presence of fear when to punishment we wed our tune."

It was then, as Tamara had turned the page, that Rooster had again begun to understand how much he still needed to learn, how far away from mastery his being remained. Yes, his skills were impressive, but did he have the discipline, the oneness of mind, the deepest commitment? Oneness of mind. What did this mean? Was it even achievable or was it a thing like Ibsen's famous onion that peels away always to reveal another layer, another layer into the perpetual, until the layers become minutia, too delicate for the human hand to ply, tiny peels that in the end defy us, our efforts, peeling themselves. The last pieces you can finger; you wonder are they two peels or more and are they distinct or did my awkward, fumbling human hand, this gross and clumsy motor mechanical thing, tear the final layer into fragments and pieces, turning the core for which we searched into a jumbled, indecipherable mess that we will never prove capable of recreating as it was before our arrival? Is every human effort bound to fail? Are we such inept, impatient creatures that we destroy everything we seek to know, to touch, to love? Ah well, and must every discovery change the state of that which is found?

Rooster had wondered if oneness of mind would be aware of itself. It seemed to him that oneness of mind, like goodness or truth, would be its own goal and its own reward. Free and independent.

He'd asked Tamara for her thoughts on the topic of oneness of mind and she'd spoke of mathematics. She'd said that numbers, in essence, do not have binary opposites.

"What about negative numbers?" Rooster had asked. "Wouldn't -5 be the binary opposite to 5?"

"No," she had smiled. "-5 is just a number. It is as whole, complete and independent as 5 is. Neither relies upon the other to exist. That adding the two together returns us to zero is altogether arbitrary. When you think of it very rationally you understand that there is nothing special about 0. It is not any different from any other number. Like any other number it is whole, complete and independent. Its relationships to other numbers are unique, as are the varying relationships of any numbers. We've simply come to a sort of collective bias that seems to prize zero or one as superior numbers. But they are no better and no worse than say 5 or 37 or 3.14 or -1,243, 864 or 10,111. Each is completely unique. So to the idea that oneness of mind is somehow better than twoness or fourness or negative eightness of mind strikes me as some type of worship for worship's sake. We're doing it to make ourselves feel better, and not because it is somehow, in some real and meaningful way, infinitely superior or preferable to the other options."

Lifting his head from her lap, Rooster had replied quickly, "But that goes against the grain of all thinking. That would mean that there is no such thing as quality. It would mean that there is not even quantity. Big gobs of numbers would just be one number, unique and independent, their relationships subsumed, but that number would be just like all of the other numbers, complete unto itself. And if this were the case then since all the numbers are now unique, you can't create any contrast, so you can't make judgments. Now, in everything being unique, it's become all the same. So it's complete all right, a complete mess!" It was not a well thought out argument and Rooster knew it. But if what Tamara had said were true, then a well thought out argument was not innately superior to a poorly thought out argument.

"I don't understand, Tamara," he continued. "Oneness of mind should not be a confused state."

"What makes you so sure of that?" she retorted. "If you are not sure of what oneness of mind is, how can you tell me what the characteristics of it are or are not? What proof would you have to demonstrate that oneness of mind would not be confused?"

"It wouldn't make sense."

"To whom?"

"To me."

"But you don't have oneness of mind, so how would you know? Or do you? And isn't that exactly what you thought in the beginning, that a person with oneness of mind could conceivably not even know they have oneness of mind unless, and this is the exception you cited, the object of their oneness of mind was oneness of mind?"

"It all seems quite hopeless to understand or achieve," Rooster had admitted.

"I disagree. It all seems quite hopeless to understand, but it seems quite achievable if one is innocent of its achievement."

"You mean as an *object* to be attained?"

"Exactly."

Both had smiled, for they had just passed through their first disagreement and from it come to understand that they were free to disagree and — more importantly — quite equal in their valuation of the other's ideas.

"We should go soon," Tamara had announced. The sun had begun to set, its round face cut from below by a horizon of distant trees. Shadows were slowly claiming the lake — large patches of dark shade trimmed at odd edges by the local milieu, creating puzzle pieces that existed for a brief span of time, in a constant state of transmogrification, matching only the progress of another day arriving at a close. Where the inoculant rays of the day still tarried in bright orange wisps, a dazzling explosion of color trickled upon the flat lake, reflecting off the sheer runway of glass. A swan gracefully descended, causing ripples to cascade in its marvelous wake.

"Just a little longer," Rooster had requested, staring directly into the sun, as is possible towards the end of the day.

"As long as you need," Tamara had answered, perceiving Rooster's sadness, adding silently to herself, *my love.*

℗

"Alexi!" His mother called from his own room, breaking the ease of his reflection. Supported by the recent memory, the darkness in which he stood no longer felt so ominous, so lonesome.

"Yes, Mother, it's me," he answered evenly, slicing through the diminutive aura she sought to cast. This darkness, he thought for the first time as he stared at the crystal amulets of the chandelier hanging above his head, has been with me my whole life. He wondered if Soli's ghost or that of his father balanced there now, swinging in observation, watchful, unsure of the final verdict.

Rooster's eyes were fixated upon the splash of pale orange light being emitted from his room. Dorothia stepped forward and stood at the threshold of the room, blocking the gentle illumination with her frame and her shadow.

"Where have you been?" she demanded.

It was the faraway, opulent look in his eyes that gave her heart a reason to tremble. She recognized it instantly, the opiate, faithful gaze, too elsewhere to be affected by the here, listless to the present, captured by a recurring memory of a sweet past and the attracting promise of an undeniable future. Retreating into the room, her absence allowed the light's return.

Rooster followed. He had no choice but to endure the impending discomfort.

Dorothia sat motionless in the rocker, her lusterless eyes consciously deadened for effect. She had rearranged his room, as though to make it more hers than his own. The bedsheets she had stripped and changed, his coffee table books of the masters, his idols — Renoir, Van Gogh, O'Keefe, Kandinsky, Rembrant, Pollack, Raphael, Solzhenitsyn, Rodin — were neatly stacked and shelved. His desk of scattered sketches was narrowly arranged, his palette washed, his oils capped, his brushes soaked in turpentine. There were colors on the active palette she had destroyed that would be impossible to recreate exactly as they had been. Rooster knew she was not ignorant to this; she fathomed the extreme care, the precision he took in developing hues, inflections of color. The half-finished painting that he now felt the extreme urge to complete, rested on the easel. His first emotion was anger for he would be incapable of completing the thing as envisioned, but then he had a deeper thought, a receptive thought. Things divide; he would create a second color scheme and paint of this deeper mode of operation, the division of things. He would work with whatever materials remained. He would adapt.

"What am I to do?" her lugubrious voice buttered the air.

Removing his coat and mittens, Rooster approached the easel. Slowly unfurling the scarf wrapped round his neck, he surveyed the unfinished painting. With long licks of the eyes he rethought its intent, its possibilities. The painting, what existed thus far, reminded Rooster of the breaking of a gray day, an amber-yellow frost radiating through subdued though dominant tones. The painting suggested to Rooster, again, the idea of the substratum, something powerful and unseen, riding just below the surface of the inimical storm. Where would this undeniable, inflammatory force finally choose to emerge?

Rooster removed two thick brushes from the turpentine and squeezed their heads in a rag. Unscrewing the caps from several tubes of paint, he pressed from the bottom as one would the last tube of toothpaste, mindful of economy and maximization. At intervals he placed potent gobs of the paint upon the palette. With a plastic scalpel, he began a blending process, searching like a scientist.

In beginning this process he always thought of the philosopher David Hume, an analytic thinker of social principle, who had by reason and argument come to conclude that there are perfect fits within this world, that a man or a woman or a color has a perfect complement for which it is intended. All unions, other than the union with the perfect one, will be but accidents and errors, some less apparent than others, dependent upon the degree of refinement of the individual's ability to discern. At first this appears a romantic concept, for fate would seem to direct this process of selection. Then we awake, becoming aware that though there are perfect fits, it is not absolutely necessary that we will find such a fit, that we will possess the vigilance or the gumption, not only to search for it, but to believe in its existence.

Hume helped others to conceive of his theory through a discussion of hues and shades of color. If all blues were laid out before the world as a rainbow is in the sky, we would see the contrasts of the varying, non-eternal, non-infinite blues, and we would be able to organize these shades in a manner that made sense to us, one after the other, like a series of steps rising to the infinite and the eternal. And when the whole scale of the shades of blue were laid out and ordered, what if, *what if* there were a single gap? What would we seek? Would any color do? Or would there be in this beautifully patterned structure, this finally explicable pathway, a single choice — no choice at all really — with regards to what would satisfy the single gap? Hume had conceived a puzzle, a puzzle of color that seeks fulfillment not through size or shape but through tone, shade and something still more rare.

And this is how Rooster thought as he blended his paint, dismissing time in a perpetual quest for quality, knowing that single gap as a chasm which he alone bore the responsibility to fill. The hue must be perfect, for within each and every key, there exists another finite world with a single gap all its own. But that gap — the gap within the gap — this, above all, must never be made apparent, never discussed. Chasms filled become pathways for another, better than us, born more innocent. And what would innocence be, Rooster wondered; certainly not ignorance of the breach but actually freedom from the breach, like a mother filled with a child in the womb.

"I'm sorry, Mother." Rooster spoke gently, resolved of conflict as he inspected the color forming in the light, its tone and hue affected by light.

Dorothia sighed the reluctant sough of surrender. She was staring at a blank wall; all the walls were bare. Rooster preferred the room sparse. It kept him relatively free of subconscious influences, of unplanned icons and idols. His picture books of the masters he would often look through for inspiration, but never for long. He sought to use them as a frog uses a lily pad, as touchstones to promote his own leaping away from the traditional, the known, the accomplished.

"I sometimes wonder if we will achieve anything at all." The words were fraught by resignation. Rooster appreciated how difficult it must have been for her to make such a confession. Gently he touched the scalpel to a ringlet of silver paint and blended it slowly with a scintilla of lavender.

"I don't want to meet that woman. Whether she wants to sell my paintings or not has nothing to do with me."

Dorothia turned the chair and gazed at her son with incredulous eyes. "Rooster, all I wanted was for you to meet her."

The conversation was not a new one. She always wanted him to meet someone, someone that could help them. "Mom, we don't have to worry about money. Soli took care of that. We don't have to impress anyone anymore. Now I can paint, really paint."

"Alexi." Dorothia shook her head. His words hurt her deeply and Rooster knew it, but he did not, nor had he ever, understood why. "It has never been about the money. What I have sought to do with you, for you, *for us*, has nothing to do with money. Yes, in the beginning maybe it did. You know how hard I worked for us to keep us going, to provide you with the best opportunities."

"I know," Rooster assented respectfully.

"I want you to be somebody, Rooster, like your father was, but nobody ever knew it. I want people to know that . . . while you're alive. I want you to know what it's like to be respected, to be honored and recognized for what you've done, what you've suffered, what you've given and overcome. I want better for you. Besides, Soli didn't leave us that much. . . ."

Rooster put aside the palette. Warm cerulean blue, born of pink and yellow dabs, mixed in the center, unique as semen, second half of the protozoan miracle.

"But Mother, don't you see?" he pleaded. "I've leprosy. Even if people know me as a painter it won't mean anything to me. No one can give me back what the disease has taken." Even as he said it, he thought of Tamara and wondered if his words held true.

"Would it have been so much to meet Irene? She loves your work. It would have meant the world to her. She flew from New Mexico just to meet you. I went to New Mexico just to sell you." He could sense that his mother was growing pugnacious, deeper frustrations emerging. "Would it be so hard for you to help a little? Are you such an ungrateful, selfish child?"

"She's your friend. Why do I have to meet her? So that she can get a good look at me? Test me? Find out what makes me tick, get some good stories about me that will help her sell the leper artist! She doesn't want to meet me. She wants to meet the painter."

Dorothia stared at her son as he uttered what had sounded to her like a mad protest. "Alexi, *you* are the artist! What are you talking about? You can't talk about yourself as though you are not what you are."

Putting aside the palette, Rooster pressed the backs of his wrapped hands to his face and pressed upon his temples. "Mother, would she want to meet me if I weren't a painter? Would she?"

"Well, no. But that's silly. She wouldn't even have a chance to know about you. She wouldn't know enough about you to want to meet you."

"Then what is she looking for? Is she looking for paintings or is she looking for painters?"

"Rooster, this is nonsense. They're one and the same."

"Are they?"

"Of course, she told me about this. She likes dealing in living artists because it is more of a risk for her. Also, the painters are still painting so she can work with them to create and meet demands in a way that you can't with dead artists who will never produce a new work."

"Then for her it is about selling as much art as she can for the highest price that she can, and that's why she wants to see me. But that's not how I paint or why I paint, so why would I want to meet her to have a conversation on how I might do it otherwise?"

"Rooster, you're twisting it all around. She wants your vision. Your way of seeing and expressing the world. She told me just that. It's not all about money. Money is just one aspect of the thing. She values your artistic insight."

"Then I don't need to paint."

"Rooster, why are you doing this? They are inseparable."

"Do you know that all I do is paint? I sit here, removed from the world, and I paint day after day, night after night, at all hours, alone in my little cubicle, painting, painting, painting. And the whole world out there moves on. What kind of insights could I possibly have into that world?"

"Maybe you have insights into another world. One that's better than the world out there. Maybe that's what she wants, access to that."

"But is that my painting or is that me, the person who doesn't paint?"

"I don't see it, Alexi. I don't see what you're getting at. All this talk makes me quite uncomfortable. You're a painter. You've always been a painter. You have had the best instruction anyone could hope for and you work at it constantly, constantly getting better. Yes, you sit in this room for hours and days on end. Yes, you don't see much of the world. Yes, you have a disease. But maybe these are the things that make you special, make your world special, make your world worth knowing and understanding for the rest of us. Yours is a blessing, Alexi."

"Dad ventured throughout the whole world, saw things I can't even imagine; I don't even leave this room. You act as though the two are equal."

"They are, Rooster. They are. You imagine things no one can see."

They sat like exhausted opponents in the dim light of the room. Their conversation belonged to the daytime, but there it was, in the embrace of the night, at a time when soothing tea should be ordered from the kitchen. Wearily, Dorothia shrugged, acknowledging that the irrational cannot be pierced through with reason.

"Do you know what your father's favorite book was?" Dorothia asked, her tone reflective and brightening, content to take respite from their ideological battle.

"No, I don't," he admitted.

From one corner of the mouth, from that part of her face that responded to memories of the spirit, she smiled. "*The Book of Tea*."

"I've never heard of it."

"No, I don't suppose you would have. It was written in 1905 by a Japanese man named Okakura Kurazowa. The same year as Einstein's paper, that's how I remember that. Kurazowa had the idea that East and West could best meet and solve their differences over a cup of tea. Because tea drinking has a rich tradition in both East and West, he saw it as a perfect metaphor, common ground among differing traditions. The Japanese have the sacred Tea Ceremony and the West has Tea Time. Your father loved his tea at the end of a day. He used to say, 'If you can share a cup of tea, you are halfway to forgiveness.'"

"You've never told me that."

Dorothia opened her palms in amenity. "I just thought of it now. It's a silly thought. I'm not sure that it has anything to do with what we were discussing. It might," she left off enigmatically, then continued, "I wish your father were still here, did you know that? I still think of him every day. You can't understand; he'd be so very proud of you, just like I am. . . ."

Rooster listened intently as his mother gazed at the incomplete painting with longing. Rooster waited, feeling her willingness to share something of value ebbing forward, close to his world.

"What is it, Mother?"

She looked at her son with loving, forgiving eyes. Tilting her head almost shyly she avoided the heart of the question, asking, "Would you trust me, Alexi? These things I do, I do of love. Will you do these things for your mother, even if you don't understand? It's so hard for you to understand the way a mother protects, so very hard, I know."

9

A GUSTING WIND BLEW through the cavernous suite composing Marcel's penthouse. Despite the frigid air, almost in protest to it, Marcel had opened all six windows and the terrace doors of the suite to create a vigorous, sweeping cross-current through the room. Standing naked in a window, he surveyed the great city of Boston. It was a clear night for sterling regret. He could see the Citgo sign of old, faithful Fenway and the blazing lights of the ballpark illuminating another night game by Kenmore Square.

Anchored to Marcel's shoulder, Prophet's feathers bristled in the wind. The crow's wings were expanded as though engaged in an attempt to remember the gift of flight. The feathers of the wings quivered in the wind, especially one feather upon the right wing that hung lower than the rest, slightly out of place, like a cowlick that refuses grooming. The minor deformation resulted from a brief tangle with an uppity housecat that had thought the bird a tender plaything for the paws. The event, for Prophet, had been formative.

They had been away, Marcel and Prophet, on retreat in Havana, Cuba. Marcel had visited the island nation many times in the past, but this time his visit had unexpectedly and undesirably succeeded in capturing the attention of the country's long time ruler, Fidel Castro. This type of attention was the last thing that Marcel craved; in previous years he had come to the country mainly for the privacy it afforded him. He emphatically agreed with George Bernard Shaw's 1933 remark, "An American has no sense of privacy. He does not know what it means. There is no such thing in the country." In contrast, it had never failed to amaze him how well the communist system, for all its failings, generally succeeded in nurturing and safeguarding personal privacy. Regardless of Marcel's keen desire to maintain the haven of this privacy, he could not ignore Castro's unusual summons. He even found himself wondering whether the leader wished to speak of literature or baseball, his own love of the game as widely known as the communist leader's.

Before meeting Castro, Marcel was told by soldiers that he would have to leave his dirty bird outside the general's chambers. He protested but gradually acquiesced; his Spanish was not so strong as the guns slung over the shoulders of the dictator's guardians. Marcel did succeed in procuring a long piece of string that he tied round the bird's leg before securing the other end to a window crank. Prophet had three feet of slack and high ground. The soldiers, prodding Marcel forward with the stiff, tappered nozzles of their menacing guns, assured him with devious smiles he did not trust that the bird would be *bueno*.

Passing through the outer sanctuary of the splendid, sprawling, bungalow estate, Marcel wondered if he had not written something in a previous book that would have caused the dictator anger. He knew it was possible, for though he could be counted on to recall all of the details, he could scarcely be expected to predict all of their effects. Pushed into the chamber by the guards, Marcel's first glimpse of Fidel Castro left a rich and indelible image in his mind. There Fidel stood, a titanium shafted putter held loosely in his hands, a stubby cigar dangling persistently from his lips. In green fatigues, a full, unkempt beard about his colorful face, the long time dictator appeared boyish. As the doors were shut behind them, leaving him alone with the general, Marcel wondered just how little effort it would take to turn a playful putter into a vicious weapon. Fidel stroked the dimpled ball across the carpet where it settled, perfectly placed, an inch before Marcel's feet.

Outside, after more than an hour of absence by the owner of the bird, the soldiers grew restless, the summer heat infiltrating their various boredoms. One of the soldiers, borrowing a bottle of rum from a recent delivery of supplies, set to work instigating a great and entertaining drama for his fellow compatriots. The man's name was Carlos Juan Carlo, and he had recently been demoted. After swallowing deeply of the spiced rum himself, he passed the bottle to the others with the exceeding generosity of one giving away the possessions of another.

This generosity was matched only by the sharp sting of his dry, scorpion wit.

"It's a day sent direct from hell when an American bends the General's ear."

The others, greedy for the liquor, nodded in agreement, understanding nothing, aiming solely to ingratiate themselves into procurement of the stolen bottle.

Carlos Juan Carlo continued. "Another manly Hemingway from the Americas wants to become a manly Cuban. Aye, deep down they are all aware that one Cuban man is better than ten American men. We have the *huervos*, eh!"

This type of bold proclamation before a friendly crowd drew beaming approval from all collected, even those who had not yet indulged in the fire of drink.

"They think they're so superior, these Americans. They throw their weight around and call it justice. Aye!"

"Aye!" the others had assented as the bottle came to their hands.

"Do you know what justice is in the Americas? Do you know what they use for a symbol of justice?"

"A pig!" yelled one man, causing a riotous outburst of laughter. More soldiers had gathered from the original three. There were six and then seven. Two cooks had emerged from the kitchen with sherry. They were immediately absorbed and accepted into the enclave.

"A dog," cursed another.

"A woman!" shouted a third, unsure of the impetus.

Carlos Juan Carlo leaped into action, pointing at the man who had offered the final annunciation, shocking them all. He peered at the man with a single, unmoving eye and an arm extended, pointing, as the bottle of rum, half consumed, dangled from the sweaty finger he had used to cork it. "That's right! A woman. And do you know why, my friend? My manly, Cuban friend?"

The man had shrugged as he lunged forward, clutching at the bottle of rum that Carlos Juan Carlo gave up freely.

"You know because you know an American man! That's how you know their symbol for justice. Because the American man is cowardly like a dog, and would gladly prefer a woman to make all his decisions."

The others had laughed. More rum was stolen. An entire case had appeared. "And now our leader listens to one! Wrapped in the pitiful American's spell." Carlos Juan Carlo spat on the floor. "American."

From the distance Prophet had crowed urgently.

"American men are cowards!" one shouted out, grabbing a fresh bottle from the case.

"They use their women as shields."

"They're dogs!"

"And pigs!" The crowd had continued to swell, having grown to thirteen or fourteen, fifteen with the children. A mob was reached at twenty. The rum poured liberally. The bird's shrill echoes went unnoticed.

A circle had formed about Carlos Juan Carlo as he held court before the lusty, drunken eyes. Two women had joined the cadre.

"American men," one had shuddered vehemently, adding her spit to the floor. She didn't spit like a man, but they'd cheer her with applause for celebrating their sentiment, their courage, their politics.

"But that's not the end of their symbol, these Americans. These *champions* of justice." The others had spurned the use of the word with a riotous chorus of boos.

"No, not only do these American men . . ."

"Boys!"

"Yes, these American boys. Not only do these American boys hide behind their women, but they blindfold her so that she cannot see."

"Because they're ashamed!"

"Little boys!" the first woman had shouted.

"Give me a Cuban man to stir my blood with passion," the second woman had added to the delight of the men.

"Dogs!". . . "Pigs!" . . . "Americans!"

"Yes," Carlos Juan Carlo crooned in approval as he had raised his bottle for a satirical toast, "To American justice, blind and weak!"

"Aye, let them always be so feminine." A shrill, violent caw.

"Give us a real Cuban man!" The bottles were upturned in boisterous celebration. A cheer was raised in unison. Carlos Juan Carlo stood drunk and triumphantly at center.

At the height of their boisterous celebration the doors blasted open, banging with a boom against the rich, carved frames. Three soldiers had entered from the direction of the general's chamber several turns down the hallway. The one in front glared at Carlos Juan Carlo.

"What is this?" he had demanded as his attending soldiers shut the doors behind them. Children, lifted upon their mothers' shoulders, peered in from outside.

Carlos Juan Carlo had surveyed the scene, calculated his odds with the confidence of a cut throat. Bolstered by the crowd, sensing that he was on the verge of possessing his own mob, his own legend, he'd swaggered forward. "We are celebrating Cuba, mon capitan. We are cursing that American dog that currently fills the ear of our great leader with lies and propaganda, the filthy, American spy!"

"It would be best, Juan Carlo, if you . . ." the captain had thought to finish his sentence with the words, *did know your place.* But as he prepared to align himself against the rebel, he saw more closely the hungry faces of the throng, and he understood that he had underestimated Juan Carlo through the act of demotion. Prepared to fight for their new hero, the mob lingered attentively on the captain's words. A terrible shift in the tide had occurred, at least for now, under the incendiary spell of nationalism and rum, a dangerous blend. The captain had thought it through in a tense moment's silence. Making eye contact with Carlos Juan Carlo, he submitted to his own temporarily weakened position. Besides, when all was said and done, the captain also resented the American's presence. "It would be best, Juan Carlo," the captain had repeated with a flamboyant wave of his hat, "if you would pass me a strong bottle of rum, that I may make a toast to Cuba with you."

The crowd had cheered in delight, reinvigorated in the revolutionary spirit of their nation.

"To Castro! He'll own the American dog before he is done!" The frenzied crowd cursed to their heart's content, ravaged in their own cause, understanding freedom, hating the American even as they knew that they could not help but love him.

"To Castro! To El Presidente Castro!" They had gaily celebrated their farce of revolution and insurrection.

And then the terrible thing had happened. One soldier, young and green and wildly drunk, charged into the room with the black bird raised high above his head. Prophet struggled vainly to escape the grimy hands, releasing shrill cry after shrill cry, the bloodthirsty screams of a woman; the most chilling sound that can be.

The young fool had entered the heart of the convocation, grinning with pride as the assembly, white with terror, stared at what he had done. The boy, Marcos del Rios, generally mild and stupid, was flushed from the alcohol that raced within his capillaries. He shouted out as he held the prize above his head. "Death to the American! Death to American justice!"

The gathered crowd fell silent as the day. The sweltering sun again made the full force of its residence known. Collectively they'd wished for the return of stale boredom. Their eyes glanced to the stolen bottles of rum, the opened crate for which there would be hell to pay. The captain had stepped forward out of habit, expecting to know what to do to put things right. A bead of musky sweat dripped down the length of his wide, pock-marked nose; no words had come. He stood as dumb as the others, shocked at the reality that had claimed them.

Marcos del Rios, not comprehending the seriousness of the thing he had said or the irony of their celebration, misinterpreted the stunned silence. Thinking that they simply did not understand what he had said or what the bird represented he frantically, zealously explained, all the while exhibiting a remarkable pleasure with himself for what he perceived a great cleverness.

"You see this bird?" he had addressed the crowd. Prophet, caught within the tight, throttling, grimy clutch, grew silent now, wise enough to tremble in fear. "This is the American justice! A blind woman. Blind, just like this bird. And weak, just like this bird. Not an eagle, a pathetic little crow. A blind, little woman." Marcos had assumed that he was not making sense, that because of his excitement and the liquor, the crowd had not understood him. He blamed his stupidity; in his head he knew what he wanted to articulate.

The crowd had understood perfectly. Their reaction stunned him, and in his impetuousness, rather than retreating, he stepped deeper into the mistake believing that this would again incite the crowd to its previous frenzy. "Death to American Justice!" he'd again proclaimed, this time spitting into the passive face of the bird.

It was then, in the terrible gap of horrid, perverse silence that followed, that Marcos del Rios perceived the unspoken essence of his nation, their great hope of liberation.

A cat from the house had clamored at the leaden feet of Marcos del Rios, aroused by a lascivious desire. Carlos Juan Carlo had felt the noose tightening round his neck. Through his single act of stupidity, this fool of the mob had transformed the moment of mythic underground victory into a terrible act of open treason. His act of heroism was now in jeopardy of being marked forever by this ignoble end. Transfixed, he'd gazed at the blind bird in desperation, praying simultaneously to Christ and the Blessed Virgin Mary for a miracle.

The prayer had received an answer, for as the crowd hung in a stuporous lassitude, the cat reared back, leaping from the floor, unleashing a million years of forgotten instincts. At least five feet in the air, it was not the force of the cat slapping at his hands but the surprise of seeing the old housecat stretched with such extreme motivation, over five feet in the air, that had caused Marcos del Rios to lose hold of the bird.

Prophet had dropped to the ground ungracefully, wings flailing in short, staccato strokes. The cat spun upon landing, peering upwards first to the dull, grimy hands of Marcos del Rios. Not spying its prize there, it scanned the floor greedily. Prophet meanwhile had bounced in circles of confusion, able to discern only the great danger of the moment. The old housecat pounced when Prophet's backside was turned, slapping at the neck with its paws, nails protracted. The bird collapsed and the two went rolling like tumbleweed across the floor in a single black mass of hysteria.

"Kill him, *Gordita!*" one of the women had cheered, shattering the paralyzed exegesis. A common housecat of the estate, the cat belonged to no one directly, and thus, it was champion of all.

The woman's advocacy broke the floodgate of the crowd. Immediately the face of the mob returned — a single, grand snarl, hungering for blood. After three rolls upon the wooden floor, Prophet, reaching round, succeeded in biting the old housecat in the neck, sending the cat scuttling backwards protectively.

"Kill him, Gordita, kill him!"

Prophet had stood in stillness, head tilted backwards and to the side in a knowing fashion, as though studying signs, accessing information unknowable to the sighted. The old housecat stalked about carefully, seeking an ideal opening for a second attack. But Prophet had turned, head twitching at unexpected moments, tracking the cat with a honed internal radar or, at the very least, a well played bluff.

The old housecat had stalked towards the bird at an angle.

Mimicking the elegant knights L-shaped attack in chess, the cat intended to cut in at the last moment. But Prophet, cowl intense with concentration, had perfectly matched the path of the cat and even leapt forward, flapping its wings, threatening to descend upon the stalker from above. With its talons spread full, Prophet had lashed at the cat, swiping at the surprised creature that slipped as it attempted to reverse course. The right talon swept downward, its razor claws slicing beneath the opponent's left eye in a bloody line that ended at the old housecat's gray nose. The hostile cat had shrieked in distress, hissing as it leapt away, its mane bristling on end.

Prophet had hopped two steps forward and the cat retreated further, frightfully shocked by this deft opponent.

The mob would not be satiated. "Kill him, *Gordita!*" someone yelled.

"Get him, bird," others had begun to urge, indifferent to the result, now that first blood was spilled. The old housecat would have been content enough to slink away, calling it a draw, but those in the circle had other ideas. Carlos Juan Carlo, ever the opportunist, stepped on the length of twine, still attached to the bird's leg, halfway along its length.

Prophet shrieked an alarm in awareness of this new attack, pecking tenaciously at the twine that snared the leg and freedom. Seeing the compatriot's restraint as an opportunity to reclaim damaged pride tempted the cat forward. It again stalked the inner circle aggressively, but the sting of the nose created doubt enough to prevent a second strike.

"Give pussy a push," Carlos Juan Carlo had shouted with drunken glee.

Bending down, hands had pushed the cat across the floor. The old housecat slid in half circles into the bird.

"Fight, fight!" the mob had screamed as blood from the cat's wound dripped upon the varnished wooden planks. "Cuba, Cuba!"

"Death to American Justice!"

"*Gordita!*"

"Get his bird, get him!"

"Little Devil!"

The spinning cat had bowled over Prophet who even fallen on its side, again under feline assault, continued wrestling with the twine cord. The cat bit into Prophet's wing and refused to let go, tugging at the wing with forceful jerking motions of the neck as Carlos Juan Carlo slowly pulled his foot backwards, thereby working in collaboration with the old housecat to draw Prophet into mutually independent and opposite directions.

Torn asunder, a mangled, twisted form, Prophet had sung out in pain, a note long and melodious, like a negro spiritual that accepts the suffering even as it affirms the righteousness of God in the here, the now and the everlasting future. The hungry crowd had pressed in deafly, consumed by their lusty fervor. Only Marcel heard the steady, piercing lamentation as he sprinted down the hallway in fear and barreled through the doorways, charging headlong into Carlos Juan Carlo, knocking him to the ground to rescue the voice of America. Prophet, now free of dichotomy, fearlessly attacked the cat, batting it away with wings and beak and talons. No one stopped Marcel. The old housecat had scurried away, disappearing, as did the mob, the crowd, the rum and Carlos Juan Carlo.

Marcel held the cold, trembling bird in his hands, stroking the feathers, calming, calming as Fidel, puffing away at a thick, well-drafted cigar, watched from the gloaming of the lightless hallway, nodding in appreciation and outright approval.

And thus the two stood, the great novelist and his plaintive-comic muse, regaled in the naked wind overlooking the city of Boston. A knock at the door called Marcel back from the memory. He noted how his eyes had lingered for all this time on the reflection of light, on the interplay of brilliance and darkness along the Charles River and the great institutes of higher learning that lined its banks. He shut the window and the crosswind died. Prophet cawed, crying out for one more moment of remembrance. A second knock at the door. Marcel set the bird on its perch, placed a peanut in the bird's beak and stroked the cowlicked feather that had never healed to its original state following the battle. On the perch Prophet flapped both wings, as though in remonstration to an improper thought.

"Caw-caw, Caw-caw!"

Marcel laughed lovingly, "Yes, Prophet, I know. I know you can still fly."

cf

Answering the door on the third knock, Marcel greeted Dorothia with a kiss. Running a hand along his chest and to his thigh, she surveyed the supple form of his naked body.

"And what if it wasn't me?"

"Oh," he shrugged indifferently, "I knew it was you. Who else would it be?"

"I thought we were going out to dinner tonight. You don't look like we're going out to dinner. Why is it so cold in here? My God, all of your windows are open."

Prophet let out two long cries of correction as though to say that not all of the windows were open, for if all of the windows were open there would be the strong crosswind, and Prophet would be remembering what it was to fly.

"That window's not open," Marcel translated, pointing at the single shut window.

Slamming windows shut, Dorothia rushed about the room. "No windows should be open! What's wrong with you? It's freezing out."

"It's 42 degrees, a perfect night for baseball. Want a drink?" Marcel stood at the wet bar, his penis dangling against the polished marble.

Grasping her cashmere jacket tightly around herself, Dorothia collapsed into a tan ottoman. "Perfect if you're a polar bear."

Marcel made her a drink. Whiskey Coke. "Here, you'll feel better. What's wrong? You want me to put on a robe? I'll put on a robe. Still, I'm imperishable underneath, like an aardvark. Look at my physique. Olympian." He preened before her.

The dimensions of his personality, conscious and unconscious, were still flowering. She sipped at the drink, wincing at the strength. He made her laugh at his apish, yet volatile playfulness. They had been with each other for over three weeks. They now shared time together on a nearly daily basis. In that time he had evolved before her, demonstrating himself to be a multi-dimensional being, capable of real emotion and relationship. She had doubted that in the beginning, though she would have clung regardless for the purpose of her goal. Now she genuinely cherished their time together, though she could have done with less drinking.

"I think they're on the tube. We can order up and watch the end of the game."

"Doesn't baseball season ever end? It seems like it's been going on forever."

"Baby, this is the playoffs. This is the year we break the Bambino's curse. I've been too nervous to even watch."

Dorothia peered at him over the lip of her glass. "The what?"

"I thought you were from here."

"I am . . . mostly."

Marcel thought about it then shrugged it off as he gulped away at his drink. "The curse of the Bambino. Babe Ruth. He cursed the Red Sox when they traded him to the Yanks in 1919. Said they'd never win another championship. After the trade the Yanks won 10 of the next 14 pennants. Red Sox didn't win one. In fact, they finished dead last 10 of the next 14 years. Bucky Dent's game winner. The ball through Buckner's legs in '86. It's all the curse of the Bambino, old ghosts haunting the Red Sox. Phantoms in the dugout. Four score plus years and no World Championship for this great city. Last time they won was in 1918. This year it's coming to an end. After the way they dug in and held on to the division pennant in the face of the Yankees' late run, I can feel it."

Vaguely Dorothia recalled the name of Babe Ruth and maybe even something about a curse of some sort. She thought it some type of cult thing. She answered patronizingly, "I see."

Marcel thought of his wife, how much colder than this room the headstone must be. "Do you?"

"I had a dreadful day today," she began, loosened by the liquor.

"Commercial. What happened?"

Dorothia sat prone to remove her coat. The effort required to remove the coat she performed with such exaggeration as to make it appear a barbarous inconvenience.

The windows were shut tightly. Already warmer, she picked up the receiver and ordered two dinners, a chicken and a fish, sauce on the side.

The game returned to the screen, post-game wrap-up. Red Sox. 4 Runs. 8 Hits. 0 Errors. Anaheim Angels. 6 Runs. 10 Hits. 1 Error.

"Damn it. They blew it!"

"Bambini?"

"Bambino."

"Is that the end of the season?"

Marcel finished the drink with a flourish of disgust. "No, it's the second game of the first round of the playoffs."

"And how many games is this?"

"Best of five. They're split at 1-1."

And then the season is over?" She was bored.

"No, if they win they go to the American League Championship Series."

"And if they win that, they'll break this curse thing?"

"No, they'd have to win the World Series."

"Which is when?"

"After the American League Championship Series."

"Like I said," she bit into an ice cube as she reached the bottom of her drink, "it seems to go on forever."

Marcel clicked off the picture and tossed the remote aside. Though he didn't say it, there was something to what she said, especially since the rearrangement of the divisions and the introduction of wild cards into the playoff picture. After all, what sense could be found in the fact that though the Red Sox had won the A.L. East, it remained a strong possibility that they would meet the wild card Yankees in the A.L.C.S.? If you beat a team straight up in your division after a 150 plus game season, you shouldn't have to play them off. Hell, he thought, maybe Kansas City will knock them out.

Legs curled beneath her on the sofa, Dorothia fingered the rim of the glass. It was a sexy pose. Ice melting.

"So what's your bad news?" Marcel asked, forcing himself to think about something other than the curse of Ruth.

"Oh, it's that bitch!"

"Another drink?" Pulling a chemise robe round his shoulders, he headed to the bar.

"I love the feel of your skin. Do you know that?"

Marcel poured two more drinks. "So who's the bitch?"

"Oh, some little hussy wants my son's money."

"So what do you care?"

"What do you mean, 'What do I care?'"

Marcel dropped sideways over the arm of the ottoman. Stretching towards her, pressing the fresh drink to her lips, he alleviated her of the burden of choice. She swallowed quickly to avoid having the bourbon drink spill upon her chambray blouse.

"I wish you were black. I've always wanted to be with a black woman."

She ignored the barb. She understood that he thrust such sentiments into space not because he wanted to hurt her but because he wanted to protect himself. Still, she did not doubt that he meant what he said. She responded with a sardonic smile. "Why not just get a psychoanalyst and a prostitute, Marcel? They'd at least pretend to appreciate your romantic prattle."

Moving to the sofa, Marcel kissed her hand as he massaged her heavy breasts through the material of the blouse; her head fell back to expose the peach cream neck. "And why is that, my dear?" he asked seductively, anticipating the wit of the punch line, fully cognizant of the buttons it would push.

Working her hand between his legs, she sighed. "That way one could tell you how good you are, while the other talks to you about your mother."

"You're a sick little girl, do you know that?"

"You'd have . . ." she moaned, "the equivalent . . . aaahhh . . . of your mother telling you . . . aaaahhhh . . . how good you . . . aaaahrre in bed."

"A perverse, sick little thing."

"And you're an absolute genius."

Slipping onto the oriental rug, they made love in undulating, dreamlike swirls, their moans of bliss rising to the ceiling and returning to their ears as splendid echoes of unrefined, uncensored, beautiful lust, the monogamous, salacious union of a man and woman. She found him soft. He found her hard. Together they were an endorphin rush and chocolate, thick, warm and sweet.

With another drink in hand he poured the contents over her breasts, permanently staining the furniture and the rug to which the liquids dripped. "Marcel!" she cried, "Marcel." Like a stricken animal, wounded by the plague and worse, Marcel shuddered helplessly, lost and helpless, a raw skein.

Both were sweaty and flushed with eyes scrolled deep within the recesses of the skull, the muscles of their face taut, like patients of electric shock. Dorothia rolled atop Marcel and covered his mouth with thin, voracious lips. Saliva dripping between them, she reached beneath Marcel, taking his buttocks in her hands, thrusting herself around him, wishing to consume him, so that he would know her to the very root and draw his nourishment, as she did, direct from mother earth.

With purple painted nails she raked his chest, arching backwards in slow, groaning delight. There was a knock at the door. "Leave it!" she commanded desperately as Marcel struggled beneath her to absorb her full breast, his greatest mouthful spilling over glutinously as she twitched spontaneously in a carriage of pain and delight.

All was silent but for the heavy breathing, the literal begging of two, holy, animal souls.

Head cocked left, Prophet listened to the communion of the cosmos.

Slipping upon the sweat, Dorothia settled with an ear turned to Marcel's firm, flat stomach where, beyond the silly, unrhythmic gurgles of his belly, she could still hear his heartbeat. Closing her eyes, she listened to sounds of the deep sea, where all movements are expounded thanks to amplification of the liquid ether. She heard a hallowed universe within and the splintering hunger of a humanity that knows no end and no limit but that which it teaches unto itself.

Marcel stroked the long, fluid curls of her golden hair through his throbbing fingers. It amazed him, the manners in which the body responded, reacting to such moments as these. He brushed his hand through to her scalp, pulled her closer in tyrannical, astricted aching, an insatiable longing that despised the turbulent, the sensate.

"You must meet my son," she said quietly. Prophet cawed. Staring into the dark, empty sockets, Marcel faced the omen of the resolute bird as it barked forward again and again in a continual and resolute strain of goading affirmation, the gray-pink tongue trilling from its beak.

"Must you be black?" he muttered softly to himself.

Troubled by the outbreak of the strange bird, Dorothia rose to retrieve the dinner cart from the hallway. "That again?" she fussed, without having heard him well enough to comprehend.

Dorothia sat down to eat as Marcel showered in steaming hot water. When he emerged from the bathroom, she wondered if he ever wore anything other than the hotel robe. She was eating the fish, a rainbow trout marinated in dill and fresh squeezed lemon served over a bed of saffron rice with sun dried tomatoes, feta and chopped cucumber. She did enjoy this life. At the bar Marcel mixed two more drinks.

As he joined her, she stated blankly, "Your first wife was black."

With the fork turned upside down, she bit into another piece of trout. It was slightly underdone for her taste.

"Yes," he answered. "Ruth was a black woman."

"And does it matter that I'm white?" she asked, chewing slowly, her eyes upon her plate, knowing full well that he would answer truthfully.

"I've never quite let go of her."

Dorothia smiled slightly. At least she had the confirmation that she had sought. "I can't replace her; you know that."

"I know that." After a short time, he added, "I wouldn't want you to."

Dorothia sipped from the water that had arrived with the meal. It took a conscious effort to conceal her pleasure, for she understood the double meaning tied within his reply. She understood that even as she could never replace Ruth, Marcel was beginning to regard elements within Dorothia that did not exist within Ruth. Whereas in the beginning he might have been attracted to her for the elements within her that were subsets of Ruth, now he was finding pieces of her that engaged him though they held no connection, no association to past remembrances. In this she found a promise. "The fish is good. Would you like some?" Marcel, for all of his abrasion, remained the most savagely truthful man she had ever met. At this point in her life, such a quality possessed invaluable worth.

Marcel uncovered his plate. "Chicken. I don't want chicken."

"Give it to me. I'll have the chicken. You have the fish."

They ate dinner noiselessly, with only the clink of silverware on china. Over the course of the meal, Marcel drank three drinks to her half drink. His brooding concerned her; still, she remained silent, waiting for him to reconnect in the new tone. She noted the scratch marks upon his neck as warm semen oozed from her vagina, slipping down her leg.

His world, she knew, was becoming her own, piece by carefully cut, interlocked piece.

"You see," he began, finishing his third drink and pushing the sloppy plate aside. "I don't want to meet your son, but I know as sure as hell exists that I must at some point in time meet him. Why, I wonder, is this such a vital necessity to you? And what in the name of God can it possibly have to do with me?" Marcel paused, half expecting an interjection from Prophet. Met by stillness only, he forged forward, limber. "So, as I begin to see it, you don't love me as you say, but you likely love what I may be able to do for your son. Though I have no idea what that might be or what you might hope since all you offer is the cryptic demand, laced with sex. At the same time, I suspect that you don't hate this girl that *wants your son's money*, as you say, but that you hate what she is not able to do for your son, or even what she does for your son. Though again, I have no idea of what that may or may not consist of. If you don't mind me asking, Dorothia, what does your son want?"

Dorothia stared coolly at Marcel, like a master card player who has been accurately assessed by an opponent, though unconvinced that the accuracy of the assessment will alter the outcome of the game. Leaning forward, she took Marcel's left hand in hers, the hand that had written the pages of *Another Day of Loving*. Her answer was simple and direct, with no sense of deception or sarcasm. "You have to ask him that yourself."

Marcel studied her steady eyes, more beautiful than ever. He sensed for the first time that he might be falling in love. But for resolve, she possessed no talent herself.

"And what is it that you are after?" he asked. This question gave her cause to turn aside and glance into the unlit fireplace across the room. "Because I'll give it to you, no matter how selfish it may be."

"You used those words in your last book."

"Did I?" He shrugged, turning aside in surrender. "Does that matter?"

"No. Nothing . . ." As she answered him the phone rang. Liberating Dorothia of her drink, Marcel swayed to the dresser and removed the phone from the hook as he swallowed from the frosted glass.

"Hello, Phrenol," he answered cheerily, the alcohol finally making its intended dent. *Jack, yes, you old rascal. What? Yes. I truly don't care to talk to you. Yes, especially not at this hour. Well, good God, who wouldn't? Don't start that trash with me. Heimmels wouldn't know shale from a diamond. Yes, well, you know where he can go. Aha, no. Yes. No. Drunk as the bastard I am. Champagne? Yes, well, when you can walk on water. Oh,* you can! What's that? What's that? It's a lie! It's true? Don't be screwing with me! Jack? Jack? Yes, I'll kill you. No, no, I'll kiss you. Well, it's overdue. You've been wonderful. Yes, I mean it! Of course, I mean it. Lord Jack, you know me. Oh hell, you can't. Yes. Yes. God bless you, Jack. It couldn't have happened without you. Well, God Jack, you're my best friend. Yes, I mean it. I treat everyone like that. Yes, I'm drinking now. Get over here. Time? Where do we go from here? Yes, yes, yes . . . yes, see you then. Yes, you're right. Yes . . . yes, Ruth would've been proud. . . . Goodnight, Jack. Thank you."

Marcel dropped the receiver to the floor, where it landed with a thud.

Dorothia approached, her wild eyes sparkling with excitement. "Well," she probed, "what is it?"

His hand trembled round the drink and tears welled forth from the rejoicing depths of his blue eyes.

"What is it? What happened?"

Marcel shook his head. His tongue stumbled. He gazed at her in utter astonishment. "I won." Prophet shuffled on the perch, dragging the lame feather, cocking its head right. "I won the Nobel for Literature!"

10

LOLLYGAGGING: IT WAS the descriptive attribute that first came to Marubrishnubupu's mind as he stood before the artwork of the 22-year-old painter, Alexi Rodriguez, also known affectionately as Rooster. "The works lollygag across the canvas as though the paints were personified individuals without a care in the world, and then, WHAM! There it is. A statement that stuns one into complete silence and awe at the monstrous gravity of that which has always existed, some portion of our own humanity, so obvious, prominent and central that we collectively denied its existence, like a consciously hewn monument that we agree to cover with an illusion we call a natural landscape."

Marubrishnubupu kept these thoughts to himself as he stood amidst the privileged crowd that maundered through Irene's home studio gallery for the official premiere of the hot new artist whom all were talking about. The images stunned him with their spiritual depth and insight. His appreciation for Irene multiplied exponentially.

He recalled the story that celebrated the virtues of the great Japanese tea master, Rainier. It was said that one rainy day a young student spoke to his master saying, "Master Shibo, why are you so humble? Your reputation is unparalleled. You are at least as great as the great Rainier. After all, in proof, almost all can comprehend the greatness of your work; it is said that only one in one thousand can comprehend the wonders of Rainier."

The master, ever humble, nodded in thanks for his student's kind words of praise, but admonished the student all the same, responding simply, "And that is why Rainier is greater."

The young student sat thoughtfully by the master's side before venturing to speak again. "Master Shibo?"

The master, organizing an arrangement of flowers for the alter, stopped.

"Do *you* comprehend the wonders of Rainier?"

Master Shibo smiled, pleased by his student's dawning awareness. "Let us be content to say, that sometimes I ask Master Rainier the questions that Master Rainier would ask of himself."

That Irene had identified the greatness, wrapped so deeply within the canvas, served as testimony to her willful discrimination as well as Rooster's talent. Marubrishnubupu resided in his spot, rooted and breathless. Others wished to see what he saw.

A balding, middle-aged doctor in a tuxedo stepped alongside Marubrishnubupu and asked in a heavy, sober tone, "What do you think of this one, Master Marubrishnubupu?"

He answered without hesitation. "There are some gifts that don't deserve our understanding."

Misinterpreting the master's statement, the man coughed gruffly, nodding in a conspiratorial tone. "I don't care much for it either. Too giddy if you ask me. Good art should make you think. This just makes me want to laugh." With this the man grew nervous as though he had said something a bit too stupid, revealed something a bit too true. He jiggled the cubes of ice against the lime at the bottom of his glass.

"Yes, you're right," Marubrishnubupu added reflectively, thoughtfully. "He does want us to be able to laugh; above all, he desires to defend our ability to laugh."

The man felt as though they were having separate conversations despite the fact that Marubrishnubupu seemed in agreement.

"So will you be speaking while you're here?"

But Marubrishnubupu did not answer, and the man, more unsure of his opinion than ever, eased warily away.

Marubrishnubupu gazed at the painting, the last in a series along the wall that were identified as being of the post-Soli period. These had arrived from Providence only hours before the scheduled opening, sending Irene into an ambitious fever to recoordinate the display to make room for the three, stunning additions. With the unexpected arrival of these three, Irene could only heap praise upon the artist's mother.

These three radiated a warmth and freedom of spirit that the others failed to wholly manifest, though the struggle expressed itself beneath the surface of the Soli period pieces that were displayed, ten in number.

Irene worked the crowd expertly, explaining motifs, guiding discussions, planting interpretive seeds, openly telling people what they should both think and feel. "Do you notice the artist's palliative use of the color red in this one? It's such a strong color for a painting that purports upon the surface to be soft; that's the contradiction. The varying shades of red counterpose the haughty dilemma of faith against reason. Reason, here being a kind of superhuman force. Notice the distinctness of the form in the red and the ambiguity here in these pastel archs reminiscent of rainbows, waves, less stable natural expressions. In the red you find buildings and cars and swords, ovens, televisions and hospital wheelchairs. The artist is suggesting that the human faith protects itself by concealing itself. It doesn't want to come to the forefront. It doesn't want to be a bold statement. It leaves that to reason. The objects of our lives are like a collective wall of brick that we are careful never to identify as a wall."

One of the listeners interjected, "It's as though as powerful as these rigid forms and passions are, this subtle little faith is moving the whole thing. I can see it. I never would have noticed it at first, but everything follows the pastels. It's like everything solid comes from that little source of softness."

"Yes, exactly!" Irene was having a ball. She had done hundreds of openings of this sort, but none had been so easy, so fluid, so spontaneously her. "The rage and love and passion that create our world, they all begin with a soft impulse, this tiny portion of faith, belief, that formless aspect of ourselves that can almost be forgotten when surrounded by all of this strength."

"Fascinating," one listener glowed, "fascinating."

Another asked, "And what about the forms? Why those forms? Why cars and buildings and swords and hospital chairs?"

Irene pressed a finger to her mouth in thought before pointing. "Notice how the artist makes these mechanical, these solid, concrete *things* fit together. Notice how he has fitted them like jointed bones to a skeleton. He's saying that everything fits together. The world is a form of human body where faith, never seen, makes all the meaningful decisions. Nothing is random, everything is natural, and solving one need gives rise to greater needs, always bringing us closer to our true purpose, that formless part of ourselves that creates without purpose."

Some wondered if the artist would truly say these things about the works. To most it did not matter. They came to know how to talk about *things* that served an aesthetic function only. Many who had lived useful lives for so many years found within themselves the formless, pastel void to which Irene spoke, that slippery portion of themselves which could be neither justified nor denied. They came and they listened to allow their imagination a living place, if only for a moment, to breathe.

No prices were set for the thirteen paintings. Instead, there were bid cards placed beneath each. The doctor bid $3,000 on the work that he and Marubrishnubupu had discussed. Five minutes passed before someone removed his bid card and replaced it with a bid card for $4,800.

Refulgent over Marubrishnubupu's presence, Irene cunningly played upon the aura of uncounterfeitable sanctity he brought to the occasion.

One woman, a 53-year-old banker's wife, approached Irene to whisper furtively, "Is he terribly attractive? I'm sure he's an absolute prince. Tell me."

These were the types of inevitable questions that Irene had not herself resolved. Some she cleverly dodged. "One kiss from you and he would be, Mrs. Mason. Now let me show you this work, called *Gentle Sorrow*, a bit more closely."

When the opportunity came, Irene glided over to the side of Marubrishnubupu, who had just successfully extracted himself from a group of Christian women who had deftly probed his secular sympathies.

"Your party has been quite a success," he complimented Irene as she joined him before the painting *Songbird*. "I wonder, though, if it is a good idea to cut up and sell these pieces. Together they are like a magnificent shrine that is taken care of by a caretaker who fully comprehends their worth. Will their worth be similarly understood by those who take them from this place in parcels?"

Irene smiled upon his charming ignorance. A glass of wine in her system, she was feeling confident and renegade. Far away from the tranquilizing pastel sunset of Taos, she refused to make concessions in her own domain. "That anyone can own art is a rarely appreciated nuance of democracy. Besides, the more concentrated we keep him, the more likely it is that we'll create a new religion. You don't really want more competition do you?"

"If he is what his paintings say he is, I would invite the challenge," Marubrishnubupu responded. "I still cannot quite believe that you failed to meet him."

"I told you. He was sick."

"It is more likely that he did not desire to see you. I am curious to know why this would be."

Irene approached the painting. "Have you noted the rip in this canvas? And the way he repaired it?"

Moving closer, Marubrishnubupu uttered a single word. "Splendid." With a mindful hand he touched the bidding placard beneath and whistled.

"Would they pay that if they didn't, on some level, comprehend?"

"No," Marubrishnubupu sighed ruefully as he turned his back on capitalism, "they would give much more."

On this night, Irene found Marubrishnubupu ironic and judgmental, not what she expected from a spiritual master who inculcated such themes as bounteous love and the freedom in equality.

"You don't like what you see, do you?"

"It depends where I look."

"What would you have me do? Hide the paintings away? Keep them locked up? Let no one but the worthy have access to enjoy them, to appreciate them, to learn from them?" Irene brushed a finger atop the green suture of paint. "Would you have this denied to the world?"

"No, not denied. But I would not sell. I would not put a price tag on the miraculous." His stale presumption irritated her. "I would advocate discernment in its display and presentation."

"Then what?" She leaned forward, her subtle fingers upon the robe of his arm. "Who would be worthy? Those who bow to you or your God? Spiritual materialism can be just as insidious as greed, just as cruel, if not more. The constant quest for spiritual laurels. Isn't that what the Tibetans did? They tried to lock out the world, the inferior world of infidels incapable of appreciating the beauty they saw. Didn't they become exactly that arrogance which they sought to rid from their world?"

Marubrishnubupu nodded. He had not anticipated that she would be versed in the concept of spiritual materialism. It made discussion harder. "You are correct. Spirituality can be used to create division as well as harmony, indifference as well as love. It can serve creation or destruction equally well. Spirituality can become, if we are not careful, the greatest and the most consuming of all the ego trips."

Irene decided then to step upon a daring ledge. In a way, she comprehended that it would be a test of the mettle of this taciturn sage who sought so much of her belief. She spoke with all the years of her experience in the art of discerning the good from the bad; she made one, single, jaded thrust to validate the illusion that spoke before her. "I like you, Master Marubrishnubupu. If you were a man, I'd . . ."

"I am still a man."

Irene played a dangerous, perhaps even a mean-spirited, game. Cruel as it may have been, she was testing him, his spiritual poise, of necessity. At the ashram as she had spooned sugar into his tea, Irene had intuitively understood the manifold manners in which the world of fear relentlessly tests and challenges any person who dares to openly believe in what others cannot see. Now she found herself, as his world entered hers, doubting and demanding proof of that spiritual poise.

A languid honesty suffused the words that the sage spoke. "I feel a full range of emotions . . . and passions. They simply do not express themselves in strictly traditional manners."

"But they do express themselves in the traditional manners," Irene responded gently as she removed her hand from his arm with an intimate touch that told them both that he had passed the most difficult portion of the test. "You express them in the masculine spiritual tradition of the East. Such a lonesome tradition. . . . It's refreshing to know, Master Marubrishnubupu, that you feel the passions that the rest of us do. In the end, only a genuine human can inspire a human."

She walked away feeling a curious admixture of guilt and relief, accepting that she had done what she needed to do.

Marubrishnubupu remained before *Songbird*. His eyes were faithfully fixed upon the physician's sutured tear. How had he not seen it earlier? He felt the strain within himself, a strain of passion and human wanting that he had believed conquered, or at least fully trained many years hence. He felt like a novice, like Shibo before Rainier. How small a man he was in this world, in this infinite *infinite* world. Standing among the milling chords of people, cognizant of his human frailty and weakness, glad for this human frailty and weakness, he began laughing aloud at the sudden awareness born from the painting: that what one may willfully choose to surrender, another may not even possess the capacity to claim. What a grand soul this painter was, that would help the world to find humor and healing in such human wounds.

Others watched him as he aged by twenty years before their eyes, transformed in a twinkle from a wise sage who seemed no older than thirty-nine to a wise, old sage who could be no younger than seventy-four. Deep wrinkles appeared in his sienna skin. His entire head of hair turned from sable to silver. As his body began to glow, Marubrishnubupu laughed louder and louder and louder still.

♐

The famine of 1934 continued through the early half of 1935, its disaffected ravages degrading cities, villages and hamlets from Moscow to Bernburg. The hamlet of Krylov suckled itself on the nectar of a sweet and widespread kindness. It was a common consciousness of the beautiful and the valuable, sustained by the fruit of Michayl's compassion-based sacrifice, that kept Krylov strong. Voluntarily relinquishing their own needs for the fulfillment of the young and old alike, villagers found deep wellsprings of human kindness hidden within.

Unknown to the Kremlin, in all of Russia, Krylov offered to the world a singular manifestation of the pure Marxist ideal. And why not? Marxism was conceived in poverty. It was a philosophy of human kindness designed to function in the midst of poverty for the purpose of transcending poverty. The famine, the dearth of 1934, represented an ideal setting for authentic Marxism to manifest, though no one in the village thought in such dry, academic terms. Few, in fact, reflected sufficiently to understand that once the conditions of poverty which had generated the need for Marxism were transcended, the need for Marxism ceased. Where the social construct lingered, social tyranny, corruption and exploitation, ultimately reigned. Marxism could not exist for the rich, the bourgeois, the ruling class. Marxism existed alone for those who were struggling together for basic survival. Again, no one thought in such terms that a Marxism properly conceived must be a democratic Marxism, regardless of the name. They knew only that their leader, Michayl, had made an extreme sacrifice they could scarcely begin to apprehend.

As the solitude of Michayl deepened due to the trauma resultant from his personal sacrifice, the inhabitants of the small hamlet united, forged by his example, to confront the challenges of the relentless season.

They learned that where divisions based in personal need dissolve, a single family, a unified social organism, is born.

In April nature turned a mollifying hand. Forgotten were the unknown sins that had provoked the accursed season of cruelty. Spring came early, caressing the rolling prairies with a cleansing rain. A lush, warm mist concealed the lilacs that grew in the plains. The rivers filled, washing clean the lingering season. Fiery cyclamen dipped their buds with morning dew. Orchards of pines lifted, turning their boughs to the sun. Walnut trees blossomed. For all the hardship, there were no dead in Krylov needing burial. Wild game thought lost or thinned returned from the mountains, stepping into the present like shaggy mastodons, magically transported from memorial time. Charging as contumacious mountains melted, the river teemed with life: pink salmon, tawny mollusks, sardines, eels. Guided by terse instructions from Michayl, the village planted early in an attempt to gain an extra rotation of selected crops. As so much in Michayl's atavistic life, the yields were modest but ample to sustain the dignity of life of the sphere he so powerfully influenced. Once again, Michayl provided health in a time when others experienced only suffering and depression.

Following the craven general's winter departure, Michayl withdrew from his public role. Some said, in his romanticized defense, that Michayl sought only to regain his soundness of body. Pursuant to the terrifying beating at the hands of the general and his night-long vigil in the blanket of snow and ice, pneumonia befell him. Others, less optimistic in their assessment, conjectured that the sadistic general had succeeded in what he had wished for all along: he had finally broken

Michayl's spirit. Like a shaman forever altered by the ineffable horror of the journey, they feared that Michayl would never return as he had once been. The women, who had strangely treated Michayl to an initial dose of cool detachment, quickly forgave him for whatever imagined transgression he had committed through his shameful performance before the general. Ever in contrast, the men, even those who had challenged him in the past, were deepened in their reverence to and for him. His display had taught them the rarest of the lessons of manhood, lessons that only the rarest of rare fathers will dare to undertake to teach.

Through December and January of that bitter winter season, Michayl remained bedded underneath the wool of sheepskin blankets. Mended socks filled with fire-heated, igneous stone warmed the space beneath the covers. Naistika nursed him, wheedling him back to the health of living, praying for him long into the night as no atheist would. No longer did they share the intimate affections of husband and wife, the soft and gentle laughter, the endearing complexities of simple personality that bring joy to a joyless world. Over time, the sweet scent of henna, the miracle of her birth, faded from Naistika. Whatever had taken place in their respective worlds on that infamous night did more than dull a desire or weaken a resolve to overcome the dividing force; it murdered a merciful memory, created a tundric expanse that all of their accumulated strength had not found a way to traverse. She loved him, but she could no longer look into his eyes.

When Michayl did successfully drive himself to rise for a few hours from the safe comfort of the warm bed, he would dodder in the village wrapped with a dirty quilt, often sitting in piled banks of white snow, seemingly immune to the cold. With dead eyes transfixed by the eternal memory of an enemy who had bought his soul for the soul of the village, he would watch a pale moon rise in the middle of the day. Wandering to the storehouses, he often checked the levels and the conditions of the remaining supplies. Content or discontent with what he saw, none could say. His world had become poetry and metaphor, long, surreal wanderings that had lost all sense of cause and effect. Interior thoughts he shared with none save one.

Solzenhitsyn alone, through an unstated agreement of father and son, was allowed to accompany Michayl on these solitary sojourns through the village. He would meander a few steps behind, his head downcast in the maintenance of an inconspicuous presence. In future years this ability to be unseen yet present admitted him access to grand ideas and wondrous words often concealed from men and women more thoroughly gifted in the art of thought. In time, Solzhenitsyn was forgotten. So well did he transform into the invisible chameleon that many stopped seeing him at all. He was like a loyal dog, a yellow shadow of the snow, death's fever.

Few could see him, and fewer still could recognize him as the son and closest confidant of the beloved leader whom none could approach. Their favorite spot to sit and rest was the round stone well in the center of the village. Reclining by his father's knee, Soli, unmoving, would share in whatever random tokens of expression his father could bear to ration in a half-broken mutter or in a stare held too long on a bale of hay, a cricket or a child whipping a hen with a swatch of wood. Despite the magnanimous adoration of the village for their great patron, he allowed no one near him in such hours. Self-quarantined from interaction, he shunned kindness with indifference, empathy with epigrams. *A man's heart provides all the rapture he will need.* Only Solzhenitsyn, the silent, stone-faced boy who had disappeared into a tight orbit of his father, was allowed by the father to father the father.

Some thought Michayl mad, though none dared to give public voice to this widespread opinion. All comprehended through the unspoken channels of community what his personal sacrifice had secured for each of them. To this they laid down an undying gratitude. Through February, Michayl went for long walks. Soli trudged softly, stoically, a step behind, his feet crunching in the pristine banks of snow in which his father walked, searching. The footsteps of his father were large; Soli could scarcely fill them, though as he followed, he learned — as any good son behind a good father is able — to match the stride. They would disappear sometimes for days at a time, returning to the village and Naistika without a word of explanation for where they had been or what they had seen. She expected no answers to the questions she did not ask. She understood what was true. In his own way, through extreme sensitivity to the subtle pains that are essence to this world, her husband had gone mad.

In March the last snow fell and the first of the starry larks returned with song. Pecking at busy feet for scattered flakes of golden cornmeal, roosters and hens wandered about the hamlet. Naistika mended a shawl beside her husband's bed. He was dying. Her hopes for his recovery were dashed. The strength he had been exhibiting in February seemed to vanished. Still, she noticed a peace in his being, an aura of serenity and wellness of which, through his whole life, he had never been in possession. She noted how, even now, lying prone in bed, emerging from these harrowed months, he appeared statuesque, massive, mythic, a transcendent, unyielding isle. Others, those who found the pilgrim's courage within themselves to enter the home to pay their silent respects, also felt ripples of this mysterious and powerful energy coming from the man. Soli sat in vigilance, Indian-style on the dirt floor at the foot of the bed. The mother could not tell if he were praying or waiting. Her ability to discern between the two had dulled. Naistika stoked the fire. She pulled the musty blanket tight round her husband's noble face. This man she had married so many years before was the only man she would ever love. She wished to live as his companion for many years hence but knew it would not be so. He coughed, wheezing for breath, his lungs saturated with mucus and yellow-spotted phlegm.

"Leave me," he commanded in a strong and sudden voice. "It is time I pass my blessing to our son."

She nodded in confirmation, resolved to be as strong as he would want her to be. As she wordlessly turned to leave, he took her wrist with all the force that she knew to be compressed within his most gentle spirit. She met his eyes, eyes wrought with the sorrow of human deficiency. "You know, woman, you know what it is I feel."

Naistika nodded once more, happy tears forming. This was their good-bye. Dropping to her knees, tears rolled from her eyes, landing on the hand that she kissed as she spread the sweet moisture into his palm with the warmth of her smooth cheek.

Once she was gone, Michayl summoned his son. Careful not to touch the bed, Solzhenitsyn knelt. The great man drew from beneath his pillow a stone-sized ampulla. With a steady focus that surmounted the sickness, Michayl poured a small amount of the consecrated oil into his open hand. Michayl smiled proudly upon his only son as he laid his outstretched hand upon the small head in an act of benediction.

Pressing firmly, he moved his palm from the eyes and over to the lobes of the ears before resting the full hand, palm to forehead. To Solzhenitsyn, it seemed that his father's powerful hand was large and strong enough to crush his skull with a single pulverizing twitch, but it was also as tender and comforting as an impenetrable helmet lined with an invincible, feathery down.

The fire crackled. Outside a fierce wind howled. Michayl spoke.

"This is my blessing, reserved for my only son, Solzhenitsyn. Lord God, Creator of all that is seen and unseen, make my words wise that they may be a reflection of your divine will. Let the best within me be bestowed and multiplied tenfold upon my son. Let all else die within this body. Let the seeds of your holy goodness be planted in my son. Let him sow the field with seeds of compassion. Let him plow the field with truth as your saints and prophets and kings have done before, and finally, when the work is done, let him reap a harvest of prosperity and love enough to share by your side for eternity. Let the light that is your grace shine forth from within his heart. Illuminate his most difficult hours that his enemies may learn. Let my son be as modest as you are great, so that he may ever understand the profound responsibilities of power and the grave power of the good.

"Let my son walk in no man's shadow save God the Father's. Allow my son the gift of knowing the unconditional love of a woman pure and true and good as I have known. Let him be a loving father and husband, free of jealousy and doubt, filled with trust and faith. Let his life overflow with friendship and his work be infused with a purpose and a meaning that does you honor. Lord, let my son not wish vainly for riches or glory or fame, but let these gifts be bestowed at the proper times when his work and life have earned your admiration. Lastly, Lord God . . ." Michayl's hand grew firm about his son's skull. "Allow my son to be keeper of the virtue that it has been the great honor of my life to protect. Let my son, Solzhenitsyn, protect this virtue without name as I have done, as my father has done, and as my father's father has done before me. So do I bless my well loved son with all that I . . . am."

Gasping a last breath, his eyes wide open, seeing nothing of this world, Michayl's hand tightened about his son's head. The oil caused the firm hand to slip, to let go. The latched door blew open. The wind swirled. The fire blew out. All was silent. Michayl Maschovich was dead.

cP

Rooster endured the trials of his own mind as he plied his concentration to the canvas with an intensity more stern and more severe than anything his prior life had known. Dipping his brush into an orange oil he stretched the fibers across the ivory sheet. Whether this work would depict an abstraction or something more realistic he had not yet determined. He knew only that he needed to paint himself through the current obstacle that threatened to throttle his very essence. Shoving the clock beneath his pillow and refusing to be distracted by the noise that penetrated from around and within, he applied the most steady and confident strokes his mind could deliver. This current painting did not depict his best self and he knew it; this was not the rendering that had he possessed full faculty and ability to actualize ideals he would have chosen. Regardless, the dedicated action represented force, thrust, energy, effort. Even if he could not move forward, he would not fall back. He thought of Freud, as little as he cared for Freud, who'd said, "When inspiration does not come to me, I go out at least half way and find it often waiting for me there."

Rooster painted intrepidly as though his soul were being fought for on the canvas. The effort was wild and blind, without structured thought or meaning. Efforts of this type belonged to hacks and amateurs and masters pressing through to a higher level.

In the orange sky he painted a series of blue angels without faces. Atop their shoulders were giant harps with strings reverberating in the still air. He painted red, plaintive waves in the air, designating a torrid heat that would not break, that would not discharge replenishment, would not yield the slightest diminishment of the torture. Into the foreground, shattering all the conventional barriers of space, Rooster drew a mountain plateau. Shorn against the crags, he depicted a man chained to the mountain with arms above his head, blood spilling from the wrists, ripped by the manacles. Red hooded vultures, men in disguise, gorged upon the naked man's entrails in gruesome detail. With talons for both hands and feet the vulture-men fed on the human feast, as the tortured being cried out in agony to the torrid sky where several headless angels fluttered at a distance singing songs. Rooster painted the entrails green and purple, creating an iridescence about the hard, shell-shaped lips of the feasting creatures, half-human, half-bird. It developed into a Prometheus motif, and Rooster, realizing this, repainted the sun so that it more resembled a candle of light atop a phallic form. Rooster reworked the angels. Under the guidance of his hand they assumed a surreal semblance. He gave them harp-like heads reminiscent of the antenna of moths. The wings he rounded to facilitate, if not invite, such an imaginative interpretation. The birdlike humanoids, Rooster also restroked, giving to them multiple limbs with the intention that a subtle suggestion would be integrated that these creatures of consumption were fire ants, hungry for the healthy, devouring. The last application of imagination and metaphor recast the entire scale of the painting, exploding it from grandeur to minutia while making the horror all the more ghastly.

Rooster trembled as he painted, resisting the extreme urges of his body to itch. The severity of the urge was a side effect of Dapsone. He battled the craving with a contesting, Nietzschean will, channeling the frustration into the painting, a painting of a questionable aesthetic and quality. Issues such as this did not matter in moments like these, when the soul was at stake.

He thought of Tamara as he painted, recalling the harmonizing effect she had upon him. What did she see in him? What could he give her? A leper? The thoughts itched within his mind, the doubts of his capacity to be a man. "I am more the angel," he thought, whitening the wings with diamonds, singeing them in the phallic candlelight, the imagery undeniable. "An angel, the bringer of solace, incapable of physical relief. I bring only the salve of concepts and ideas. I bring a song and feeling, but nothing real, nothing tangible." He brought the angels, through careful manipulation of lines, closer to the flame. He exaggerated the terror that contorted the face of the chained man. No, he thought again, it's not exaggerated. It is finally realistic.

When finished, he pressed the maulstick aside and studied his art. His own first look as a witness startled him. It was deformed, hideous, incongruous, a queer version of hell. He smiled for he knew it to be good, courageous, unlike anything that had come before. Simultaneously, he feared what he saw, wished to distance it from himself, deny that what existed on that canvas mirrored some portion that existed within. Still, his soul, if such esoteric thoughts are believed, he had preserved.

What will I name it, he mused casually, pleasantly noting that the severe craving to scratch his leprous sores had subsided. He gazed into it pensively, balancing his thinnest brush against his chin. Pondering, he listed for himself the elements his eyes perceived: heat, sun, candle, moth, flame, music, harp, angel, cow, ant, microbe, mountain, chains, orange, wings, pain, vultures, rooster, hood, entrails, worms. The name came to him. *Sublime Awe.*

It fit and he knew it.

Standing, wobbling, he crossed the distance to his bed, removed the clock from beneath the pillow and pushed it to the floor. He collapsed in exhaustion. It had been an outstanding effort, an exercise of will over canvas. Inspiration had met him halfway, just as Freud had suggested it would.

♍

Tamara woke him with a gentle kiss upon the lips. Opening his eyes to her buttery smile, he remained flat and motionless as her fingertips brushed against his cheek. He had green eyes into which she searched, exploring like a voyager without a line to safety, the quintillion souls that lived within. Moving her fingers through his hair, past scars in the scalp, she dipped again downwards to meet his lips, pressing them softly, slowly with her own.

"I thought I dreamed of you and now I wake to the dream. Can such dreams be true?"

"Aye," she nodded with mirth-filled eyes, "it can be true."

Sitting on the edge of the bed she held his wrapped hand. "The bandages need changing." Blood and sebaceous puss, anti-bacterial ointments stained through. The exertion of the act of painting, the contortions required of the hand, resulted in an exacerbation of the condition. The shingled scabs seldom had ample chance to heal, so actively engaged was the hand in strenuous activity. Often the shingles would crack and the hardened shingle, with no place to go, confined by the very gauze intended to heal, would carve into the raw flesh beneath like a cold shale splinter. Thus the hands of Rooster suffered most. Never allowed to rest, they never healed; they suffered perpetually, a never-ending font of agony and revelation conjoined, the very limb of

Moses spilling lesson upon divine lesson into the noumenal. Such an accursed gift, wrapped, sheathed like a virgin sword, raging with potency enough for all the nebular woe.

Gradually, tenderly, like a nurse touching the clothing cauterized to raw, human tissue, Tamara unfurled the wrap from Rooster's painting hand. He withdrew, but she held him near knowing that she was not hurting him. She hushed his fear, whispering encouragement, prose of peace. Such was the intimacy they shared as the gauze grew thicker, caked and rigid with dark excrement, ringlets of iodine extending into puddled ripples of blood. Watching, Rooster saw maroon pools of oil seeking release through the sensitive cracks of a drought blighted field, the humanity that is found beneath humanity.

"Hold it up," she urged, wrapping the bandage, unwrapped from his hand, round her own. Sitting erect, he lifted his arm. The hand hovered in space between them. The outer bandage came closest to her own skin as the inner bandage, moist and dry, simultaneously became, as though transformed, her outer skin. She did not shudder as the flesh beneath, blanche and gray, charcoal and tawny-spotted, crimson, exposed itself. The crisp, bloody crust reminded her of images televised from lava fields, where the outer membrane of the running lava, exposed to the air, turns hard and black, magnesiums and nitrates infusing the atmosphere with a vile, nauseating, resonant scent, an archetypal summoning back to our deepest, pre-historic, amniotic pools.

"Please don't look."

"Sssshhhh. . . ." Coagulated and coagulating blood seeped from the cracks as shifting shingles, geographic platelets of God's hand, settled.

What she saw, the anguish, awed her. How did he paint with this below the surface, with this as his hellishly inspired, tormented substratum? — And with such beauty as one could scarcely imagine oneself to comprehend. Tamara held the hand at the forearm. To her it seemed a burnt mass, an eviscerated piece of meat pulled prematurely from a searing pan of margarine. Yet, in the next instant, before sorrow could overcome her, she looked to the new painting, *Sublime Awe*, and knew that beauty and ugliness are seldom what they seem, that a piece of golden fruit plucked from the drooping branch of a comfort tree is sustained by the work of the roots, buried in the soil, segregated from the light, communing with nightcrawlers and worms and oracles of death. So are beauty and ugliness married in truth, when one can recognize the other for the comfort that it gives.

"Where are the fresh bandages?" she asked, moving gracefully forward, allowing neither a pause nor a gasp for doubt and confusion to seep into the chrysalis of their connubial sacrament.

"Beneath the bed," he answered. The answer did not surprise her. She smiled as she kneeled, falling prostrate to the floor. This makes sense, she thought, perfect sense that the bandages would be here, beneath the bed, such an intimate place for such an intimate, pure and clean, piece of apparel. A bathroom would have been too far removed, too suggestive of something else.

Drawing a large basin from beneath the bed, she stared at the compendium of health supplies and medicines. Gauze and tape. Cotton swab. Iodine and a multiplicity of ointments and creams. Opaque jars of prescription pills. Petroleum jelly, ice packs and water bottles. Thermometers and syringes. Rubber ty-offs. Injection vials and gloves. Clear bars of soap. Aspirin and diuretics and sugar pills.

She paused over the basin of items. So this is what it meant? A constant battle for sanitation. And just who was anesthetized against whom, she wondered, selecting two packages of gauze and tape.

"Do we use an ointment?"

"The blue-labeled one."

"Is there anything else I must do? Tell me everything."

Rooster paused, unsure. He gazed at his hand as it lingered in center space, a focal point. The longer it remained there, the less repulsive it became, the more common, the more acceptable and understood, the more justification in reality it accrued.

"Tell me everything," she repeated.

Nervously, he responded. "Sometimes I'll soak them in warm water with lime juice.

"Lime juice?"

"And linseed oil."

At this they could both laugh, as though his sickly condition were but a superstition, one prayer removed from healing, one alchemical concoction away from mystical transformation.

"Lime juice and linseed oil," she echoed, quipping, "is that in the medical journals?"

"It's a nice dish over a bed of pasta." They both looked at his hands and understood that laughter was their solace, their goodwill and their salve of consolation.

Awkwardly following her lead, he went into the kitchen where she filled the sink with hot water. As the water level slowly rose, she poured a quarter cup of lime juice and several capfuls of linseed oil into the sink. Waiting for the sink to fill, Tamara unfurled the right hand as she had done his left so that both were wholly exposed. Rooster stood like a surgeon after a vigorous scrub, waiting for gloves, touching nothing. His hands were useless, unprotected and defenseless.

Furled in neat balls, Tamara placed the old bandages, vestiges of her own skin now, in plastic bags which she tied tightly before disposition in the trash.

"I burn them usually," Rooster added.

"Here," she coaxed, unbuttoning the sleeves of his shirt, rolling the sleeves above his elbows. She saw more scars along his forearms but no signs of active wounds or scabs. It appeared to her, from what she saw of his body, that the disease was restricted to his hands alone.

"Now dip them seven times."

He cast her a curious, quizzical glance, half believing.

"Seven times," she repeated with authority. "I want you to dip your hands seven times, slowly. No matter how hot the water is." This was her mathematical moment.

Rooster stared at her as though she were crazy. The stern confidence of the eyes that met his did not convince him that she was not.

"Do it," she demanded, "as an act of consecration."

And he did.

He dipped his hands in once thinking that if she could do this for him without protest, without recoil, then he could oblige this secular peculiarity, this ceremonialization, this modest ritualizing twist. The water singed, much hotter than warm, but she stood by him, compelling him with a hand to plunge them deeper. It was a searing, disinfecting pain that shot up and through his arms. Rooster looked to her, pleading for release, but she held firm and aloof, responding to his appeal with two words. "Seven times."

Finally allowed, he raised his arms hurriedly from the water. For the first time he noticed the thick steam drifting upwards.

"It's a bit hot," he suggested, with no intention of masking his goal to get the water cooled. "I soak them in *warm water*, not boiling water."

"Down," she pressed forcefully, unmoved by his protest. The water burned more than the first time. The pain, no longer derived simply from the novel nature of the experience, throbbed in sharp currents as he gained a thorough knowledge of the details, each more acute than the previous. The lime juice began to take effect, tingling frenetically. She whispered in his ear, a demonic hush, "Viscous little animals consuming your flesh." The acidity of the lime thrushed his hands like whetted blades causing him to forget for an instant the terrible heat. She pulled him free.

He trembled. "What are you doing?"

"Relax," she offered, "relax." And down she thrust him once more. The pause in between, seeming a cruel mode of relief that did not count, did not meaningfully exist. Once more the shooting pain, his nerves were on fire, scorched and burning. "Where do you feel it?" she interrogated. "Where do you feel?"

"What do you mean?" he begged, exerting pressure upwards. "What do you mean?"

"Where do you feel it?"

"In the hands. In the hands," he groaned. The rawness beneath was unreal, beyond his ken, incomprehensible.

"Not good enough. Where else?" And she pulled his hands from the water, gazing into his eyes, as he considered her in fear. "Where else?" This time it was she who pleaded and he who began to understand.

"In the arms . . . and, and in the mind. I feel it most in the mind."

"Do you remember our talk about oneness of mind?" Again she pressed his hands downwards. This time his body did not fight. "Where do you feel it?"

Despite the monstrosity of the pain, he managed a slight grin. "It's in the mind. That's where the pain seeks its release. That's where it runs for relief. It's not just the hands. It's in the mind."

"Breathe!" she commanded him.

And he did.

"Deeper."

He settled himself into the pain, acknowledging the battle occurring in his mind, confronting the temptation to retreat from the pain and settling deeper into it with each breath, wondering when he would break, sensing that he must but knowing that if he could control the pain for one instant, he could control it for every instant. The pain was ridiculous, the water an extreme temperature for exposed flesh. He imagined raw chicken in water of such a temperature turning white. He felt sure his hands were cooking. It terrified him and he attempted to withdraw. "Breath. Relax." Her voice brought him comfort. He began to count the seconds until she would allow him to extract. It was cruel, sheer cruelty. This thought was false. She pulled him free.

"Oneness of mind," she repeated.

"I can't do it again," he implored her.

"What's in there? What's in there?"

His eyes were bugged with fear.

"What's in there?"

"Water. Lime juice . . ."

"What else? What are you forgetting?"

"Linseed oil. Oil."

For a fifth time she forced his hands into the water, each time they were easier, more willing, more pliant though Rooster himself felt his resistance heightening.

Linseed oil, he thought to himself as though remembering an important secret. The oil acted as a soothing emollient. It smoothed the abrasion and alleviated the torturous scourge of the leprous affliction. He found comfort in this thought, the thought of the oil mixed within the sink, acting as a thin, protective sheen, permeating the water, following into the crevices between live and dead flesh where the lime juice had cleansed a path, corroding debris and rust. Yes, his hands were like mechanical pieces of equipment plagued with rust. The lime juice dissolved away the leprous rust and linseed oil soothed the joints, easing their repetitive movements, enabling endless motion. For just a moment, as he focused upon the lubricating properties of oil, the water was bearable. Then his mind shifted; he fixated upon a second characteristic of oil. It burns. It catches fire and burns. Even in or on water it can be ignited and so it was in this sea, where his hands like a burning bush were aflame. He began to tremble and Tamara raised him up.

He was unaware that his hands had been submerged without effort for a full minute.

"Seven times," she impelled him as he rested, restoring his energy, refocusing his mind, determined that the pain he had been through would find meaning in completion.

"How many is that?"

"Five." And she pushed down once more.

Focusing intently in the water he asked, invoked clarification, an impatient edge forming in his voice, "That was five or this is five?"

"Six," she answered blandly, refusing to budge, to be moved by the comic animation of his emerging will.

Rooster emptied his mind and waited patiently. Words from Marcel Phrenol's pages entered the stillness. *The bottom is crowded with good people, only bastards and cream rise to the top.* A halcyon smile stretched across his face as he watched oily, saponaceous swirls bobbing on the surface.

She withdrew his hands from the baptismal font. They appeared cleansed of blackness, cleansed of dried, coagulated bloody clumps, softened. Rivulets of watery serum dripped in a common direction. The hands glistened. Tamara submerged the hands a seventh time, preparing him completely for what would come. He waited peacefully, his mind clear. *But miracles happen anywhere.* She removed her hands, and Rooster allowed himself to linger in the soup. Turning them beneath the water, he admired their gracious structure, their wondrous form, a part of him, magnified in the blood of earth. When he lifted his hands from the water they were vaporous, emitting the very heat and power they had absorbed. They were forged masses of flesh, purified, fresh from the fire. After allowing the air to do its work, Tamara wrapped each hand slowly. Some of the scab and shingles had fallen free in the water and were floating upon and within pods of sebum. The inner skin, cream-colored and pinkish-tan, microscopic veins laid bare, glistened with moisture.

"Do you want ointment on spots like that?"

"No. Not this time."

Tamara worked from the wrists to the palms to the fingers, proceeding from pinkie to forefinger to thumb. He watched her intensive progress.

"What you are doing is courageous." Afforded the rite through the extension of her touch, he gazed intimately upon her. She ignored him, dedicating her concentration to the given task, her left eyebrow ruffled.

With her method of wrapping, each hand required two packages of gauze. Beginning high upon the wrist, she ended at the thumb leaving the knuckle unveiled.

"Your thumbs aren't bad. I'd like to leave them uncovered. They can gage the rest of the hand, and you'll have a bit more freedom of touch."

Rooster nodded. He had never thought of it. She held a hand. "It amazes me that you never get paint on your hands."

"I used to all the time. And then this happened. I had to learn to paint all over again. How to hold a brush. How to pull a line."

"How do they feel?"

Thinking first of the early pain, he contemplated the final product, chuckling and serious, as he held his hands before him, flexing the thumbs in the open air. "Good. Very good."

"We'll have to go to the arcade," she joked.

"Or I can box," he jabbed back, fluttering at the air. "Float like a butterfly."

Tamara drained the sink by removing the stop plug with a knife.

"Let me take you to dinner," she suggested as the water spun downward in a cerebral vortex.

Rooster stopped in mid-action as though his imaginary opponent had succeeded in stunning him with a blow to the chin.

She pursed her lips in a parody of thought. "Dinner. You've heard of dinner, right? Maybe you've even done it once or twice?"

"I can't go to dinner. I can't go out, Tamara."

"Why? Who told you that?"

"What do you mean, 'Who told me that?'" he retorted defensively.

"I just don't understand why you can't go out. We've been spending time together. We've been touching." She was washing her hands. "So it's not only the disease."

"You . . . well," he stumbled to explain. "It is the disease. But you know how to be around it. You're comfortable. Others, well . . . others."

"What about others?" she demanded. "Others won't even know. You'll be just another customer ordering a meal, eating a meal and paying a bill. Oh, your hands? They'll think you burned them or that you scraped them real bad diving head first into third base. Don't you understand, Alex? It doesn't show the way you think it does. Most of it's in your head."

He exploded with gale force. "Leprosy is not in my head! Look at you! Look at the way you have to protect yourself from me!"

Flabbergasted, she tossed the soap aside. "God, Alex, I'm taking precautions, common sense precautions, *because* I want to be with you." They were silent. "And I didn't say leprosy was in your head. What I said was that it doesn't have to keep you confined. People don't see it. They don't notice it the way you think they do, and there is no reason that they have to. The way it is now you can have a normal life."

"A normal life!"

"You can go out into the world! People aren't calling you a freak. You're doing that yourself. Who is it that you think you're going to offend if you go to a restaurant? Who are you going to hurt? You take care of yourself. You're not trying to spread it. It's not the middle ages. You take your medication." She pleaded with him in earnest. "You have a right to have a life outside of that room. You have a great gift, Alex, and it's not only what you paint, as wonderful as that may be, but it's you. I fell in love with you."

"Love! What do you know about love? What do you know about me? How could you love me?"

It was steel in her eyes. A dull, roundly polished steel of resolve that knew it would not answer a question so easily answered. Saturnine resolution pervaded her answer. "How can you ask such a thing?"

His cheeks sagged with terror at the thing he had said. "Tamara, I didn't mean . . ."

"What did you mean, Alex? That you won't let me? That you won't let anyone?" Forlorn, he gaped into the white encasement of his palms. How had it unraveled? Come to this? Oh Soli, what did you want me to know about love?

She spoke with more tenderness now as she saw him in a new light. How fragile was the soul of this man? This was the reason a woman fell in love. "It's in your mind, Alex. Can't you understand? It always has been."

☞

Even before Dorothia could find the new wrapping on her son's wrists exquisite, she paid a visit to The Amber Artist to inquire about the delivery girl who had, until quite recently, been under employment. The information she desired came to her without begging the necessity of a bribe, for which she was prepared to dole substantial sums.

The ex-co-worker who provided Dorothia with the information appeared quite willing to support any effort of ill-intent towards Ms. Tamara R. Browne. The ex-co-worker with bright pimply pistils shooting from his face resented being turned down by the young math whiz who fancied art and artists. Sensing Dorothia's malevolence as a dog senses fatty bacon, he supplied Dorothia with complete photocopies of the young woman's job application, including previous employers, references, et cetera, et cetera.

The boy remembered that the owner, Sal Gentiles, had vacillated on hiring the young woman and had placed several long distance phone calls before finally making the decision. "A strange thing for a low skill, low wage job," he had commented. After that, the boy could tell her no more of the details, despite his relish to collaborate, if not converge, on the topic, his young lust pushing him to penetrate the consciousness of the marked target by any means possible. Dorothia purchased a few supplies to create a cursory feel that her visit could have been something more than anti-social.

"Tamara R. Browne," Dorothia muttered to herself as she marched into a phone booth and grabbed at the bound yellow pages. "Let's see, H, K, M, Q, P. Here it is. P. P. P. P. I." She looked up as a well dressed man passing the phone booth gawked at her attractive calves. "P. I. Private Investigator." She ran her finger to the first listing: AAA Private Investigation, Zephaniah Maxwell. "How creative," she thought sarcastically as she slipped a quarter into the slot.

An hour later she sat across the desk from a balding, gruffly handsome man who was thoroughly preoccupied by the sight of her curvaceous breasts. The leather gun holster wrapped about his shoulders was unfastened and empty. "Find out everything you can about this girl. Here's her information. Everything! And I want it fast."

Lounging behind the desk with strong arms laced behind his head, the man had rectangular, gambler's eyes: the kind of eyes that are constantly scanning the scenery in search of the triple cherry. He had cold coffee in a Styrofoam cup and a fedora hanging from a hook on the door. The file cabinets were in the corner. There was dust on the floor and a bloodstain on the wall. Buzzing flies were slapping against the window. "Fast ain't no trouble. No trouble at all. But it'll cost extra."

When all was said and done, she liked his style. He didn't hem and haw or coat his motive for profit with platitudes. Hard cash to cut through the bullshit — she could appreciate his kind, his hard and fast and dangerous style.

"Name it," she commanded, and he did.

"Cigarette?"

"Just get me the information. I pay extra for dirt," she answered coldly, rising from her seat and walking towards the door.

Eyes on the ass in the tight skirt, Zephaniah Maxwell whistled, stating flatly, "You're one icy bitch. This girl really must have pissed you off good." Tossing aside the cellophane wrap, he slapped a cigarette from a fresh pack. Her back to him as she stood at the half open door, she turned. Scrutinizing the black man with a half-hearted grin, he could see that she recognized the words for the compliment he had intended them to be. "Yes ma'am," he repeated, "one icy bitch."

With a long, painted finger she adjusted the bright red lipstick at the corners of her mouth before replying with a hint of disdainful conceit. "Why Mr. Maxwell, you haven't a clue."

11

ZEPHANIAH MAXWELL POUNCED on the information provided. He liked his work; it gave him ample opportunities to exercise the more atomic elements of his consciousness.

Zephaniah had been born in a shanty town eleven miles outside of Mobile, Alabama in 1961. The whiskey breath doctor who performed the delivery had come to the poverty-stricken home only reluctantly and on the promise that he would receive the meat of a healthy sow in the late spring. Following labor, the doctor took a single look at the baby and declared that the child looked like, and was sure to be, a screw-up. Understanding how such an inauspicious pronouncement can curse a child for life, the grandmother took the child from the doctor as soon as the umbilical cord was cut. She wrapped the newborn in a blue sheet and stared deep into the babe's face.

She spoke aloud so everyone in the room could hear. "No, Doctor. You're wrong." The grandmother's statement was bold, for it was a white doctor whom she contradicted before the family gathered in the room. At 71 years of age, it was the first time the Baptist woman had ever contradicted a white person. Years later, on her death bed, she would reflect upon that day with a smile saying simply that the holy spirit had moved her. "This child is part of a special plan. His name will be Zephaniah, right from the Bible. Do you know what that means, Doctor? Do you know what 'Zephaniah' means?"

The doctor ignored her. He repressed his disgust, thinking bitterly, "Another sign of the times, ungrateful niggers. Pretty soon they're going to start thinking they're as good as us."

"It means, 'The Lord hides,'" the grandmother had stated with shining eyes to the approval of the room. "Yes sir, the Lord has got a secret plan for this child, a secret plan, indeed."

"I'm sure," the doctor muttered as he stepped over the snipped umbilical cord laying on the floor and left the rickety shanty. "Part of a secret plan to ruin my Sunday afternoon."

Many years later, well into adulthood, Zephaniah still had not decided who was right. For all of his effort, he found it easier to think of himself as a screw-up than as an important part of God's secret plan.

This at least was easy stuff Zephaniah figured, pushing aside the coffee so that he could dig into the new case. Mining information on a 23-year-old girl with a highbrow education shouldn't take a heavy spade. How sharp an appetite for the depraved could the Stanford math and physics crowd really have? Strip chess in the study lounge? Calculus on crack? Getting dirty information, that could be the hard part.

"Tamara R. Browne." Scanning the job application, he repeated the name to himself, searching for a lead in the syllables. B.S. in math, high honors. Scholarship. Whistle. Graduate work in physics, limited. No real work experience. Teacher's Aid. Lab Assistant. Six month gap. General staff at Danforth Institute of Fine Art, seven months. Employed at the Amber Artist, weeks.

"She's a damn Girl Scout cookie!"

Zephaniah reasoned it through, constructing an initial profile to prime the old thought pump. Self-motivated. High achiever in the abstract sciences. Goes on to grad school, meets up with some bad drugs, follows Phish or joins some cult for a while, tries to find herself. No, he corrects himself; she's not the drug type. Rechecking his premises, he returns to grad school. Here she is floating along, bright as a sun, life's a joy and then all of a sudden — boom! She drops out. Why'd she drop out? She was on a damn scholarship at Stanford, easy street for life. What happened at grad school? That's the question. Zephaniah feels a joy. A few shards and he can read a life, so he believes.

So she drops out of grad school. Six months of nothing. What did she do in those six months? Finally, she appears in Vermont at another high brow institute, only this time she's on the periphery, working a menial job that demands nothing of her mind. She's free to think whatever she wants to think. No one to tell her what's right or wrong, no one to throw "proven" scientific history at her. Zephaniah begins to like her. She'd taken a stand, moved from west to east, much as he had moved from south to north, from Mason to Dixon. Only for her, for Tamara, it was science to art, from linear to lateral. What caused her to pull the psychological 180? Did she fall in love with the arts? Or was she working on some damn thought experiment too abstract for the general population? People as prime numbers. Art as the rational. Something freaky. Had she gone over the edge, into an abyss? Six digits in education and she wants to pedal a cash register. Had she overthrown social capital in her mind? Independent thinker crap? Is that what this boiled down to? Couldn't hold down a job or didn't want to? The latter seemed more likely. Perceived no value in it as compared to her real work, whatever that might be.

Zephaniah wrote a note to himself on the application — *Proposition 1: Psychological 180's don't happen; it just looks that way from the outside.*

So how has my sweet little Girl Scout cookie been messing with the Ice Queen? It didn't make sense. No sense at all. "I hate it when they give me none of the facts. Raw data, not a shred of context."

Zephaniah decided to begin by tracing the trail backwards. Placing the job application to the Amber Artist aside, he put in a few calls to Danforth. Unfortunately, no one appreciated the virtues of gift giving over the phone. With a very short list of names, he hopped on the I-95 freeway. He reckoned that a trip to Vermont would do him good, help him to clear his head. After all, his wife had just cleared out their apartment. He knew because the furniture was gone. He knew it was serious because she took the green gripped can opener. Detective work, in the end, brought him as close to himself as it did to his clients. Sharing and uncovering secrets with strangers gave him raw material to project himself through. God could have served the same function, but clients paid better. And this one, with her heaving breasts, what a ringer!

Autumn swung fully, a swift scythe eradicating summer. Zephaniah put down the hood and blasted the heat. Expenses. This was a New England autumn to the core. Red Sox in post season and foliage in all its glory, peaking. He'd been up north now for six years but never made the scenic trip about which people rave. New England in autumn. In six years, you'd think I could have done this with Carol. She'll be happier without me. The horizon blazed in brilliant colors, a radiant display of fireworks in leaves. Shades of color he'd never seen. Shades he could not name. The landscape was literally ablaze, awash with an aura, a bursting energy that defied explanation even as it demanded the attempt.

"It's a painting," Zephaniah thought out loud, "or what every painting tries to be." An explosion of life. A last celebration more magnificent than spring, sharing wisdom from the precipice of death.

Zephaniah did not allow the separation from his wife to affect him. He knew that his workaholic, philandering ways justified her desertion. Still, it would have been nice to share such a bounteous splash, the drive north. Shaking his head, Zephaniah dismissed the intimations of self-pity, telling himself that he welcomed the opportunity of a new beginning, whatever that meant. The car zipped along. The wind felt good upon his skin.

"No more womanizing," he admonished himself, fully aware that this was a straw resolution, constructed purely for the delight of tearing it down.

There were a multiplicity of shades of red that when patterned together he could not call red, yet he did not know what else to call them. Some of the shades were crimson. This came to mind easily enough. There were brick and magenta. Fuchsia, vermilion and vermeil. An orange-breasted robin flew across the sky. It had been years since Zephaniah had seen this beautiful and simple bird. "Aw hell!" Zephaniah mused, "it doesn't matter what the technical names of the colors are." That was academic. What mattered was how the colors made him feel. He thought of Tamara again and conjectured that this was what the young girl must have been thinking as her world became a complex mathematical puzzle, a lifeless equation of academic, mechanistic physics that made her feel nothing. *Proposition 2: Irrationality can be based in reason. A logical decision has led her towards art.*

At the Danforth gate, the guard refused him parking access without a sticker or a confirmed appointment. Parking along a residential side-street, he walked the distance to Danforth. It ran through his head, "The rich thrive on controlling space." He did receive stares, nothing too obvious. A few nervous glances. This affluent town, he could surmise, was not accustomed to the sight of a black man. In this, a fair amount of modest pleasure existed, a corruptible pleasure that recognized the correlation between notoriety and celebrity. The more attention he drew, the more Zephaniah understood that they expected him to be bad. The more he fulfilled their expectation, the more they could celebrate in their sense of knowing all without knowing at all. Northern racism, he had long ago come to recognize, possessed a very different face from southern racism. In the North they hated the individual, saw a menace, but loved the group. In the South, it was the exact opposite. They loved the individual but hated the collective group. Of the two, Zephaniah found northern racism more dangerous and, at its core, more insidious. One did not dare play black, particularly in the deep *Naurth*.

"I can get you a job application to fill out, but I don't think we're hiring." The Office of Student Housing and Regulatory Affairs marked the fourth point to which Zephaniah had been run. Why did the detective work always look easier on television?

"I'm not looking for a job. I need to speak with whoever the person is that coordinates your maid and general labor staff."

The silver-haired woman who stood on the other side of the barrier surveyed him over spectacles and a wrinkled nose. "No."

Zephaniah waited as she shuffled her papers, marking small boxes with X's. When it became clear that she considered her work done, he pressed himself over the counter.

"What do you mean, 'No'? No, I can't see him, or no he's not here?"

The woman stroked her chin as though considering an answer that truly wouldn't matter. "No, he's not here," she finally responded.

Zephaniah stepped back from the counter. "Oh, I see, it's just that he, Mr. Morgansterne," it was the name he had read on an official looking piece of mail. "Mr. Morgansterne wanted to see me about, well, the paternity finding."

"Paternity finding?"

"Yes, I, well, I shouldn't really be telling you. One of the students here at Danforth. He wanted to speak to me about the parents' concerns."

"One of *our* students?"

"This is Danforth, isn't it? Boy, I'd sure love to go to a school like this. Must take big cash!"

"One moment, Mr. . . . ?" The woman fumbled, picking up the phone.

"O'Shaughnessy. Daniel O'Shaughnessy." Adding the Irish represented a transparent touch of madness. Perhaps one did play black in the deep *Naurth*; perhaps that was the very best place to play.

Ringing the extension, she whispered, "Mr. Morgansterne, a Daniel O'Shaughnessy is here to see you . . . yes, O'Shaughnessy, Daniel. About the," her voice descended two octaves, "paternity. Yes sir, yes sir, I'll send him right in."

The gamble worked. Hitler's advice: the greater the lie, the more likely it is to be believed.

"Mr. Morgansterne will see you now. Down the hall and to the left."

Like a fellow conspirator, Zephaniah leaned into her. "Back from lunch already?" He received no answer.

Already way out on a limb, Zephaniah opted to double down as he entered Morgansterne's office.

From behind his oak desk, Morgansterne, resembling a curarized curmudgeon well-suited to a wax museum, smiled without warmth. He rose with an extended hand. "Mr. O'Shaughnessy. O'Shaughnessy, is that correct? Please, take a seat."

Shaking the clammy hand of the administrator, Zephaniah controlled his impulse to cringe by substituting exuberance for disgust.

"Yes, Mr. Morgansterne, thank you for seeing me today. O'Shaughnessy is correct. My father, God bless his soul, an Irishman with a thing for the black woman. I got my mother's genes but my father's sense o' humor. My papee used to say when I was a wee lad, Danny Boy, there's nothing like a dirty potato to bleed sugar, don't you ever forget that. What a world it is. What a world."

"Yes, indeed," Morgansterne replied disapprovingly as he settled back into his leather chair, a storm of skepticism clouding his brow. The thin gray man with a bloodless face and effeminate lips spoke without emotion. "And what can I do for you today, Mr. O'Shaughnessy? I'm very busy."

Zephaniah glanced at the empty desk and wondered what Morgansterne could possibly be busy with? One o'clock dusting, two o'clock tea, three o'clock golf match, four o'clock pee.

Reading the expression of perpetual boredom in the face of the minor dean, Zephaniah experienced wonderment in understanding that Morgansterne's job was to sit in an office all day and look official. Outside the window, groundskeepers were raking the colorful leaves from the manicured lawns.

"Yes, I'm sure you're busy, Mr. Morgansterne. My papee used to say, don't waste the time of busy men, they have a lot to do that most of us wouldn't even want to." Zephaniah pressed forward onto his seat's edge. "Let me get to the point, Mr. Morgansterne. Getting to the point, my papee used to say it's what many a woman wants and a few men too. It's such an urgent matter I find myself in. You see . . ."

"Paternity, Mr. O'Shaughnessy?"

Zephaniah had to admit, Morgansterne's arrogance made their interaction much easier. Since Morgansterne assumed he knew everything and Zephaniah really had nothing to tell, they were a fine match.

Morgansterne sighed wearily, as though he had seen it all before. "This won't go well. What is it you seek for silence? Which one of the students is it?"

What is it you seek for silence? The smug presumption, even from this listless lumpfish, astounded Zephaniah. Only in such an insular petri dish could such a view be groomed and proffered without any sense of self-irony. Zephaniah needed time to think. Anything he said now would strike Morgansterne as trivial. The gallantry of the office possessed an austere and foreboding quality that belittled the sinecure who sat behind the desk. The artwork on the walls was splendid, if not pedantic. So the old bird thinks I'm here for blackmail. And he's listening! What type of a studio is this? If the old man thought they were in some sort of bargaining stage, then they would bargain.

After a thoughtful pause, Zephaniah continued casually, "You have a whole lot of employees here. How many do you figure it takes to run an operation like this?"

"We currently have 46 members on staff."

"So you probably don't remember them. They're probably just a lot of faces without names to you."

Bristled by perceived insinuation, dander up, Morgansterne grew defensive for the first time. "My job, Mr. O'Shaughnessy is to provide the best conditions possible for the living and learning of each and every student of Danforth, sparing no expense. We do that, Mr. O'Shaughnessy, by being on intimate terms with all members responsible for this charter. Our staff is of the highest quality and I take responsibility for their performance personally."

This was getting good. Zephaniah forced himself into calmness, willing his muscles to relax.

"Then I'd bet you remember a girl named Tamara Browne."

Morgansterne tilted backwards, exercising his long term memory. His lips moved but slightly as he recited the name softly to himself. He thought they were still in negotiation, the larger issue of paternity and extortion not yet addressed.

"Tamara Browne, yes, I remember her. About five foot-six, pretty features. Quite a rare find. A bit of a tragic case really. She came to us after a bit of a stint stateside. But that's not news to anyone. Completely innocuous to anyone but herself. Brilliant thinker, really. We were pleased to have her on our team. We had hoped to eventually move her into some mathematical mentoring, perhaps teaching. She wanted nothing to do with it though, complete breakdown. Such a sad story of wasted talent. We'd hoped her brilliance would rub off in intangible ways on some of ours."

"Stateside?"

"McLean, Mr. O'Shaughnessy."

"McLean?"

"McLean Hospital. Loo-loo bin as you might call it. An insane asylum, Mr. O'Shaughnessy." Morgansterne pressed forward, clasping his hands upon the desk impatiently, the gray wrinkles of the face contorting, thickening as he spoke. "What student, Mr. O'Shaughnessy?"

"A mental hospital?" Zephaniah muttered in awe, forgetting his role. So this Tamara had a few tomatoes stewing in the old brain, a loose cogswell cog, a few cards short of a full deck; she takes a hit on eighteen, laughs at a funeral, watches the commercials instead of the programs.

"I don't think I like you, Mr. O'Shaughnessy," Morgansterne pronounced suddenly, gazing at the man with a lively suspicion. "You're too smart for a dumb man; you're not what you seem to be."

With the eyes of a deer, Zephaniah gazed at the stiff board of man. He had done it again! He had succeeded in compromising his cover as soon as he had obtained the information he wanted.

The bookshelves were filled with leather bound titles, probably first edition classics of the classical canon. If the authors were dead and white and men, then they deserved a spot in history. These were the gods of academic men like Morgansterne who had come to know the world they claimed to love through leather bound books. But they had not known the mean and gritty streets, the rage of hate that clings to physical violence, blood on their finest trousers, church burnings, the intimidation of the hanging cross and the long-term indignation of second class citizenry.

"I'm afraid I've misjudged you, Mr. O'Shaughnessy." Pressing a button, Morgansterne, a glib, bestial snarl upon his lips, called for a security escort.

It was his damn Achilles heel. Every time, sure as Doris Day, Zephaniah pissed away his good work because he couldn't maintain the illusion that had gotten him what he wanted in the first place. Zephaniah's wife, ex-wife, used to kid him that he'd make a great bank robber. He could always find a way to get what he wanted, but he always failed to pull off the graceful exit. What was it Carol used to say?

"What's the use of success, if you can't ride into the sunset to enjoy it?"

Zephaniah got so caught up in his purpose of reaching his goal that he never gave much of a thought to what he would do if he succeeded.

"Riding off into the sunset gracefully has to be a part of the goal. That's what people want, Zephaniah. That's what I want."

Zephaniah didn't doubt that she was right.

"This world don't care about us, Carol. It's never going to give us that chance. This is America, Carol. All the happy endings are for Snow White."

On one of his last assignments, he'd ended the job with two broken ribs, a punctured abdomen and a broken nose. But he had gotten the job done.

Zephaniah laughed out loud as he thought about Carol. Other than his work he no longer had a life, and that feeling of having nothing left to lose made him feel something more than dangerous.

Fright contorted Morgansterne's pale cheeks. This was the face of the slaveowner, the slavetrader, the pale criminal.

Zephaniah rose, leaning forward on the desk. "Do you know what, Morgansterne?" A hundred years of violence flamed in his tired eyes, hopeless eyes with no place left to go, defeated eyes that knew the game was rigged, eyes that knew there could be no sunset and no horizon on the classical stage.

The door opened and a guard in powder blue stepped in.

"What's that, Mr. O'Shaughnessy?" Bolstered by reinforcements, the question was saturated with a mockery that filled the speaker with pleasure. Morgansterne's gnarled face evinced pride in mastery of the upper hand, the hidden ace. With a rigid, grim, bony hand he halted the guard's approach.

Eyes locked in combat, Zephaniah and Morgansterne confronted one another, each filled with hate and longing and history. Zephaniah felt a layer of himself unfold. How tired he was of being seen as an ape at the verge of extinction. In Morgansterne he saw all the ghosts of the Klan, all of the weak, insipid, pale judges.

"I'm a free man, Morgansterne, free!"

Despite the irrelevance of the strange statement, Zephaniah's heart soared. The old man flinched. Zephaniah could not tell why.

Shaking with impotent wrath, the old man sputtered vehemently, "Get out!"

The guard approached but didn't dare lay a hand as Zephaniah turned. "A free man, Morgansterne, a free man! Try to say that about yourself!" There was an atomic madness to their encounter that both could feel. Falling into his chair, Morgansterne gazed at the inspired works of artists hanging like victims — bought and sold and put in frames — from his walls.

Zephaniah got back into his car and drove south. On the highway he wove back and forth across the dividing lines, his borders a little broader, the limits less limiting. He had made a graceful exit. Carol would have, for once, been proud.

Two days later Dorothia called. She and Zephaniah met late in the afternoon. He offered her a drink as she took off her coat. She declined. Slowly and in regulated detail, he reported on what he had learned. A brief visit to McLean and a few well-directed calls to Stanford proved even more fruitful than the visit to Danforth. It wasn't quite dirt, at least not dirt of the worst kind, that which is self-inflicted by the individual, but what he had discovered greatly satisfied Dorothia. Grinning at the prospect of the young girl's fragile mental state, Dorothia finally relaxed. "Keep talking, Mr. Maxwell. Your voice is making me giddy."

Zephaniah Maxwell gazed across the desk at the sumptuous woman and realized for the first time, awakening, that he did not like her; she was too much like him. He did not like her at all.

12

O
N AUGUST 23, 1939, the Russians and Germans signed a secret
pact of non-aggression. Following the signing, Ribbentropp,
the Nazi Foreign Minister, and Stalin drank copiously into the
night. The secret Nazi-Soviet Pact ushered into existence a new era of
relations between the two nations. Previously, Stalin had been one of
the Führer's more vocal critics, calling through the League of Nations
for a strong, unilateral response in resistance to the fascist dictator. The
treaty was signed in the drafty Kremlin after a long and veiled discussion of spheres of influence. The deal, in the deftly metaphoric language that has remained fresh since Caesar's time, stabbed Poland in
the back.

To Hitler's joy, Germany received immediate assurance that the
Soviet Union would not join Britain and France if Britain and France
honored their treaty obligations and came to the aid of Poland should
Poland be attacked. In part, Stalin felt forced into the treaty. The Anglo-
French diplomats were doing their best to force the war eastward; they
cared little for the interests of the Soviet regime as crisply demonstrated by Chamberlain's appeasement of Hitler in Munich in 1936, a diplo-
matic roundtable from which the Anglos had deliberately excluded the
Russians.

Matched by France's willful failure to meet her treaty obligations to
Czechoslovakia — a move that fundamentally represented the moral
bankruptcy of the West — Stalin had great reason to believe it profoundly unlikely that Western obligations to Poland, a country where
the Anglicanized West had even less at stake than in Czechoslovakia,

would be kept. The seemingly odious deal, made behind the backs of the Anglo-French delegations, provided Russia with some much needed *peredyshka:* breathing space. Unfortunately for the West, it also gave Hitler the necessary incentive to surge through Western Europe, uninhibited by the fear of a two-front campaign.

Peredyshka lasted but a short time, as Stalin later claimed he had suspected it would. On June 28, 1941, with the Balkans occupied by German forces and the war with Western Europe largely won, Hitler attacked the Soviet Union. As news of the advancing German blitzkrieg reached Moscow, the Russians, embarrassingly underprepared for the act of betrayal, conscripted. The armies that marched from Moscow and St. Petersburg grew as they accelerated towards the front, consigning soldiers as they fatefully advanced to meet Mother Russia's need. Solzhenitsyn, at age 16, thus found himself caught between three converging armies. He waited, eyes to the plains, as did the other men of Krylov, for the first army to arrive. For the first time in their lives, they were actively hoping to see the Russian army. The men waited in the village for the purpose of protecting the women and children, woefully cognizant that if the Germans first arrived, any resistance they offered would be delusive.

To the joy of all, in the early days of September, the Russian army arrived from St. Petersburg. Fifty-one men were selected from the village for service. They had three hours to prepare for their march; most had been ready for days. By the time the army moved through, the tears were already shed. Naistika watched her young son in silence. For the past seven years, she had found him to be her single pleasure in life. She refused in a time of war to weaken him with the burden of tears.

Despite his age, Solzhenitsyn had earned the stature of being one of the most respected members of the village. Upon the day of his father's death he had become a man. Some said later that young Solzhenitsyn had never in fact been a boy but had been born a completed man. These were, of course, wild exaggerations from those who believed and hoped that young Solzhenitsyn might grow into the respectable semblance of his father. Occasionally there were glimpses that affirmed such a possibility. After his father's death he became garrulous as his father had once been. He would enter the company of men, working side by side with them on the hardest projects of the village, freely expressing his thoughts and ideas, giving his unsolicited opinions. Initially, the men patronized the boy out of respect and compassion, but soon they grew impressed by the force of his will that somehow allowed him to keep pace with the elder men and nearly match their strength. Some said that Michayl had not died but simply entered the son as a ghost invades a body. Others said that in the last months, Michayl had planted all of the seeds the village would need to thrive in the head of the boy. Solzhenitsyn paid no attention to such talk. Amongst the children, he already walked as a distant legend.

Some had thought it best that the men of the village go into hiding until the armies had come and gone, thus attempting to avoid the war altogether. It was young Solzhenitsyn who said, to the surprise of all, "We would do better to fight our enemies with a gun given to us by the Russian army than with a carrot plucked from our own field." The statement drew wide support from the villagers. They cheered Michayl for the words he uttered through his son. And so it was with young Soli that he was never himself alone but always his father and his father's emissary.

And so the guns did come on a hot Tuesday in September as fifty-one men were marched from the hamlet to a site where they would receive their basic training before, as quickly as possible, being sent to reinforce the Russian front. Dressed in blue fatigues, Solzhenitsyn excelled in the training camp, proving himself to be an apt student in the tactics of war. To the pleasure of the instructors, he never had to be told a second time to aim high with a gun and twist with a knife. He didn't complain. He was silent and focused, often found standing near the commanders of the camp listening to their conversations. They would laugh at him, and his eyes would tell them that they had no reason not to laugh. Then one day as they were laughing, Solzhenitsyn interrupted, "I want to be in Yusherin's army."

They grew serious and eyed Solzhenitsyn grossly. "Yusherin's army? Why would you ask for such a thing?"

"Yes," another added, "you're a young boy. You want to come out of this thing alive? The war will pass. All things do. Yusherin is a black-souled dog. No one wants to be in his army; they all want to get out."

A wry smiled turned the corners of young Soli's lips as his eyes darkened with intent. "Then it shouldn't be a problem getting me in."

The men laughed nervously at what they saw but did not want to believe they saw in the eyes of the young imp who should not have been capable of such a knowing look. Soli remained unmoved, waiting for an answer.

The ranking major finally stepped away from the clownish crowd. "Listen, boy, you seem smart enough in other ways. Russia needs her smart sons alive, not dead. I'd recommend you stay as far away from Yusherin as possible. But if you want his army, God knows, I won't stop you."

"It's what I want."

"It's your funeral."

One of the others chimed in deliciously, "The pup's got a taste for war is what it is!"

Three weeks later, Solzhenitsyn stood at attention, a single man amongst a sea of faces as the commanding officer approached on horseback. Soli had not seen the face of Vladimir Gorcinov Yusherin in six years. After the death of his father, Yusherin returned only once more. Soli remembered the general demanding that Michayl come face him. The general thought it a lie when the villagers reported to him the death of their honored leader. The general grew angry. He ordered the storehouses seized in full. He tortured several men. He raped Naistika — violently. Soli had rushed to attack the general, to confront him; only the efforts of several men of the village tying him down, gagging him, prevented the boy's assault. It was the only time the men truly treated him as a boy. After that season, Yusherin never returned. Another representative from the army came each year, an aristocratic man, groomed and paunch-bellied, who had won his title and position through political favors. He hated the role he needed to play and viewed it as a temporary inconvenience and a mild necessity to be carried with dignity until assuming a position more worthy of his grace and upbringing. He turned out to be corrupt and easily mollified by a few sparkling trinkets of jewelry, just as Soli said he would be.

Alongside dark army jeeps and other pieces of heavy, camouflaged equipment, General Yusherin rode a beautiful Arabian stud with an orange mane. Surveying the new troops from the brave steed, the general was and would remain an anachronism. The new troops had just intercepted Yusherin's army which had been recently ordered to drop back from the front to make ready a tactically advantageous position from which to challenge the forward momentum of the German tide. For weeks the dreaded German blitzkrieg had steadily progressed, their collective will seemingly irresistible. The brightest Russian strategists, far from public view, devised a scheme to lure the bulk of the German military deeper into southern Russia so as to stretch the supply routes. Baited through a series of subtle gambits, three hundred miles into Russia, constricted by the merging of two rivers, the Russians would hunker down to fortify an unmapped position named Dostoyevsky's Ridge, a forty-foot high, five-mile ravine that faced directly down into the sharp cuts of a gravel gulch. The Russian strategists pinned the hopes of Moscow on the ability of Russia's finest to make a decisive, committed stand against the main glut of the German artery at this strategic point. If they could halt the German onslaught, at least stall the powerful, uninhibited war machine, then perhaps they could shift momentum in their favor.

Yusherin's face, dark hollows below the eyes, was cruel, crueler than it had been six years ago; recent time had wrung all traces of sentiment and decency from the man. A chill traveled down Soli's back. He questioned for the first time what it must have been like for his father to look into the eyes of this vile monster even as he questioned whether he would possess the mettle to stand where his father had stood. Yusherin emoted more than a bitterness. Had it been mere bitterness, Soli would have been prepared. Bitterness, like a radish, possessed substance, pungency; it is something to which a person can react. Yusherin had no substance.

As the general reviewed the troops, he conveyed no sense that he saw the men who stood in line. They were a collection of shells, without personification, and he was the gun. "We are going to kill Germans, you and I," he began. "We are going to kill them because we want to. We are not killing them to protect our children or our wives or our family or even Mother Russia. We are going to kill them because killing is good. Killing affirms our right to live. Killing confirms our existence. Killing is good. That is the lesson of my army. If you follow this lesson, if you live it, if it is the one thing you keep in your head, you will live and they will die."

He drove the horse down the ranks, his voice booming. "War is simple, just as men are simple. It was Nietzsche who said that a true man seeks only two things: *danger and play*. A good war gives us both!"

Soli listened against his will, and to his own shocked dismay he found that he did not wholly disagree. He found that an eccentric charisma existed in this banal beast of a man, that to his own terror, they shared in part a common language.

"Killing is good. With every German you kill, you become better. Take pleasure in the killing like a carpenter takes pleasure in cutting a board or a farmer takes pleasure in chaffing wheat. Killing is good. The carpenter kills the tree. The farmer kills the wheat. It's the one thing that no one wants to tell you. They fear that it will make you what they want to be but cannot become — powerful! But I will tell you; killing is good. The Germans thought they would kill us, but we will kill them. We have the advantage. Do you know why? It is because they think that they are trying to win a war, but this is not about a war, and it is not about winning. This is about killing. By crossing our borders they have given us a great opportunity. They have given us the freedom to kill them. To kill as many as we can, as fast as we can, with as much cruelty as our spirits can muster."

The men were nodding in excitement. Soli felt it too; the voice that came from the general came from a lost portion of his own soul. He could understand it, this language, this language that no one had ever dared speak to him. Yes, this is what it was to be a man. To kill. To be the master of death, just as the woman through birth is the master of life.

"But words are cheap things. Life, like women, is a cheap thing to be forgotten. Words can never wholly communicate the essence of the thing."

Yusherin waved his gloved fist and a grim-faced soldier stepped from the seasoned ranks, dragging forward what had once been a man. Stripped naked, feet bloody from a forced march, arms bound by rope, purple bruises, grisly, gaping welts about the head and chest, his visage was a declaration of terror. Led before the general, the beaten being stood in bondage before Yusherin who fiercely took the rope of the blond-haired man's life into his own ardent hands. "Yes, life is cheap. Look at this pathetic creature. Is it a Russian? Is it a German? Take off the uniform and it means nothing. That is why you need only remember that killing is good." Facing the prisoner, the general addressed the man with a mocking, sweet voice. "Speak to me in German, will you? Speak to me in German. Tell me of your superiority."

The prisoner gazed upwards in dumb horror, his eyes wide and white as the general leaned forward on his horse, resting his chest upon the orange mane, reciting for the prisoner the German words he wished to hear. "Speak to me of how strong you are. . . . *Was nich micht umbringt, mach micht starker.*"

The terrified man stared at the general with imploring eyes that comprehended the words but sought desperately to avoid connecting them with meaning. "*Was nich micht umbringt, mach micht starker,*" the general repeated again, a gross mockery in his tone. The prisoner implored in the broken utterances of an alien tongue swollen with blood. The general tugged at the rope, jerking the German forward. Soli cringed, thinking the arms pulled from the sockets. "He may as well be a dog for how well I understand him!" the general shouted for effect. "Another species all together. And if he had kept in his mind that killing is good, he wouldn't be here; he wouldn't be at the hands of death! This is the price of softness! Of forgetting your one purpose, of forgetting that killing is good!"

"*Was nich micht umbringt, mach micht starker. Was nich micht umbringt, mach micht starker. Was nich micht umbringt, mach micht starker.*" The general shouted at the man again and again and again, a relentless repetition that caused all to believe General Yusherin mad. The German creature shook his head in fear, his comprehension of the general's intent gaining in clarity. Kicking his spurs into the horse's side, the noble horse lurched forward. Nearly immediately, Yusherin yanked at the silver bit, reining the horse in, but not before the prisoner stumbled to the ground, dragged for several feet, crying out in despair. Finally the prisoner broke, fluidly repeating the German phrase with the speed and mindless repetition of a Catholic rosary. "*Was nich micht umbringt, mach micht starker. Was nich micht umbringt, mach micht starker.*" With each recitation he shook his head, attempting as though to deny the words and his belief in them. Yusherin grinned in the delight of sadism.

"Killing is good, is it not?" the general asked the troops, invoking the mantra. "This German should have remembered what you will never forget." The general again tugged at the man's hands, urging him to speak again. *"Was nich micht umbringt, mach micht starker. Was nich micht umbringt, mach micht starker."* Each time the man paused — unsure of whether to continue — the general jerked at the cord, urging the prisoner to repeat the phrase over and over again as all but a few who witnessed the criminal scene wondered what this terrible phrase could mean.

The general gazed at the man and spoke with a voice so clean of mockery that it made the statement all the more baneful. "I'm going to let you die a poet. You should thank me."

Soli watched. So this was a zombie, a living ghost, already dead, white as a sheet, without contrast, beyond pity, transformed. Killing one such as this, Soli thought, would be an act of mercy. *"Was nich micht umbringt, mach micht starker. Was nich micht umbringt, mach micht starker. Was nich micht umbringt, mach micht starker. Was nich micht umbringt, mach micht starker."*

Facing the assembly, the general probed the eyes of his men. Many shivered with fear, hoping only to avoid direct eye contact or anything that would draw the general's attention to them. But in that moment Soli's human senses left him. Staring directly at the general, he was thinking exactly what the general wanted him to think. *Killing is good.* When Yusherin pulled the horse and the German to stop before the line, Soli met the cruel eyes. Each man maintained a steady gaze upon the other. Soli noticed the color, stone gray. The general flinched, narrowed his lids so that his eyes peered from thin slits; he focused them upon the boy's face as if trying to remember something that had meant something once, something that had made a piercing impression long ago.

"Do I know you?"

"No, sir, you don't."

"But you understand what I'm saying, don't you?"

"Killing is good, sir," Soli responded promptly, gaze unwavering.

"Yes." Yusherin unconsciously patted the horse in approval. "Yes, killing is good. You want to kill this one?" The seductive quality of the voice was repulsive. Yusherin brought the German around the horse so that he stood in naked form, pink-gray scrotum shriveling between his filthy legs, separating Soli and the general.

"Was nich micht umbringt, mach micht starker. Was nich micht umbringt, mach . . ."

Had the general not looked away to swing the prisoner around the ass of the horse, Soli's face might have revealed his deeper truth. Instead, by the time the general's brimstone eyes fell upon him once more, Soli had transformed his face to iron. *"Was nich micht umbringt, mach micht starker."*

"So, you want to kill this one. Good. . . ." Yusherin commended. "I like my soldiers hungry and simple. Come here." Solzhenitsyn stepped forward, eyes locked steadily upon the general though his knees were quivering mightily with a fear he had never in all his life experienced. "You'll be rewarded for that." Soli stood at boot level to the man who had killed his father. Eyes upon Soli, Yusherin withdrew his sword. The steel released a single shimmering chime as it slid from its sheath.

"Was nich micht umbringt, mach micht starker."

With a deep, slow breath, Soli steadied himself. Is that what his father had felt? Fear to the core. A paralyzing fear to be overcome, driven out by a single-minded resolution of the heart to do whatever needed to be done. *"Was nich micht umbringt, mach micht starker. Was nich micht umbringt, mach micht starker."* For a moment, as the blade glistened in sunlight above the general's head, for just a moment as the sterling blade danced in the sun, Soli suspected that the general had recognized him. Yusherin lowered the blade for Soli to take, the sharp end inches away from the general's exposed neck. With a single movement he could have grasped the sword and plunged it forward, slicing Yusherin's throat open wide. As Soli took the sword by the gilded hilt in his hand, the general stated once more, his voice phantom-like, eerily kind, "Killing is good."

"Was nich micht umbringt, mach micht starker," the prisoner repeated like a prayer.

The blade exposed, Soli felt a gnarled pit in his stomach. Heavy as an anvil and absent of meaning, the whole of his being quaked with fear. He could still kill the general. With a leap he could sink the sword into the general's side with a slice between Adam's ribs.

Was nich micht umbringt, mach micht starker.

What was the meaning of these horrible words?

Solzhenitsyn felt the weight of the steel in his palm. This was the hilt, ornate with golden asps, that had beaten his father into submission. Looking at the German dog, he tried to see Yusherin. But all that he could see in that strange moment was his own father's weakness. Why had father willfully submitted to such a treatment? Why had he not fought like a . . . The sword was strong and light, suggesting simplicity. Soli glanced at the general as he proudly surveyed the troops who watched the developing performance, the evolving, traumatizing moment that would scar them all, stripping away their innocence, bringing them into full and undeniable awareness of the existence of good and evil. With a combination of awe and fear, the newly trained soldiers watched, unsure of what it would finally mean, knowing only that it was as if they themselves held the sword before the bleating German. *Was nich micht umbringt, mach micht starker.* The only way to stay close to Yusherin was to complete this act, Soli urged himself. Looking into the terrified eyes of the human creature, Solzhenitsyn raised the sword, still undecided. Would he strike to the top of the head or to the side of the neck?

These are the choices one begins to make after one has decided to kill. For power or hatred, for greed or mercy; these are the choices.

"Gott das gute! Gott das gute! Gott das gute!" the German screamed, his eyes locked shut so that nothing, no horror of evil, would corrode this final paroxysm of the spirit, the final return.

A gun shot rang out as Soli brought the sword swinging forward. Propelled backwards like a sack of flour, the body of the German bobbed, alone and disoriented, like a rooted tree that bends but will not break. Soli watched in slow, breathless motion. The wide, fixed eyes were in neither pain nor peace. They were only searching, searching for something comforting, something to safely recall upon waking from a nightmarish dream, something worth carrying from this world to the next. Never finding what he sought — and such a look of existential terror it was — the German collapsed into Soli's arms. The bullet through the forehead struck an inch above the brows, dead center to the eyes. Yusherin allowed the pistol to linger in the air so that all would remember its source. Dropping the sword, Soli caught the man, struggled in the attempt to ease him downward as blood poured upon the flesh of his palm. The naked man lay in the mud, chest rising with irregular gasps. The cloudless, azure sky drifted above, indifferent, simultaneously inviting.

"Gott das gute, Gott das gute, Gott das gute," the dying man strained, clutching at Soli's shoulders, passionate that if he could take nothing good with him, he would leave something good behind. So these are the choices of life. From the hole in the head blood trickled as water from a bubbling aquifer. *"Gott das gute,"* the man whispered. His spirit withdrew.

From the corner of his eyes, Soli saw Yusherin's hand as it picked up the golden asped hilt of the sword. Without thinking, knowing only what needed to be done, Soli reached to his belt for his own dagger and plunged it into the stomach of the prisoner, now free, that convulsed once more, wordless, silent, breathless, thankful. Soli twisted the knife deliberately; it gave him time to bow his head against the cold heel of the dagger and pray. *Let his most difficult hours be illuminated by your guidance and instructed by your will.*

"Not much of a poet," Yusherin proclaimed to the assembly.

"Killing is good," Soli mouthed the words mechanically.

Kneeling, the Yusherin took the knife from Soli's bloody hands. Upon his own shirtsleeve, the general wiped the blade clean. "The last words of a man are a dangerous thing. You want to kill, but you don't have the killer instinct . . . yet." Returning the dagger to Soli, he added, "Next time, be quicker." Standing over him almost protectively, the general patted young Soli on the back, as a father training his own son might do.

ℰ

Tamara had no place to go and nothing to do; she wasted her days wandering upon the gravel walkways at the zoo. The oriental panda bears had recently given birth to a pair of fat cubs, first generation Americans. Already, news coverage of the event had faded. Tamara found herself wondering for prolonged flights of time about the natural habitat of the panda, a mammal indigenous to the mountains of China and Tibet. Where would such a black and white camouflage serve them and how? In the jungle of night and day, on the front lines of a Zoroastrian engagement? Ruminating over eucalyptus branches, patient as clever monks, the masticating pandas resembled learned sages, deep in the maintenance of deliberative trances induced through

the ingestion of copious quantities of minty eucalyptus. Even the
young novices with sleepy eyes steeply pondered the complexities of
light and dark. Tamara watched them for hours upon end, waiting for
their insights to be revealed. When it became absolutely necessary, she
would get another job for as long as absolutely necessary.

At Stanford, as a graduate student in physics, she had held a job. It
was to think about physical problems from a theoretical perspective —
to prove or disprove postulated truth-functions through the meticulous
testing of propositions (most frequently achieved via methods of negation). In particular, she deliberated postulates that arose in relation to
the causation and nature of curved space. Her job, even as a mere student of spatial curvature, was to solve selected puzzles and/or provide
insights towards the solution of selected puzzles. Every proof or denial
of a proposition solved a puzzle, thus creating a picture of reality, what
could rightly be called a fact. She worked on and in spheres and planes
attempting to construct a picture of the reality of spheres and planes.
She lived on and in expanding points attempting to construct a picture
of expanding points that held true without exception.

Without exception, this was the crux; she sought to discover facts
that held true without exception. In this, she had never, not once, succeeded. All day and all night, she created alphanumeric formulas, twenty tedious, straight lines — as straight as straight had ever been — long.
She realized one day halfway through a statistical equation to prove
proposition k (the truth or falsehood of the proposition depended solely on the truth or falsehood of k) that she was living *in* the equation.
She was not solving it; it was solving her. Or put differently, for the
equation to exist, for the equation to get from one place to another, it
relied upon her; she could not be extracted as a factor — if not *the* factor — of the explored term. To explore the truth-function of k was to
explore the truth-function of herself. And if k were proven to be false
then she was proven to be false; for to know enough to question the
proposition of k, was to know k. And if k were proven to be false, then
what was proven was that that which proved k to be false knew that
which opposed k, the underlying proposition that proposed to challenge the truth or falsehood of k. As k was negated, that which opposed
k was affirmed. However, if k were affirmed and proven true, then that
which opposed k, let us call it j, was denied. [But Tamara understood

even more deeply; she understood that a straight line, the shortest distance between two points, was always defined as the straightest possible line from the point of view of the creature that was traveling from point to point. She understood that to invalidate k, for instance, was to invalidate j. Propositions were not a matter of "either/or," but matters of "and." Either k and j were false or k and j were true. For just as to know enough to question k was evidence of a knowledge of k, so did the antithetical proposition of k, j as we have named it, in knowing enough to propose itself as antithetical to k, demonstrate a complete knowledge of k. K and j were proven true or proven false together. K and j were true or k and j were false.]

From the perspective of one not traveling within the line, the line was curved space, spherical. This was the effect that gravity, or at the very least Einstein's interpretation of gravity, produced. The perspective outside the line was able to see the relationship of third points and alternative forces upon the line. And yet, how did one resolve the fact that the outside perspective was itself a third point and an alternative force that impacted, through its own projected interpretation, the curvature of the line?

Tamara Browne began, though not completely, to understand that all of life could be seen as an equation, a truth-function intending towards a singular fact. And since every equation needed human beings for its very existence, these humans should choose very carefully the equations they wished to bring into being by starting with the end they desired and building the equation around that desired end. The end — selected at the beginning — possessed within it the seed of every mean.

Tamara began to understand that life is lived backwards and that we should not concern ourselves with straight lines, as they are in great part deceptive. The essence of all that "is" is just an idea that at one point in time sought to be real. It is through building backwards from the idea that we arrive at the beginning of a successful equation that will lead to the actualization — or physical proof — of the idea. Mathematics has always been this way, she apprehended, once the epiphany landed; mathematics has always been about entelechy. The idea is posited, and the idea is to make the idea plausible or even real — wholly true in all its seemingly differentiated parts — if one is good enough.

From this point Tamara began to search for ideas that, if true, would contribute to the well being of the world, that picture derived from facts. Facts that do not clearly improve the well being of the world are false; it became this simple. She began to see a pattern, an idea emerging from the puzzling proposition she now forwarded: from an interior perspective there are no straight lines; all is curved space. One cannot see in a straight line. One cannot walk in a straight line. One cannot travel in a true, straight line. Look at a scene outside your window. The transparent glass has affected the line. Look at transparent glass. Do you see the transparency or what is behind the transparent? What does transparency look like? Look at a point within the distance. What gets in the way? Color? Air? What color is air? Is it also transparent? What color is transparent? Reach out and touch the distant point. Does that which touches the point travel the line you imagined? Walk in a line. Is there no curve to the floor? No curve to the earth beneath the floor? No spin to the earth? No orbit of the planet? She stopped concerning herself with rationality or logic. She began with an idea that she believed in, an idea worthy of realization. From this, she decided to find a way to prove it real. But here she saw another challenge. Would proof of the idea come from numerical abstractions? Had she not set herself up to get lost in another puzzle, to succumb in service to another formula? She finally concluded that to pursue her idea she would have to leave the world of abstract numbers and prove it by way of an existence more tangible, more real, and most importantly, more human. After all, her idea for a better world began with those who would define what a better world would be. Humans. Humans are where she ended, where she found her conclusion. Humans make definitions.

The irony that this idea to dismiss the world of math had come to her in the midst of a mathematical equation was not wholly lost upon her. Odd, she thought, that when the epiphany struck, she was engaged in an operation whereby she resolved a deep mathematical paradox through the introduction of negative radical one into the equation. She did not know how long she had been working on the equation. Her watch had stopped working.

Her goal remained to create a formula for the human being that would in and of itself improve the human being even if the human being never arrived at a solution. The solution was a worthless thing to pursue if the process of pursuit of the solution itself did not itself produce the desired solution. She had written the equation as initially conceived in a notebook. It was almost laughable; still she persisted, knowing that her intentions were true. W=E. The Way is the End. Or she could conjugate the formula transversely. E=W. The End is the Way. Regardless of how silly it seemed, W=E was her idea, her simple atomic proposition. Her professors began to worry when this phrase began to appear within drafts of important papers that she wrote. She constructed extensive, elegant equations where E=W over 1 would suddenly be presented as a critical, lynch-pin footnote. It was like watching an artistic film that culminates with the three stooges suddenly appearing on the stage for a circular stint of playful shtick. Tamara would introduce long and brilliantly structured logic trains of thought, propositions that would seem as childish gibberish if not for the fact that they worked. A reader suddenly confronted with her E=W proposition would enter thinking nothing of it and exit wondering why it was there, while being fully unable to find a clearly articulable reason to deny that it belonged. From a strict mathematical world view her methods were proper, though her subject matter was nearly universally identified as immaterial, juvenile. M (mean) equaled W(way). Thus M could also equal E or W. Each could be substituted. Tamara began at one point to turn her equation at a ninety degree angle or even upside down to demonstrate that E (end) looked like W (way) or even M (mean) and vice-versa, when orientation was altered by even a minor curvature of the flat page. From this, it did not take her long for obvious reasons to make the correlation that 3=W=E=M.

Her professors, who tended to see themselves as intellectually independent and free, were initially more curious than dismissive. Some questioned her on these odd anomalies; others simply chuckled, reasoning that she could add the minor proposition so long as it did not alter expected results. Perhaps, some thought, her work was grounded in some esoteric mathematics that she had simply misunderstood. Perhaps, they hoped, this was part of an elaborate mathematical prank. The greater the mind, they knew, the more imperative the need for play. To the dismay of her mentors, it was not a prank and there were no esoteric sources to which she could point as a basis for these rudimentary terms (clauses) she proposed.

Tamara argued for her idea first by reasoning that the introduction of her terms did not in any way alter the given proof. This was true. Regardless, her professors reasoned that they were unneeded, inefficient and irrational introductions. Tamara suggested that her professors found them unneeded, inefficient and irrational introductions not because they were unneeded, inefficient and irrational introductions but because they — and here she said a curious and what turned out to be an inflammatory thing — *lacked the courage to believe in a line they could not see.* This was the statement that turned many against her. They argued that the idea was simple, that it contributed nothing to realms of known and accepted math and physics. She agreed with both the latter and former portions of their statements. They told her that they had no choice but to take points off for such an inane stunt. She agreed, duly noting that this verified her proposition. They told her she was talking nonsense. Again, she agreed, declaring the first conic principle of what she boldly declared to be a new, physical, mathless mathematics: "All human beings become the functional applications, the original truth-functions of their thoughts."

The physics department convened for a special meeting. Tamara was not on the agenda as a topic for discussion; however, she was discussed in detail. Some thought that her position, though excessive, could be sensibly defended. This group found it helpful to define her expressions as a radical, albeit immature, form of intellectual freedom that deserved to be honored and even incubated for the fruit it might someday yield.

"We're mathematicians, not farmers," others argued, saying she was making a mockery of their profession. They argued that if there existed any validity to her claims, then from a scientific methodology others would be able to meaningfully follow the path her thoughts constructed somewhere beyond a meaningless loop. Still others called her works revolutionary and progressive.

"Yes, like the scribblings of a five-year-old."

"It's poetical. At first it strikes one as foolish, but then one sees that it remains unflawed in principle."

Others scoffed. "But what does it add? That's the real question. As far as I can see it contributes nothing to our collective understanding."

"Other than to bring it to conclusion."

"She's making a mockery!

"Well, what does it subtract?"

"We should be capable of withstanding a little mockery for what we do. She has!"

"Have you noticed how when she introduces these terms into her equations, they control the flow of time? I think she's trying to say that conic representations of curves and lines are more important than curves and lines in and of themselves. I spoke with her about the assumptions of her ideas in depth. She said an interesting thing to me. She said that the only puzzle we need to solve is how time pours space."

"She said the same thing to me!"

"And what does that mean?"

"She's making a mockery!"

"I don't know, but it's extremely provocative. Don't you think?"

"You're all missing the point!" shouted the department head, pounding a heavy fist upon the table. "This girl has not earned *intellectual freedom*. She's a graduate student. She's flying off on wild fancies before she has mastered the basic propositions. If you remember, she came here touted as a genius. Maybe she is a genius, but she has lost all connection to the community, the *sensus communis*. And what do we do with a genius who loses all sense of common sense with the community? Remember Kant? What do we do when wild wings begin flapping too high?"

A quiet voice answered, complicitous in the conspiracy of shame, "Clip the wings."

"That's right," the department chair, Rudolph Weimer, declared. "We clip the wings for the safety and well being of the community. We grow steadily and methodologically. We are not in the business of pursuing the wildly fanciful leaps suggested by the overly-fertile minds of 22-year-old nubiles. No more of this gibberish. It's dangerous. I don't want to hear another word about Tamara Browne. If she doesn't conform, fail her."

Tamara attempted to conform; she truly did. Repressing all of her thinking about W=E=M=3, her professors enthusiastically commended her on the increased quality and clarity of her work. Inside, she was dying from the meaningless efforts. Her graduate course work complete, she addressed her thesis. She attempted with all of her will to keep it simple and uninspired; that is what they sought. Halfway into the argument of her thesis, she dropped the pen with which she was writing, exhausted by the futility of denying her own thoughts. She delivered the 60-page fragment to the desk of Professor Weimer, the department head who had proclaimed the conditions of her sentence — *If she doesn't conform, fail her.* Accompanying the incomplete thesis was a single sentence letter of withdrawal from the university that stated simply:

"And I agree."
Sincerely,
Tamara R. Browne

The letter infuriated Weimer.

ℐ

Tamara ascended to the top of the orange painted steps. Six hours of aimless wandering about the city had left her hungry and tired. The weariness she had sought. Approaching the door to her dilapidated apartment with her keys jangling in her hand, she discovered it wide open. For a moment she hesitated, speculating upon the possibility that she had not closed and locked the door, unsure of whether to proceed forward or go for help. Stepping cautiously over the stoop, she called into the hollow where the white sunlight of late afternoon refracted off chipped floorboard.

"Hello?" She called out nervously, poised on a heel to retreat if necessary, her own edgy voice saturating the emptiness. "Hello?"

"Oh, yes, yes, hello, dear. Come right in."

Directly ahead the short hallway dumped into a tiny living room. At the end of the hallway, Dorothia appeared, a tall glass of yellow lemonade in her hand. Dressed in black linen pants and a lime-green cashmere turtleneck, her saccharine smile oozed obtrusion. Her thin fingers, busily engaged, were playing with the solid gold cross dangling upon the swells of her chest.

Tamara closed the door slowly.

"What are you doing in my apartment?"

"Oh?" Dorothia feigned. "Is this your apartment? I had no idea. I thought that what was yours was mine, or was it the other way around? I get so confused. Was it you who thought that what is mine can be yours? Can I pour you a lemonade?" Turning her back, Dorothia entered the living room, disappearing from Tamara's sight. Tamara could not help but notice what a gorgeous body the woman had and how much easier such a body, at any age, with all the obvious advantages, must make life. Easier yes, she assuaged herself, but there is no guarantee that it makes it better.

Taking a deep breath, Tamara dropped her backpack to the ground and entered. "So how did you get in here?" The words filled the sparse apartment.

Dorothia sat on a piece of plastic lawn furniture with her legs crossed. Placing her drink on a milkcrate she stated flatly, "Love what you've done with the place. It has a certain mathematical charm, doesn't it? Must get lonely though."

Tamara checked the mail that Dorothia had brought in and placed on a beaten coffee table. Circulations for cosmetics, flyers, solicitations, junk. "So how did you get in?" The nearly completed puzzle — one corner piece missing — of the Bavarian landscape lay by a wall on a pile of finished puzzles, one atop the other like pages of a draft manuscript, ascending over one foot into the air. Dorothia remained silent as her eyes lingered on the striking pile in something approaching a respectful amazement. In another corner of the room, an assortment of unpiled, scattered books lay by a cheap reading lamp. Dog-eared, highlighted pages were open and lay flat upon the floor, as though the story or the idea or whatever alimentation the girl found on the pages was expected to arrive in simultaneity from a multiplicity of sources. There were philosophical and math texts, physics and poetry, a few novels and histories, maps, biographies and spiral notebooks. Sitting by the eclectic collection there reposed a wooden monkey holding a human skull in its outstretched palm as though to say, *We've come a long way.* The long wooden tail wrapped itself in three and a half turns as it lifted a carved quill into the air. A wooden monkey playing Hamlet, Dorothia thought, much amused.

"How did you get in?" Tamara demanded a third time.

"A friend of mine who specializes in such things. Amazing what a man will do for a woman who meets his simple little needs. A woman is a hole, Tamara. Fulfill a man's need to hide and you fulfill the man. Once we accept the little truth of this, it is so much clearer. But I don't have to tell you, do I? So tell me, Tamara; I can call you, Tamara, can't I? What is it exactly that you want from my son?"

Tossing the mail aside, Tamara surveyed Dorothia closely. Seeing a smug, arrogant face that knew the most nuanced rules in the game of manipulation, she refrained from responding to the prattling bait.

This prompted Dorothia, smoothing her linen pants as she leaned forward, to continue. "Because you see. You can't have it. Whatever it is you want. You're wasting your time." Dorothia inspected her manicure; the russet polish was impeccable, not a single smudge or parting line. That little shop on Thayer Street did impeccable work.

"Why's that?" Tamara asked.

Dropping her nails in an overwrought gesture of exasperation, Dorothia held the girl in a steady, deliberate, condescending, possessive gaze. "Because, dear Tamara, you're fucking with me, and if I have to, I'll tear your pretty little eyes right out of their cute little sockets." It was the coolness, the aplomb with which she made the threat, that caused Tamara to shiver, and in the shiver, blink.

Tamara said nothing, just as Dorothia wished. Standing, Dorothia took the floor like a lawyer who has been granted the freedom to lay out the entire argument, uninterrupted, before judge and jury.

"You're a quaint girl, Tamara, aren't you? A little bit queer, underappreciated; people don't quite know what to make of you. In another world I might almost feel pity for you. But unfortunately, this is my world and I don't because I can't afford to." She meandered to the window that overlooked the small, fenced in backyard of the suburban community. A pear tree with rounded leaves rose from the hard earth in the center of the court below. A tire swing hung from a low limb. Dorothia found the white walls of the thick rubber swaying in the wind awfully romantic. "We've spent our entire lives, Rooster and I, getting ready, preparing for this moment. You can't know the extent of the sacrifice, the willful humiliation we've put ourselves through to make it this far. He's on the verge of becoming someone who will live in history. But you know that already, don't you? He's on the verge of history. I don't even think he realizes this himself. It has taken me years to condition him to become what he is becoming. You think it just happens? You think a great artist just emerges? Of course you don't. You have much to learn but not that. His entire world is created for him, shaped in a specific and deliberate way to cultivate a particular way of thinking that the standard conditions of the world are incapable of producing. I've gone to the best. I won't tell you what I had to do to get there, though I suspect you might even be able to understand. A woman is a hole, Tamara. We allow ourselves to be filled with the best that we can find."

Dorothia paused to watch a dead leaf fall from the tree, twirling downwards to land directly beneath the swaying tire. A boy and a girl ran into the yard. The girl entered the tire ring. Stepping on the leaf, the boy pushed her from behind. "Do you think I'm really going to lose control now? Do you think I'm going to just let some random element off the street come in and jinx all the work we've done? Do you think I'm just going to stand by and take the chance of letting you ruin everything? Do you? Could you possibly be so stupid?!"

Dorothia faced Tamara, commanding her with words, almost kind. "Look at me."

Tamara looked. "He is everything you're not. Everything you want but fail to be. Every thought you think you have, he is." Unable to hold the gaze, Tamara looked away in desperate shame, knowing that Dorothia spoke the harshest of truths. "I know where you are. I've been there. And as much as I may feel for you, I won't allow myself to feel it for you. I won't let your desperate needs drain him of that which makes him great. I gave you the chance to walk away yourself. But now I'm telling you. I'm telling you, Tamara: stay away from him. He doesn't need what you think you're offering. Do you understand? I know you do. I know you understand. You're not giving him a damn thing; you're just here for the having."

Tears spilled down Tamara's cheeks as she protested. This was the negation she did not know how to accept. "That's not true. I love him. I love him."

"You love him?" Dorothia mocked her, instantly hardening against the protest. "Hhmmm, I like that." Again studying her fingernails, she asked, "What is it you love about him?" She ripped at a cuticle. "You love the fact that he's a leper? That he's a homebody? You love his mind? That he'll never have children? What is it that you're so everlastingly in love with?"

"Stop it! He completes me! We complete . . ."

Dorothia snapped, ignoring the girl. "Or is it his painting? Are you in love with his painting? That I could understand. That would make sense. You love his painting, just as you should. It has more soul than the Himalayas. He carries more tragedy with him on a daily basis than most people carry in a lifetime. And he's innocent of it. He doesn't even know what he carries, and that's what makes his work such a miracle. And that's what you want to destroy? You want to open up his world, Tamara? You want to give him a reason to feel all the sorrow that we can't fathom he doesn't presently feel? You want to give him that kind of reason? You want to touch him with the pain he doesn't even know he carries? You want to make him just like the rest of us?"

"It's a lie!" Tamara objected weakly. "I wouldn't hurt him! He's not just some animal whose world you control. He's more than you let him be. There's more to him than a paintbrush!"

"And you're going to show it to him?" Dorothia tossed the lemonade in the girl's face. "Wake up!" she commanded. "What are you going to do? Are you going to turn him into a man? Are you going to make him normal? Are you going to take away the one thing that makes him more than a goddamn freak?! The one thing that protects him from their hatred?"

"He's more. He's more," was all that Tamara could muster to reply.

"He's more, all right." Dorothia hurled the glass across the room, shattering it against the wall. Fragments landed upon the landscape of puzzles like glistening sickles of transparent ice. Tamara covered her eyes in fright. "Stay away from him, Tamara. Do you hear me? Stay away from him. I swear I'll kill you if you don't!"

The two combatants grew quiet. The heavy liquid trickled down the wall. The wooden monkey in the corner watched. Each woman breathed with her own anxiety and cumbersome anguish. Between them something palpable had come into being, something that had nothing to do with Rooster. Lifting her eyes, Tamara stared at Dorothia.

"He's the one thing that keeps you from hating yourself. Isn't he?"

Cold and inert, her entire being limpid, Dorothia responded, "Don't flatter yourself, honey." She smiled treacherously. "Even he can't do that."

Picking up her coat from the radiator where she had kept it warm,

Dorothia drew a manila envelope from the pocket. "One more piece of mail, deary. Special delivery." She tossed it across the room where it landed at Tamara's fingertips. "Do the right thing, for all of us. Sorry about the glass, deary. Next time, don't go so cheap."

Her heels clicked down the hallway, and then she was gone, leaving a nightmare to drip down the eggshell wall. Quietly shaking, Tamara lifted the package and held it against her wrist. Within the package something terrible awaited, something that would cause her to wither in sorrow. Praying that it would not be what she feared it was, bent upon the plastic milk crate, she slit the seal with a dull butter knife.

cP

On the day following Tamara's eighteenth birthday, her parents had filed for divorce. Two years and several months later Cynthia Browne, her mother, died of lymphoma of the central nervous system. She had been the Gibraltar of Tamara's world. Popular myth has it that boons, providential blessings of good fortune, come alone, while bad luck arrives in waves of three. The diagnosis of lymphoma followed the divorce by less than two months. Cynthia had been performing a self-examination of the breast when she noticed the hard nodule, like a large pearl comfortably settled in an oyster's flesh. A biopsy confirmed malignancy and led to the dread diagnosis of a non-localized, non-Hodgkin's lymphoma.

Cynthia's doctor, a compassionate woman in her thirties with astute eyes and varicose veins, declared, "It's in the food we eat, the water we drink, the air we breathe. I've even come to believe that it's in the television we watch and the radio we listen to. It's terrible to say, but it's become an accepted part of the human condition. Just one of the prices we pay for an advanced civilization." They were detached, somewhat disinterested words that the doctor spoke, hardly comforting in their meaning, and yet — oddly — they pacified Cynthia, as though the statistical reality that she was not alone, that she carried a modern burden that many were asked to carry, that she had used artificial sweeteners, stripped her of the right to experience outrage or hysteria.

On the day of her diagnosis she became part of another species altogether, one that had always existed though she had never invested it with much thought. She was not alone; there were many just like her, and they were waiting to embrace her as soon as she accepted the new identity.

Her divorce had been a similar event. Not a tragedy, only an event. How could anyone get too upset about a condition that affects fifty percent of all marriages? Statistically, it was bound to happen. *One of the prices we pay for an advanced civilization.* She felt a cultural malaise. She accepted the words of the doctor. So this, she mused as her body entered a humming tube for an MRI, is the new human condition. Disappearing into the tube, she felt at peace. She wanted to stay inside the humming tube and not come out. After twenty-two years of marriage, her husband was sleeping with his twenty-six-year old secretary, a woman who could not even perform adept dictation. Why return to that world? This world, amidst the steady hum, felt safe. Following consultation, the doctors began her treatment with an aggressive campaign of chemotherapy.

Deadened to the emotional pain of the experience, unable to even recognize the third bit of bad luck when it came, Cynthia slogged dutifully from one day to the next. She learned to walk like a zombie, to avoid judging the events of her life. *It's one of the prices we pay for an advanced civilization.* She could join a single's club or a support group for those battling the same disease. Groups existed everywhere, for everything she could imagine, and she had earned the exclusivity of membership by mere virtue of statistical calamity. The chemotherapy made her vomit and drool. Her thick custard hair fell out in tangled clumps. She wore a wig and joined a support group for men and women battling cancerous lymphoma. There, with others of her kind, she could freely — within reason — pity herself. For the first time in her life, she experienced community.

Henry Browne was an affluent and powerful financier who had built himself from nothing to become a highly respected political force in San Francisco. A philanderer more by virtue of mid-life crisis than long-term nature, he resigned himself to his wife's misfortune, acknowledging no personal responsibility. Tamara argued with him, telling him that a human being persisted as a holistic, complex unit full of cause and effect relationships that we have barely begun to understand.

Six months after the diagnosis, Cynthia's doctor declared the chemotherapy treatments unsuccessful. Cynthia did not cry. From seed, she had started the garden she had always wanted but never had time to grow. She had planted pole beans and peppers and plum tomatoes. She discovered that the moon will affect a seed's germination and that it is best to plant two days after a full moon.

A partial mastectomy of the left breast removed the node and the surrounding cluster that Cynthia had first identified in the course of her self-examination. That the invasive surgery could not stop the spread of the non-localized lymphoma did not matter. The partial mastectomy was almost a symbolic measure. Even symbolically it did not work. Removing the first cause, the source of the nightmare's beginning, did not restore a sense of hope. There was no going back to do it all again, differently, better. Cutting away a fragment of the disease left behind a scar. Cut the hand off if it offend thee. It will still offend, even in absence.

"We can rebuild it afterwards through plastic surgery," the compassionate doctor told Cynthia, who had made the decision alone.

"Haven't implants been known to *cause* cancer?" It was a moot point; she would never have reconstructive surgery and she knew it. But such a fact did not matter; such things could still be discussed. The possibility regarding what could have been becomes vital as the end grows near.

The doctor smiled reassuringly. "That's not a concern. We don't use silicon anymore. We use a saline water." Cynthia watched and waited as her body weakened by degrees. Hair grew back, slow and curly. She wondered if it had anything to do with the state of the moon. For close to a year the lymphoma remained in a near dormant state.

Making the drive north from Stanford to San Francisco every weekend, Tamara became her mother's rock. Cynthia continued to meet with her support group. She laughed more. Her tomatoes and peppers grew. Her beans, brought to gestation too early, died. She allowed others to feel pity for themselves. She encouraged grieving, telling people that grieving was a natural state of any world, modern or other. She accepted a date. It did not go well. She laughed more. She began experiencing painful headaches. A cat scan revealed a large, inoperable lymph nodule at the stem of the brain. By Christmas of the second year, just shy of three years from the date of her divorce, she was dead. On a peaceful December day, deep in the wine valleys of northern California, they lowered Cynthia Gezel Browne's casket into a frozen earth. There were orange-beaked cardinals and small drifts of snow.

☞

Henry Browne signed the legal papers that committed Tamara to McLean for thirty days of observation. Subsequent to the funeral, their relationship, despite her father's attempts, deteriorated. The memories of her mother's suffering, a suffering of which he held himself all too innocent, were too fresh. When they talked, Tamara's words were bitter. Sadly, the more she pushed her father away, wanting nothing to do with him, the more he struggled to embrace her, to communicate his love and to stress the importance of family. He became, in his own way, deluded, convincing himself through the sheer desire of his ego's projection that his daughter needed him. He required, as it turned out, only the slightest reinforcement to justify and validate his position, for if his daughter were sick, then her hatred for him could be interpreted as part of the sickness. And if it were a mental sickness then perhaps it could be healed, and with such a healing the misunderstanding between them would dissolve and her love for him would return. So he believed in the recessed fathoms of his warped psyche.

The reinforcement that he required to support this belief came after two full years of alienation from Tamara, when the dean of the graduate physics department at Stanford called him on the phone expressing concerns, "parent to parent," about Tamara's mental health. Tamara was a brilliant student, Professor Weimer stated, with an incredible gift and the potential for genius. Having entered college at seventeen, she had completed her course work in three years and at twenty-two was poised to continue her ascent. But her work of late revealed signs of mental duress; "anomalies" is what Weimer called the incidents that had caused him and other members of the department concern. In fact, only hours before, she had attempted to withdraw from the university, the circumspect Professor Weimer finally stated.

Henry Browne arrived at Stanford the following morning. Those selected to speak with him painted a grim portrait of a girl caught within a spiraling, nonsensical vortex. Upon Professor Weimer's encouragement, Henry visited his daughter at her apartment.

"What is it you want?" she'd demanded through a closed door.

"To talk to you, please. I only want to talk to you."

"Talk. I can hear you."

He'd plied the edges of his hat in nervous, fidgeting fingers. Boards of banks he could address with absolute confidence; his daughter reduced him to this. "I've spoken with some of your professors. They say you've left the university. They say you're . . ."

"I thought you wanted to speak to me," she interjected hotly. "Or are they the ones who want to speak to me?"

"It's me. It's me. . . ." He had paused, trying to think of how to rephrase what he wished to know. He didn't know what he wished to know. "Are you thinking clearly?"

Inside he heard her whistling in short, tweety bursts.

"Clear as a lark in the dark," she had replied.

The sound of her laughter, so rare to his ears, warmed his heart, gave him hope.

"Please open the door, Tamara, please."

"No."

"I'm worried about you. Have you received my letters?"

"Like you worried about Mom?" The words were hard, inflexible. "Are you still seeing your secretary? We must be about the same age. Maybe I'll come visit. We could all go out. We'll hit it off just splendidly, I'm sure. She'll be just like a girlfriend to me."

Henry had snapped. Baited just as Tamara had intended, he raised his voice. "Now this has nothing to do with . . ." But he bit off the name, fully aware that the words were twisted, that they were a world away from the topic and sentiments he had hoped to discuss and feel.

"It has everything to do with her!" Tamara had shot back, refuting her father's denial. "Go back to her, Daddy." The mockery was visceral. "She's mommy and daughter rolled into one. You don't need me anymore. You only think you do."

Pleading, he had pressed his fingers to the door. "Baby, that's not true. None of what you say is true. You . . . you're not feeling well. You wouldn't be thinking these things. . . ." His words trailed off as he stated his silent conclusion to himself alone. "You're sick, Tamara, sick."

A sudden and overwhelming weariness overcame him. His legs felt like dull slates of stone. He experienced a numb throbbing in his shoulder and shortness of breath. Placing his hat upon his head he shuffled down the hall, feeling very old, very old indeed.

It surprised him how quickly and easily having his daughter committed proved to be. With the beneficent aid of Professor Weimer and others like him, Henry found the whole process simpler than a loan application. On the recommendation of those who knew more than he in such matters, McLean was selected as the hospital. Dr. Weimer, having procured the support of Stanford's psychiatric services, established himself as a great benefactor.

"I couldn't have done this without your guidance, Dr. Weimer."

"No need for thanks, Mr. Browne. We all want the same thing. McLean will be perfect. It meets your every requirement. It's connected to Harvard Medical School. She'll receive the best treatment. It's considered more of a sanctuary for the highstrung than a mental hospital. It's a type of Betty Ford clinic for the intellectually gifted. Many famous people have gone there for its special R&R."

"Like who?" Henry asked, greatly intrigued, beginning to feel that his daughter would thank him for this experience.

"Famous people, fragile genius types . . . like your daughter. What a mind she has. Tender and darling. It's hard to imagine what people of her caliber might be thinking or the burden of it."

"Like who?"

"Oh," Weimer reflected, "Robert Lowell, Sylvia Plath, Ray Charles, John Nash. A lot of great ones. We've used them before. Think of it more as a retreat for your daughter than a hospital. I'm sure that after a short time, she'll be as good as new and ready to complete her thesis properly." Professor Weimer looked at Henry from the corner of his scurrilous eye and hoped that the father did not fully comprehend what he had so sloppily revealed. But Henry's mind drifted elsewhere, barely listening to the troll of a dean.

Henry was engaged, attempting to calculate the odds that news of his daughter's need for a retreat — "Yes, a retreat for the intellectually gifted," he reinforced for himself — would ever leak into his business and social circle. If it did, it could cause quite an embarrassment. Being on the opposite coast made things easier.

"The university will be discreet?"

"Of course, Mr. Browne. Our goal is to preserve her mind and the reputation that goes with it. The reputation and the mind, that could practically be our motto."

"Good. Good. She won't be hurt, will she? I mean when they take her?"

"No, Mr. Browne, a light sedative I'm sure, if she even protests. She might not. Some don't. It's exactly what they really want, deep down inside."

"Should I be there?"

Professor Weimer tugged at his goatee as he peered at Mr. Browne over sharp, moon-shaped spectacles. "It's not necessary. What is necessary is that she see you at McLean, that you help her to understand that this is for her own good."

"Yes, it's for her own good, her own good." It pleased Henry that he did not need to convince the professor of this. Weimer made a mental note of Mr. Browne's eagerness to agree.

"The university representative and the staff psychiatrist have already signed," Professor Weimer stated as he moved the papers across the desk. "Everything is ready. With your signature we can proceed."

Inside Tamara's apartment they found eighty-one white mice scurrying about, over and under and through obstacle courses, fields of play constructed of toys.

Thirty days of observation were extended into ninety. Ninety days became one hundred and eighty. Weimer visited once, attempting to coerce her to finish her thesis work. He brought her first draft and many supporting texts that he presumed would be necessary for its successful completion. He urged her to finish the thesis, so full of promise, and return to the place where she belonged. She exhibited little interest in the thesis and no interest in Weimer.

On the day that Tamara entered McLean, her father was there to be quickly disillusioned of the notion that McLean was, despite the best of spins, anything other than an institution for the mentally disturbed. When Tamara saw him, both knew beyond doubt's shadow that she would despise him forever.

He visited on the last weekend of every month. His secretary waited in the car when he entered McLean. She stroked him when he re-emerged, always quite upset, speaking backwards. "Can't do this anymore, I, my daughter, she's."

"You're doing the best that you can do for her. It's called tough love," she cooed. "Now come on. Let's get away from this dreary place. Have you ever thought about dying your hair?"

At the end of the second ninety-day period, Henry, with a new head of auburn hair, met with the two young doctors assigned to Tamara. Conclusively, they could make no diagnosis of poor mental health, though they expressed suspicion of a mild psychosis.

"The more talented and exceptional the individual, the more diffi-cult these diagnoses become. Your daughter is recognized as brilliant within the domains of math and physics. You have to understand that in these cases, there can often be creative intelligences at work that we can't recognize. It's too close to call. That's the nature of the cutting edge. If we diagnose her, we could be interfering with an extremely pro-ductive, free thinker. What we can say that is quite positive is that she doesn't appear to be a threat to anyone. We've identified a minor dis-position towards sadism and masochism."

"Sadism and masochism!"

"But again, nothing abhorrent, nothing outside the standard cultur-al deviation."

"Standard cultural deviation?"

"It could simply be part of an intellectual experiment. We just can't tell."

"What are you telling me, doctors?"

"We're telling you that your daughter, but for some eccentricities that we would expect to find in anyone of talent — anyone that's an exceptionally intelligent, free thinker — is normal."

"So she should be released?"

"We didn't say that."

"That's your decision," the second doctor added.

"We don't consider her a threat to the social order."

"We can continue observations on your authority as parent under-signed by the university. Her withdrawal was never made official."

"So what does that mean? In laymen's terms," Mr. Browne asked wearily.

"In the loosest sense, they have intellectual claims to her."

"Weimer won't be happy," the second doctor noted to the first.

"Weimer? What does he . . . ?" Henry rubbed his forehead. They were in a ventilated room with no windows. "Cut her free."

"We'll need your release."

The increasingly typical lassitude setting in once more, Henry clasped his eyes shut against the incoming migraine. "I'll sign. I'll sign."

cℱ

Tamara emptied the contents of the manila folder upon the unvarnished coffee table. Inside were three separate pieces of paper. The first was a temporary restraining order issued by the Providence Police Department. The second was a blank "Letter of Commitment" form from McLean, blank but for the line marked "PATIENT." Dorothia had taken the poignant liberty of printing the name TAMARA R. BROWNE upon that line. Tamara unfolded the third piece of paper slowly. In large, fluid and elegant script on a photocopy of Stanford letterhead, Dorothia had written:

Deary,

I had such a very nice talk with your father. What an interesting, broken-hearted man. He certainly loves his daughter; the very last thing he wants is to see her spend more time at that awful McLean. I wonder what he would do if he were to learn of this restraining order. It is such grim evidence of an anti-social pattern of behavior. The courts are very sympathetic to the needs of invalids who are cautious and sensitive to their impact upon society. Ex-patients of mental hospitals do not inspire them with goodwill. You are a smart girl. Stay away from my son. This is a puzzle you should have no problem solving.

Dorothia

P.S. — Since we won't be seeing each other anymore, I've left you a gift. It's in your bedroom. You see, deary, I don't doubt that you love his art. In fact, that's a proper role for you, so long as you keep a proper distance. It is a divine gift he brings, and you will best serve through worship from afar.

Trapped in the foggy maze of life, Tamara drifted into the bedroom without thought, prepared to behold any cruel horror that such a heartless woman as Dorothia could conceive. Futon, reading lamp, alarm clock, piles of folded clothing. Hanging from the eggshell wall, light from the outside illuminating the emptiness, was Rooster's religious painting, the depiction of Rabbi Baal Shem Tov and his student visiting the home of the messianic leper.

Tamara collapsed before the painting. She felt the vacuity of the apartment, of her life, of her soul, now filled with meaning. The hidden messiah, the rabbi, the student peering in. Don't let me be crazy, she prayed. I'm not a hole to be filled. She did not want to return to McLean, not for another day, not for another moment in that hellish reformatory of the mind. Gazing upwards at the painting, she thought of the Chinese panda bears, patient as monks, peering beyond the savage jungle of black and white, good and bad, night and day.

cP

Marubrishnubupu was winding down the crowd, bringing them safely back from the mysterious regions of the mind to which he had led them, helping direct them towards a practical understanding they could now apply.

"So you see, the deeper we go, the less resolution we are likely to find. Con-centration — against centralization — is like that. The more we centralize, the more we run a course against centralization. We need to stop concentrating. The God that we seek is ever expanding and quite comfortable to do so. It is the human impulse that seeks the triteness of closure. We require it because we are unable to believe with an absolute and perfected faith that death in this world is not death at all, only another transition. And even for those saints who may acquire, through years of careful dedication and commitment, the absolute faith of which we speak, even these men and women will have a desire to know. What comes next? Will I recognize my last brother or sister, my mother, my father, my childhood friend? And that is what we truly fear. This is the place where our faith is weak.

"We fear that we will not recognize or be recognized by that which we once knew. But I want you to remember something; love is a transcendent force. It is not reliant upon time or space. Love will be recognized in any form. It is the very force of freedom swimming out from the current illusion of this life as well as any illusion that may cloud our perceptions in lives to come. You have been such a good audience. If you will, let me close today with the words from a great lover of life among us. This comes from Marcel Phrenol's book, *Another Day of Loving*.

"He writes, 'Abstain from the vanity of fearing what you may lose. Rather, spend your life searching. Seek always to re-identify with what may already have been lost. For as surely as your search will lead you to find the spirit of lost love, so in the same breath will your future like a rose bloom before you. My character walks to the foamy sea of brine and there feels her caress in the trickle of the turquoise tide, struggling to advance, destined to retreat. We make love in this way, ever grateful for the subtle embrace of a thoughtful good-bye.'"

Marubrishnubupu bowed. "My friends, thank you."

13

IRENE SAT FOR CHAMOMILE tea and finger sandwiches with three potential buyers at a popular restaurant in Beverly Hills. She had called for the meeting to discuss Rooster. It was a risk. Together, these three were her most discerning, influential and moneyed buyers. They were not asking to see the product; they understood that what lay beyond the product was far more important to their investment. They understood influence. They respected Irene and her reputation.

"What I can't understand, Irene, is how you can promote so aggressively when you have not met the artist personally. It seems an imprudent risk. Very unlike you." Margo Halscome, a Modernist proponent with tight lips and silver hair, knew good art and could pay for it. Her commentary was astute and accurate.

Irene decided to wait for the initial barrage of criticisms to wash over her before beginning.

"I agree," J. J. Goldberg, Texas oil man, spouted. "We've worked well in the past, but we've always had a concrete foundation on which to stand. This is not a town where the smart money is spent on fantasy. You know that. I agree with Margo, Irene. It strikes me as imprudent."

Irene's third buyer, Frederick Schleigger, heavily rumored to be an underworld pornography kingpin, tickled the pink feather on his hat as he listened. The most flamboyant of the three, he also possessed the truest raw instinct. "What you're asking us to do, Irene, is put our reputations on the line. You know how unforgiving the art world can be. One bad decision and your reputation's mud."

"That's right," J. J. concurred. "A reputation is worth more than money in the bank. We just can't do what you're asking at this time." As usual, J. J. attempted to predict the group's final verdict, confident that if he stated it first, such anticipation would demonstrate superiority over the other two. Even here, at the table of possibilities, there were gains to be made as well as losses.

"I wasn't finished," Schleigger continued. "I was going to say that you understand that, Irene. Your livelihood is even more dependent on your decision in such matters than ours. It's the core of your world, not fully so with us. What I want to know is why you are so willing to place your reputation into the arms of fate."

Margo Halscome, a proud woman of shrewd origin, leaned forward in evident agreement with Schleigger's assessment. J. J. Goldberg watched with ambivalence. Because he had already rendered a verdict, he was now trapped, forced to defend his initial opinion regardless of what followed. However, Irene knew that if Halscome and Schleigger gave their support, he would, given the slightest face-saving opportunity, fall in line. As much as he wanted to be the most influential of the group, he wisely wanted to be in the most influential group even more.

"I'd like to know the answer to that question, also," Margo stated, pushing aside the tea that, once poured, no one drank. "You've taken a significant risk even approaching us with this. Why?"

Irene bent forward, emerging from her psychological shell with the fresh fierceness of one who has securely waited out the lashing of a storm. "I can sympathize with your concerns. They're quite admirable. And you're right. I am putting a lot on the line. I've spent a career discerning worthy art from the unworthy, making sure that none of the latter contaminates the former. I'm the gatekeeper. One wrong move and every prior decision is open for reinterpretation. Entire squadrons of worthy artists and their buyers can have their reputations tainted because one unworthy passes through. So why am I willing, so anxious to pass this one artist through the gateway without, what we might call, a genuine security check?" They were listening around the table. What she was saying made sense. The world of art was like a game of chess where one wrong move can completely ruin an otherwise flawless game. She took a deep breath. "It's a judgment call. One of those moments in an art dealer's career — there are only a handful of such moments in a lifetime — when all the conditions, the total state of affairs, come together to demand a judgment despite the fact that all of the evidence is not yet in. I believe that in a sense I am in what we might call a metaphysical moment of truth."

"What do you mean?" Margo probed with a deep interest as J. J. Goldberg folded his arms and rolled his eyes towards the ceiling.

This was it and Irene knew it. "For instance, metaphysics consists in the discovery of truths, true propositions about the world and the laws of our universe that are not empirically dependent, truths that can only be known through an active application of the cognitive powers of the pure mind."

"Pure mind? But it's not even wholly accepted that metaphysics is possible," Margot pointed out.

"Count me in that group," J. J. chimed.

Casually interested, or so it seemed, Schleigger chewed on a plastic toothpick as Margot continued. "Some argue quite convincingly that *every* cognitive thought is dependent upon empirical experience. The mind can never be pure for it can never be free of the sensate environment that teaches it."

"That's true," Irene acknowledged, leaning into the table, the small cups of her bra pressing upwards. "But I've always held that if we defeat metaphysics faith is meaningless, and I'm not ready for that sort of world. Metaphysics is about more than ideas. It's about the capacity of the cognitive powers to accurately know what ideas are true and what ideas are untrue, even when we have no empirical evidence per se upon which to render a judgment. For instance, I've never had sex with Frederick in a pool of jello, but metaphysically I hold it to be true that it would be delicious." The subtle twirling toothpick went static. Frederick, expression unchanged, nodded his head in acknowledgment of her brilliance.

Margot smiled demurely and sipped her tea.

Turning to J. J., Irene paused until he looked from the ceiling to her. "Which brings us to the larger issue of beauty and fine art. We all know that what is agreeable or disagreeable to one person need not be universally agreeable or disagreeable to every person. And yet it is our job to make universal judgments that we claim can be held true for everyone *without exception* at all times. That's fine art. That's beauty. It is art that makes a moral claim upon the viewer, a moral claim that transcends any individual taste. If it is beautiful, it is beautiful now and it is beautiful always and everyone must recognize it to be so now and always. Its beauty, the degree of its refinement, is a metaphysical fact, a universal truth that cannot be morally denied."

All three were listening attentively.

"I'm putting my reputation on the line on this one because I must. The universe, for lack of a better term, has directed me through a moral imperative and I am thus obliged to act without reservation upon that imperative. I'm making a judgment — not a personal decision — *a judgment*, a moral claim that the art of this painter is beautiful, and I am demanding that everyone must agree with me. It's not a matter of my opinion. It's a matter of metaphysical truth." She paused to give them time for reflection.

"It's not queer art, is it?" Schleigger suddenly asked. "Because as wonderful as queer art may be, it has a real ceiling."

"No, it's not queer art," Irene replied, smiling mildly, appreciative of Schleigger, knowing she had accomplished what she needed to accomplish, knowing she had won.

"And you really believe it's that good?" Schleigger probed.

"I really do."

"Even without meeting the artist?" J. J. appended, as though an afterthought, searching for a pause, a flinch in her response.

"Even without meeting the artist."

J. J. tugged at his chin. Margo drew her tea closer. Schleigger tickled the pink feather.

"We're going to do business," the most influential of the group announced, and the others, confident, nodded in full agreement.

14

I T ALL CAME DOWN to the Boston Red Sox and the New York Yankees in the American League Championship Series. Having captured the final playoff spot from the Orioles with a head-to-head win on the last day of the regular season, the Yankees had entered the playoffs as a wild card, but they weren't playing like one after beating the daylights out of a tough Kansas City club (98 wins to 58 losses) during a three-game sweep in which they outscored the opposition 27-4. On the other side of the bracket the Red Sox had struggled. After dominating the division throughout the majority of the season, they had limped into the homestretch, capturing the division over the Bronx Bombers by only a single game. In their opening round playoff series they looked tired, like a team unraveling. Their average margin of victory in the four-game series was 1.33 runs, but considering that two of the Angels' starting pitchers were on the disabled list, the series win did little to convince fans that the team had recovered from its late season swoon. Entering game one of the ALCS, the Yanks were favored despite the fact that Boston had home field advantage.

The 37-foot-tall Green Monster, the Citgo sign, the red Coke bottle in left field, the flags stiff to center: all were invitations to the long ball. A capacity red, white and blue crowd rose, right hands across their hearts, for the singing of the national anthem.

"Your Boston bums are going to take a beating, you know that, don't ya'?" Jack reclined on the sofa, Walker Blue in his hand. He had just arrived from New York to spend a few days with his favorite author in preparation for the public release that would announce Marcel Phrenol as a Nobel winner. He wore an olive suit fashioned of silk in France and tailored on the West Side. He wore a sheer silk shirt with 24-carat gold cufflinks. He wore a silk tie with navy octagon discs outlined by slim olive lines that matched the suit. He wore an onyx-faced, platinum Rolex with twelve diamonds symmetrically placed. He picked a piece of lint from his lapel. Twittering his fingers, he sent it fluttering to the floor. He sipped the warm, peat-flavored malt from the cool crystal glass as he watched Marcel move across the room in steady, graceful steps. This is the best of life, Jack thought to himself, fully appreciating it as he seldom took the time to do. He worked too hard to appreciate it — such was the nature of the machine — except in small quantities of such an extraordinary quality that he never regretted, not for a single second, the personal sacrifices he made.

"We'll see," Marcel retorted to the jab. "This could be the year." Jack had positioned the television so that it faced the coach. The two men had wordlessly decided to relax after a long afternoon of tedious preparations. In the morning, the awards from Stockholm would be announced; by noon, Marcel and Jack would be with the media for a release.

Marcel organized his desk, bookmarking several texts that he was simultaneously reading. As always, he was conducting his own form of research, preparing thoughts to express the particular and pregnant depths residing within all personal experience. Opening his journal, Marcel scratched a line and scribbled another — *Meanwhile I'll be here waiting to wait for you* — without sitting. From the desktop he picked up two premiere tickets for the game about to get underway. A day earlier he had spontaneously purchased them with the erstwhile intention of taking Dorothia. Afterwards, he thought of Ruth and questioned the decision, wondered if going with Dorothia would be sacrilege. Fortunately Jack had called, providing a plausible excuse for forgetting that allowed Marcel to abandon the wrestling match of his mind. Slipping the unused tickets into the crevice of an unwritten sheaf, he closed the leather bound pages and placed them into a drawer.

"You know, the best thing you could do now is wait. Don't write anything for a few years. At least don't release anything."

Marcel ignored Jack's comments, though he suspected that they were seriously intended.

"Need another drink?" Marcel asked, pouring himself a short martini.

"Don't think so."

The Red Sox trotted onto the field on the chilly October night. The fans were huddled, wrapped in thick jackets and scarves. The announcers were commenting on how unseasonably cold the New England autumn had been, the coldest autumn of the century for the Northeast. Breathing a vaporous mist from his flaring nostrils, the Red Sox starting pitcher, "Crazy Horse" Watson, hurled BBs at catcher Mike Bardick. Simply watching the warm-ups, fans could understand the name, "Crazy Horse." At 6'5" and lanky, with long black hair and a neck that moved the head in swaying arches, Watson's entire being communicated power and unpredictability. If the Red Sox had an ace in the hole, everyone agreed it was Crazy Horse Watson, a fiery, impassioned survivor from the Black Hills of South Dakota, a man with a troubled past, who claimed and often proved to thrive on pressure. The prior evening at a press conference he had gone so far as to announce that he would personally see to it that Ruth's house crumbled. It was an incendiary prediction that did not produce the headlines one might have expected. The Boston papers had lived through enough drought; the last thing they wanted to do was incite the old spirits by kicking dirt on Ruth's grave. But this was the mentality of Crazy Horse who had, by a matter of course, been traded to the Red Sox two seasons earlier, with a World Championship ring in tow, from, of all teams, the New York Yankees.

Marcel sat. "Listen, Jack, I don't want to have to say a lot at the press conference tomorrow. I'd prefer not to even be there."

"Sorry, no can do." Jack finished his drink and rose to make another. "You're following my rules this time. This one's too big. It's an honor you have to honor."

"I know, I know. But I'm not saying much."

"That's fine; just be there. The public wants to see your face. It'll help them sleep at night. Do you know the last time an American won the Nobel?"

Marcel curled his brow. "Toni Morrison, 1993. Before that, Joe Brodsky, 1987."

"Hell," Jack interjected, "that's pretty good. Another drink?"

Twinkling his glass. "Sure."

Kicking high, Crazy Horse struck out the Yankees' lead-off hitter, Raines, on three consecutive fast balls. It sent the Fenway Faithful into a frenzy of delight.

Marcel released the mute button and the crowd roared through the room as the camera panned the throbbing stadium. The announcers were already playing the stage for all its worth.

"Crazy Horse predicted that this would be the year. He has come out to make a statement tonight. If that wasn't a challenge, I don't know what is! Look at these Fenway fans. This is the loudest that I have ever, in all of my years in broadcasting, heard Fenway. It's pandemonium!"

So perfectly had it been used, Marcel wondered if the announcer might actually know what "pandemonium" really meant, its literary origin. Prophet cawed wildly from the perch.

Jack pointed at the bird. "Red Sox fan?" Marcel simply nodded.

"LOOK AT THAT! Crazy Horse is pointing to the sky! He's pointing to the sky! This crowd is incensed. It is pandemonium here at Fenway. Crazy Horse is shaking his finger at the sky. Absolute pandemonium! I have never seen this, never!"

The crowd thundered as Crazy Horse, intimidating engines of furnace steam billowing from his nose, curled into his knotted, gnarling wind-up. Meadows, the Yankees' first baseman and number two hitter, dug into the box, intent that his .366 batting title would silence the crowd. Crazy Horse heaved the pitch with all his might, straight down the center of the plate and into the sweetest point of the hit zone. Meadows swung perfectly and missed completely. The ball whizzed past the bat a hair too fast for the snap of Meadows' muscular wrists.

The assembly remained standing, pounding their feet against the bleachers, against stone, raising the dead in rebellion. Crazy Horse took his position. Bardick did not even dare attempt to call the pitch. Crazy Horse called it with the flamethrower in his eyes. Fast ball. Heater. Down the middle. Again, Meadows swung and missed. He had faced Crazy Horse in batting practice hundreds of times and had never seen this. Meadows dug in deeper, opening his stance to quicken his swing, choking up on the bat. In all of Major League Baseball, he had never witnessed a force of this nature. I'm a .366 hitter, he told himself, the best batter in baseball.

Crazy Horse bore down, his head dropping forward in preparation.

Rearing backwards, his body contorted into an unnatural cord of energy. In a single instant it unleashed a blur from its center. Meadows saw
it coming down the center pipeline as though in slow motion. Pulling
the trigger, he swung with all his might. The pop in the catcher's mitt,
the soft leather surrounding the ball, was all he heard as the crowd
exploded like a ton of dynamite taking down a mountain.

"*SSSTrrriiikkkkeee, yyyeeerrrr ooouuuutttt!*" The umpire emphatically charged, lunging with the arm as though stabbing a beast that has
refused to die. Bardick whipped the ball around the horn; his catching
hand was throbbing.

Prophet bobbed on the perch. The crow's neck pecked at the air,
testing its wings in an orgy of excitement. "CAAWWW, CAAAWWW,
CCCCAAAAWWWW."

"Can't you shut that bird up?" Jack protested in aggravation.

Marcel could not move. His eyes were transfixed on the screen as
Crazy Horse fired an imaginary bazooka into the sky. The crowd
watched the fireworks that Crazy Horse was creating. People hugged.
Meadows slammed the bat in frustration.

"Unbelievable! Unbelievable!" the announcer screamed into the
microphone, all pretense to decorum freely abandoned. The Yankees
were stunned. The Yankee skipper, Eddie Martinez, called over the
third batter, designated hitter Daryl Walker, and whispered into his ear.

Walker took his stance. As Crazy Horse went into the wind-up,
Walker turned, showing bunt. Crazy Horse blazed his seventh pitch of
the inning. It plugged off the bat and bounced up the middle. Charging
off the mound, taking it on the second bounce with a bare hand, Crazy
Horse aimed for first. The runner barely out of the batter's box, he waited, pumped once and stopped. Placing the ball in his glove he turned
away from the play and strode back atop the mound as Walker hustled
across first base for a bunt single.

For a moment, it silenced the stunned crowd, just what the Yankees'
coach, Eddie Martinez, thought he wanted.

But Crazy Horse stood on the mound in the center of the field and
grinned inanely as he gazed into the heavens, shaking his head as
though to say to the Sultan of Swat himself, *It just won't work!*

The fearless crowd roared, urging their inspired hero onward as the
Yankees' clean-up hitter marched to the plate. Justice Crowe had just

finished a dream season batting .333 with 63 home runs and 157 RBI. He was the most feared batter in baseball. The crowd remained standing but grew hushed, succumbing to the tension of the game. From atop the rounded tumuli, tall and silent, Crazy Horse surveyed the diamond. He had promised that he would bring down Ruth's house, raze it to the ground, and he meant to do so. He intended to win. Focusing on Bardick's glove, he entered his rotation with a slow, burning calm. Accepting the challenge, Justice Crowe leaned his shoulder into the plate. The announcers simply watched. Prophet glided from across the room and landed soundlessly atop the television. Jack watched the blind bird in stunned amazement. Marcel held his breath. The pitch came, another fast ball down the center of the plate. Crowe flexed his knuckles and swung the thick pine bat.

Pop! *"SSSTTtriikkkeee!"* The umpire danced as Bardick pulled his hand from the mitt to shake off the sting. Crowe spun in disbelief, incapable of comprehending that the ball had gotten past him. The Fenway fans once more erupted. They already knew what Crazy Horse had done. The curse was broken; the rest needed simply to complete itself. Marubrishnubupu watched his screen, finally comprehending; it's the beauty of the perfect repetition. Once can be a fluke. Twice can be luck. But three times, three times is more than a charm; three times is mastery.

Two more pitches, fast and directly down the center of the plate, duplicated the first. Justice Crowe went down without even swinging the bat, the first two pitches so paralyzed, so completely overpowered him.

"Three pitches to three hitters for three outs."

"Don't forget the bunt," the color man added, to which the incensed lead commentator responded, "That doesn't even matter after this. That doesn't even matter."

Under the lights, Crazy Horse tipped his hat to the sky as the Fenway Faithway poured thunderous applause, adoration and thanks upon him.

Marcel was staring at Prophet. Having drifted across the room with the open wings of an angel, the bird had landed atop the television perfectly.

"Ruth," Marcel whispered in stunned recognition as the sightless bird, now silently perched above the screen, turned its head to better hear.

Jack brushed bothersome lint from his suit as he seated himself once more. His own eyes downcast, his only commentary was hard and New York. "Nothin'. That was nothin' but dumb blind luck."

♋

The Red Sox were leading 6-0 in the fourth inning when Dorothia arrived. She used her card to swipe open the door. Marcel, his skin flushed, appeared surprised to see her. Dorothia had not previously met Marcel's publisher who, having already been up to mix drinks, stepped to greet her at the door. Extending her lithe hand with the traditional social grace, she noticed him wantonly appreciating her breasts. She found no pleasure in meeting Jack. His agenda and her agenda were indirectly antithetical. The naming of Marcel as Nobel Laureate, Dorothia wisely accepted as a boon. The timing she loathed.

"Drink darling? Hell of a game. Sox are putting on a clinic."

Dorothia waited at the open doorway to see if Marcel would rise or if he would simply sit there like a dope, reveling in boyhood.

"Don't listen to him," Jack asserted. "It's a seven-game series. They still gotta' travel cross town. How bout' it? Want me to make ya' a drink?" Drunk, obviously incapable of holding his liquor as well as Marcel, Jack slapped the author on the thigh. "Ya' got yourself a beauty there. If you need any help . . ."

Her disgust for Jack grew exponentially. At times like these she understood that it was not the words Marcel used but what he wrote of and how that made the words worth reading.

Dorothia sat on the arm of the sofa and ran her fingers through Marcel's hair. "I didn't know we'd have a guest tonight."

"Oh Jack," Marcel explained comically. "He's no guest. He came down today to go over some of the press arrangements. The thing gets announced tomorrow."

"You seemed surprised to see me. Weren't you expecting me?"

Taking her hand, Marcel turned away from the game reluctantly. "Baby, of course I was expecting you. What'd you think? I just got off routine with Jack in town. That's all, just off routine."

Philip Rand, the Yanks' right fielder, lashed a line drive into the chest of the Red Sox shortstop for the second out of the Yankee fifth. With the exception of the bunt single, Crazy Horse had faced the minimum number of batters without allowing a hit or a walk.

"Come on, watch the game. Watson's pitching a perfect game."

"He gave up a hit. It's not a perfect game," Jack objected.

"Not a perfect game? Crazy Horse let him take the base! If he had wanted to throw him out he would have thrown him out. Hell, think about it, that makes it even more of a perfect game!"

"So he didn't want to throw him out, is that it?" Jack feigned incomprehension poorly.

"Please, Jack, you saw it. Watson wanted nothing less than to strike out the side. If your Yankees had faced him like men . . ."

"Oh lovely. Macho night," Dorothia commented as she settled in next to Marcel with her hand about his shoulder.

"It still ain't a perfect game. They're not gonna' say he could have thrown him out in the record books."

"Then I might just write that book."

Plopping next to Dorothia on the sofa, Jack delivered a round of drinks. Resigned to simply delivering herself to the mental state she could not combat, Dorothia swallowed without relish. She could taste the sloe gin, a bitter-sweet, diluted syrup in carbonated water. Jack checked the time, though she knew he was not interested in the time. Consciously, she relaxed, allowing the alcohol to do its best work. "That's a beautiful watch," she commented just as Jack had hoped she would; this was, after all, the reason he had checked the time. He pretended not to care about the brand, the name he mentioned twice. In subsequent moments he put his arm around her, touched her knee, brushed against her breasts.

Without beads she said a silent rosary, praying that Marcel did not expect what Jack was hoping to achieve. She suspected and thanked God that he did not.

The final score of the game was 9-0. Crazy Horse Watson, with the exception of the bunt single that he willfully allowed, or so the debate of the baseball pantheon would go, pitched a perfect game. Over the course of the event he had faced twenty-eight batters, striking out fifteen. Doing a lap around the field to a standing ovation, Crazy Horse pointed to the sky in jubilation.

Preparing to take his leave for the night, Jack swallowed the last of his drink as Prophet cawed a ceaseless string of high-pitched, staccato chords. Stumbling out the door, Jack pointed to Marcel. "Get some sleep. I'm going to see if I can't still find some pleasure at the bar." Dorothia rolled her eyes. "Sugar, why you with a loser like him?"

"Just lucky I guess."

"Goodnight, Jack."

"Tomorrow, Boston. Next week, Stockholm."

With the menace gone and the game over, Dorothia clicked off the television.

"I wanted to see the laps," Marcel protested with no real energy. "What a game. Down comes the house. He did it. He did it just like he said he would."

With Prophet perched upon her arm, Dorothia wandered about the apartment, pensively feeding the bird shelled peanut halves. "When were you planning on telling me about Stockholm?"

He gazed at her with glassy, happy eyes that claimed contentedness as their prize. Even knowing the limits of Marcel's astounding tolerance, she could tell that tonight he was authentically drunk.

"Do you know what happened out there tonight? Do you know the nature of what happened?" he asked.

"No, I guess I don't." Dorothia returned Prophet to the wooden perch. Bobbing, the bird cawed its thank you. Slipping from her clothes, Dorothia entered the bed and closed her eyes. The drinks had her dizzy. "I guess I have other things on my mind. Please turn off the lights."

She heard Marcel sigh as he approached the bed and sat by her side. "What did you think? I have to go to Stockholm. That's what they do. They make a few phone calls and say, 'Come to Stockholm. We have something for you.' I go. They give me something. It's simple really. What did you think it would be?"

"And then you come back here?"

He paused, and she knew that it was meaningful. "Eventually, yes. I may stay in Europe for a spell. I've been feeling a need to engage a new landscape. I feel invigorated. I'm ready to begin a new book. I can write again, but I can't write it here."

"I see." And in all sincere honesty she did. The events did not bother her, only the timing. Her eyes still closed, she asked for the one thing she needed. "Will you come to meet my son before you leave?"

"Of course, of course. . . . I'll meet your son. You keep hounding me. If it's so important, I'll meet him."

"It is."

"Then I'll meet him." Still fully clothed, drunk, he collapsed with his head in her chest and drool spilling from the side of his mouth.

"Promise," she stated firmly.

Raising his head he looked in her eyes. She pressed her fingers through his hair and knew that she would miss him. The first gray strands were appearing. She could bear this but not the absence of the other thing. "Promise," she insisted again.

He wiped his chin against the blanket. Crawling to her lips he kissed her. "I promise."

"I read Blake today," she uttered softly. Reaching over his body to turn out the light, she drew the percale sheet about their shoulders. The glow of the city illuminated the suite. A pale aura of gray-blue light cut rectangles across the room, dividing the most natural of borders.

The globe of life blood trembled
Branching out into roots
Fibrous, writing upon the winds,
Fibres of blood, milk and tears,
In pangs, eternity on eternity
At length in tears & cries imbodied,
A female form, trembling and pale,
Waves before his deathly face.

All eternity shudder'd at sight
Of the first female now separate,
Pale as a cloud of snow
Waving, waving . . . waving . . . I can't remember the rest.

She knew it did not matter. Slumberous as a log, his body lumbered atop her. With his promise now, she was as close to fulfilling her promise as she had ever been.

"Marcel?" she whispered. Vigilant and on guard, aware and poetic, Prophet listened in the darkness as Marcel dreamed the dream of perfection in words.

℘

The army arrived at Dostoyevsky's Ridge a day ahead of schedule. It had been a beautiful land through which they had marched, a beauty not often associated with Russia. Rolling plains of gold stretched into the ever distant mountain ranges, their hazy purple peaks always at the end of a serene horizon, detached and indifferent to the nameless suffering of nameless men. Soli knew the meaning of deep emotional detachment. And because of this, the grueling march as a faceless drone amidst the rows upon rows of sentinels could not disturb him. His father's powerful silence had sown within him a lesson that transience could not truncate: deep emotional detachment indicates a deeper emotional commitment. Crossing the plains Soli experienced an intimate feeling for human history, a feeling that seemed to be speaking to him directly at the molecular level, entering him through the solid earth upon which he marched in endless repetition.

Rain often fell midday. This, Soli thought after the third day of marching as he watched a rainbow fade from the sky, spoiled the men who had quickly come to expect it.

On the fourth day of marching, exiting the plains, they traveled old roads that winded through the forests, roads overgrown with stiff, sweetly smelling lemongrass and fern, roads untraveled for many years. The tank squadrons trammeled the old forest roads, flattening the overgrowth for the soldiers who marched behind. The tanks opened a doorway to a past that had nearly been sealed. New meaning came with a gun.

The forest and the road ended forty yards shy of the ridge. Ghosts were alive here, ethereal doppelgangers of ancestors and past lives. This was the type of place that men and women had once been proud to call home, a place of peace, a place to be content to live, to bare offspring and to die. Once upon a time, before the river had dried up, Soli could see how this crooked line along the ravine would have been the ideal spot for a village, an ideal spot to share wisdom. Dostoyevsky's Ridge ran parallel to what, thousands of years earlier, had been the powerful path of a life giving river.

Now, buried in the naked gorge below, there existed only the dry, brittle, ivory bones of the ancestral mothers and fathers, their words of ritual — perhaps even their language — forgotten, buried in the parched red clay of wind-cleft arroyos. Soli could feel the spirits in the land that cracked beneath a merciless sun. A just and gentle wind moaned from the basin, rising over the ridge, subduing hardness, summoning Soli, telling him that the sole purpose of the war was to bring him here.

Why? He could not fathom why.

General Yusherin's second-in-command informed the men that the Third Reich, it appeared, had decided to attack from a southern route, pressing north before veering eastward for the Kremlin. The Russians believed the Germans had blundered by entering the Russian Federation through the Ukraine, just north of Kiev, too far south of the major roads leading into Moscow. Still, if the unorthodox approach worked, as it had in the initial phases of the attack, the gamble would gain the Germans time and a supreme tactical advantage.

Seen from German eyes the great danger of the innovative approach existed in the fact that it demanded their army press forward through poorly defined terrain. One stretch in particular, about fifteen miles — the last leg that would pour the German forces onto a major road to Moscow and validate the daring strategy —· cut directly though Dostoyevsky's Ridge. The Germans found the antiquated route marked on an old map of the Russian Federation dating to the Sino-Russo war of 1905. The sparsely marked route of the map made no note of Dostoyevsky's Ridge.

Dostoyevsky's Ridge was the best weapon the Russians possessed. For even if the Russians could not decisively turn the tide, if they could hold the ridge, they would at least stall the German machine, push the Germans off course, cause them to lose precious time. It was still only September, but with each passing day the Russian winter drew closer, the winter the likes of which only the memory of a Russian or the imagination of a poet could appreciate; the monstrous, fascist Führer was neither.

Yusherin intended to drive a wedge through the heart of the enemy army as it emerged from the forest road. Surprised by the steep ridge before them, the steep ridge not indicated on their maps, the Germans, Yusherin reasoned, would have limited options.

First, they could retreat. A retreat into the forest would be unlikely.

Second, the Germans could conduct an infantry assault, attempting to scale the steeped incline and overwhelm the entrenched Russian forces with sheer numbers — feasible, but a difficult prospect even under propitious conditions.

Third, the Germans could string out along the ridge and build a defensive rampart of men to mirror the Russian position from the forest's fringe. This was the best option available to the Germans, and Yusherin planned his forces based on the likelihood that this was the option the Germans would choose.

Working from the forest's edge, the Germans would then scout for vulnerable points of engagement, potential breaches in the Russian position. The most susceptible points thus located, only then would the Germans flex their military muscle for a direct assault. Once this structured, calculated assault began, the Germans would willingly sustain high losses for the imperative gain. Such a strategy, calculating but aggressive, would be a typical expression of the German mind.

The Russians, like a millipede whose legs have become guns, were positioned upon the edge of the ridge, hand dug into concave pillboxes in the soil, in an extended lateral line without great depth. Armed with superior position and the advantages of preparation and surprise, Yusherin believed his army stood a good chance of controlling the battlefront, of halting the blitzkrieg. Focused only on killing, perhaps they would even succeed in repelling the German onslaught. Soli saw the men lying in wait, belly down in their hand-dug entrenchments. With the voices of dead ancestry rumbling in his head, he could not help but think that for many among them, simple village men with red clay beneath their fingernails, they had just dug, without a sense for irony and with no trace of ceremony, their own graves.

Reports from the front indicated that advancing German tanks outnumbered the Russian tank force 6-to-1. If this held true and if the Germans were able to utilize their tank capacity to a fraction of its potency, the Russians would have little hope of victory. If a single German tank succeeded in mounting the top of the ridge, the Russian position would be lost.

The outcome of the battle would be determined by the German tanks. As long as the German tanks were contained below the ridge, their shells would be largely futile. Either they would explode into the side of the ridge or rocket over the heads of the Russians. The Germans could try to lob the shells in, but such tactics were difficult and statistically ineffective. Morbidly, Yusherin would have invited such a waste of valuable munitions.

Having studied the entire ridge tirelessly, Yusherin determined that the German tanks would be capable of negotiating the bluff's rise at only three points. Yes, the cruel general surmised with his impressive military mind, a mind that understood how to violate a landscape like a woman, there existed three assailable points along the five-mile ridge. Yusherin cursed the barren rivulets that had once emptied from the plains to slice these passageways into the bluff's austere face.

The general took personal responsibility for overseeing the defense of the violable points. Two of the points were located within a quarter mile of one other, towards the last third of the ridge's southwestern shoulder. Yusherin intended to protect these with a massive force. It was here that General Yusherin desired Russia to make her stand.

The third access point worried Yusherin. As the other two points were where he desired the battle to be drawn, the third point represented the only true vulnerability. Located a hundred yards from the dead center of the ridge but two miles away from the dual breach, the third site, from a military standpoint, was a scarcely defensible nightmare. Where the two breach points existed in near proximity, the land curled into a natural, bowed crescent. Yusherin liked this feature of the land. But at the third point, the geography of the ridge was more linear, meaning fewer soldiers could be effectively positioned in tactical arrays.

Had Yusherin been leading the German force, had he been tasked to assess the ridge from an offensive perspective, he would have without hesitation committed his troops to a pyrrhic assault on the single point. Although the two-breach position ostensibly offered more opportunity for a successful assault — two vulnerable points within a quarter mile of one another — General Yusherin understood that ambiguous choices arising in the midst of battle can be more dangerous than guns. Choices in the midst of battle divide the will, create questions that lead to doubt, doubt that leads to fear, fear that leads to defeat. Singularity, choicelessness and certainty forge the will with the extreme courage that leads to victory. It was a common sense military principle that in war, where human emotions are a factor, it is easier to conquer one point than two.

Yusherin anguished.

If he prepared a massive contingency to defend the position, he would be confirming the critical nature of the position for the enemy, practically unfurling a red carpet for their assault. He could ambush. This idea he also dismissed. Against a smaller force it would have been a solid strategy, but against the German army it would be nothing but an act of desperation.

General Yusherin reviewed the situation. Outnumbered and outgunned by the German army, Russia's success depended on their ability to get the Germans to go where the Russians needed them to go. If he were the German commanding officer, Yusherin would have wanted to attack this single point in the bluff, regardless of the human cost. This meant one thing; if the Germans concentrated their attack here, the Russians would lose.

General Yusherin had only one choice. He had to minimize the attractiveness of that single point on Dostoyevsky's Ridge. He had to make it appear as less than it was. He had to destroy its appeal. Insane as it seemed, Yusherin had to make that single slope in the ridge appear as indistinct as possible. He had to find a way to ensure that the enemy's attention would not be drawn to it. But how? Such madness! Impossible! If he had seen it, what could possibly make it so they would not?

Pacing upon his Arabian steed, his hand unconsciously plying the orange mane, Yusherin stared at the vulnerable point. How does one make what is so, not so? Gripped by a postulate, a possibility, Yusherin ripped into action. Vengefully, he ordered all of the tents brought to the basin. He ordered them sullied, gouged, scrubbed in dirt and sticky needles of pine. Soldiers trained in killing were set to sewing as the Russian army constructed a massive sheet of thick canvas. Once sown together, Yusherin commanded the sullied canvas pulled across the gap in the ridge's face. He intended to create an illusion, the appearance that the ridge was not broken, that it was one continuous, imposing, steep bluff. Word of what Yusherin sought to accomplish burned through the ranks. The soldiers were stunned. They thought it mad. It'll never work; he's high on his own power the men grumbled to one another.

The point of entry they needed to conceal had room enough for two tanks side by side to ascend the ridge. The final product was 37 feet high and 27 feet wide. It took a hundred men to sew it together and forty to string it up. The general watched from the ravine's bottom, shouting directions to the soldiers atop the ledge. Young Solzhenitsyn lingered at the general's side through much of this. Due to his youthful vigor, he had succeeded, following the murder of the German prisoner, to ingratiate himself sufficiently with the general to serve as a runner. As the giant canvas rose, the debacle became apparent. Though it concealed the inviting slope, the façade, a laughable fiasco, fooled no one.

Upon seeing the product of his thought, the general swelled with violent rage.

"Rip it down!" Yusherin boomed in disgust. "This is where we'll fight it out. Where we'll live and die as men."

Standing by the general's boot, Soli gazed at the drab canopy that had been pulled too stiff to resemble a natural apparition. "Let me paint it, General." The words erupted without thinking.

The general turned to the boy, iron branding in his gaze. "What did you say?"

The presumption of the boy was insult enough. But Soli thought only of Krylov, of his mother and his father's sacrifice, of the past that reached out to him from the canvas like an unanticipated calling from God.

"I can do the fresco," he stated, simply and unafraid, his eyes impassioned, alight. He did not know from where the word *"fresco"* had come. In all of his life, he had never used it. The landscape was alive, speaking to him, commanding him, summoning him to fill it with his spirit. "Let me paint it, General. Let me make it real." Soli's eyes tarried on the botched canvas. His mind saw not what was there but what he would manifest.

Brandishing the reins of the horse, the general prepared to assault the young soldier for the affront. Glaring at the boy, Yusherin intended to bend Soli with intimidation, yet it was he who was intimidated. Yusherin saw the profile and in the profile he saw the fully revealed impression of the one man he feared, the one man whom with the resolution of a pure and consistent spirit he had been incapable of breaking, Michayl.

Yusherin yanked furiously at the reins of his Arabian, escaping the ghostly reflection, veering towards his second-in-command. "Do it," he ordered vehemently.

"General?" the captain asked, confused by the sudden shift of mandates.

"Get him whatever he needs."

The captain paused, still unsure, incapable of interpreting the concession.

"Do It!" the white-eyed general roared, spitting forth the caustic, delirious wrath of a commander not in the habit of giving orders twice. Spurred by terror, the captain raced into action. Peering over his shoulder, Yusherin galloped away, towards the two-breach site, as Soli, palladium eyes wide open and receptive, awakening medium to the mystical substratum, studied the canvas of his dead father's living soul.

Soli had only a day to complete his mission. The materials were limited and rough. Undaunted, he entered the work overflowing with an intense energy, his purpose clear. Without reflection he drove the men about him, much older, bending them before the directives of his will. He shared his sense of purpose, shared it through his lack of respect for the needs of the individual. Oddly, every individual felt their greatest desire met. From the dirt and clay, deep brown shades of varying consistency were mixed into mud. Black: motor oil from the jeeps and tanks. Yellow: gallons of mustard. Red: tomato paste. Corn starch was used to thicken and whiten specific pools that Soli ordered mixed. When his paints were readied, he ordered four-foot paint brushes cut from swaths of evergreen pines. He required more gray and commanded soldiers by the hundreds to chip away at limestone from the ridge until he had vats of gray, stone flakes at his disposal. The canvas was scrapped of Yusherin's work and flipped; Soli would work on the other side.

Once the materials were prepared — the paints, brushes, the massive canvas stretched in the arroyo's basin — he washed his hands and began painting. He permitted only two men to aid him in his efforts. Two men, whom he hand-selected for their honest faces, to pour the paints upon the canvas from aluminum cooking vats. With a stark, selfless diligence, these men prepared his brushes and kept his supplies fresh so that he could focus and never stop painting. As night fell, his comrades, acting without orders, positioned floodlights to shine from above so that Soli could continue working on the immense project. A second set of assistants were selected. He screamed at them for incompetence. "Concentrate! Concentrate completely on what you are doing!"

They worked with pride, with integrity, with the dignity that noble purpose brings. As Soli worked on the project he realized that he would require more stone flakes. Men were roused from sleep to accommodate the need, the whim. Many volunteered; they were not sleeping anyway but watching from the ridge, witnesses of their own birth. The general came only once. Alone, in the middle of the night, he stared down upon the canvas from a lonesome spot upon the ridge. He watched the deliberate and thoughtful movements of the painter, the painter who rejected all the manipulative claims of exhaustion as he painted the canvas upon which all of Russia's hopes were pinned. The general watched from the darkness, feeling human.

At sun-up, a report came in that the German army was only hours away. Scattered gunfire could be heard in the distance as select Russian squads initiated spotty engagement, luring the Germans forward. Fueled by an increasing energy and excitement, pulled forward by the anticipation of completion, Soli worked without sleep. He was lost in the world of the canvas, oblivious to the advance of the Germans. No one dared intrude upon his work with questions; all wondered if there would be time. The vats of stone flakes were still untouched. The men, as they watched, could merely conjecture what they were for.

Soli stood amidst the completed canvas. Unawares, he had painted himself not into a corner but into the canvas' center. Dead center. This was his father's living soul, his son, legacy to the world. Solzhenitsyn walked boldly, without hesitation, off of the canvas. Leaving footprints behind he ordered it hoisted. The top was fastened by thick twine and long iron stakes driven like nails into the land. He ordered slack as the men below, following his direction, stretched and shook the canvas. Atop the ridge and with the aid of strong-willed men, he dumped limestone flakes. Downwards, gray cascaded as the colors ran. It was a living canvas, becoming natural, transformed from a work of man to a work of nature before their very eyes.

"Shake more vigorously. With all of your might!" Soli bellowed into the gulch below. A fine, dusty powder, sparkling flashes of zinc-yellow and gray, rose from the canvas like spirits released. The men let the canvas fall flat and watched in awe-filled silence as Soli poured more flakes of stone downward, a waterfall of ashen dullness until the canvas bottom rooted.

Gunfire grew closer, but the men who worked with Soli worked with courage and conviction. The work made them intrepid. They believed no bullet could do them harm. Protected by the will of God and the prayers of the forefathers, Soli ran to the edge of the forest to see from a distance what the German men would see and would not see. Standing below, reviewing the work he had done, he was the last man in the ravine. The Russian soldiers — men and boys — held their breath and their guns. Their eyes, with all of their love, lingered upon him from above. Soli gazed upwards at the canvas. Once more the spirits were speaking to him, easing his human fear. He nodded in appreciation of his comrades' efforts. From the distance, he could see nothing worthy of attention. He saw only the obscurity of the sublime — a single, continuous, unbroken, ever so close to revelation, steep bluff — so grand we cannot see it.

Gunfire closer, Soli sprinted forward. Until he was halfway there, he could not find the seam that divided the representation from the represented. Stepping behind the canvas, his creation, the creation of all the spirits of goodness that had once lived by this dried-up river, Solzhenitsyn disappeared as the first German, a hundred meters down, appeared from the solid wood. Down the line, upon Yusherin's command, the Russians opened fire, battering the emerging force that scurried for cover. German tanks could be heard, their steady mechanical roll razing the young forest. The business end of the turret guns arrived. Two worlds collided.

The first Germans to enter the barren ravine were mowed down by bullets hailed from above. With the first drop of red river blood spilt upon the earth, the land was transformed. Just as the general expected, the first tanks drilled shells into the side of the ridge's steep embankment in futility. The land shook. The Russians clung for life.

Taking defensive coverage in the trees, the German soldiers spread themselves in a long, flat, parallel line that mirrored the Russian front.

Clawing his way up the slope hidden by the canvas, Soli saw the general atop the ridge, staring down from his prized, orange-maned Arabian. Upon sight of Yusherin, Soli stopped. He had forgotten this man as he had worked, but now he remembered. Now his memory recalled everything. His stomach hardened into a knot.

At the same time, hatred filled the cold eyes of the general, hatred without limits.

"There's a promontory seventy yards to the right," a sneering Yusherin stated. Soli looked. Precariously extended over the ravine, he had noticed it before. "I want you and these men to take that position."

With a stoic's discipline, Soli saluted. Completing his ascent, he joined the three others, the assistants who had helped him. Ragged, they carried a crate of grenades among them. Each struggled to express gratitude to Solzhenitsyn. Each struggled to make an apology for what the general now asked them to do. They had been commanded to take an offensive position that was perfect, perfect in that their small band would be in an ideal position to kill the enemy. The problem was that the promontory, extending over the ravine below like a banner soliciting target practice, was also a perfect place to be killed.

"It's suicide," one of the men declared after Yusherin rode off to give other directions along the line. The gunfire intensified.

Without listening to the protests, Soli drove forward, grabbing at the handle of the crate of grenades as he slung a machine gun over his shoulder. "Come on; we need to create a diversion."

"A diversion?"

"So they don't have time to see our bluff." He ordered the other men now. "We need to draw their attention to us. We need to pull them down the line so that the canvas becomes a blind spot. It blends in well. It's hard to see, but we don't want them lingering for a good stare. They'll pass right by it if we get them coming for us."

"What good will that do if it gets us killed?"

"We're going to kill them first. Killing is good, remember?"

The four men took the position. The promontory was larger than it appeared from the distance, and it gave them hope.

"A tank could drop this whole thing."

Soli ignored the fear and led the men to the edge. He led, once again, by example, as he had done throughout the night. Other Russians were along the ridge, aiming at the Germans. They watched as the four men crept out upon the ledge; their wills were forged with a resolve not to let their valiant comrades die. Killing is good, they thought as a collective organism, leaning out farther, courageously daring from their spots of hiding, bringing themselves to the center — or were they bringing the center to them?

Lobbing grenades, they traded fire with scores of Germans for nearly an hour. As a group, they proved to be extremely talented at killing.

Working as a single mind, the Russians eased their way gradually left and gradually right of the painting, leading the German line, creating a gap of inactivity at the exact point they wanted.

Amidst the collateral gunfire, the swearing, the sweat and sulfur, a breathless moment came when one German emerged from the treeline awestruck. Mesmerized as though by a dream, he wandered from the hemline of forest that offered him protection. Arm raised, he was pointing at the canvas, his incapable lips struggling to articulate what he saw. Soli and the small squad could see the German from the distance. What type of extraordinary eyesight did the man have? One of Soli's men took a bullet in the arm, dropping the live grenade. They all watched as it rolled in a shaky line down the stony ridge. At the last moment, one of the men gave the deadly device a kick, sending it off the ledge just as it exploded beneath them. When the group from the promontory finally looked back into the ravine, the German soldier, riddled by a violent multitude of bullets, was dead.

They were so good at killing that for fifty yards left and fifty yards right of the painting, the German forces were dominated. Seeing nothing but a losing proposition in that stretch of the ridge, the German attack progressively subsided. The blitzkrieg, though not yet stopped, had been effectively stalled. Their crate of grenades empty, the four men, exposed to the burning sun's eye, lay still upon their backs, each finally experiencing the reality of the terror through which they had, thus far, bravely lived. The sounds of gunfire were fading down the line, more distant, a shriveling dream. Enemy tanks were silent, desisting from earlier attempts to gage the exact trajectory from which to attack the forces atop the uneven ledge. A messenger traveling along the Russian front on motorbike informed the troops that half their numbers were to report down the line. The Germans, it appeared, were reconcentrating for a massive offensive at the dual slopes of Dostoyevsky's Ridge, exactly where Yusherin desired the attack. "It worked! It worked!" the messenger cried out when he saw that it was the young painter. "You've done it! They believed it! It worked!"

All along the line, the fighting receded as the bulk of the German force reconstituted for a second wave. Their bluff had not guaranteed victory, but it had assured that the Russians, already outnumbered, would be able to fight from their self-determined, best strategy. "Be brave!" the messenger cried out above the muzzling roar of the cycle's engine. "Gremikov's army is a day away."

"Gremikov's army is coming here?" the stunned Russians asked. But already the messenger was racing down the line, his helmeted head ducked, just in case. Stripping the cloth lining from the empty crate, Soli bandaged the bleeding arm of the wounded man. High above, part of his world, he watched as a steady winged hawk cut circles in the sky.

♉

The winds outside their home howled. A bright red scarf tumbled down the street. His windows, transparent bars of prison glass, rattled. It was 2:00 a.m. when Rooster completed his third painting of that day. Battling the sluggish pull within for just a few more moments, he swirled his brushes within empty sauce jars filled with murky turpentine. He understood why Soli had been so insistent in telling him, "Painting should exhaust you. It should leave you empty, used, *worthless* . . . with nothing left to give. . . . It's not enough to rise early, Rooster. You must also work late." This he had done and had been doing for three days now.

Too drained to even address surging inflammation, he circled the room, pausing before each new painting, before shutting off the light switches and crawling into bed. Again, the desolate winds rattled at the windows as they had done all night. His bloodshot eyes shot through the clear panes of glass hoping to glimpse the magical. Nothing, *nothing* but the mundane streetlights, patient sentinels, streamlined colossals. He had not seen Tamara since the evening when she had cleansed his wounds, three days now.

A ghost amidst the darkness, he lifted the wrapped hands before his own gaze. The subtle warmth of light from the street intensified their irradiate sheen. He admired the wrapping of the bandages, remembering her touch, summoning it to linger upon him still. Closing his weary mind, the passion she evoked stirred within him. To see his own hands, nursed through her touch, was to reconnect with the divine. He imagined her constantly as he painted, conceiving of her hand wrapped about his, moving the brush, selecting the tones. Tonight, he fully believed that she would come. His intention was to surprise her by completing as many works as humanly possible between the time she left and the time she returned. Following his muse, he completed more than this. Each time along his journey, if his body ached or his concentration faltered, he recalled the tormented anguish she had inflicted, dipping his raw and sickly appendages into the steaming bath seven times. He recalled the pleasure and the pain, extreme dimensions of the same bliss. The memory itself suffused him, sharpened his insight, his edge, his oneness of mind. Placed within the grander context of agony and ecstasy that she revealed to him, he felt reinvigorated. He redoubled his efforts, directing all of his enthusiasm to the single task of delighting her through an uncommon display of exertion that he humbly intended might nearly equal the piety of her gift to him.

Lying in the darkness, the chaste wrap about his hands, he reflected upon the last three days without her. He could remember nothing but a single blur of relentless forward momentum dedicated to her influence. An emptiness to which he refused to succumb sagged inside his heart. He had been sure that tonight she would appear. Three days, he felt, symbolized some sort of limit. Rooster squeezed his fingers slowly; it was the hands, refulgent with her presence, that gave him faith.

Alone now, with no painting functioning as companion to draw forth and ease his soul, Rooster pondered their last exchange. Wrapping his arms beneath his head, he smiled at the ceiling. Their strange night had altered him forever. Her remarkable efforts made it possible. How hard had he worked to push her away? How much vital energy had he expended in protecting his insulated cocoon? Tamara had finally helped him to see the truth. Tamara helped Rooster see that he was not protecting the world from himself as he so believed. He was protecting himself from the world, creating an alternate world in response. What had she said?

"The world of your canvas is glorious. But don't lose the world outside your door. Teach them. Teach me. Don't remove yourself so completely. It's not an either/or. There doesn't have to be an opposition. Lord, if anyone can make it work, if anyone can unite the contradictions, it's you. Your mind makes it happen. You're more than the painting on the wall. Do you understand? No matter how wonderful a painting may be, never believe that it is more than you. The whole world is your canvas. I could say, 'don't deprive us of that,' but I won't. The world will have your paintings. Don't deprive yourself of the world. You're a healer, Alexi. Don't you even know? You've healed me. God yes, there is a heaven, but there is also life."

Rooster thought fondly of her words. He felt short pangs of shame remembering how he had accused her. "What do you know about love?"

"How can you ask such a thing?" she had responded with emblazoned ferocity. "Is it that no one can come close to you, or that you don't want anyone close to you?"

"I've let you close. I've allowed you into my life."

"You've allowed me! Yes, yes you have. You've allowed me into your little sphere in a way that you won't allow any other. That's true. But do you trust me enough to enter mine? Will you open up your heart and trust what's outside that door, outside this house, beyond the edges of your oils and your canvas, beyond the easy frames?"

Rooster had lifted his hands in demonstration and protest, "What more do you want from me, Tamara? What more do you need?"

"Everything." Her answer had come without hesitation or self-consciousness, without irony or regret. "Is that so impossible for you to understand? I want everything you are. I want to face the world with you, to explore it, to know it, to discover it. I want to be unafraid, as unafraid as you are when you paint. And when it's needed, I want to be afraid. I want to turn outward with you and engage the world in whatever it wants to give, good or bad or indifferent. But I want to do it with you. Do you see that? Can't you understand that little distinction? Can't you risk a little more? I don't want to change you, Rooster. I just want to share it with you."

"But what?" he'd pleaded, genuinely lost. "What?"

"But I can't! I can't paint with you. I can't experience what you experience in the moments of creation. That's yours! I can't be there. So what do I share with you, Alexi, if you aren't willing to share the world with me? I love your art. I love what you do there." She had paused. "But I would throw it all away for one hour fully lived in the world with you."

He'd listened in a state of disbelief. Since as early as he could recall, for his whole life and then some, he had been told he was a painter and that his paintings were the best part of him. He had been told this, and he had believed it without question. Now a woman stood before him, a young, beautiful woman with glowing eyes who honestly loved him, telling him that he was more than a painting. Like so much of life's mysteries, even as he heard it, he did not doubt it, but it was hard to accept as true.

"Help me," he had whispered, stepping from the ledge of his heart. "I can't do it myself."

Taking his hand, she had searched his face, a wonderful canvas of innocence and fear, sacred trust and faith. "You don't have to."

For something so obvious, it was the first time since his master's death, Soli's death, that Rooster believed it true.

A cab had taken them into the city. Crisp lights had reflected off the gentle mist that swirled along the glistening wet city streets. Rain drizzled. Golden cabaret reviews had alighted the theater district with flashing intermittent bulbs. People bustled to and fro. Old babushkas waited in the plastic enclosures of the bus station. Young Latino men jaunted in the streets as a motorcycle gang ate hot dogs from a circus trailer. The outdoor skating rink had just opened for the season.

Tamara had pointed and the cab rolled to a stop. Rooster tapped his pockets apologetically. "My mother," he stumbled over his tongue to explain. "I have a trust from Soli . . . and even some sales but . . ." For the first time, he found himself wishing that he had control over his own money. "She manages it all." His voice had trailed off. "It's never been an issue."

Tamara had laughed, paying the driver.

After skating, on Tamara's playful lark, they had entered the most expensive restaurant in town, the type of place where the ambiance is thick as the porterhouse. In the corner, the violinist led the cellist. The maître de had informed Rooster that jackets were required. In the bar, cigar smoke drifted upwards, dancing in and out of tractor beams of light. For all its ambiance, Rooster had thought it a colorless place as he appraised the quality of illuminated portraits lined upon the walls. When the maître de returned with a coatsleeve prepared to receive Rooster's arm, the painter paused nervously, so well had he trained himself to avoid physical contact.

"He's a boxer," Tamara had told the maître de as she dropped a book of the house matches into her pocket. It horrified Rooster to have direct attention drawn to his hands. The maître de only nodded without interest, skillfully slipping Rooster into the sportscoat.

Tamara had woven her arm into Rooster's arm as they were led through the candlelit room of white table clothes, austere waiters and attractive waitresses. The people provided the color he'd realized as they had walked through the room; the background should be black and white. In his own mind he felt paranoia's prick, as though everyone in the room knew he was a leper. Tugging at the sportscoat, he raised it higher round his shoulders in a useless attempt to conceal the only visible signs of the disease: healed scars about his neck, chin and earlobes. Tamara pulled out a chair for him, causing the hostess to suppress a grin.

Suddenly aware, Rooster blurted, "I'm supposed to do that for you."

"You? You're too nervous."

They sat at the café table, flickering candlelight defining the space between them. The edge tremored as the flame danced. "Everyone's looking at me." He'd buried his hands beneath the table.

"You're so vain," she'd joked, but it had not made him smile. His discomfort had been a palpable thing. "Give me your hands."

He'd given them to her, noting that the tablecloth was not white, but off-white. Held in contrast to the white gauze about his hands, the white of the white tablecloth diminished. What did pure white look like? Did it exist? If he now held his hands against snow, would he see that the snow was not true white? Would it be the gauze that would set the evolving standard? And if after one hundred years in a cave of darkness, he entered into the light once more, would his definition of white be purer, more refined? Would he have seen in that time the ideal in his mind's eye, the ideal never known in the world . . . or would he forget, and in forgetting emerge from the cave to see white even in the darkest ash? What is white? And does it have anything at all to do with color?

"There's not a person in this room who can create the beauty you create, not a single one. Of course they're looking at you. I'm looking at you. Why wouldn't we look?"

The waiter had approached the table and introduced himself. Without pause he had begun rattling off the evening specials like a practiced actor in perfect control of his lines.

"Lobster thermidor," Rooster had blurted out.

"Sir?"

"Lobster thermidor. That's my order, lobster thermidor."

Glancing at Tamara as though for reassurance that all was well, the talented waiter had assuaged the rough lines, "Excellence choice."

"I'll have the same," Tamara had quickly added. Menus disappeared.

She'd watched as Rooster fiddled with the utensils. They appeared within his hands as foreign objects, tools possessing an enigmatic purpose he could not fathom. When the waiter had left, she leaned forward. "Are you all right? We can leave if this is too much."

But he had surprised her with a rimose smile, for he was finding strength in the thought of Soli and the last meal that there had been no time to share. He'd then made confident eye contact with a woman at another table whom he had caught looking at his hands. "I'm a boxer," he'd explained to Tamara's delight. Scurrilously, the woman returned to her squid appetizer.

"Lobster thermidor."

"What?" Tamara had asked as a natural grace began to infuse their space.

"Lobster thermidor. I've never had it. It was Soli's favorite."

They had talked into the evening, ordered a bottle of wine, then coffee, then a sumptuous key lime pie. Like moths to a candle they had spoken intimately, letting go of the threat of the world around them, blending in, quite ordinary, the hardest thing for each, when alone, to do.

"I knew you when you were at Danforth," Tamara had suddenly admitted as they were sharing the chiffon slice of key lime pie. Since Rooster offered no reply but for a questioning stare, she'd continued slowly. "I was a cleaning lady, staff help, laundry, kitchen, whatever they needed. I used to mop the dormitory floors in the early morning."

The memory of solitude and simple but steady achievement had caused her to smile. "Everyone else would be asleep. I'd start each day at 4:00 a.m. It's such a lonesome time and beautiful all it once. I think, if not for you, it might have been just lonely. But you were there, always awake. I'd go into the dorm and the first thing I would do is walk by your room to see if the light was on. I'd heard about you. I'd know that you were painting and that I wasn't alone. And I knew that no matter how alone I might feel at that early hour, you were probably feeling it too, being awake, working in solitude at such a lonesome hour. It was comforting to me.

"You won't believe this, or you'll probably think it was strange, but I used to imagine that we were connected in a grand, cosmic effort and that as I moved my mop from one side of the floor to the other, you were moving your brush, covering the canvas with wonderful, delicious lines. I used to imagine that my rhythm was yours too, so I tried to create these perfect lines, absolutely mathematically perfect lines with the mop. It's how I knew, or at least had a tiny sense for what you were going through. Some mornings I couldn't get it right; I couldn't do anything right. I couldn't even make a straight line with my brush. . . ."

She'd blushed in embarrassment of her slip. "My mop," she'd corrected. "But that's the kind of effect you had on me, even then. Before I ever saw even one of your paintings, you made the mundane magical. That's what I was seeking."

Rooster had remained silent and that silence had made Tamara nervous, causing her to reveal more.

"I met Soli once too."

Shocked, excited, "You met him?" he'd asked.

"Yes, it was the day you made a scene giving him your sketches. He kept them in his arm the whole night. Did you know that? The students were so angry and jealous. They thought it was their night, but even then they couldn't beat you. They couldn't beat your ghost. Soli only wanted to know more about the lunatic in the courtyard, the passionate artist who had approached him. You were the only one there he called an 'artist.'"

Rooster had stared at her with the intensity and focus reserved for painting. She'd trembled, her legs weakening from that look. "And you told him something, didn't you?" The question was neither angry or pleased. It merely probed for truth. With her eyes staring in the black depths of the coffee cup, she'd nodded.

"No one wanted to talk about you to him. He couldn't find out what he wanted to know. We knew all of the gossip, the behind-the-scenes, on the general staff. They hated you at that school. . . ." Sipping from her coffee, she'd allowed the words to waft between them. "When Soli was alone, I got near him. All that I did was ask him if he wanted to know about the artist who had done the sketches. He said yes and we met behind the building." She'd stopped. It was all that she could tell him.

"I have to know, Tamara. What then? What did you tell him?"

She had smiled, suddenly understanding that there was one more thing she could say. "Oh Rooster, I told him that you worked in the night to create the day." A tear formed in her eye as she met the intensity of his stare with an intensity all her own. "I told him that since you had left, mopping was mopping, night was night, being alone truly was being alone."

Rooster's voice spoke in an ethereal hush. "And he understood?"

In the corner, the violin led the movement of the cello. "Yes," she'd answered, "he understood completely."

Three full nights and three full days had passed since their key lime pie. Three full nights and three full days of waiting for her return, a waiting full, a waiting pregnant with expectation. Why hadn't she come? Was this another threshold? Was she trying to demonstrate that she had no intentions or desires to interfere with the production of his art? Glancing out the window, he craved to see her form born from shadow and street. He didn't have her phone number or know where she lived. Now it seemed a stupid thing, but at the time, neither need nor purpose seemed to exist for such surety. Tamara appeared when she appeared, always at the proper time, finding him receptive. Such was the nature of their unspoken routine. His eyes growing accustomed to the lightness in the dark, he reached across the bed, picking up the corner puzzle piece from the flat stand of his night table. There were two smooth edges forming a right angle and then a contorted side, seemingly unable to determine what it sought to become. If it had possessed a will, would it have become a triangle or a square? Or would it have chosen to remain a perpetual puzzle? The odd edge always defines the whole, he thought. Tomorrow she'll come, surely tomorrow. We'll go to the lake. We'll do whatever she wants to do. We'll go wherever she wants to go. I'll get her address, her phone number, some money so that I can take her. This won't happen again. No more division, he decided firmly, closing his eyes and attempting sleep.

Thirteen paintings in three days time due to her inspirational splendor. Tomorrow, she'll definitely come tomorrow. Until then, I'll paint for her, to her, of her. And so Rooster dreamed, perceiving a world of future hope, slipping effortlessly between the curtained realm of the real and the courageous imagination of the supreme.

15

THE PHONE RANG on a bright day. The sun shone. Rooster was painting feverishly. Tamara had been contained. Marcel had promised to see her son. The world for Dorothia Rodriguez could not possibly have been more perfect as she picked up the phone, readjusting petunias in a rose colored vase. On the other end of the line Irene anticipated the answer. The two women chatted delightfully for several minutes about topics unrelated to art before Irene eased into a review of her meeting with the buyers. In enthusiastic tones she explained to Dorothia what it meant to have the unilateral advocacy of the three. "It's like having the U.S., Russia and China agree," Irene illustrated.

"I've never heard of any of them."

"You wouldn't have. These are the behind-the-scene players. They're the ones who have the power to set market value. These are the people art critics listen to as they define their own opinions. These three don't just make or break artists. They make or break art movements. When they're in disagreement, they kind of check and balance each other, but when they agree, their judgments rule the entire cultural landscape."

"That's just not possible," Dorothia exclaimed, titillated by the prospect that it might be true.

"You wouldn't think so, but it is. I've been in this business long enough to know that there are people, not many and not very well known, with levers that are long enough to move the world. Individually they don't, but collectively, these three wield that kind of leverage."

"It's amazing. It fascinates me." Outside, the rays of a crisp sun filtered through the craggy limbs of the trees. Most of the deciduous leaves had fallen, acceding to the undeniable approach of the winter season. Those few leaves that still clung to the wrinkled branches were fading in color. The brilliant reds, oranges and golds had given way to lusterless shades of ocher, brown and puce. A coven of crows temporarily dappled the sky before descending ragtag into the distant trees by the lake down the road. Irene's news was simply another flower for Dorothia to arrange in her bouquet of recent achievements. "That a few people can hold so much influence, it doesn't seem possible." The words did not communicate the smile of her understanding, for to Dorothia's reasoning, if the three influenced the masses and Irene influenced the three and she influenced Irene, then it was she who applied slight pressure to the lever with the greatest effect.

"Your son has succeeded in generating a tremendous stir out here. His art is going to redefine the surreal."

"Yes, my son," Dorothia replied with fake warmth, feeling slighted that Irene appeared so oblivious to the obvious.

"What we really want to do now, Dorothia, what we really need to do, is meet Rooster. I've taken this about as far as I can go without a personal connection. I'm out on quite a limb for the both of you."

Dorothia tugged at her pearl drop earring quizzically. "On a limb?"

"Well yes, these things I've been doing for your son are quite unique. For myself personally, the aggressiveness of the approach I've taken as an advocate for Rooster's art is unprecedented. That's why I'm saying, it really is time for me to meet him."

"I see," Dorothia responded carefully as she attempted to deftly assimilate the new insight. "You said 'We.' 'We need to meet Rooster.' Who were you referring to? Not anyone besides yourself, I trust." Her fingers, devout and guarded, stroked the satin texture of the flower petals. She knew that she had just laid a severe burden on Irene, and it pleased her.

An intermezzo of silence filled the line from Providence to Los Angeles. "There is at least one, maybe two others that I would be bringing with me."

"Out of the question," Dorothia sternly ejaculated. "Absolutely out of the question. Three people to meet my son? Do you have any idea of the stress that creates?"

"For whom?" Irene fired back with a rebellious ire that Dorothia did not expect.

"For my son! Why, how dare you suggest . . ."

But Irene was already soothing the gap she had of deliberate necessity opened. "I apologize, Dorothia. I didn't mean to suggest anything. I just need to make sure that you see how important this meeting will be. This is a critical juncture for all of us. If you care about your son . . ." Irene slowed down, gambling on the full depth of what she believed she understood. "If you care about making something of his name, then you'll concede to what I'm asking. It is absolutely critical if I am to be successful in fulfilling my mission for your son."

Dorothia plucked a petal and rolled it into the shape and feel of a satiny cigarette. For a long draining span of electrified time, she did not answer.

"Dorothia? Are you there?"

"I'm here," she responded perfunctorily, apathetically.

Prudent to remember Dorothia's propensity and ability to manipulate, as demonstrated through her pouty fit in Santa Fe, Irene proceeded from a position of intellectually poised confidence. "This is something we need to do."

"Who is it?"

"What's that?"

"Who is it you want to meet him?"

On the other end of the line, Irene took a deep breath. She had won this very important concession. "One of the three buyers would like to be with me when we meet. They'll decide themselves who to send."

"And who else?" There was a distance in the voice, a deep and resentful distance.

Irene paused. For all of her prepared introductions of this topic, she had never figured out an approach that she thought ideal. She fumbled for how to frame Marubrishnubupu.

"A friend."

"A friend?" Dorothia responded, a spark of the old self returning.

"Well, more than a friend. He's actually . . ."

"What is he, your boyfriend? What kind of friend are we talking about?" The words were hasty and emotional, precipitous with envy. Irene needed to literally withdraw her ear from the phone.

"He's a guru."

"A what?"

"A guru, a spiritual guide, a Hindu monk. He tours all over the United States giving talks on spirituality and meaningful living. Oh hell, he's a friend of mine."

"Yes, you said that. What does all of this have to do with Alexi?"

"Master Marubrishnubupu has had dreams."

"Dreams?"

Irene felt as though she were speaking to an echo. Everything seemed to repeat itself.

"I can't explain everything to you now. Master Marubrishnubupu is a very special man. His interest in your son is spiritual, a spiritual interest." The words felt odd coming out of Irene's mouth, as though they expressed a sentiment in which she herself had not fully committed to believing.

"Is he buying my son's art?" Dorothia shot out rudely, her intent and suggestion clear.

"He doesn't believe in buying art . . . or selling it."

"So what does he want with my son? And what is this business about dreams?"

"Dorothia, please trust me. I have only your son's interest in mind."

"Oh, I believe you on that." Dorothia made her assertion sound like an acknowledgment of a dirty thing. Irene could hear the frustration mounting in Dorothia's voice.

"May we come?"

"Oh, of course," she mocked. "Bring the whole state. We'll make a circus out of it. I'll hire a few clowns and a dancer, maybe a juggler and magician. We'll have a party. Yes, let's see, who else can we invite? Are you sure that's enough? We can make room." The sarcasm stung. Irene, despite the fact that she did not comprehend this disease of leprosy, felt once more confirmed in her original evaluation of Dorothia. If not for the art, the damn quality of the art, she would never have agreed to working with such an inconsolable client.

"Just the three of us. There'll be no more."

"I sincerely hope not." The proclamation possessed a ring of finality, as though Dorothia had made the decision and set the conditions. Irene shrugged. Once she met the artist, once her anticipations were confirmed or denied, Dorothia would no longer be so important. Perhaps this was exactly what the mother intuitively feared.

"We'd like to fly in on Friday and meet with you both in the evening, about seven."

"Well, if that's what you would like to do, by all means that's the way it must be. Let me get the red carpet from the attic for your . . ." Dorothia broke off in mid-sentence. "You know where we are. We'll be here waiting."

The stamen of the petunia that Dorothia had been stroking hung limply. Without petals it was as bald as a Buddhist or a Nazi. The petals had been torn and dropped on the table. Dorothia despised the concept of being beholden or dependent. Once the art was out there, she could cut Irene free. She thought of a direct line to the buyers.

"We don't need you to do anything in preparation for Friday, Dorothia." Irene spoke again. "We just need you to be yourself. We just want to spend a little bit of time with Rooster. Even ten minutes will be enough. The goal is not to cause stress in his or your life."

"But you need to do this to represent his art on the level that you want it represented." Dorothia finished the thought perfectly.

"Yes, that's exactly right."

"Don't worry, Irene. Bring your buyer and your friend on Friday. Everyone will get exactly what they want. I promise it." There was a draft by the windows where Dorothia spoke. Irene felt it in Los Angeles.

"No hard feelings; we'll see you then."

"No hard feelings," Dorothia echoed as she hung up the receiver, snapping the fallow petunia's neck.

☞

General Gremikov led the Russian army that approached from St. Petersburg. Widely held as the most brilliant and talented strategist in the Russian army, as well as a respected leader who could motivate troops to any and all measures from respect and love, news of Gremikov's impending arrival heartened the troops. Rumors, widely believed, spread among Yusherin's army that once Gremikov arrived they would be united into a single force under Gremikov's command.

For many who served in Yusherin's army, the notion of following a leader other than Yusherin meant as much as staying unpierced by German bullets, both, some joked, being equally painful.

"Gremikov, ahh, that's good news," Soli's comrade declared as a weak spit drooled from his chin. "He's a soldier's general. He doesn't treat human beings as though they're cheap bullets."

"If we stay alive long enough," a second comrade warned.

"Don't talk like that," Soli commanded. "Don't even joke about death. We'll stay alive. We'll drive those German bastards straight back to Berlin and shove a bomb up Hitler's ass."

"Aayyye," the men laughed, thumping the butts of their rifles into the ground. They decided that two would go to the front as ordered by Yusherin's messenger. The injured man with the hole through his arm and Soli were elected to remain behind.

"You haven't slept." The men argued with Soli, refuting his protests at being chosen to stay behind.

"Aayyye, you've already saved us all. We'd be dead if your painting hadn't worked. You just stay and make sure it keeps working. We'll take care of the rest."

The lines along the ridge were thinning as men in full battle gear trotted in pairs and small squads towards the consolidating hive. Soli watched the soldiers pass, their eyes on the men before them, one following the other into the heated heart of real war. What was amassing would not be a skirmish. It would be head-to-head assault with absolutely nothing held in reserve. Sulfur and screams and agony and lost limbs and men amidst it all still seeking to conduct more killing. What a species we are, he thought; my father saw this. It is what he understood and what he spent his whole life fighting against: the barbaric code of humankind.

Soli checked the bandaged wound of his comrade, Private Vladimir Rohnechenko. The bleeding, though it surely had not stopped, was at least successfully plugged. "It will clot. Can you move the fingers?"

"Aaayyee, it's nothing. I'll kill the Germans with my one free hand." The bravado was appreciated. It served a necessary function in times like these. Soli stared as the men headed toward the mounting battle line. The second wave would be worse than the first. This was the German way. Test to understand, to analyze. Then, having assimilated the knowledge, breach the weakest point. The first wave had sought not victory, only information.

Vladimir was a hearty man in his early forties, a farmer with thick gray hair that grew in coarse patches upon his leathery face. Typical of most Russians, the life he had lived had been hard. He had a long scar from the cheek to the forehead and a lazy left eye marred by a perpetual spot of blood. A horse had bucked on him, wildly kicking its legs into the side of his head the first time he had ever tried to apply a horseshoe as a young man. He considered himself lucky for having survived.

One of the main reasons he had volunteered to work with Soli was that as a boy he had always wished to draw. Using coal on gray stone he had once created fantastic images. Machines, he said, that would make farmwork obsolete, a thing of the past. Vladimir's father, so many years before, had beat him for wasting good coal, thus killing Vladimir's impulse to draw — or so it had seemed. So many years had passed, meaningless years of working in the same methods that the father had worked. As Vladimir saw what was occurring in the preparation for war, a flame re-ignited within him, that burning sense that life is a place where possibility above all else should exist. He did not distinctly remember the events of his childhood; he saw only the act of painting that had somehow been transformed into a useful, productive act of war. Simple Vladimir, somewhat incoherent Vladimir, rendered a bit senseless by the cleft hooves of that horse, simple Vladimir who had all the men crying "Aayyyee," looked to Soli in the same way that a young boy looks to a father.

"I should go to the lines," Soli asserted. "There's nothing more to be done here." Vladimir's protests were unsuccessful. "Aayyyeee, why get yourself killed? You've done what you can do. Aaayyee, let the general fight his war now. You're just following orders."

Over a mile away the heavy shelling had begun. Solzhenitsyn knew it was the work of both German and Russian tanks, volleying for advantage. "Stay here, stay here. A German could come by and discover the ruse. You have to stay to kill that German. This is a foothold."

But Soli knew that the reasoning was flawed, that nothing could alter the chain of events already begun, that all would be decided at the dual breach points of the buzzing hive. Their bluff had succeeded, but they had not won the war. He picked up his pack. "You'll have to kill him for me."

"It's suicide you're committing. Wait for Gremikov. Follow orders. Be smart." Vladimir cursed the dirt for Soli was gone. "Keep your head down!" the simple farmer shouted, doubting he was heard, gazing into the light. "God bless that boy."

At the front, smoke filled Soli's eyes with running tears of irritation. The noxious stench of charred flesh and the tortured cries of soldiers filled his senses. Covering his mouth, he choked down his own vomit, commanding his legs to move forward. Grown men howled for water, their anguish untouched, disoriented. Soli saw the strained pupils of men who did not understand what had happened to them or how. He stepped on a hand and looked down, ready to apologize. The body was not there. Doctors rushed about, screaming for supplies, unable to attend to the numbers.

Thick smoke covered the landscape, turning the terror of black and white into a gray mist of obscurity and confusion. He could know the enemy only from front and back. If they were coming towards him then they would be German. Russians would be aiming down the ridge, off the slope, their backs to Soli's approach. He saw backs mostly and knew that this ridge still held. A mortar exploded. Soli ducked his head before the incoming whistle of sound ceased to exist. Something struck him. He searched himself. It was just dirt and mud, not steaming shrapnel. It had all been moving slowly until the first mortar struck nearby. Now Soli knew that he was standing in the midst of it, in the heart — if it could be called a heart — of hatred and rage. No longer was he participating on the fringe. He had, without even being aware, entered the midst. A man called to him, frantically summoning him, shouting and waving his arm simultaneously. Soli did not know how long the man had been calling, but from the face of desperation Soli understood that the man was experiencing and living an urgency that was not yet his own.

"Get over here, God damn you!" Soli dashed forward and grabbed the mass of metal to which the officer pointed. "Over here, over here, over here!" Soli did not even know what they were moving. To him it was only a massive object. Only when they had placed it down and his hands began to mechanically respond to the vilified orders of the offi-

cer did he perceive that they had moved a stationary rocket launcher.
"Get the shells, get the shells, get the shells!"

Soli raced back to where they had been. A crate of red-tipped rockets lay on the ground half open, a shingle of wood pried from the cover.
Blood smears stained the box. Unaware of its weight, he dragged the
crate along the ground. The crate snagged on a raised tree root. He
yanked with all his might, falling backwards. Pushing himself from the
ground, he pried the crate free and continued struggling forward. Back
with the officer they prepared the shell. Soli had performed the act in
training weeks before. Now his hands moved in a perfect rhythm,
matching the efforts of the officer. "Down, down, down, down!" the
officer screamed as the loaded launcher tipped down the slope. The
man shoved Soli to the ground as he flipped the switch that initiated
the rocket and sent it firing away from its weighted base. Only on the
ground did Soli begin to comprehend just where he was and what he
had been doing. A tank had climbed three-quarters of the way up the
slope, impervious to Russian machine gunfire. Soli was at the top of
one of the two slopes, the focal point of the attack.

Striking the left tracks of the tank, the red-tipped rocket exploded,
jarring the tank, its right track spinning in futility. In that moment Soli
imagined Vladimir as a boy, struck by the thunderous blow of a mature
horse's hooves, permanently changed. The tank's turret turned forward,
simultaneously lowering, as the combatants inside took aim at the
rocket launcher.

"Again, again, again! They're firing!" Jumping to his feet, Soli was
once more working with the officer. The rocket was halfway prepared
as the tank's barrel took position. Their hands moved with speed and
precision. Soli heard his own voice as he and the officer dove aside, into
the ground, and he released the second rocket. "Again, again, again!" It
had been his own order they had been following. He shut his mouth,
stopped shouting. The second rocket erupted into flame, striking within a joint of the turret. They both watched from the ground as Germans
emerged from the innards of the metal beast to escape the fire.
Emerging into Russian space, they died instantaneously, met by
Russian soldiers riveting the vulnerable slope with bullets.

"Good job, painter!" the officer cried out, darting in a new direction. "Now support the lines." The presence of mind of the officer

inspired him. Soli rushed forward, leaning with others over the ridge. In the distance, like a wraith from the smoke and fog, Soli thought he could hear Yusherin's scratched voice chanting the mantra for the troops, establishing once and for all the final proof of his ultimate proposition. "Killing is good! Killing is good! Killing is good!"

Soli allowed the rattle of the machine gun to rip through him, shaking through his hands, vibrating to his toes. The position he held was solid; he aimed downward into the ravine over a corpse that now functioned as a bunker bag. He listened to the general. It did, in spite of the message, help to have a voice directing, holding his thoughts and actions. The mantra kept it simple, clean, free of complication and moral ambiguity. The Germans were blasting away at the ridge from several positions. The destroyed tank now blocked part of the path. At this slope at least the Russians had regained a certain advantage. Obliteration of their own tank or a widening of the path or some combination of the two emerged as the German plan. The Russians did their part to make the German enterprise exceedingly difficult. Yusherin found it a pleasant turn of events. As the Germans sought to destroy the remnants of their own tank, clearing it from the path, the Russians had great latitude in working to destroy them.

The battle raged for hours, a relentless stalemate. German forces assumed a less aggressive posture, apparently not convinced that the ridge could be taken frontally.

Gremikov blindsided the Germans. Attacking from the ravine, he took the German forces by complete surprise. The sudden Russian counter-offensive sent the Germans into disarray. German forces had been sent the long way round to attempt a flank of the Russians. Gremikov's appearance trumped that secret offensive. The Germans, attacked from above and now pursued on the ground, initiated a full scale retreat. Yusherin, hesitant to abandon the superior position to chase the Germans on the ground, ordered his troops to hold the ridge. It was Gremikov himself, surveying the landscape from the porthole of a tank atop the ridge, who altered Yusherin's perspective.

A barrel-chested man with ferrous eyes and a full, black beard, Gremikov wasted no time in asserting his presence.

"General Yusherin!" he shouted as the tank halted atop the center slope. The tank that swallowed his lower half appeared, to those who watched his forceful approach, to be more of a natural appendage than a vehicle from which he could detach and exit. "Why aren't you sending tanks into the ravine to pursue the enemy?" The questions possessed a cantankerous edge.

"General Gremikov, good to see you, sir! I didn't want to abandon the superior ridge position, sir."

Gremikov brushed a hand along the three stars on his collar as he stared dismissively at the single star on Yusherin's collar. "So you were going to wait until the enemy found a way up here?"

"Sir?" Yusherin asked, genuinely perplexed.

"They're Germans, General. If they're not going forward, you damn well better have them going backwards. Keeping them put won't work with the krauts. Send all regiments down. Keep the heat on them. The Germans will move. We want to make sure they're moving in the right direction."

"Sir?"

"As long as they're in Russia I want them hunted like dogs." The troops for the first time cheered. Soli stood at the edge of the tank staring upwards with a smile on his face.

Yusherin scanned the grizzly scene. Russians and Germans alike lay in contorted, bloody, unnatural heaps. The groans of the wounded ached for mercy. Below, Russian tanks were pressing forward into the forest, launching rockets. "So where's this painter I've heard about?" Gremikov hollered from the tank. "Still alive?"

"Here I am, sir." Solzhenitsyn stepped forward from the smoke.

Gremikov appraised the boy with admiring eyes. "I understand that you're fairly well responsible for the success of this little party. Brilliant work. You'll have to do my portrait after the war."

"I'm not really a painter, sir." Soli responded quickly.

Gremikov stared warmly at the boy, stating with munificence, "Yes son, yes you are a painter."

"General, how did your troops get down there so fast?" Yusherin's question was desperate, anything to get the attention away from Michayl's son.

Steel and ice pervaded Gremikov's gaze as he addressed the interruption. "General, what do you think I just said? What keeps one man out, allows another man in. We used the painter's pass." He turned again to a beaming Solzhenitsyn. "So what's your name, son?"

Soli looked to Gremikov and then to Yusherin. He thought of his father, his mother and Russia, of all that he had seen and so painfully learned. "Solzhenitsyn Maschovich, son of Michayl Maschovich of the hamlet Krylov." He saluted the general. "They call me Soli, sir."

"Well then," the general asserted. "I can see that. Solzhenitsyn is a bit long. Dreadful Russian names. Too many syllables. We'll call it Soli's Pass. Have it noted, General. Preserve the canvas."

"Yes, sir," Yusherin responded.

"Sir?" Soli took another step forward.

"What is it, son?" Gremikov asked, settling his eyes squarely upon the painter.

Soli paused; he felt the pain and death about him and found the heart to speak in honor not only of what had been achieved on this day but also of what had been lost. "Sir, I'd like to make a request, sir."

General Gremikov listened with admiring eyes that allowed Soli to continue.

"If you are going to name the pass. I'd like to request that you name it 'Michayl's Pass,' sir."

The general held his eyes upon the boy. He smiled that even in the midst of such carnage, honor and value held true. "Your father?"

"My father, sir," Solzhenitsyn affirmed.

"So noted, son. So noted." The general raised his hand to his forehead, his fingers tight, and saluted the young man who had served his father and Mother Russia so virtuously. Tall and proud, Soli saluted in gratitude to all who had come before.

Snapping the hand to his side, the general turned to the troops. "Well done, men. You're spirit has made us proud today." Gremikov hollered inspired words from the tank. "But there is much to be done before Mother Russia is safe. We will pursue the enemy until they are driven from our home. Mother Russia is inviolate! Love her with your heart, men, and you will find your courage. Stay strong, and stay alive." With that Gremikov ordered his own tank down the slope, trickily maneuvering over and past the battered German tank. Behind the tank stood Vladimir Rohnechenko, machine gun slung over his shoulder. Now Soli better understood as he smiled at his brave, wounded friend.

Yusherin gripped Soli's arm, causing the painter to wince in pain. "Go to the pass! Wait for me. That's an order." The cold general swept away from Solzhenitsyn, showering an angry cavil of commands upon subordinates as the troops prepared for pursuit.

"Aayyyee. What was that about?" Vladimir asked, a grave, deeply perceptive concern in his voice.

The order, if Soli properly understood, was a threat, a date with destiny that he intended, once and for all, to keep.

Soli smiled wryly as he patted his friend's good arm and lied for the first time in his life. "He's promoted me, that's all. Go with the rest, Vladimir. I'll catch up." He folded his hands. "There is one last thing I must do, my friend."

రా

A conic fold of time and space away, Tamara scoured her record collection for the 45, "A Little Bit Country, a Little Bit Rock n' Roll." She felt like a complex ragdoll, a Dorothy of Kansas tossed against walls of wind in a twisting cyclone of dust, unable to find stable land, something credulous. The numbing mathematics that had ended her promising career before it had started had brought her to the brink of a terrifying nihilism. No act of denial could circumvent her own fact-based comprehension. The very faith that had led her to dare was now conclusively refuted by spacial geometry. She had come to believe against her own desire that we exist in a theoretical, relative world where nothing remains as it is and nothing is as it appears. The tautology of the mathematical had brought her to a more refined conception of the material. If she could have rejected what she had discovered, she gladly would have. To be an imbecile would have been preferable to being a genius coming to her conclusion. Sometimes she suspected that if her mind were sufficiently elegant, she could have cleverly disproven the theorem she had discovered, buried it in a complex argument, a sixty-line formula. But she couldn't do that to the truth, make it less complex, less powerful than it was.

She desired to believe in faith, but in her efforts to give it an empirical basis, she had collected nothing but detailed proof against it. The theoretical ideas, incapable of being touched or held in the hand, were like the immovable winds of a hurricane or an endlessly rising silo of grain, indifferent to the debris caught within. The silo she saw in her mind was always appearing to the eye as tightening in the distance, growing slimmer, coming to what would be a head, a tip, an apex, the beginning or the end, the conic. But this was illusion. It was reality that flowed. From the inside, one knew that the more one moved forward through space, the longer the silo became. Begin to measure points. Attempt to calculate the apparent distance from conclusion. What was thought a cone becomes a cylinder, a pipe with no end, only the promise of an end, or the idea of an end. The limits of what we can see or think, these were the only conclusions, these were the data points, the facts and statistics, arbitrary, like stopping in the middle of an ocean or the eternal desert and claiming that point to be significant. These were the acts of faith. These were the delusions, the privileging of one point in space to another.

Space led to time, of this she was convinced. All time is a manifestation of inadequate measurement. The very act of measurement produces time. $W=E$. Tamara had stopped seeking to measure, to quantify. The habit was strong, a lifetime of social conditioning, a lifetime of hypnosis, of illusion to be dispelled. Her mind tempted her to see cones; she unwrapped them as they formed, looked beyond, sought to perceive the eternal silo, feeder — to what?

The lemonade that stained the wall dripped towards a gravity that, for all its clever tricks, did not deceive her. Tamara tossed aside the 45's that were not exactly what she sought. What had Rooster said about Hume and the search for a single color, the only fit, the perfect match? If there was one piece of her soul missing, if she were that close to its completion, then yes, there would be only one perfect match in the universe that would deliver completion. No replication, no imitation, no forgery could fill the space perfectly. Only the one authentic hue within the spectrum of color or being or morality or emotion or time. What a complex piece it would have to be, what exactitude. And yet, for the single piece that fits, there could be no task more simple. And yet again, how lost it, like her soul, would be, until it found its perfect compliment. She caught her mind, chided herself for finding solace in the idea of this metaphysical keystone, another conic imposition, a chimera, false hope. The 45's spun across the room in wild, eccentric circles. In and out of their sleeves they slapped against the wall and fractured into multiplicity like all of the extracted, brittle, ossified vertebra of an experimental nursing home. Euthanasia, what a rage. The vinyl landed on the floor with shards of glass and 1,499 pieces of a deconstructed Bavarian landscape. A wobbling Elvis gyrated across the room, a UFO, exploding on impact with the flattened plane of the wall. Was this the immovable object? Were there no points, simply flat planes? Silos intersecting silos? Tamara did not find destruction to be a source of pleasure. She was simply reorganizing pieces, still searching for a solution, for faith. Perhaps nothing was missing. Perhaps the pieces she had were adequate, fully sufficient for completion, perfection. Perhaps they only needed to be rearranged, accepted, deeply accepted, deeply deeply accepted, received with gratitude. Perhaps we have all of the pieces to the puzzle at any time, but we have made an error in our assumption of how they are organized. What would Hume say of this? What would Rooster say? Nothing is missing. We have simply misorganized the pieces. If there is a gap, surrender to it, fill it with yourself. This is nature's way.

She had not slept, had not eaten in three days. Across the street gales wailed against brick and a long-haired collie on a leash barked at nothing. She owned thousands of 45's. Collecting from the age of ten, at a time when other children were watching TV and experimenting with lip gloss, she was collecting the miniature vinyls from the crowded attics of neighbors she barely knew. Chubby Checker, Roy Orbison, Glen Miller, Tammy Terrell: they were all created for this moment. Why not, she thought, as she launched them across the room, leaving them to spin in the breeze, their songs imperceptible vibrations of some ethereal, forgetful void. Smash. Smash. Crash. Why not this point in time above all others? An enthusiastic bang, incrimination of the somber whimper. Why not a faith like Joan of Arc that claims this point in time, me! Tamara found the 45 she sought at the bottom of the pile. Placing the black disc on the turntable, she set the needle above the groove. Cued, the sound of rhythmic static ached from the speakers. She stood listening, jealous, her fists balled into fierce weapons.

Even static has a rhythm.

"Oh my mama said skip don't you do it, don't you listen to that skip and roll, but mama can't skip you see it, I got the country skip my soul."

Her own life had none.

"Yeah, I'm a little bit skip country and I'm a little bit skip rock and roll skip and even with dear Jesus skip that dang devil skip my soul. I done skip *the best I could, dear mama* skip *can't* skip *see? But the devil* skip *he got dear* skip-*us, and now* skip *he's coming for me.* skip. *Oh I'm a little* skip *country, and I'm a little* skip *rock and* skip *roll. So don't you* skip *up waiting,* skip *I won't be coming* skip *home."*

She experienced the usual anger that came at the limit of her limits, when reason could bear no more of faith's mockery. All nihilism deserves an answer. With knotty, adrenalized arms she tore the turntable free of its socket in fury. The flailing cord whipped her in the eye as she hurled the unit across the room where it crashed impotently against the wall. Her pulse raced with an uncommon strength. She kicked aside the coffee table, sending Dorothia's blackmail papers fluttering to the floor.

Two days had passed after Dorothia's threat before Tamara had worked up enough courage to attempt to steal a visit with Rooster. She'd wanted him, at the very least, to know of Dorothia's threats. Perhaps together they could find a way to diffuse the mother's wrath. If cones could not exist for her in the positive, why should she believe in them as more than transitory illusions when they manifested in the negative? Tamara had approached the house late at night. A snow squall had dusted the roads, tiny flakes blew up the road like ghostly tumbleweed. Dorothia's car had been gone as Tamara had expected it would be, her knowledge of the woman's schedule still accurate. Peering from the street, she had sought to spy a view of Rooster through the window. Hunched before the canvas he had worked with a stable concentration, his arm unsupported by the maulstick. Silently she had admired him, his stability, his permanence, from a distance. A supreme sense of peace had washed her over. He looked well.

Reaching for the gate, she'd heard the steps and then the heavy voice of threat. "I wouldn't do that if I were you." A hand had touched her hand and removed it from the latch.

She'd turned to see the intimidating figure who had stepped from the shadow, flakes of white snow striking against his dark cheek. He wore a Yankees ball cap and a long black overcoat. "You're Tamara Browne, aren't you?" He was tall, a thick-shouldered black man with spreading flesh and eyes deliberately intended to convey danger. The question was strictly rhetorical.

"Who are you?" she'd asked, having to look upwards to see his face more clearly.

Taking her by the arm, he had removed them both from a direct line of sight before the window. "That doesn't really matter now does it? The only thing that matters is what I can do. See, I could bring you down to the police station right now for violation of your restraining order. And that would set a particular chain of events into motion that would send you back to McLean, back to the loo-loo bin. Now you don't really want that, do you?"

"No," she had answered. "That's not what I want."

"See," Zephaniah had impelled, leaning into her, letting her feel his weight, "it's not my job to judge people, to decide who's right and who's wrong, who's sane and who's crazy. I don't get paid to be a judge. I get paid to enforce." She had felt his breath on her cheek. "It's my job to make sure that you don't go near him."

On the other side of the street a couple had strolled past. They'd glanced furtively at Zephaniah and Tamara. The woman had shaken her head.

"Smile nice," Zephaniah had commanded, casually raising his arm upon the fence, creating the appearance of intimacy. "You're on a date having a wonderful time." Tamara had forced herself to smile. "Now, look at me. Don't you look at them."

The couple passed from sight, and he'd congratulated her. "That's good, that's good," he'd cooed. "So let's say you make this easy on both of us. You don't try to make any contact with him, none at all, do you understand?"

Moved by the coercion of the threat, she had nodded.

"Say it," he'd commanded. "None at all. I want to hear it."

"I won't try to make any contact with Alexi."

Zephaniah Maxwell had bore down sternly upon her. "I don't want to hear his name. I don't even want you thinking his name. Now say it to me again."

She'd looked at the ivory orb of his eyes. "I won't try to make any contact with him." She'd paused, gazing at the cracked pavement in shame, adding submissively, "None at all."

"Good, that's good. Now we got an understanding, don't we?"

"Yes," she had whispered softly, "we have an understanding."

"I'll be watching you, like an eagle." He'd pointed adamantly at his gambler's eyes. "You so much as whisper his name and you'll be back at the loo-loo bin."

Tamara had stood in terror, not simply due to the man before her but due to the prospect of returning to McLean. She knew they could do it, and now any doubts that she harbored about whether they would were fully abandoned.

"Now get out of here. And you remember, I'll be watching."

Zephaniah had hated himself for doing such things as this, for acting this way, but this was his job, what he was paid to do. Staring into the window from the street, Zephaniah had observed the painter whom he was now being paid, in essence, to protect. "I'm not free," he'd thought. "But that kid in there, he's free."

Zephaniah had walked away from the still life, towards his car parked two houses down, as Rooster stretched his tired arms and glanced into the empty street before dabbing his brush in turpentine. Rooster had thought, strongly hoped, that Tamara would come to see him tonight, three days having passed. He tried not to worry. Immersion in the ferocious concentration of painting helped. He yawned, confident of her love, reaffirming his resolve to be inspired by her in both her absence and her presence.

Two days had passed since Tamara's encounter with Zephaniah, and it was now five days since her beautiful evening with Alexi.

Tamara smiled as she lingered above the heap of broken glass, vinyl and stereo components she had just destroyed. In a state of wonder, her fingers investigated a hole in the wall. The stereo had busted through, her throw a perfect bulls-eye into the center of the lemonade stain. With her fingers dipped within, feeling the chalky plaster and the splintered wood, she thought of Doubting Thomas — the scientist, the skeptic of good intention, the truth seeker so committed to the empirical and the sensate — his hand in Jesus' side, the side where the devil had sought to set a hook. Just maybe, she thought, her first breath of hope in five days, maybe there is a way.

∽

But several more days passed, several more days and nights alone in hell to contemplate betrayal, insanity, resurrection and the higher good. Time lost all meaning as Tamara resorted to her prior training, to the life she had sought to leave behind, to the work that made the physical world seem less and less likely. It seemed many years ago that she had attended Stanford on a fellowship to work in the realm of theoretical mathematics. All of her work there had been theoretical, and yet all of her work was based on the belief that the mind can discover knowledge, truth about reality, without direct empirical evidence.

This was the history of Euclid, who first conceived of geometry in the sand, though these sand drawings were hardly sufficient as empirical truth to make the assertion that all triangles consist of 180 degrees (a reality pure math has since proven false). Regardless, he used the work of his theoretical mind to come to that conclusion, a conclusion destined to be shattered and then replaced, becoming the foundation for a stronger model. But faith alone had not led him to such cognitive feats. To call the work of theoretical scientists such as Einstein or Euclid or Newton "faith" would be preposterous. If faith were a factor in the equation at all, it was only a faith in the pure cognitive faculty of the mind; it was only a faith that held that truths might possibly be derived from a point that did not begin empirically. Each of them understood a truth first in their mind, theoretically; from this they developed experiments that allowed them to validate or invalidate the veracity of what they knew to be highly probable based on the theoretical point from which the thinking of the cognitive mind had led. They held faith in metaphysics, *a priori* knowing, their right to postulate. All else was rigid science. Thus, even God, the ultimate postulate, was something reason-based, an appreciation of a truth of being, the right to postulate, from which cognition begins without conclusive, empirical knowledge. From this appreciation, which can only be metaphysical, the empirical basis for the proof or disproof of a specific, postulated truth can be and generally is garnered through experimental demonstration. For Tamara, until now, the collection of all the necessary elements that set the conditions for the truth to be manifested had been the easy part.

Conceiving and organizing the difficult and problematic distinction between faith and metaphysics caused Tamara to leave theoretical mathematics behind. To postulate, in and of itself, was an act of faith — or was it an ultimate act of reason? She knew that it was difficult to conceive of an effective metaphysics without faith, but simultaneously she could not deny that it was hardly impossible or even implausible. Tamara wanted faith, not metaphysics, but nothing in metaphysics, the central training of her life, gave her cause to believe in faith. Faith to her was that hollow and hallowed cylinder, that silo without end in which one loses the self in a perpetual, disintegrative state of grace.

Every problem has a solution she told herself, has a correct and proper answer that is true. She approached her dilemma systemically, attempting to hold the emotions beneath the surface at bay. The problem as she defined it was an either/or. If she saw Rooster, she would surely be sent back to McLean. She did not question Dorothia's heartless resolve. In addition, her father would be in favor of such a course of action, especially backed by a court injunction that made Tamara look like some sort of maddened stalker. Henry wanted nothing more than an excuse with which he could control Tamara and over time bring her round to his way of thinking. Having her hospitalized for mental imbalance was the best way, the most efficient construction, to prove that his way of thinking was superior to her way of thinking.

In the end, Tamara knew that Henry cared very little about her mental health; unconsciously, he sought only to confirm his own dubious and ruthless mental state. Like so much of his business career, he received the validation he needed through the act of crushing a perceived opponent, even if that opponent became his own daughter.

Yes, Dorothia would do it and her father would be all too eager to comply through crocodile tears. If she saw Rooster, she would end up in McLean. This solved the first half of the first move of the equation. The second half of the first move needed to resolve what would occur if she did not see Rooster. First of all, she would maintain her freedom. The idea of spending more time in the hellhole called McLean caused her sleepless nights and fits of emotional anguish. What good was a life without freedom? This part of the equation was only slightly more difficult for she had to first address a disparity of scale. Already, by Dorothia and her thug, Tamara's freedom had been imposed upon. If she could not see Rooster due to the imperative of another's force, was she not already imprisoned? Tamara knew the answer to be yes. She was being asked to compromise, to concede the one point for the game, to relinquish the quality she saw in Rooster for the quantity of a free life, a quantity so great that theoretically it would return the lost quality in full and surplus. But if the way were the end as she maintained, then would not the concession of one point be the game?

Dorothia had given Tamara Rooster's painting *I Give You My Word.*
Wasn't this a payoff for throwing the game, for being smart enough to
concede, to get out of the way so that another's end could be achieved?
Or was it a social issue? Did Tamara, Tamara asked herself, detaching
herself from herself, have a social responsibility to Rooster and even
Dorothia and even her father that was being neglected in the pursuit of
an individual freedom, in pursuit of her desire to gain experiential evidence for the metaphysical truth in which she so believed and in which
she had already sacrificed so much? Wasn't this faith?

Tamara pulled the equation back before it grew beyond her control.
Already it was stretching the limitations of her mind to keep the vari-
ables organized. If she compromised her freedom by not seeing Rooster
as she wanted to see Rooster, then could it ever be said that she lived a
free life? If she followed the requests of her own will and passions and
saw Rooster, her body would be imprisoned, but not her spirit, for she
would have followed its desire. The moral fault would lie with those
who sought to restrict her freedom by imprisoning her at McLean.
McLean, the very notion of the place, with its pills and needles and listless haze and ghoulish attendants, horrified her.

She checked her assumptions; every math equation leads to a truth.
Every truth, though the solution can appear extremely complex as we
seek to solve it, follows the simplest and most obvious path. In retrospect, the solution always appears as obvious; the bias of the solution
seeker is what generally makes it complex. If this assumption were
true, and Tamara wholly believed this to be the case, then any pathway
that resulted in the physical incarceration of her body necessarily indicated that the solutions to the prior portions of the equation were
flawed. Puzzles of truth do not lead — should not lead — to dead ends,
to conic endpoints that go no further. If there is an entrance into a
problem, then there is an exit. If the problem leads to a dead end, then
the problem has not been solved and the solution is inaccurate. If not
compromising her freedom in the moment meant incarceration and the
loss of freedom, then it could not be freedom that she was being asked
to compromise. Irrespective of her choice, the loss of freedom, she
decided, is predetermined.

Tamara felt that she finally understood something significant and
that the first portion of this mammoth equation she was parceling into
workable pieces was solved.

She moved forward. If my freedom is already lost regardless of what I do, then what is the value of not seeing him? Why have I not seen him for eight days? It's not better for me. Not seeing him does not bring me happiness. Is it better for him? That's what Dorothia keeps trying to tell me. Is she right? But if she is right, then his painting is more important than his person, and I can't believe this. But what if his person is not as important as something else? Is it possible that he is greater than his painting, and there is still something else that is greater than both him and the painting, a something that benefits from my not seeing him?

Again, Tamara had to reign in her ideas before they grew out of control. She had to be on guard, to recognize the eruptions of her emotions into her logic, for if her emotions got into her logic, her ends would be off balance; and if her ends were off balance, then her means were off balance; and if the means were off balance, then she was off balance; and if she were off balance, then perhaps she did belong in McLean with the pills and the horrible needles and the tools of restraint. She brushed a fly from her face. If in the end it all led to a mental instability, then why shouldn't she see Rooster? O Christ! There is no end, she reminded herself. There is no way.

If her freedom was to be lost to her no matter what, shouldn't she spend the little time she had remaining following her free will? *Free will?*

But maybe this was exactly Dorothia's point. Maybe Dorothia saw my illness, if it is an illness, Tamara thought to herself. Maybe Dorothia wants to keep me away from Rooster because she fears that my imbalance could unbalance him. Could she be right? Do I serve him better from a distance than I do from his side? And what if I really deserved to be there, at McLean, the first time? Maybe I really was insane. Maybe my ideas were all wrong, about the way equaling the end. That was the idea that landed me at McLean in the first place, the hellhole of torture and boredom. But if the way equals the end is wrong, then everything is wrong. If the way and the end have no relationship, then I'm already in prison. I'm already in an insane world. For if the way does not equal the end, then that's exactly what the world must be: insane. I'm the one sane person, Tamara thought to herself. That's impossible. But if I were the one sane person in an insane world, wouldn't the insane want me locked away? Isn't that the nature of truth? It destroys our world even as it brings a new one into being. Things feel so right when I'm with Rooster. Maybe he's sane too. Maybe that's why they want to keep us apart. Tamara pressed her emotions into her psyche.

She needed to make a decision. To see Rooster or not to see Rooster? The answer to the problem did not lie in the issue of freedom; she now knew this. The matters of her own freedom and her fear of McLean were of little consequence. What mattered to Tamara was that she did the right thing for Rooster. What would be best for Rooster? Was Dorothia right? Did she serve him better from afar? Was that the best way to love him? Would her imbalance, if it was an imbalance, imbalance him? Or did he need her now more than ever? Did they need and balance each other? Was there a reason even for this deliberation?

"I know the way equals the mean," she whispered to herself. "This is the one thing I believe with all of my soul. That means I'm here, in this position, for a reason, but what is that reason?"

Every equation has its true answer in the simplest path. That path isn't always obvious until afterwards, until we reach the end.

"I know I'm not crazy. So what don't I see? What is it that still remains hidden? O God, if you can hear, please help me. . . ."

16

THE WEEK HAD been trying for Dorothia. During the hardest moments she refreshed herself with advice from Dr. Schuller's *Hour of Power:* "A plan must be made; the course must be stayed." She chided herself to stay focused. The moment of fruition was approaching. Mentally, she reviewed her checklist of things to do. One, check in with the private investigator. Two, check in on Rooster; get him working on something new. Three, and most importantly, pin down Marcel on a time for his visit with her son. Already it was Thursday and by Monday he needed to be in Stockholm. She cursed the tight time frame but remained confident. She had his promise, after all.

Dorothia paid sweetly to keep Zephaniah on round-the-clock surveillance of Tamara. In actuality, the money, like so much of the funding for Dorothia's activities, came from the trust that Soli had left Rooster in his final will and testament. She calculated the charges in her head. The exorbitant figure only strengthened her resolve. I can't take any chances while these meetings are hanging over my head, she told herself, picking up the phone and dialing Zephaniah's cell number.

"Maxwell here."

"Mr. Maxwell, this is Dorothia. How's it looking?" She whispered so as not to be heard by Rooster in the other room. With her toe she straightened the frazzled tassels of the oriental rug at the base of the stairwell.

"She just sits there," he replied, bewildered by his own report.

"What's that?"

"She just sits there watching the pandas, day after day. That's what she does. That's all she's been doing for the past, what is it . . . five, six days now? Ever since her fit, she's calm as a gravestone."

"She watches what?"

"The pandas. Panda bears. I'm at the zoo."

"What do you mean she just sits there?"

"Just what I said," Zephaniah raised his voice. "First thing in the morning she comes to the zoo. She sits by the panda cage, just sits there watching them. She doesn't go anywhere. She doesn't eat. She doesn't get up to stretch. It's freezing out there. She doesn't even go to the damn bathroom. She just sits, sits until they close the zoo. I think she really might be insane. I didn't think so before, but I do now. It ain't human. It ain't natural. Girl's got problems."

"Because she watches the pandas?" Dorothia asked, caring precious little for his assessment of her psychological state.

"The zebras sometimes too."

Whether Tamara was or was not mentally unstable meant nothing to Dorothia. "So she's trying to turn an instinctual decision into a rational one. Can't trust her own emotions."

"What's that? She's what?"

"Don't worry about it, Mr. Maxwell," Dorothia responded in a stale tone. "What does she do after she leaves?"

"Nothing," Zephaniah stated emphatically, increasingly sickened by Dorothia's total absence of empathy. "Far as I can tell she goes home and goes to bed. Actually, that's not completely true. She spends a lot of time in front of that painting you gave her. Kind of weird. She lights a candle, then she lays there staring at it. That's how she falls asleep. At least, I think she falls asleep. She just lays there and the candle goes out, then I can't see any more. She must fall asleep. Yeah, she must. There's not really much to see. Miss Rodriguez, I honestly think this girl needs help."

Dorothia ignored him. "Just make sure she stays away for a few more days. That's all I need. Then you can bring her to a shrink personally for all I care. You just make sure she keeps her distance from my son! We're almost done. Do you understand? Do that and there'll be a fat bonus in it for you."

It disgusted Zephaniah but even as her coldness repulsed him, he answered, "I understand." This was some of the easiest money he had ever earned.

"Good, now don't you go getting personally attached," her saccharine voice admonished again. "This is business, nothing more. Business."

"The girl needs help."

"Don't go soft on me."

Zephaniah was silent.

Getting off the phone, Dorothia moved to the second item on her list. Gently she knocked on Rooster's door. Inside, a stillness reigned. It permeated the door and touched her very skin. She was worried about Rooster, more now than ever before. Furiously, through a thoroughly controlled violence, he had produced in two weeks more works and of a higher quality than anything he had ever done in all his prior years combined. Standing at the door and knocking lightly, she realized that she feared him. The thought came and she purged it from her mind as fatuous paranoia. How could she fear her son? Irene's visit would be a tremendous success; Dorothia felt confident of this. With all of the new paintings — thirty-six in ten days' time! — how could anything go wrong? She had contemplated sending a handful of the new productions to Irene in advance, but she ultimately decided not to, choosing to leave the splendid surprise for the visit.

"Rooster?" Dorothia called out in the sweet melody of a mother, straightening the dress she wore for Marcel. She knocked again as she turned the nob cautiously. The past five days did not equal the production of the prior ten. He had been working on only a single painting, a dark and disturbing work that Dorothia cared not to see. Dorothia knew that Tamara's absence had something to do with his melancholy, though in her repressed emotions she sensed that the current mood was something more dangerous than melancholy. Thirty-five paintings in nine days, then he had spent the whole tenth day painting *Study of the Beautiful*. It was, in a word, magnificent! In a sentence, it was the very best he had ever done.

Characteristic of early impressionism, the masterpiece of the tenth day represented an intensely daring lesson in the courage of form in light. Relying heavily upon swirling, staccato brush strokes, favoring quickly splashed vortexes of minutia to careful lines, unrefined by confinements of the past, *Study of the Beautiful* evinced the inimitable flame of originality. Set where night and day co-mingle at neither twilight nor dawn, the stunning result depended on innocent colors. The exquisite depiction alchemized bronze and pink, ordering a union that released luminous possibility while igniting wonder. Conceptually abstract, *Study of the Beautiful* possessed a multitude of particular, striking, distinctive features that bordered on strict realism emerging in tiny pockets of rebellious, irrepressible freedom. From the shimmering illusion, compelling, non-prescriptive images made love to an unbridled imagination. At center a pink man with swollen feet sat on a tree stump, leaning weakly upon a crooked, emaciated arm. The body was undefined but for white wounds leaking black blood.

Gazing curiously at the pink man from the branches of a nearby tree, a bronze bird nervously ambled from a branch to the single, outstretched, inviting finger of the man. More than a mere invitation, it was an appeal for mercy. The hands and the face of the man in the painting were realistic and powerful focal points of the penultimate masterpiece. The face composed an almost ghoulish pall, a dull ivory skull ripping forth from an abode of pink fabric. The bronze bird had one talon upon the tree branch and one upon the bony metatarsal of the grim, pink figure. Mild and tame suggestions of the erotic pervaded. Illuminating the scene, extraordinary beams of golden light spewed from the bronze eye sockets and the bird's black jaw, opened in rapturous bliss. Amidst a navy background, an orange-red moon was floating in the upper corner of the canvas. The bronze bird flapped nervously, its fiery wings emitting pale blue flame. Ignited in holy rapture was the green tree. Nascent light came from many sources.

When Dorothia first saw the radiant canvas, she interpreted it as heavenly validation of all her difficult, controversial choices. Could he have brought *Study of the Beautiful* into being with that tramp slaking around? Surely her choices would be difficult for him to understand. Surely he desired a physical relationship and the warmth of intimacy. But he could not understand how such intrusions could cause him to lose focus from his art, and with it all of their dreams. Dorothia needed to make the difficult choices, even if it hurt her son in the short term. In the long term he would thank her, though she did not intend for him to ever know the full impact of all she had done.

How fortunate he is to have me watching over his shoulder, protecting him from distracting influences, she told herself, poking her head into the room. He'll forget the girl. Without me, he would be nothing.

Upon entering, the sight she witnessed disturbed her to the very core. Rooster's maulsticked arm shook violently as he addressed the brush to the canvas. All of his effort and an ungodly concentration struggled to tame the unruly shaking that caused the hickory maulstick to tremble at its roots.

"Rooster, Rooster, my God!" She ran forward, taking him by the tremulous arm, containing its contortions, stopping it from further revolt, protest and demonstration to the war he fought within. "Stop. Stop!" she pleaded, hugging his arm, its tremoring quakes beyond her powers of restraint.

With opaque, mucous glazed, obfuscated eyes, he studied the woman before him. Dorothia could not tell if the dull appearance of the eyes was a strange effect of the weak lighting; of fear she convinced herself that it was. His gaze terrified her. She felt like an unrecognized stranger before him and drew back in horror.

"Mother?"

"Rooster, what are you doing? What are you doing? Rest." Again, she looked into his eyes and saw their filmy coating, a sure sign of sickness. "What are you doing? What are you doing? You need to rest."

"Mother?"

She struggled to lead him to stand, but he would not budge from the chair. The solidity, the immovability, astounded her. She stopped, helpless.

"Mother, I'm all right." A calmness pervaded his voice. "It's all right." Dorothia could smell the odor associated with the affliction of the skin, but his face appeared lively, peach, vigorous.

"Are you having an outbreak? Is it advancing? Have you taken the medication? Your eyes, Rooster." Dorothia scurried beneath the bed and pulled forth the plastic containers of medical contraband. Quickly, with the professionalism of a nurse, she counted the vials of Dapsone and Rifampicine. "You haven't taken any medication. She grabbed at two vials and ripped a syringe from its plastic sheath.

From behind her the voice spoke. "I don't need any, Mother." This was not the voice of her son.

"Rooster, you should see your eyes. Can you close them? Are you having clouded vision?"

"My vision has never been better." He blinked once and then twice. "It's just the work. I've been working very hard."

"Yes, I know," she stated, glancing round the room, overwhelmed. "But Rooster . . ." She paused, unsure of what to say next. "You can hurt yourself working too hard."

Dorothia turned to see her son uncurling Tamara's gauze wrap from his hands. "I want you to see something." The gauze fell to the ground in flutters, coiling on the floor like a boa as it dropped away. Dorothia watched as his movements, a bit sluggish, revealed the hands beneath. Breathlessly, Dorothia waited, preparing for a ghastly disclosure. The dark colors of the current canvas overwhelmed the room, swallowing the light. As the gauze lay on the ground he wiped his hands roughly with clean paint rags. She approached, easing forward as the skin beneath the flaked scabs, the dried blood and crusting shingles, was laid bare, pale blue as a newborn babe.

"Rooster," she cried, clutching at his fingertips, enthusiastically inspecting the warm palms and white knuckles. They were stalwart and unscarred, not a single abscess, boil, blain, pustule, infection or shingle, not a single puss-filled, carbuncular wound or deformation. They were a picture of perfect health, his hands, a lordly canvas. She gazed at him in wonder and amazement. "You're better. You're completely better. This is miraculous. There's not a single sign. Your hands . . . Is it . . . ?"

"I'm fine, Mother; now let me paint. I need to finish what I've begun." She did not hear the otherworldliness of the voice or see the gazeless gaze of his lonesome eyes, bloated with vitreous humor, as they searched the canvas for the source of the emptiness within.

"Yes, yes," she exclaimed with excitement, rising from her knees, unwrinkling her dress, touching the dove-shaped silver broach on her blouse. Scuttling from the room, she was solaced, more than happy to leave, content to believe in her own failure to comprehend. Stepping past *Study of the Beautiful*, her prior instincts returned. She paused, her mental checklist returning. *Study of the Beautiful* was not magnificent. It was magnificence. Pride swelled within that such artistry should come from her womb. "You should paint more like this. Put that dark thing you're working on away. People don't want to look at things like that, much less think about or feel them."

Lifting his brush once more, his reply was strange, empyrean. "People see the colors they need to see."

"Your hands, Rooster. It's wonderful."

His brush already at work upon the canvas, he replied, "Yes, Mother, it is."

She exited the room full of hope. Her son would be great, great, great. One of the greatest. She closed the door. A fine click echoed in the hallow hall of the Spartan antechamber.

Refusing out of habit to linger on celebration, her mind jumped to the next item on her list. Marcel. She needed to secure his visit. From the hallway she called to her son as she pulled on her winter coat before the full-length mirror. "I'm going to see my friend. The buyers are coming tomorrow; don't forget." It did not matter if he heard her. In fact, she fully expected that he had not. Temperatures were dropping rapidly. Everything was going splendidly.

Only with an act of will did Rooster place the brush upon the palette after Dorothia left the room. The entirety of his being burned. An acid suffering to the bone afflicted his body. He could barely blink. For at least a day now, commanding the eyelids shut demanded a painful, strenuous effort. His mother had been a blurred form, a fuzzy sphere of disseminated color. He listened as the car pulled from the driveway. She was gone now, through the night and possibly well into the next day. This, at least, offered temporary abatement. He had aspired only to get through her visitation so that he could continue, uninterrupted by her curiously motivated sympathies.

It was keratitis. He knew the condition of the eyes — a raw, burning inflammation of the cornea — and the risks associated with it: permanent damage, even blindness. As the condition worsened, his perception of form and line transformed. It was a beautiful alteration that gave to him the ability to see what in the past he and Soli had only theorized. What had become clear before him, he interpreted as direct, unmediated communion with substratum. His first instinct as the altered vision set in was to administer medication. This, he realized as though a savage ape waking from a dream, had been his first instinct every time another region of his body, flaring up with its demanding, violent itch and searing presence, ordered his attention. He felt during those five agonizing days and nights that his body was battling the canvas for his soul. And the canvas, to Rooster's own pleasure, was winning.

He rejected the claims of the body, willfully denying the ardent urge to administer relief from a bottle. After such struggles, the last thing he wanted was someone else, Dorothia perhaps, forcing the false remedies upon him. This was why he feigned health in the face of grimness. He could feel the body consuming itself. Denigration of the flesh, it did not matter now. Nothing of their world remained as objects for his belief; only the canvas mattered. Only love could save him. Tamara, like a dwarf of a mythical childhood fantasy disproved, crossed his mind. The pain the memory aroused in him contrasted the body's pain, the ravenous leprosy he hid. Nothing the body proposed could compare to her torture, the way she had entered, slicing his soul wide. Pouring forth upon the canvas was consuming blackness, unalterable, untamed and unmastered. This is my destiny, he thought without regret or fear. Soli had always known. He tried to prepare me for this, for the hour when I would cling to the act of painting though it would no longer matter. But how could anyone prepare anyone, for this?

Picking up the brush with the flesh of his own hand, Rooster reapplied his valiant effort to the eddied mask upon the canvas. *In some future world I shall choose this; this will be my face.* Within its gracious prophecy, he saw an unfettered cradle, a place where one could lose oneself for an eternity, without delusion or hope of ever being more than what one is, what one is born to be. It's a simple matter of destiny, he thought, the strained muscles of his face spasming from the effort required to blink. But for his eyes and his hands, the rest of his being he ignored, already left behind. In the next world, only his eyes and his hands would be necessary. He rolled the brush upon his palm, *my palm.* He spoke aloud to himself now. The canvas heard. "I suppose I can thank her. Yes, for this at least I can thank her." Dictator to the brush, he pressed the wise paint forward, commuting his spirit through the dispelled illusions of space, of time, of identity. His purloin paintings had known it long ago. Now he also knew.

ℐ

They awoke in the morning after a long and deeply satisfying night of making love. In Marcel's arms, cuddling within his curled chest, the musty scent of dried salt on his flesh, Dorothia felt safe. For a night, she had surrendered to sumptuous weakness, accepting that in the morning all would, as need demanded, return to what it had been. His bow legs intertwined with her own, she soaked in the warmth of his luxurious body, for once allowing it to give her true comfort, acknowledging that she received from it a breath she could not breathe alone. As soon as they awoke, she would have to raise the matter of her son, the painter, the young master. She closed her eyes, imagining for an instant that the outside world did not exist, that it held no bond upon her, that there remained no obligations or duties, no higher good, only arms entwined in arms, loving embraces and sumptuous sleep.

In such moments, with sun breaking through windows, at dizzying heights that diminished even a city, the necessity of companionship seemed obvious, true. She could hear the song of a morning lark and wondered from where it had come. Perhaps she only thought she heard the song of a morning lark, the song of a bard, a morning singer of Shakespeare, of Sarum and Salisbury plain, of Winchester and Devonshire.

Prophet slept beneath a veil drawn like a shroud over the cage. For a blind bird there is no difference between light and darkness, day and night; and still, they know when to sleep and when to wake. How different are their cues? For if not cued by light and dark, sunrise and sunset, what breaks that they may know the time to come, the time to go? Marcel awoke soundlessly. From beneath the black veil, the crow released an unruly cry.

"Aahhh," he uttered dreamily, plying her hand in his. "You're radiant this morning."

She smiled as she rubbed the fingers of her hand against the stubble of his cheek. For the first time she saw him: the smile wrinkles about the eyes, the strain of too much thinking in a furrowed brow, tender lips, a sorrowful manner of looking into the world, past it, like a refugee searching for love amidst rubble, though he believes it dead. Faith among the faithless, hope among the hopeless, she counted rare indeed.

"Cigarette?"

"No."

They lay in bed, smoke drifting upwards. Both were experiencing the fullness of the something on their minds that each of their own accord had postponed for a night. On Dorothia's lips were the words she would use to broach the necessary topic. She needed completion, a date, a time, no more delay. No more messing around.

"I leave this afternoon," Marcel began, casually sucking at the cigarette stem as Prophet stretched morning wings. "I wanted to tell you. It came so quickly as these things often do. Jack had to book me. No international flights over the weekend, that's all. That's all there is to it. What a character he is. *Marcie,* he said, *the royalty in Sweden won't wait for a fool who plays with a pen. . . .*" Slowly he released the first lung of smoke, considering what that might mean. "Anyway, that's all there is to it."

For a long time she sat pensive, still. She did not reflect on all of the obstacles she had overcome already. There was only, once again, this moment, now, the ever eternal present and the trial it presented. She expressed no shock at the injustice, no visible sign of anger. She remained cold, cold as a killer with one thing in mind, cold as a killer who has planned so deep that the double-cross has been foreseen.

"Is that right?"

Marcel had not known what to expect. He knew only that meeting her son was important to her though he still did not know why. That she did not explode emotionally caused him relief as well as slight concern. Maybe she was not the worthy woman of insurmountable strength he had believed. Her reaction surprised him; perhaps, he contemplated with an author's analytic poise, it had even disappointed him.

"Yes, that's right," he continued. "Things are going so fast. It's an amazing time. I apologize that I won't be able to see your son. It's just not possible now. Everything has crept up on us it would seem."

Marcel Phrenol was an evil man.

Inside Marcel Phrenol one goal existed. A goal that, as far as Marcel was presently concerned, had nothing to do with meeting Dorothia's son.

Reaching over, Dorothia took the cigarette from Marcel's hand. She now understood that the great writer had never planned on meeting her son. She reflected on the talk of passing ships, of enemies lashed together to sustain a treacherous storm in mutual safety, of moments in time auspicious to particular events, of symmetry in the solar sky, of a metaphysical window of opportunity that remains open for but a transient speck, a sniffle in eternity. Dorothia knew that their romance was over, the legitimate romance that had budded without being sought. She had desired to meet Marcel to accomplish an aim; along the way she had allowed herself to feel more, a familiar warmth, a yearning for past comforts. Perhaps he, in his own way and for his own reasons, had done the same. Now at the end she would revert, as all things do, to what she had been in the beginning.

Soberly, she dragged off of the cigarette; her gaze lingered on the ebony shroud draped over the bird cage.

Detached, unemotional interest in her voice, she asked, "What was it like?"

The cigarette lingered in the air between them as she returned it to him. "What was what like?"

Exposing them from beneath the covers, Dorothia squeezed her own breasts, twisting the dark nipples with indifference. "Being with a black woman, a negro."

They were like two opponents who no longer had reason to hide their motives and intentions and prejudice, the end being determined. It pleased Marcel that Dorothia was not making an obscenity of being used, of being lied to. She knew as well as he that people share company seeking insights and gratification, fantasy fulfillment and 1,001 other modest forms of mutually fabricated and sustained delusion. He knew as well as she that sometimes the insights sought could not be found among the common lot. Relationships were like mentors; we submit ourselves in order to appease esoteric callings within. Marcel mused as he held the smoking tip before his lips, "I'd be lying, you know, no matter what I say."

She thought about it, conceded, "Yes, I suppose I knew that."

Turning on his side, he placed a hand on her breast and squeezed.

"The negro woman is more passionate in bed, wilder, more primitive. She has no European inhibitions. She's savage. She believes in the hard arch; that's why she was stolen from Africa."

"You're lying now."

"Yes," he replied, turning his back.

"You loved your wife, Ruth. You still love her?" she probed with the efficiency of a physician.

"Yes."

"I can understand. You never had children?"

"No."

"Was it because you didn't want to put the child through the racism that comes with being in the middle? Half and half, identityless, neither one nor the other?"

Marcel scoffed. "Please! That's the fascist lie; the one they use to divide us. That's how they turn the life urge against us."

"Yes," she assented, finding a reason for pleasure in the morality of his indignity.

"Why are you asking me these things?"

Unwrapping herself from the sheets, she sat on the edge of the bed. Marcel wanted her. He could not have her now.

Dorothia thought without regret of the way she had driven herself between Tamara and her son, wishing to prevent the girl from infecting him. Stretching, she cracked her neck and ran her hands along the curves of her milky body, admiring and taking pleasure from her own form. Her body was a tool, and she was the one who used it.

Marcel pressed again. "Why are you asking these things?"

"There are things I want to know."

"What do you want to know? Why are you asking?"

She turned and patted his cheek. Then she softened, weakened, and ran two fingers across his brow and down to the tip of his nose. "You'd have made a good father, Marcel." The arched eyebrows of his aged face revealed surprise, a twinge of sadness. The morning can be unflattering when we look upon ourselves. It is, after all, nature's time, never our own, an unguarded awakening, her porticos inviting, when she is most wont to reveal secrets, at least one, and maybe two.

"You read to me once about Urizen." She spoke of the mythic vistas created by the remote poet and artisan William Blake, a quaint figure rejected by his contemporaries, a blacksmith discovered and deified after his death. They say he saw angels, viewed the world in the fullest sense of heaven and hell, an active battlefront of the eternal which could be seen if we only would allow ourselves to be receptive. "You said," she continued, "that he had a leprous face."

Marcel smiled an ironic smile, a smile that judged the moment, in all of its splendid imperfection, to be fitting. Closing his eyes as though to read from a text scripted upon the inner lid of his eye, he recited the words to which she referred:

> The heavens melted from north to south; and Urizen
>> Who sat
> Above all heavens, in thunders wrap's, emerg'd his
>> Leprous head.

Quietly, Marcel rested against the backboard of the bed, his eyes still closed, content.

Dorothia remained upon the edge of the bed. In another life, a more blessed one, she could have loved him from cradle to grave.

"I've told you before that Blake was a visionary," he continued. "A true visionary, prophetic. Do you truly wish me to unwrap his words for you?"

Since she did not reply, he expounded. "The truth is always before us, Dorothia. It is never hidden. That's the beauty of it. The truth stands right before our eyes knowing that if we do not want to see it, we will not see it. With truth, nothing is hidden. Since the dawn of time, everything is apparent. That which is hidden, is hidden only by our own desire not to see. I could tell you everything about Urizen and Los and Orc and Enitharmon. But you wouldn't see it. Beyond heaven you are powerless." Marcel smiled as he said these words, treating them as they were, cause for joy.

She did not pursue. She knew well enough not to pursue a poet into his world.

They passed the morning together, talking generally about such nonsense as fills the lightest hours of a couple's day. Two large suitcases emerged from a closet and Marcel began the ritual of packing as Dorothia read the pages of his journal that she concealed behind the pages of a fashion magazine.

"Jack is coming at one," she heard him say, slipping two suits into a garment bag.

Desperation enthralls us, guides us like slaves in welded chain towards molecular beauty; immortal cells we fear; our want for courage shining forth, to see. Imagine, imagine the sea itself as a worm that wrinkles, creeps

& crawls, so is the indelible desire to express ourselves beyond the current
limits. Imagine imagination reaching out beyond imagination.

She turned another page where Marcel had written the words of the
French poet Valéry, *"La définition de beauté est facile; c'est quoi conduit à*
témérité déserpérée."

At noon Marcel entered the bathroom for a shower. Removing herself from the sun in which she sat naked, Dorothia returned the journal to the desk. She dressed smoothly, mechanically, while listening
with pleasure to the Nobel winner as he hummed bars of classical
music. She laughed to think that she had known him, would keep the
memory of knowing him, like this. The shower water lapped at the
ceramic as rain to stone. She pulled on her pumps, wiped her inner
thigh with the bed sheets and lifted the veiled bird cage from its hook.
The crow beneath remained silent, silent as an accomplice, as they
dipped from the room without goodbye.

Dorothia took the long way home. She drove through Kenmore
Square, down Beacon Street and through Brookline. She drove along
the T, racing with the C-line before cutting up to Commonwealth
Avenue and sidling along the B-line. She was driving backwards along
the route of the Boston Marathon, past Chestnut Hill and the golden
eagle of Boston College. She drove through Newton, rising and
descending along the torturous stretch that composed the four-mile
span known as Heartbreak Hill. *Heartbreak Hill.* What did the runners
learn about themselves in a place like this? The drive was peaceful. She
took a left onto Route 16, past the red brick firehouse on the corner, to
the exact point where Heartbreak Hill began its fastidious ascent. In the
front seat, she uncovered Prophet's cage thinking that God is like an
ever-present resource upon which we can draw. Still, she mused, in her
own poetic world, we should not be absolutely dependent upon this
resource. The Creator fulfills every prayer, but this does not mean we
should pray every wish. Sometimes, she thought, touching the cage, we
need to rely upon our own resources; God respects pluck.

"If he had just kept his promise this wouldn't be necessary," she told
the bird, expressing complaisance. "If he had just kept his promise, I

would have let him leave. Now we have to do it this way, the hard way. You understand, don't you, Prophet?" The bird marched along the wire, clipping with its beak, attempting to snap the prison bars. "Yes, I know you understand what it means to wish to break free. Personal freedom is our only moral obligation. Everything else is a lie. That's why I can't be angry at Marcel. I can only respect him. I would have done the same thing in his place. We all want that kind of freedom, don't we, Prophet? Don't we?"

Dorothia did not know why it bothered her that the crow was more interested in battling the wire than listening to her voice. Checking her hair and lipstick in the rearview mirror, she steered the car onto Route 95 South heading for Providence. A sharp, bitter edge permeated her address. "Why do we act like you care, Prophet? Why do we act like you understand? All of Marcel's mystic mumbo-jumbo, I suppose. He's as vulnerable as any man." The bird tilted its head in a display of estimation but gave no reply.

The sun was already setting as Dorothia, returning home, checked her wristwatch. It was only 4:00 o'clock but the sky was turning to dusk as the first bitter welts of winter worked past her nerves and into a core of bone. In only a few hours Irene would arrive with her small cadre. Stripping off her coat, Dorothia tossed the mail into a kitchen draw. She needed to hold her scheme together for only a short time longer. Of this she remained confidently convinced. Once this thing was done tonight, she could let go; it would be her son's life from then on — his future assured, her work complete. The things a mother must do.

She entered Rooster's room carrying the cage. Much as he had been a day earlier, Rooster sat at the canvas in poor light. His hands were unmoving upon his lap. Dorothia found it a staid, oppressive atmosphere, an ambiance different from anything she had experienced emitting from her son before. The plastic tub she had pulled from beneath his bed remained just as she had left it, as did the gauze that had until so recently encircled his leprous hands. The bed had not been slept in. She strongly suspected that he had not eaten.

"I brought you some company," she ventured softly. He seemed unaware of her entrance, wasted with unfulfilled effort. Placing Prophet next to him on the floor, she glanced over his shoulder. The painting had been transformed overnight. A white border contained the black foreground. The black had been completely contained within the white, and yet her first impulse — or was it insight — was that the white was in greater need of containment, was more complex, more confused, more desperate for subjugation. They were strange thoughts, but her first thoughts.

She put a hand on her son's shoulder. Instinctively he pulled away, a movement of such unexpected violence that she instantly recoiled. She did not know who this was before her. Stunned, she began, "This is Prophet. Prophet belongs to that friend of mine I told you of who wants to meet you."

Rooster stared at the canvas unblinking. Without genuine interest he glanced in the direction of the bird. "What would I be, Mother, without my painting?"

Rushing across the room, Dorothia cracked a window. "It's gotten stale in here. Let's get the air flowing again: You've probably been working too long on that one painting. I told you to put it aside, didn't I? 'Start something new,' I said. You're hung up. Put it away and return to it later. You'll see it with a whole new set of eyes."

The air that rushed into the room from beneath the crack was bitter cold. Dorothia found it refreshing. "Fresh air. Fresh air, that's what you need to get going again. Out with the old, in with the new. That's our mantra. Every painting can't be a masterpiece. Let that one go."

"What would I be?"

Coming closer, she touched his hand. He did not look at her. "Why, Rooster, please, you'd be my beautiful son, my beautiful, magnificent son."

"What else, Mother, if I couldn't paint? What else would I be? What else besides your son?"

She took a deep and irritated breath. Desperate, she pointed at Prophet. "It's like asking what a bird would be without flight."

"But I'm not a bird, Mother. I'm not looking for similes. What would I be, Mother? Me. What would I be besides your son if I couldn't paint?" There was resolution in his voice and purpose in his silence.

Grappling against the atrocity, her frustration mounting at the fact that her greatest beneficiary held her in contempt just in the moment when she most needed his support, she blurted outwards, "You wouldn't be anything, Rooster. You'd be nothing. And that's what makes you a great painter. Everyone else out there, they go from event to event, activity to activity, job to job. They commit to nothing and they can't understand why they don't become anything. You stand for something, Rooster. You mean something. You've put everything into your painting, and so have I. I believe in you. Take away the painting and you're nothing. Take away your painting and I'm nothing. That's why it's so important; that's what makes it meaningful. That's what makes it worthwhile. Do you understand? Don't focus on the fact that without the painting you're nothing. Focus on the fact that your painting has made you something! And it's going to continue to, Rooster. Oh yes, it's only begun."

He listened. "So I'm a great painter?"

This question pleased her, as though his expressions were finally returning to the proper and relevant perspective.

"Of course you are. That's what our lives have been about," she stated matter-of-factly. "Don't you know that?"

"And I'm nothing more."

She smiled as she moved her hand from his hand to the brush to the canvas, her finger touching the black center. "To be remembered for the images you capture . . . What more could you be?" Her fingers lingered on the canvas. A moment of drifting passed before she remembered her son and where she was. Pulling back, she added lightly, "Look at me. I get lost in your painting. What a gift you have." She watched her son askance, hoping that her words had a positive effect. "What is it, Rooster? What's wrong?"

Raising the brush, he corrected the spot that her touch had tainted. "Nothing." And before she could speak again, he added, "I'm looking forward to meeting these people. We're really going to show them something tonight, aren't we?"

Dorothia beamed as she heard the words. "We'll show them who's the best."

"We'll show them something, the whole world."

"Oh, my beautiful son, yes, yes we will." Hands folded over her heart, she held her breath in joy. "How I have waited to hear that!" The blind crow let out two tepid caws, the cords of its throat taut with an unsuccessful effort to strike a higher note.

"How wonderful. I have to get ready. They'll be here soon." Rushing about, she pushed the plastic container beneath the bed and picked up the gauze from the floor. "You'll be ready, won't you?"

His eyes still locked on the canvas, he answered quietly. "Yes, Mother. I can see the end now. Leave me. I want to finish before our guests arrive. Thank you for all you've done."

Dorothia stood at the door, upon the threshold of an exit. "You're not still mad about the girl, are you? That's not . . ."

"I'm a painter, Mother," he interjected quickly. "Why would I be upset about a silly girl? Please, let me finish."

Dorothia pressed upwards, giddily on her toes. From the hallway she rushed up the stairs, excited as a teenage girl preparing for her first date. No, no, she thought, excited as a bride, arranging for the wedding night.

Inside the room Rooster sat with a certain knowledge of who and what he was. He arched his stiff shoulders, struggling to loosen the muscles as he continued studying the canvas. *Someday,* Soli had told him, *you will need to put yourself within the center of the canvas. No more hiding in the backgrounds. You will stand courageously in the foreground for all to see and judge.* Rooster's life and all of its battles were recorded on the paintings scattered about the room. So much of the room was taken up by the paintings that there was little room left for him. On the other side of every artist who seeks to convey a vision or create a new world is a human being desiring to paint or write or sculpt or play his or her way out of existence, to overwhelm a room with such expressions and intricacies of quality that a person can disappear within, blending in as it were with the scenery, so thorough has nature been.

Rooster felt no feeling, thought no thought. All thought and feeling had been emptied into the world around him. It was, at least, a pleasant environment, one that he could understand. Even if he could not paint his way through the gateway of existence, he could create a myriad of wonderful pathways, everything for which a soul could hope and then just a little more, enough to keep one going, enchanted. He returned to the painting before him and recognized it for what it was. Emptiness. Exhaustion. That which consumes for the end of consumption. This was what he had been painting towards, and now it was here, more canvas than he could paint in a lifetime, in ten thousand lifetimes, more emptiness than a thousand leprous souls could fill. To know the hunger of the world, this is what it is to be full. It would never be enough. Hunger grows and with it need, voracious and nondiscerning. Soon it all becomes the same, nature, a massive table with a single purpose: to fill our need. There is no distinction between the dishes, among what is good and what it bad. There is no taste. There is only the rage of hunger, of insatiable need and the fear that comes from the deep knowledge that it cannot be fulfilled because we have not learned how to stop.

Free of thought, Rooster reached down, opened the gate and reached into the cage of the bird. Skittish, sidestepping on wire to the back of the cage, Prophet sought escape, still unsure of this new setting. "Don't worry. Don't worry," Rooster cajoled, taking the crow with both hands. Coming forth from the cage, the bird nipped nervously at the thumbs. Holding the bird round the body, Rooster studied Prophet before the light. Unable to blink, Rooster could still make out impressions. Looking closely, then probing with a finger, he recognized that the bird possessed no eyes. "Blind?" he asked in amazement. The bird grew calm, respectful of an owner who would so intimately and intrepidly share such a sorrow. Prophet listened, cocking its head at curious angles, as Rooster stroked the wings with a steady, healing thumb. "I guess you're a leper, just like me."

For several minutes they sat in silence as Rooster held the bird and surveyed the painting, largely a swirling mass of sensory impression for him now. He wiped his eyes, but the mucous layers were thick. "I should consider myself lucky. I can still see better than you, old bird." But Prophet cawed in protest, causing Rooster to laugh, feeling as if the bird had understood and rejected the suggestion of infirmity.

Like a child, Rooster raised the bird before him in an effort to achieve a fuller introduction. "What did my mother say you were called? Ah yes, Prophet. What a wonderful name. How fitting. I wish you could tell me a bit about what happens next. I am finished as a painter. I'm through." The bird released a shrill cry.

"Well, what then?" Rooster asked, playfully engaged. "What should I do?" The bird remained still. "Silent as the Sphinx, eh?" Rooster smiled as he slowly released the bird, guiding the old crow to perch upon his curled wrist. "You know everything wise, but you'll teach me nothing, is that it?" Rooster jested before turning serious. "Just teach me a little about the hunger, about how to battle the hatred of the emptiness."

"Caw-Caw!"

Raised far above Rooster's head, Prophet flapped, unsure of the height and the perch. Testing its wings for flight, the mystic oracle released its spondaic message. Without warning, the bird dove. Swooping downwards, Prophet plunked into the heart of the oppressive canvas that had been devouring Rooster for five days. With desperately gallant wings that warred against all oppositions of the physical world, Rooster watched in fear and awe as the wise old crow struggled in midair against the canvas. The bird maintained its loft, suspended by a sheer and beautiful, unflappable will. Temporarily but successfully, Prophet demonstrated the way in which one resists gravity's spiteful urge. The wings battered the canvas with the force of a thousand brushes. Each wing pronounced its declaration: This is commitment. This is affirmation. This is redemption.

"Caw-Cauw!"

The frenzied effort, the courageous wings drew the white border inward as feathers slapped the canvas. What had been divided now came together. Upon the white background midnight black was shown for what it was, a rich and noble purple, the color of spiritual calling. Rooster witnessed as a field of amaranths bloomed before his eyes beneath the ocean, below the midnight moon. The bird wailed a wretched cry as it bumped from the canvas to the floor, its attack repelled. Greatly concerned, Rooster reached out to help the disoriented champion. But Prophet was not done. The wise old crow had barely begun. Now in the midst of its selected work, the bird dragged its battered wing. Fumbling away from Rooster, Prophet refused to give up. Flapping its wings, determined to fly, the bird hopped forward. Guided by the current of air streaming into the room, Prophet leapt successfully to the windowsill. The wise old bird unleashed a cry, celebrating a minor victory, as though to assert, *I still got it!* Difficult as it was for Rooster to focus, the room a nebulous blur, he dashed after the surprisingly nimble crow.

"It's O.K. It's O.K.," he reassured the bird. But Prophet had entered into a dazed, furious, dervish, life-affirming, Dionysian state of shocking grace. Plunging into the current of air with a warrior scream,

Prophet wriggled through the thin gap of the cracked window. Rooster's heart thumped as he saw the fuzzy image disappear. Rushing to the window, he thrust it wide open. A fulsome gust of chilling air struck him full in the face, blowing his hair in wild directions. First stars, ancestral, eons distant, some already dead, revealed themselves from the blanket of night. Orion's belt sparkled.

The white-tipped, painted wings flapped for flight. The wise old crow made it only so far as the iron gate before meeting the brutal resistance of the palisades. Knocked down again, Prophet stumbled in a circle like a boxer unable to find the proper corner. Fearing the bird's escape, Rooster scuttled from the window and leapt into the crisp, fallen leaves of winter's garden. Matching the young painter's efforts, almost taunting youth, Prophet squeezed through the rusted iron bars and staggered into the guttered street.

Struggling to fly, Prophet progressed down the street, a handicapped comic, flapping and flapping, flapping and falling, leaping and flying and falling. Several times the bird flew directly into the chrome wheels and dented doors of parked cars. The bird simply bumbled about, a punch drunk fool too stubborn to give up. Each time Rooster came close, arms extended, Prophet expended another effort, exhibiting a final burst of energy that like all of the others before was not the final burst. Rooster hoped each time the bird went down that it would stop. Just stop! Rest! Quit! But the wise old crow never did, never. Instead, with each beating delivered by a car or a telephone pole, the silly bird paused for only a moment, shaking off the dizziness of doubt, before again flapping forward. Rooster tried calling the bird; he tried creeping upon the bird; he chased quickly and walked with slow measured steps. The magical bird, he thought at times, was toying with him, keeping him close, teasing him, inviting him to play a game he could not win. At the end of the street, Prophet stood in the center of a four-way intersection. Rooster surged forward as a brown sedan screeched to a halt before the bird, the empty eyes oblivious. For sure, the crazy bird had reached the end of its rope. Hearing the angry horn, bouncing off the tire, the bird hopped beneath the car, bumping its head on the radiator pan. Fearing the worst, Rooster stood paralyzed as the sedan drove off. To his amazement, the white-tipped wings, unaffected by it all, were flapping their way down the street, flying in ten-foot spurts directly into traffic, playing daredevil, challenging fate; the draped, wounded feather of the wing swept forward, utilized as the automotive matador's bold cape.

Approaching the edge of the forest, Rooster escalated his attempts to capture the bird. At the hem line dividing street from suburban wilderness, Rooster came within inches of the spry bird, diving down with his hands outstretched. Prophet bound away with a peevish cry. Rising, Prophet struck its head upon a branch, collapsing in a heap on Rooster's back. Lying in red clay on his stomach after the missing dive, Rooster clutched a single black feather in his hands. The white paint smudged upon his fingers. Making fun of the failed attempt, Prophet cawed in Rooster's ear before springing into the woods, discharging a shrill caw with every flap of the wings. Rising from his dirty belly, Rooster chased the old crow as it flew as though by sheer, dumb luck at least thirty feet before crashing into an oak with a solid thud. Had it not been for the radiance of the white wing tips, Rooster would have lost the bird. Again, just as he came within distance to pluck the crow from the ground, Prophet took off. Their game of emancipation continued on and on, deeper and deeper into the patient woods until they arrived at the still edge of the lake.

Dashing down the slope as Prophet burst into open space, Rooster began only then to sense the degree to which his sight had been damaged by his own negligence. Unable to see across the lake, he had no sense of where it ended. For all his lack of perception, it may as well have been an ocean. The reflection of the rising blue moon created a cool, frosty palette before his eyes. He felt for the first time how cold it was. So incensed had he been by the bird's escape, he had charged into the wintry night without a coat. He shivered, admonishing himself that he was running out of time to capture the lame old bird. That bird should want to get caught; it could never survive out here, Rooster told himself as he reached the lake. He stood by the limb of the fallen tree where he and Tamara had spent some of their first hours together, where they had first kissed. Touching the limb he smiled, almost glad that the foolish old bird had dragged him out here against his will to remind him of this special place. What had they discussed? Substratum and oneness of mind. He loved her. Why had she not returned? Why had he never told her?

Prophet dropped from the sky onto the frozen ice of the lake, ridiculously spinning and sliding to a comical halt. From the distance, the bird released a dull wail that Rooster had not heard before. The soft moan summoned Rooster from his melancholy with the urgency of the moment. Unsure of what to make of such a plaintiff, mournful sob, Rooster searched for signs of the bird. The cranky moan, a wounded trochee saturated with warning and instruction, broke from the darkness a second time. Rooster focused upon his sense of hearing. He felt it sharpen, intensify, grow increasingly acute. But for a gentle haze cast from the moon above, Rooster could make out nothing. The lament rose a third time, a dirge of mourning for the lost. Oriented by the call, Rooster stood nervously at the frozen edge of the lake. Letting go of his hold on the limb, he stepped out to test the ice. Thumping a foot he felt secure as he sidled forward six inches at a time. Finally he could see the bird, or what he reasoned must be the bird, white tips like stars in the sky.

"Stay there, Prophet, stay there. This is dangerous now. It's not a game, Prophet, stay there," he urged, easing forward, quite afraid of the void. Moving into the darkness, away from the safe edge, Rooster noted how suddenly warm and comfortable he felt despite the freezing temperature. Sweat dripped down his brow even as his breath turned before his mouth to a snowy mist. "Be a good Prophet. Stay there; I understand now. I understand."

The distance increasing between himself and the shore of the lake, Rooster tried to think of the month and the date. Was it early for a freezing over? Was this the expected season? He paused, like a fox on delicate ice, unsure of whether to continue. He could not even remember the month. What is the month, he demanded of himself? Prophet released a low, odd, wheezing cry, a modest elegy. Summoned, Rooster continued forward. He could more distinctly intuit the form of the bird now. His eyes were locked wide open, though he could not tell whether this was due to the intensity of the moment or the sickly condition that had cleansed his sight.

"Work with me, Prophet. Work with me."

Gazing back to the disappearing limb of their embankment, Rooster thought of Tamara. He thought of how she had entered his room the first time, how she had dared to let go of the doorknob, how difficult that must have been, what an extraordinary act of trust, what a bold act of faith. He thought of what his life would have been like if she had not dared. He took two steps forward. The ice seemed firm, strong, deeply secure. There's nothing to be afraid of. What did she say to his fear as she dipped his hands into the scalding water? Rooster watched as Prophet hopped towards him, a promising sign that galvanized Rooster to progress one and two and then three more feet, sliding gradually into Prophet's circle. "That's it," he cooed peacefully. "That's it. Be a good Prophet." The wise old crow appeared nervous. It hummed its low wail, keeping anxious notes trapped within the throat. Trapped within the gray haze, Rooster could no longer see the shore. The bird was close. "Good bird. Good bird. Stay right there. Easy, easy. . . ." His arms were stretched forward, outward. The bird could nip his fingers. "Easy. . . ." Prophet extended the white-tipped, painted wings to fly again. Rooster heard the feathers bristle with movement.

Lunging, he wrapped his hands about the bird. Prophet struggled, but Rooster held the bird close, encircling the crow's body in his arms. "I got you. I got you, Prophet. It's O.K. It's O.K. Relax."

Proudly, Rooster held the bird in safety. Prophet, peaceful, dispossessed of the struggle, answered with a meek, guttural groan.

It was only the sound of a splinter crack, followed by the thunderous echo of a surreal burp emitted from the hollow belly of the lake, but it caused Rooster's entire body to stiffen. He immediately knew it to be the unmistakable roil of ice plates cracking, readjusting to expansion, temporarily weakening in a movement toward strength. Sound became a material force, tangible as the crack of the branch with which one has balanced a life over a chasm's dream. The single splinter multiplied as Rooster stood, still as a hunter now hunted by the prey. Beneath his own feet he could feel the vibration, the shifting of frozen plates. He could see silver electricity trapped in the ice. Cracks spread at the surface, widening the interconnected reach of a patterned web of indifference. The definitive lines erupting from below seemed alive to Rooster, intent upon touching him, approaching him, enclosing him, *him*. A single streak of splintering electricity, powerful and violent, attacked from the darkness. The lines, crooked and cracked, slithered like an eel without skin to his feet. The slithering splinters seemed a slow, insidious thing as they passed by him, continuing on directly beneath him. The lake roared as its massive, solid block broke in two.

Rooster watched, unable to react, as his left foot disappeared, taken away, into a cold and murky depth. It seemed not real. As though on a spring his right foot was propelled upwards. He lost his balance as the last vestiges of the center came free. What was ice and what was water suddenly became clear. They were opposites, completely unrelated and in perfect collusion, one serving to feed the other. A mouth opened within the lake. Through the savage season of a hungry world, the pain vanished. He felt the chilling lap of the water beneath. She enfolded Rooster within her liquid womb, her inconsolable hunger an unconditioned love. Prophet cried out, pounding wings of despair directly against the buffeted sky, pulling, pulling free from the hold of pendulous earth.

℘

"Oh yes, my, Master Marubrishnubupu, it is such a pleasure to meet you finally. I've heard so much about your inspired work." They shook hands. Dorothia wore a yellow dress accentuated with cream pearls and her million dollar smile. Pressing aside a strand of wispy hair with the back of his sienna hand, Marubrishnubupu listened intently, striving to connect directly with the complex emotions that surged beneath the surface. This, he knew, was where true stories reside. Dorothia had suffered much. She was determined not to suffer. He could sense the depth of her suffering far beneath, buried below a tremendous resolve. It was this suffering to which Marubrishnubupu imperatively needed to speak, to reach.

Her own nerves peeling away with anticipation, Irene concluded a cheery ring of introductions among the peculiar group.

"And this is Miss Margo Halscome. She has come to represent the West Coast buyers I told you about."

"Miss Halscome . . . Margo . . . yes, Margo. Please, please then, call me Dorothia. What a lovely broach. Stunning." The two women opened their arms, embracing with smudgeless kisses to the cheek.

"Petunias, why yes, they are. Your favorite, are they? Mine too. How grand! These have just lasted forever."

The four stood in the antechamber basking in the successful pleas-
antries of the first meeting, each quite naturally excited by the
prospects and promise the evening offered.

"Won't you please sit," Dorothia continued, prattling so as not to
allow a conversational pause. "Relax for just a bit. Rooster . . ." she
laughed with trite, accomplished gaiety. "I mean Alexi. Imagine a
mother calling her own son Rooster, ludicrous! But that's what he
prefers, Rooster. I suppose we could all say his art is a wake-up call.
Rooster, ah, but that's my son, he's just finishing a new painting. He has
been a slave to it for days." Lowering her voice she whispered as
though it mattered. "He wanted to finish it for you all, as a tribute to
your visit. You've all come such a long way."

Like a light-hearted loon, Dorothia drubbed her forehead with a
palm. She did not appreciate the way this Marubrishnu fellow stared,
guru or whatever he claimed to be, so intense and uncivilized. And
what a tasteless attire, Dorothia thought to herself, as her eyes glanced
again at his small body draped over by a coarse black robe. How very
lugubrious for a festive occasion!

"Oh, how miserable I have been. What a miserable little hostess,"
she asserted. "May I take your coats? This New England weather has-
n't gone too deeply into the bones, I trust. What a lovely robe. You get
used to it though. How quaintly mystic of you. May I get anyone tea,
coffee, juice, water?"

"Tea would be lovely. Just what I need to get warmed up."

"One tea, yes," Dorothia responded. This Margo was a charm
though, through and through. "Irene, Master Marubrishnu . . . ?"

"Bupu."

"Bupu? You go by Bupu?"

"Marubrishnubupu," he offered humbly, dipping his head and
extending his upturned palms.

"Marubrish . . . nu . . . bupu. Yes, I see, may I get something for your
worship?"

Margo Halscome suppressed a slight smile. She also found this
Marubrishnu . . . bupu fellow to be a social flaw and wondered why
Irene had invited him to attend this critical meeting.

Dorothia, much as she desired to convince herself that she was not nervous and that her scattered hostess routine was all routine intended for affect, felt an authentic anxiety. Steady as a compass, all of her hopes, dreams, efforts, prayers and sacrifices had been faithfully directed towards this night. That Rooster would impress them, she had no doubt. His paintings were of a beauty, magnitude, and inimitable originality that no contemporary, young or old, man or woman, marginal or privileged, could touch, challenge or compare. No rules existed to paint as Rooster painted. The night, she knew, would be more of a victory celebration than an appraisal culminating in judgment. The hard work had been done; receiving accolades in a graceful manner was all that remained. Tonight her dear, cherished son fulfilled a role handed down by destiny.

"I'll admit," Dorothia continued as she took the coats from her guests, "I was nervous about having the three of you into our home. Irene can tell you that. It wasn't easy for us, no, it wasn't easy. Rooster works hard to stay to himself, focused, true to his art. We don't like to open up his world to strangers. I've worked hard to keep him away from all those influences that can turn life into a soap opera. But you're not going to be strangers, are you? Oh, it is wonderful now that you are here. We'll meet him in just a minute, I'm sure; as soon as he's finished you can all meet him. He's quite excited! I'm so glad that you are all here. It means so much to us both. You just can't know!"

What completely astounded Irene was that, despite everything she had learned about this controlling mother, she believed Dorothia to be, without exception, absolutely sincere.

Margo Halscome found Dorothia overly deprecating but delightful nonetheless; she attributed it to the puritanical roots of the region. Calling Dorothia like a friend to her cherished side, the two women spoke intimately of the pride of motherhood, something Margo, with three children of her own, could understand.

"He's worked so hard in recent days. I'll think you'll be pleasantly surprised by how far he has come in such a short amount of time. Maybe I'm just being a mother. I don't think so though. It's more than that; it's more somehow even than I can explain."

Margo placed a cool hand on Dorothia's arm. For a detached, analytical woman by nature, it was what Margo considered a warm gesture.

"I'm sure you're not exaggerating. Irene has been your son's greatest proponent, and Irene's judgment in such matters has always been impeccable."

Leaning forward, Marubrishnubupu asked, "Your son is sick, Ms. Rodriguez?"

Dorothia looked at the odd man. Puzzling to comprehend the fit of this cultural anomaly, for several seconds she did not respond to the rude intrusion but tried rather to understand from where this curious manifestation had come and why.

Straightening her posture, her voice hardened. "Alexi has battled with a rare disease over the past few years We have real reason to believe that it's a battle he is winning."

"How wonderful, good for both of you," Margo ejaculated, discretely guiding the disturbing, inappropriate question towards more genial topics.

Irene cast a cautionary glance at Marubrishnubupu. The question was tactless, raw and unbuffered. Over the prior days, Marubrishnubupu had not been his usual self. Usually detached and reflective, he had recently exhibited an irritating poignancy.

"Master Marubrishnubupu sometimes forgets that he's not in a lecture hall with one of his students," Irene explained to Dorothia.

But Marubrishnubupu began again, interjecting despite even his own misgivings. "Is your son . . . Is Alexi suffering, Ms. Rodriguez?"

For a moment Irene thought to mediate once more, but the icy gaze that Dorothia held between the narrowed lids of her eyes was so sharply focused upon Marubrishnubupu that Irene did not venture to place herself in that line of sight. Margo, holding Dorothia's hand in her own lap as they had just been discussing the joyous vagaries of motherhood, reclined, allowing Dorothia full breath to respond. The vapid gaze she held for Marubrishnubupu was of the type that one would hold only for a spited enemy. The rest of her face, detached and separated from the eyes, smiled derisively.

She struggled to sound pleasant, although no one in the room, including Marubrishnubupu, would have held failure in this attempt against her. "No more than any great artist, I presume, Master Marubrishnu . . . bupu."

For a rigid moment, each expected her to say more. She did not. She rose from the divan where she had sat at Margo's side. "Now if you don't mind, I'll get that tea I promised." As Dorothia marched away, Margo and Irene scowled at Marubrishnubupu.

He responded with supplicant hands. "Something is not well here."

"Yes, you!" Margo censured.

Poking her head from the kitchen, Dorothia called to the room, echoes of her words carried down the hall. "I understand you have dreams, Master Marubrishnubupu."

Standing nervously, he spoke to the blank corridor as though to fill it with a faith that emptiness would need to understand. "I do, Ms. Rodriguez." Receiving no reply, he continued, "I hope that my questions have not . . ."

"I have dreams also, Master Marubrishnubupu." Dorothia cut him off as she emerged from the kitchen with a tray of steaming tea. "Perhaps you are skilled at interpretation? I've always believed that having a dream is not nearly so important as being able to interpret it properly. Your religious training — *where it is so very necessary to believe you see what is not there* — helps you in these matters, I'm sure." Placing the tray on the table, she extended the teeming teapot to Margo. "Do you like Russian tea?"

"I don't believe I've ever had it," Margo stated, holding a teacup and saucer towards the spout. "What a pretty kettle."

"I hope you enjoy it. It's an Eastern favorite. Apple juice, orange juice, pineapple, a little lemon peel, sugar, water and courant. I let it steep for about an hour. I have regular tea also if you're not a fan. Don't be afraid to hurt my feelings."

"Oh no! It's tasty. How different!" Margo asserted upon her first sip.

"Irene?"

"Yes, please. Thank you."

Dorothia turned to Marubrishnubupu, forcing him back into his seat with the piping, hot teapot. The guru reached for an empty saucer and she poured the tea from its pewter pot as she spoke. "I can understand the power of a dream, Marubrishnu . . . bupu." Filling the cup high she caused Marubrishnubupu great effort to keep it from spilling. "For instance, I dreamt years ago that Alexi would make something of himself. His father was a wonderful photographer. Another maker of images." Again, she sat by Margo. The group adjusted to face her, listening to her cutting dialogue. She continued slowly. "I dreamed that Alexi would be known for something special, for doing something that no one else could do. I dreamed that he would be world famous. What a silly dream. The silly dream of a mother, isn't it, Master Marubrishnubupu?"

Marubrishnubupu said nothing. He simply listened, paying close attention with large, round eyes, waiting.

"But here you are, come from New Mexico and India. It is India, Master Marubrishnubupu, is it not? Or Nepal?" she asked, as she extended the teapot once again to the cup from which he had barely taken a sip.

"Tibet, I was actually born in Tibet."

"Tibet, yes, all the way from New Mexico to Tibet. That's what I dreamt of, Master Marubrishnubupu. And here it is come true, world famous in a way. At least, it's a good beginning. How wonderful, don't you think, a world where the silliest dreams of a mother can come true? Isn't that wonderful, Master Marubrishnubupu? Isn't that absolutely wonderful?"

There was a sincerity in the question that caught Marubrishnubupu off guard. He was about to reply when she added, returning their conversation to the source of their theme, "And what is it that you dream of, Master Marubrishnubupu, if you don't mind me asking?"

Raising the saucer to her chin, she sipped the Russian tea.

Margo and Irene both watched, their pleasure neatly contained; they felt confident that Dorothia could extricate the gloom and doom where they had proven unsuccessful.

Holding his tea with both hands, he stared straight into her eyes without mistake or confusion, intending for her to understand that what led him forward even now, unpopular as it made him, was not personal, regardless of whether she thought it to be so. His words were precisely measured. "Ms. Rodriguez, I have dreamt of a great disaster befalling a person of the quality of which you speak, a very special person." Placing the cup on the table, he warned, "I have much reason to believe the person of whom I speak so highly may well be your son."

Dorothia gulped hard before glancing into her saucer where drips of tea had accumulated in a tiny puddle. Tersely, her upper lip stiffened, she pursued the conversation. "And what happens in this dream?"

"Dreams. It has been many dreams."

"Yes, to be sure. What is it in these *dreams*, Master Marubrishnubupu, that leads you to this mistaken conclusion?"

He tread carefully, as even angels do, upon his words. "At first I dreamed of baseball."

"Baseball, Master Marubrishnubupu?" Dorothia exclaimed in amusement, thinking of Marcel. "I think you've come to the wrong house. Alexi is not a ballplayer. Perhaps you should go to Boston. I understand they are having quite a run in the playoffs."

Unfazed, displaying neither appreciation nor offense for the barbed humor, he continued. "I was dreaming of the death of the Babe Ruth and of a curse. For a long time, as the dreams came to me, I believed it was about baseball. But it was not. Little by little, the imagery grew, as though my dreams were being painted. Every dream I have had ends with a painter whose face I cannot see sitting at a canvas without edges as though the very world I have been dreaming was his canvas all along. And I see his palette run dry. He's all used up, torn by two worlds. I have come to protect him, if I am able." The tone grew ominous. "We will lose him again, if we do not care for him." Marubrishnubupu pressed forward. A hand upon his long silver beard, his walnut skin tight and lively, he closed the gap between them. "We will lose him, Ms. Rodriguez!"

Dorothia gulped hard at her tea, suddenly aware that she had been fully transfixed by Master Marubrishnubupu's words, also aware that in being so taken by the Master's warnings, she had revealed something of herself. She reacted to the tender vulnerability in the only way she knew how, as a lioness might react to a human who has come too close to the wounded cubs she cannot heal.

"I'm afraid you'll be disappointed, Master Marubrishnubupu," she responded curtly, more than a hint of anger suffusing her words. "My son is quite healthy, healthier than he has been in quite some time. A dry palette, all used up, torn between two worlds, in need of your protection? I assure you, Alexi's work has never been more sound and his palette runneth over. And his health — my goodness! Just yesterday, in fact, his health took quite a turn for the better. One that I am nearly tempted to call miraculous. But maybe that's the prejudice of a mother, I'm sure you would say. What does a mother know, when you are having holy dreams?"

Marubrishnubupu bowed his head, his eyes reflected within the swirl of tea, his hair falling forward in silver wisps. She had not heard the most important parts of what he had said; he acquiesced to the natural order of things. "A mother has a right to her prejudice. I am pleased to have been so wrong."

Irene and Margo in that single moment, witnessing the scorn Marubrishnubupu accepted without protest, could not help but admire how willingly he played his part.

Margo experienced a chill upon her portly ankles and shivered. Feeling it herself as an ominous doubt in the pit of her stomach, Dorothia approached the door to Rooster's room. "Do you feel a draft?"

"Yes, I do, just a little one," Margo lied, wondering why she had not felt the draft earlier.

"He has his window open," she explained, smiling anxiously, checking Marubrishnubupu's attentive eyes, her confidence fading. "If you don't mind, I'll check on Alexi now. See if he's ready to see us. That's quite a draft . . . quite a . . ."

They rose tensely to their feet and watched as Dorothia stood before the door, her hand on the knob, outlandishly afraid. Turning pale, she gazed at Marubrishnubupu in terror, unable to move, stricken by a foreboding intuition of silence. "Something's wrong! Terribly wrong!"

"Be brave," he counseled.

As he spoke, a piercing scream broke from the street. Margo Halscome rushed to the window. Pushing the drapes aside, she declared, "Oh my goodness, there's a fight!"

"A fight?"

"He just hit the man."

"Should we call the police?" Irene clamored above the rising tumult.

"They're fighting over a girl!"

Irene headed towards the phone as Marubrishnubupu and Dorothia stared at one another without moving or speaking, each one knowing that all the events were related, that all the seeds that had been sown were coming for harvest. Her cold hand still on the doorknob, Dorothia's eyes pleaded with Marubrishnubupu for a mercy he could not give.

"They're coming this way!" Margo Halscome shrieked, retreating from the window in a state of fear and horror. "Oh my goodness! Lock the door! Someone lock the door!"

"Hello police? Yes, I need the police!" Irene shouted into the phone as the front door burst open, crashing violently against the inner wall. An icy wind filled the room causing petunia petals to shudder on their stems. Blood dripping from a cut at the bridge of his nose, Marcel stalked forward, forcing his way into the antechamber with determined strides.

"Where's my bird?" he bellowed furiously, oblivious to the gathering and the intimidating effect of his bloody face. "Where's Prophet?"

The group remained at attention, pinned where they were by the rage of the commanding presence.

"Where's my bird? Goddamn it!"

Trailing only a step behind, Tamara dashed into the room. She was white as a ghost, thin as a rail and haggard, like a rabid, frothing creature that has not eaten or slept for days. Her frantic eyes, sick with passion, searched the room. In her frail hands she held the unframed portrait *I Give You My Word*. She was the one over whom the two men had been fighting in the street.

"The address? The address? Oh God, I don't live here. I don't know the address!" Irene lamented into the phone.

"You can't buy me off!" Tamara shrieked as she stood in the center of the room, staring down Dorothia. The force of her words drowned out even Marcel's furious protest. The author drew back, stunned. Tamara's blanched knuckles shook as she held up the painting in her wrenched fingers as tears of torment dripped down her face. "You can send me to hell for all I care! But you can't keep me away, you rotten bitch! Do your worst; I love him!"

The room became still and for an instant each person waited for someone else to speak, but no one did. Through the hush, the wind gently blew, cleansing the room, confirming the young woman's declaration. Irene dropped the phone.

"Who is this?" Margo finally asked, stepping timidly to Dorothia's side.

Before she could get an answer out, Zephaniah Maxwell rushed in. Blood dripped from his lower lip where Marcel had split it wide with a

firm right cross that had knocked him dizzy to the ground. He was prepared to attack Marcel when Dorothia commanded firmly, "No!"

Zephaniah stopped as Marcel raised his own fists. "I tried to stop
her, Ms. Rodriguez," Zephaniah explained as he wiped away the blood
spilling from his lip. "I had her before this maniac . . ."

"It doesn't matter anymore," Dorothia interrupted, preventing
Zephaniah from the continued embarrassment. The men dropped their
guards.

"What is this?" Marubrishnubupu whispered, gracefully removing
the painting from Tamara's trembling hand. As the others were drawn
deeper into the unfolding drama, Marubrishnubupu held the painting
before him in a state of awe. This was one of the vague images of which
his cosmic mind had dreamed. The first image, the trinity. An over-
whelming psychic hot flash transported him into the canvas.
Transported to another lifetime, Marubrishnubupu sat at the abscessed
feet of the wise leper, bending on a knee in the dirt, listening.

"Prophet is safe, Marcel. I'm sorry I had to bring you here this way.
You gave me no choice."

"Prophet?" Marubrishnubupu echoed without thought.

"Just what is going on, Dorothia?" Margo Halscome pleaded for an
answer that would dissolve the chaos.

Irene attempted to respond, fearful that her position and reputation
was in jeopardy, "Let's just forget all this. Let's meet the artist."

"It's all right," Dorothia asserted once more, the stale calm returning, pervading the entirety of her demeanor. "This is exactly where we
needed to be. Even you, Tamara. Even you. It doesn't matter anymore.
It's like Marubrishnubupu said. Nothing can stop it now." Turning the
knob, all fear of the unknown thrashed, she opened the door. "I suppose it had to come to this."

Marubrishnubupu removed his eyes from the magical spell of the
canvas just as Dorothia disappeared from his view. Entering the room,
she was calling out as the congregation followed, "It's time, my son.
Rooster, dear God, it's time."

$\backsim\!\!\rho$

Inside she found the gilded bars of a dream outgrown. Drawn to the center of the room by the irresistible notion of creation, Dorothia stood helplessly, listless arms limp at her hips, as an impotent reason sought sense from the senseless. The window was wide open, fanning the drapes aside like white robes hanging from a clothesline. Scattered about the room, one leaning atop another, were the multitude of paintings completed in the amazing span of sixteen days. For the first time she saw the various paintings as one synchronous flow. *Generous Solicitude, Hecatomb* and *Thermidor. The Cry of Tharmas, Sweeter Rage and Sun there Shall not be.* A miasma of self-digested dereliction receded and she understood that the paintings of an artist are composed like the pages of a book or the individual notes of a symphony. Only taken together is the full tale told, is the depth and reserve of emotion expressed, is the movement complete.

Prophet's empty cage lay on its side. *Physical Dust; Bird Outside; Outside; Bird; Birds Sing.*

Looking backwards down Rooster's road, she saw the void from which all the bright laughter of childhood ends and begins, where emptiness gives bloom to birth. In *Af Taken* she saw life and hope conceived in an adoration of color, adoration most luminous when mixed with modest hues. Upon the canvas of *Sastruga* she saw this life grow bold and alive, blissful and overflowing, healthy and surging with a profusion of faith. In *Blue Hands*, where a small chimpanzee reached with blue hands for ripe plantains at the edge of a pink jungle, she recognized the imaginative courage of Blake's Los, the libidinal drive of a redemptive creation. There was *Return from the Oppressed* and *Leander's Purse, Pestilence Sobbing* and *Shadow of Regret, One Touch Bestowed, Sacrifice Willing* and *Several Thoughts on the Quality of Desire*. Her eyes lingered on a painting called *A Billion Buzzing Bees*. He had completed eight paintings that day, so many that she had not really looked at what he had accomplished. *1941, The Complex Appetite of Clear Milk, Obscure Mice, Gauze and Minor Miracles, Hysterical*. She had on first glance, quick as it was, thought *A Billion Buzzing Bees* a pleasant swirl of red, black and yellow. Only now did she see it for what Rooster intended, for what he layered so carefully beneath the surface — the magnified face of a young girl being viciously and systematically and bloodily swarmed. There was *Gracious Blade* and *Distinct Delusion, Purple* and *What Came After. Euripides, Come Out and Play, Mule of the Dalai Lama, Alice through a White Glass* and *Sublime Awe.* She saw compassion culminate in *Study of the Beautiful*, a study of love and forgiveness, of complete submission and acceptance, of a resigned commitment to reality in all of its variations.

She looked to the last of the paintings, a consumptive maelstrom, a dark mime in which she saw the abysmal reflection of her own transcendent dread. The painting she had so despised and wished for Rooster to put aside seemed to her a filthy depiction of pure honesty. But now she understood. Her knowledge penetrated. How had she not seen? How had he painted this before her eyes, a testimony and will? Like the bird beneath blindness, so too his world had become a structure dedicated to the interior, with limits made beautiful by a divine beauty not meant to be held. Dorothia looked to Tamara as the young girl pressed past the others into the room — not a room, the essence of the inexpressible, a sacred chamber, scattered repository of the living soul. Dorothia could not remove her eyes from the last canvas upon which Rooster had worked, from what it said, from what it predicted and promised, from what it revealed and confessed, from her role in suffocating the boy in a world without light. "What have I done?"

Marcel stood amidst the others, his mouth agape as the colors, the images, the disturbing spirit of a poet more than he had ever dared or dreamed to be, overwhelmed him. "What is this? What is this?" he asked again and again, bewildered by the splendor of the garden. He was not seeing paintings; the paintings were the very last thing in the room that he would see.

Irene dropped to her knees before *Sublime Awe.* In it she recognized the aim and vision of her life; she understood that this representation was but a single step along a higher mountain. She thought of Aristotle, of truth's arrow piercing the eternal heart of the disbeliever. Touching the canvas she caught her breath. So surreal. So sublime. So perpetual. Margo, with a hand on Irene's shoulder, said nothing. Her own eyes on *Pestilence Sobbing*, a locust-ravaged plain in the palm of a child, she simply thanked God to be present.

Marubrishnubupu did not even enter the room. He remained stationary on the sofa, the painting trembling in his hands. Tears poured down his cheeks in a stream of measureless oneness. No tear was individual but each was part of the whole, a continuous wave that swelled. He could not rise and did not believe that he deserved to enter the room. He knew without seeing that Rooster was not there, that he had not succeeded in stopping this thing. So little was his worth, so rich his reward.

Tamara looked at *Black Mask* and saw the hallowed belly of the lake. Zephaniah saw the chasm between white and black and the sacrifice of humanity that would reconcile the tragic division. Both saw the struggles of a bird at the very center.

There in the room, all could share him, whole and complete. They met him as he was and as he always would be.

"Where is Prophet?"

"I know where he is," Tamara told Marcel, pulling him by the arm. Holding the empty birdcage in his hand, Marcel suspected that they were not talking of the same person. "Follow me," she commanded.

Together they dashed out the front door, past Marubrishnubupu who gazed up from the painting for only a moment, his sorrow intensified, his pain multiplied as he re-entered through no choice of his own, the suffering of existence. "He gave this to you?" The words rolled from his lips but Tamara, dragging Marcel, was already flying past the ancient guru, fashioned in the moment, as though of stone. With the painting in his hands, he chased them from the house, pursuing with frantic footsteps. Turning into the street at the gate, his robe felt quite warm, though his breathing, for all of his meditation, labored, so unused to rigorous exercise is a holy sage who like all others will pounce enlightenment without decorum.

Seeing the procession surging past, beneath streetlamps and spherical cones of light, Margo Halscome impelled Irene. "They're going to see him. To see *Him!*" Responding mindlessly to the urgent behest of her friend, Irene followed. Tossing coats round their shoulders, they hastened with abandon into the street, the oncoming night, winter's verge. They could hear Marubrishnubupu hollering to those ahead. "Wait for me! Wait for me!" Refined in the threshing wind, they followed the fleeting voice of the will-o-wisp, the spiritual urge, a distant call.

Held in abeyance before her son's final work of art, a maddening

desolation wide awake and unafraid, Dorothia was oblivious to the dis-
tended cortege flashing before the window like wisps to a comet's tail.
"What have I done, Zephaniah, what have I done?"

"Come on," he implored as she collapsed in his arms, her fists flailing against his chest, her psychic necrosis turned within. "Come on."

"Where? Why? What have I done? Alexi, Alexi!" she cried out in
anguish as her eyes locked upon the final product of his brush. "What
have I done?"

Zephaniah squeezed her in his gigantic hands. He felt how small she
was, small and crumpling before his exhortation. "The girl knows
where he is! She knows where he is!"

"Rooster?" she asked, bewildered, the blood of Zephaniah's lip now
on her fingers.

"Yes, yes, your son."

She seemed distant, lost, like a creature without meaning, without
purpose — a derelict dispossessed of secular duty. "My son?" But the
words meant nothing as she collapsed to the floor, unable to stand.
Aghast, her eyes spun around the room. Palettes of color organized into
infinity consumed her. She giggled aimlessly. "My son? My . . ."

Zephaniah waved a hand before her glazed, listless eyes, but she did
not see him as she released a terrifying cry of separation from the very
bottom of her heart.

17

TAMARA ARRIVED AT the lake screaming his name. "Rooster, Rooster!" Marcel also called the name of a bird into the darkness.

"I'm sorry," she cried. "I should've known. I should have come earlier. Rooster!"

The intense events transpiring about him were sufficient to help Marcel to understand that Dorothia had been right. He had needed to see her son. Against his own will, the stubborn mother had re-forged his broken promise. *Damn you, Dorothia. Why didn't you tell me that it was like this?* Dodging through the sparse forest, he struggled to keep pace with the frenzied young woman. For sheer fear that if he lost her he too would be lost completely, he found the will to match her pace. Surging forth in his aged body, he discovered limits and strengths he had thought long depleted, exhausted by the vastness of the world.

Emerging from the forest he stumbled, toppling down the slope in a painful, bouncing heap, tearing his trousers on a jutted, cragged root. Mud mixed with a maroon blood that dripped upon his expensive Italian shoes. He cursed as he checked for broken bones. The girl had stopped upon the bank of a beautiful lake set in the dipping hollow of a valley. Its frozen surface was illuminated by a full harvest moon. Pale silver luster, a dull pewter haze pervaded the night. The moon was still of the valley. The harsh wind capitulated in the basin, willfully relenting. Tamara paused, rigid as a granite marker. She stood upon the ice, a step away from the shore's thick sand. Attentive to the lake's center, Marcel wondered what she expected to find.

A feeble wail rose from a constricted throat.

"Prophet?" Marcel muttered hopefully as he stepped to the young woman's side, gripping her protectively by the arm. "Careful."

Kismet had led him to defend her at the gate against Zephaniah, but she ignored him now as his eyes, adjusting to the shimmering glimmer of the moon, brought into focus what she saw: a dark, unmoving mass at the center of the lake.

"Rooster?" she pleaded breathlessly.

Another low groan, the guttural groan of a dying animal, traveled through the flat, stale, lifeless air. "Look." Marcel pointed to a sharp crack in the ice, a splinter from which the dark water below seeped upon the ice, overlaying the frozen surface with a cool breathing mystery returning from beneath. One ridge of ice was lifted over the other ridge like a clean snapped bone; the pattern of each broken half was a perfect, mutual fit. "It's not safe."

Tamara glared at him brutally and unleashed her most recent conclusion. In her voice he could hear the rippled remonstration of his lost wife Ruth. "It never is."

Marcel's grip wilted as she tore free of his protective grasp. Rushing forward, she skated to the edge where a ten-foot gap of murky water flexed, separating the solid ice into two distinct shores. Tamara knelt at the edge of the black, watery partition.

On a small island, floating free from both shores, an island unapproachable, a silver tile protected by a rippling moat of numb fluid, Rooster's beveled form lay in a naked mass. His clothing lay in drenched piles strewn upon the ice. A pant leg floated helpless and quiet in the chilling water. His body, shivering periodically in violent spasms, was a swollen lump of sores and sickness. Greenish puss oozed from patches on his torso, the soft edges defined by tiny, dilute rivulets of blood. It appeared that his body, a single wound of sores and shingles, could be taken apart piece by piece. It was not a body but an assembled puzzle, a fragile structure made to resemble health. The illusion had come undone. Purpose fulfilled, the picture complete, the individual pieces were free to disengage. This was not an unhealthy body, not a sick body. It was healthy pieces made to appear unhealthy and sick through the force of a terrible tension, a horrible union into which the pieces were committed for a higher cause, a greater good, a more divine intention. The individual pieces were becoming distinct once more. The union that had held together under immense strain no longer wished to be. But while the union had lasted, it created such beauty as had never been imagined.

Tamara gasped upon seeing the violent degradation of the body. His legs, his arms, his belly. His chest and loins and back. His neck and chin were marred by scarified boils, furuncles of a ravaged flesh. Only his face and hands were spared the leprous insurrection. *His hands*, she mused as her eyes descended upon them. The hands at least, like his waxen lips turned blue, were spared. "Rooster," she whispered, her voice breaking through the tremulous shock. She could see his face, a gently curved smile upon it, the look of tranquillity, the serenity of innocence. His eyes opened; all suffering was gone. His opaque eyes held her in their gaze. His purple lips trembled. His was like the souls of the righteous in the hand of God, untouched by torment and affliction of the body. From his bed of ice, from waxen lips preserved, he spoke a final word, "P . . . P . . . Peace." Smiling angelically, he shivered. Releasing the struggle, he breathed no more.

"Rooster, Rooster," she whispered through her tears. "Rooster, please," she uttered again. The wind wailed as his spirit blew through her. "I will always love you."

Upon sight of the body, Marcel vomited into the lake. Irene made the sign of the cross. Ambulance sirens sang in the distance.

Tamara, small but calm, looked from Rooster to Marcel as he cleansed the dripping bile from his lips. "You're Marcel Phrenol," she stated, unafraid, recognizing the stern, manly face from the back of the book that she and Rooster had read together at the lake. For her there was no sense of surprise, no sense that his presence should make anything but perfect sense, no sense that everything did not fit.

He looked at her, met her steady gaze, answered as he drew a handkerchief cross his lips. "Yes."

"You'll write his story. You'll write it. You'll make it known what happened here."

He knew that it was not a matter of choice but a matter of fate, of the life and destiny that finds each of us in time. "Yes."

"I'll teach you what I know of him. The rest will be found in his work."

Water lapped against the white, transparent ice.

"Who was he?" Irene asked.

"Another child of God," Marubrishnubupu answered. He stood upon the isle of ice with his hand upon the boy's head. They stared at him in amazement. The ice isle had drifted to the other side, a pyre docking upon the other shore of the continental lake. Marubrishnubupu sighed as he ran his hand along the thin blue skin, adding regretfully, "But we were not ready . . . so he has gone home. Home."

With a muffled caw, Prophet dropped from the sky, crashing with a forceful thud into the ice. "Prophet!" Marcel declared with joy, lifting the disoriented bird into his arms. "What is it you've found?" Marcel wondered, taking a small item from the bird. Too dazed to fight, the crow released the puzzle piece from its beak. An upper right corner. Marcel looked from Tamara to Irene to Marubrishnubupu to the lain body of the dead painter stretched upon the ice. Moonlight reflected off the waves of the water, but there was no bridge. Prophet released a bold, courageous cry. Caw-Cauw!

Marcel stroked frost from the feathers of the wise old bird. "Yes Prophet, I hear you."

Caw!

"You were right all along."

Cauw!

"Now I see."

18

H IS LABOR HAVING survived the war, Soli waited for Yusherin in the dry ravine. He wanted to feel whole but he did not; he felt more incomplete than ever. Digging his boots into the sandy soil, he watched pebbles roll aside beneath his muddy boots. Looking to the canvas of his creation, he realized that nothing would ever be adequate again. Only when he had been painting, *painting like that*, had he felt right in the world. It did not seem fair that he could go through these recent experiences without a conversion of some type, without some minute epiphany of being. Neither pride nor exhaustion did he feel. He did feel an emptiness, not an exhaustion but only an emptiness, as though he had given only what he was naturally able and nothing more, as though a proper limit had been met and received — and nothing more. The emptiness, he thought, was likely worse than exhaustion. At least with exhaustion there is a sense that one has gone too far, and so one must return, at least a little bit. But with emptiness there are no such sentiments; there is only the feeling of having played a part and the sad, yes, truly sad sense that there is nothing left to play, that one's time has been expended. Nothing is left to give and nothing more is asked. This was worse than the feeling of having been used for a terrible purpose. This was the feeling of having no use.

Soli arrived at the conclusion that something should have changed, something should have been affirmed. But staring down the distance of the ravine, seeing the scattered bodies of the Germans lying face down in sand, there was no affirmation, no place remaining for Soli to go. He rubbed his eyes of soot as Yusherin, with sword of antiquity drawn, sliced a portal through the regal canvas that concealed Michayl's Pass. Gazing at it now, in the aftermath, Soli wondered how the Germans had not seen the façade. Was this a psychological effect of war? How does the mind react? What does it see and not see in stressful situations? Soli saw now what his unconscious self had done. Deep in the pattern a monumental assault upon the psyche appeared, a reverse swastika. Soli saw the slice in the canvas and drew his knife. The general swung the blade. Soli met the swinging hand, holding it at bay as he drove his knife into the general's shoulder, the tender tissue beneath the collarbone but above the breastplate. The two men withdrew. A moment later, plunging his knife into the general's stomach, Soli thought only of his father, a good man who had sacrificed his life for the belief that killing is not good, that the way of peace is better, more noble, harder. Yes, harder was the way of peace than the way of war. Killing is not good, Father, Soli thought, twisting the blade, evoking a gasp from the general, but it is not all evil.

The sword fell.